THIS MAY END BADLY

THIS MAY END BADLY

SAMANTHA MARKUM

WEDNESDAY BOOKS
NEW YORK

First published in the United States by Wednesday Books, an imprint of St. Martin's Publishing Group

THIS MAY END BADLY. Copyright © 2022 by Samantha Markum. All rights reserved. Printed in the United States of America. For information, address St. Martin's Publishing Group, 120 Broadway, New York, NY 10271.

www.wednesdaybooks.com

Designed by Devan Norman

Library of Congress Cataloging-in-Publication Data

Names: Markum, Samantha, author.
Title: This may end badly / Samantha Markum.
Description: First edition. | New York : Wednesday Books, 2022. | Audience: Ages 13-18.
Identifiers: LCCN 2021051028 | ISBN 9781250799180 (hardcover) | ISBN 9781250799197 (ebook)
Subjects: CYAC: Practical jokes—Fiction. | Dating (Social customs)—Fiction. | Sexual abuse—Fiction. | Single-sex schools—Fiction. | Boarding schools—Fiction. | Schools—Fiction. |LCGFT: Novels.
Classification: LCC PZ7.1.M37243 Th 2022 | DDC [Fic]—dc23
LC record available at https://lccn.loc.gov/2021051028

Our books may be purchased in bulk for promotional, educational, or business use. Please contact your local bookseller or the Macmillan Corporate and Premium Sales Department at 1-800-221-7945, extension 5442, or by email at MacmillanSpecialMarkets@macmillan.com.

First Edition: 2022

10 9 8 7 6 5 4 3 2 1

FOR MOM

THIS MAY
END BADLY

CHAPTER ONE

We only have a few hours before sunrise.

I should be tired, but adrenaline pumps through my veins, forcing my eyes wide open. I work on shoving another stake into the soft, damp ground.

"Hurry up," Gemma whispers with some urgency. She's anxious, but then again, she's always anxious.

"I can see security," Jade says from my Bluetooth earbud. "They're rounding the south side."

"South side?" Sumi's snort echoes through the earbud. "Doe can barely tell her right from her left. You think she knows north from south?"

"Shut up, Sumi," I say, banging the last stake into place. "You just worry about yourself."

"Nothing to worry about," Sumi says, sounding pleased. "I've been done for ten minutes."

Gemma lets out a panicky hum. "I think I see flashlights!"

"She's staying home next time," Shawn says from my side.

"No!" Jade protests. "I can't focus on anything with her teeth chattering in my ear."

I glance at Gemma. Sure enough, she's got two fingernails in her mouth, hammering at them with her front teeth.

"Will you get her out of here?" I say to Shawn.

"We're almost done," Shawn reminds me.

"*I'm* almost done. The only thing Gem is about to finish is a nervous breakdown."

"I'm fine," Gemma says, her voice shaking.

I give Shawn a look.

She laughs. "Okay, I got you."

Gemma gives a meek protest as Shawn grabs her arm and hauls her out the front gate. They duck around the side, and I hear Sumi say from my earbud, "Oh, hey, guys."

I stay crouched behind the Winfield Academy sign, working the last stake into the ground. Shawn was kind enough to attach the ropes, at least—because I do hear footsteps, and they're closer than I expected.

"You've got company," Jade says. "Shit—*shit*. You've got real company. Where did this guy come from?"

"Get out of there, Doe," says Sumi.

"I'm almost done," I say.

"You'll be done for *real* if you don't get out of there," Gemma says from the earbud.

I grit my teeth. "Someone get her off the line."

I secure the last stake and look up, triumph squelching the nervousness creeping in. But then I spot the beam of a flashlight headed my way. I freeze, crouched in the dark. I could slip out now, but I'd be spotted for sure, and any close investigation would reveal what we've done. I can't let that happen—not before the first car arrives.

Somewhere on the other side of the building, a dog howls. The flashlight swings in the other direction.

I sprint out the front gate, hurtle over the trip wire, and duck around the corner, where I collide with Sumi and Gemma.

"Where's Shawn?" I ask.

The dog howls again.

Jade laughs in my ear. "She spent all summer perfecting that."

"Her neighbor got that hound dog," Gemma says.

"It woke me up every goddamn morning." Shawn huffs a laugh from my earbud.

I shoot Sumi a grin. "Let's get out of here."

We duck away from the light of the streetlamps as we sneak to the building across the road. Shawn meets us as we dart through the entrance.

THE WESTON SCHOOL, the sign overhead reads. AUT VIAM INVENIAM AUT FACIAM.

I will either find a way or make one.

When we meet up in the stairwell in the morning, I feel like I got about two minutes of sleep. Somehow, Gemma looks even worse off. Circles as dark as bruises drag practically halfway down her cheeks, and her pale skin looks almost gray. Even her freckles have dulled.

"You look like death," I say.

She laughs, the sound brittle. "I didn't sleep."

To be fair, Gemma isn't a great sleeper on the best of days. During the school year, she spends most nights up studying, hours after the rest of us are asleep—except maybe Sumi, who could be awake at any time of night for any number of reasons, none of them similar to Gemma's.

Things have gotten especially bad since this summer, when Gemma came out to her parents and two older sisters. From the few details she divulged, things went well. But revealing a secret, even one taken well, has a way of creeping into a person's anxieties.

Shawn appears at our backs wearing a pair of overalls she

cut into shorts, looking like a summer-tanned farm girl with her sandy brown hair tied in a messy topknot. She's balancing four coffees in a holder in one hand and a fifth in the other. "Take these."

Gemma grabs one and pops it open to blow on it.

"Did you sleep?" I ask Shawn.

Shawn grins, rosy-cheeked and glowing. "It's move-in day."

That's a no.

But unlike Gemma, who probably would have slept last night if she could have snatched a few hours, Shawn draws her energy from pulling a good all-nighter every once in a while.

Sumi and Jade arrive, looking disheveled and only half changed out of pajamas. At least I'm not the only one who wasn't too anxious or excited to sleep.

I unlock the service door and prop it open, letting them pass.

Sumi yawns, takes a long pull of her coffee, and promptly spills it down her chin.

"Hot, hot, hot," she says, swiping at her mouth with her sleeve. She's wearing a bamboo sleep shirt she got on her late-summer vacation in Florida, and it's caught in the waist of a pair of cotton shorts. She's shoeless, stripes of lighter brown skin crisscrossing the tops of her feet from the sandals she wore all summer.

Jade is still dragging herself up the stairs, practically on all fours. She's in a silk shorts pajama set, long dark legs looking like they should end in dainty slippers, but she's stuffed her feet into clunky Doc Martens instead. Her hair crowds her face like a fluffy black cloud, and she tosses her head to get it off her forehead. It flops right back.

"Rise and shine, ladies," Shawn says in her best impression of Mr. Tully, our wellness teacher. "I want to see bright eyes. I want to see bushy tails."

"He wants to see bushy something," Jade says.

Gemma shrieks.

We spill out onto the rooftop. It's already baking in the sun, and I squint against the glare.

"Sunglasses," Jade says. "I always forget sunglasses."

"You say that every ti—ime," Shawn sings as she passes her.

Jade glares but doesn't argue. Jade's eyes are notoriously sensitive, what she refers to as her "eternal curse" from her Danish father. Already, moisture has gathered at her lash line, ready to spill down her cheeks.

"No fighting," I say. "This is a sacred space."

The roof is pitched on all sides and flattens at the top, where the service entrance juts from the center like a cake topper. Four tall chimneys cap each corner of the roof, connected by a five-foot-tall brick barrier around the edge.

At one corner is a collection of old dorm beds, desks, chairs, and tables all stacked together in a haphazard mass of junk. You can see it from the street if you know you're looking for it, but the maintenance staff is pretty meticulous about maneuvering it just right behind the chimney.

A long time ago, when I first came into possession of a key to the service stairs, we staked our claim on it as our hideout. A kingdom of forgotten furniture. Every so often, the collection grows, but as long as we've been coming here—two years now—it's never gotten smaller.

"Who's fighting?" Shawn follows me to the other end of the roof. "No one's fighting."

"Someone might be fighting," says Jade, her voice hollow.

Shawn pouts at her. "I brought you coffee."

Jade sighs. "Fine, I forgive you. You don't have to beg."

Shawn makes a small, outraged noise that skitters into a laugh as Jade hooks an arm around her neck, dragging her sideways.

Gemma pulls a flamingo-print bedsheet from under her arm and works to secure it over the space between two old dorm bunks while the rest of us organize some chairs in our makeshift fort.

"Welcome back to the Kingdom," Shawn says, banging her fist on her chair before dropping into it. She takes a swig of coffee, coughs, then drinks again.

"Hear! Hear!" says Jade, holding her cup up in salute.

"Anyone got the time?" Sumi asks, craning her neck to peer down the street.

"Seven fifty-six," Gemma says, falling breathlessly into her chair.

Shawn sits up a little straighter. "First car should roll in any second. There's always that one family eager to get their kid off their hands."

I snort. "At Winfield? I'd be begging them to open up a summer session."

"Guys!" Sumi rushes to the edge. "We've got a biter!"

We follow and crouch down, peeking over the bricks at the front entrance of Winfield Academy.

Move-in days at Winfield and Weston are always separated by at least twenty-four hours, alternating each year for first move-in. My first year at Weston, someone rigged the outdoor speakers to blast the last minute of "Girls" by Beastie Boys on a loop.

The next year, the Winfield boys arrived to bras tied all along their front gate and in the trees.

Junior year, Winfield repaid us by vandalizing every statue on campus. The Weston School has commemorated some of the greatest female minds in the nation with statues and busts. The boys from Winfield dressed them in aprons and bad lingerie.

This year, we will not be outdone.

I grab Shawn's hand and squeeze. She lets out a little squeal of anticipation.

The car is nice. Sleek, black, dark-tinted windows, with at least a $100K price tag.

It glides over Sumi's trip wire, and our sign unfurls, covering the Winfield Academy entrance gate.

WELCOME BACK, LOSERS

"Beautiful." Jade shoots Sumi a shark's grin. "Well done."

Sumi shrugs, brushes her nails against her shirt, and blows on them.

It takes all of ten minutes for the next car to arrive and our sign to garner attention. We cackle as the Winfield headmaster comes out with a pair of desk scissors and tries to hack away at the ropes. Someone gets the bright idea to pull out the stakes, but the sign only half falls, partly blocking the entrance, so every car pulling in drives right under the word LOSERS.

We fall over each other laughing.

"Oh, wait, wait." I shush them, grabbing onto the ledge. "They've got it. The last stake is going."

The others practically pile on top of me.

"Here we go," says Shawn.

I see a familiar silver car roll in, and the timing couldn't be more perfect. As Winfield's headmaster finally gets our last rope undone, the sign over the gate falls.

As it does, it pulls the second trip wire.

A new banner unfurls, made from five bedsheets tied

together, and hundreds of unsheathed tampons rain down over the new arrivals.

In red, the banner reads:

WESTON GIRLS TAKE NO PRISONERS

And standing there under the sign, a little white tampon stuck in his hair, is Nathaniel Emeric Wellborn III.

I pull out my phone and zoom in as he turns and looks right up at us.

"Say cheese, dickwad."

I snap a picture of his grimacing face, and the five of us dissolve into laughter.

The question of which came first, Winfield Academy or The Weston School, is a bit of a chicken-and-egg situation. According to the Delafosse Historical Society, The Weston School was built almost a century before Winfield Academy was even a dream in someone's mind.

It started as a family home on the outskirts of the small Midwestern town of Delafosse, occupied by generations of Westons. When Mallory Weston finally took ownership in 1882, unmarried and the last of her family line, she used her inheritance and the house to start a school for girls.

By that time, Winfield Academy had been running for a few decades—a school for boys from the nation's most elite families. Mallory marketed The Weston School as a finishing school, and with what would become the nation's most eligible bachelors just across the road, she had no problem pulling in pupils. But with a curriculum of science, math, and literature made available for those girls with a certain inkling, Weston amassed a legacy of students that would span generations.

Upon Mallory Weston's death in 1922, the house was granted to a trust and the school to a hand-selected board of trustees, and the finishing school front was dropped entirely. By then, pretty much everyone knew what girls got up to at The Weston School, so there was no point in pretense.

Since, new buildings have been tacked on and the school has grown into a sprawling campus, but the original house, now Mallory Hall, remains at its heart.

As for Winfield, no one really knows when the rivalry began. Some say a Weston girl was deeply scorned by a Winfield boy long ago, and that's when the animosity started. Others say it's simply the way of the world when you put two of anything across the road from one another—one always has to be better.

After a long nap, I head out for food and gossip. Some of the other seniors in my hall have their doors flung wide, socializing. Seniors at Weston are blessed with single dorms, like a gift before college. One year to cultivate a sense of privacy before we're thrust back into the world of roommates. Although Shawn and I were never roommates who impinged on each other's privacy.

I pass Shawn's new room and quickly backtrack to her open door. She's stretched up over her bed, hanging a string of pictures on the wall, and still dressed in the same overalls from this morning. Her room already looks halfway back to normal—bed stacked with a few colorful pillows, string lights coiled over the single window, and her sunflower-shaped rug rolled out in the middle of the room. Under her lofted bed is her reading nook—a fluffy pink beanbag chair and a small shelf stuffed with books.

It's quintessentially Shawn—sunny, colorful, and packed with sentiment. It's weird seeing her making her space in a separate room. For the first time since I started at Weston, Shawn and I are living apart. I don't know if I'm ready to be responsible for my own dorm room yet.

I clear my throat. "Decorating already?"

She looks over. "Oh, hey. Welcome back to the land of the living."

"Did you sleep?"

She shrugs. "A little after we split this morning. In the wee, wee hours."

"Please don't say *wee wee*."

She snorts. When she finishes hanging the pictures, she flops onto her beanbag chair.

"So, how'd it feel seeing Three bombarded with tampons? Everything you hoped and more?"

"We couldn't have timed it better. The gods were on our side."

"We'll get an earful at assembly," Shawn says.

"Worth it. Cotesmore secretly loves this stuff. She's a Weston girl, too—don't forget."

"How could I when she makes such an effort to beat it into our heads every chance she gets?" She puts on her best Cotesmore voice and adds, "When *I* was a student in Storey House, it was simply the berries. Don't forget, we're Weston girls forever."

"That much is true, at least. Weston girls till we die. Hey, you hungry?" I grab a scrunchie from her desk and try to wrangle my snarl of curls into a ponytail. My hair has reached new, frizzy heights, and dark strands snare around my pale fingers as I wrestle the mass atop my head. I try to remember the last time I brushed it and draw a blank.

Shawn shrugs. "Nah, I ate. I'll go with you, though."

I wave her off, heading out. "Stay. Decorate. I'm just grabbing a snack."

"Hey, Doe?" she says.

I turn and lean in the doorway.

She smiles. "I know this will be hard for you. But *don't* text him."

I scowl. "I wouldn't."

"You would. Just to gloat a little."

"To gloat a lot," I say with a grin. "But I won't. I left my phone in my room, anyway."

"For the best," she calls after me.

It's blistering hot outside, but nothing can bring down my good mood. I'm going to print that picture of Three with a tampon in his hair and plaster it all over my dorm room. All over the hall. All over the *school*. As place mats in the dining hall, on bookmarks, maybe even a banner to hang over the front entrance of Weston so everyone knows his shame.

If Winfield is Weston's natural enemy, Three is mine. The oldest son of one of the most distinguished Winfield families, he's the epitome of a Winfield boy. And even though he'd never admit it, he was desperate to make a name for himself at Winfield that first year. Our legacies worked in opposite directions—mine, a desperately-held golden ticket, his, a long list of expectations.

After we pulled off our first prank, it came as no surprise to find out my friends and I were marked. And with Three looking to secure his spot at the top of the social food chain, it only made sense he'd be the one to hit back.

The first time we met, I thought he might become a friend. We were at the outdoor ice rink Delafosse puts up every winter. One of my skates had come untied, and Three practically threw himself into my path on the ice to warn me before I face-planted.

We bonded over hot chocolate while my friends kept skating. We talked about school, what foods we missed from our hometowns (Provel cheese for me, Skyline chili for him), and what our friends were up to that year.

That was how he figured out how to hit back at my friends and Weston at the same time. For Three, saving me from that small humiliation was just a means to an end.

He made his move months later at our first home softball game. The four of us turned up to support Shawn, only to find our team had already forfeited after they opened the equipment shed and found everything missing. And not just from there—lockers had been ransacked, storage closets cleaned out.

There wasn't a bat or ball or glove to be found.

Shawn was devastated.

When I saw Three a week later, he greeted me with a self-satisfied smirk and a "Great day for a softball game, isn't it?"

It was as good as signing his name on it.

Had he only struck back at me, things may have been different. I might have respected it.

But he hurt Shawn, which is unforgivable.

"Hey, Doe!" someone calls behind me as I make my way across the lawn toward the Brick, our student lounge. It's the only place on campus to get a decent snack when the dining hall isn't serving.

I turn. A girl in a Weston Rowing shirt jogs across the lawn.

"Hey," I say.

There must be confusion on my face, because she giggles and says, "Sorry—I know we don't know each other, but he asked me to come and get you."

"He?"

My heart hammers. It's stupid—it shouldn't matter. But I'm almost sweating with anticipation.

She jerks her thumb toward Mallory Hall. "Yeah, one of the Wellborns. He's at the front gate."

I try to bite back a grin but can't muster the self-control. He really should know better.

"He wanted me to give you this." She reaches into her pocket and pulls out a tampon. "He said it's his calling card."

I snatch it and twist the string around my finger. "I guess I'll go see what he wants, then."

I start to stroll away, feeling like a champ, and the girl calls after me, "Hey, nice job this morning, by the way!"

I turn back, give her a sly thumbs-up, and walk off laughing.

I practically skip to the front gate. Technically we aren't allowed off campus without permission. It's pretty easy to get a day pass into town as a senior, but when it comes to Weston-Winfield relations, there isn't much point in exerting the effort. We can talk just fine from across the road.

If Three crossed the road, that means he's either breaking school rules or went to the trouble of getting a pass. Either way, he's an idiot. I will lord this over him until—

I stop short.

The boy leaning against our front gate begins a slow clap for me.

I'm annoyed that he looks so at ease as he toes our campus line. A breeze rumples his mess of brown hair, and his dark eyes are narrowed in amusement. How can he look like he's never touched a hairbrush and also like a golden-skinned autumn prince at the same time? It reeks of unfairness.

"I see he called in his guard dog," I shout as I come down the path.

I should have known—*one* of the Wellborns. Even though there are only two with the Wellborn last name, there are technically five of them—no, wait, *six* with an incoming freshman this year. A band of cousins whose Thanksgiving table I would certainly never want to sit at. *Wellborn, Biermann, Page.* They're names to steer clear of.

But for some reason, I can't seem to stay away.

"So hostile, and on move-in day?" Wells says when I reach him. "With a win like this morning? I thought 'Welcome back, losers' was all you had for us, and I must say, I was a little disappointed at first." He reaches into his pocket and pulls out another tampon. I'm only kind of dying to know how many tampons he has on his person at this very moment. "This was good. Wasteful, but good."

I admit nothing to Wells, because—and I say this without a trace of exaggeration—he could be recording me. And even though our schools' administrations know what we get up to on move-in day, no one has ever outright admitted anything. I imagine there would be a steep punishment if someone were stupid enough to get caught.

Although I'm positively *itching* to tell Wells that for every box of tampons we bought for the move-in day prank, we bought another to donate to the nearest women's shelter.

But I don't have anything to prove to a Wellborn, least of all this one.

"Are you gonna get to the point soon?" I ask. "I was on my way to find a snack."

He grins and holds his arms out. "Well, you found one."

I make a big show of rolling my eyes. "Okay, this is clearly a waste of my time. I'm going."

I make it half a step when Wells says my name, and I turn back. He looks like he's about to come through the front gate.

A warning noise jolts out of me. There's no real campus boundary line at the front gate, but it's so well understood, it may as well be painted in neon. I point at it, imagining it glowing against the pavement. This is the line no boy can be caught crossing.

Wells lets his foot hover there, smirking like he's won something, and slowly retreats to the other side.

"He'd like to open a dialogue."

"He can kiss my ass."

"I'm sure you'd like that."

I imagine it—Three on his knees—and quickly shake the thought from my mind. I don't know what it is about him that winds me up so tight. Of the five older Wellborns, he's not even the cutest. In fact, he's not even the second cutest. He's third, which is only fitting. Right after Christian Page, but before the Biermann siblings, whose family looks were cultivated over generations of what was probably inbreeding.

The best looking Wellborn is, unfortunately, standing in front of me. God, what an annoying thought.

"Is there something you *need* from me, Gabriel?" I ask, crossing my arms. I use his given name in a sad attempt to throw him off his game. "A signed letter to bring back with you? *'Take your dialogue and shove it up your ass. Love, Dorothy'*?"

Wells grins. "He'd probably want it notarized."

Wellborn boys hate having their full first names used against them, but Wells doesn't seem bothered. So, I use the only weapon I have left.

"I'm leaving," I say.

"Oh, come on, Doe," Wells calls after me. "I know you want to laugh at that!"

I do, but I'd never give a Winfield boy the satisfaction. I only allow myself a grin once my back is turned.

I wave over my shoulder as I round the corner, collapsing against the wall once I'm out of sight.

Open a dialogue? I wonder as I catch my breath. Something

about interacting with Wells always does this to me. Maybe because he's so emotionally removed. It makes me feel wildly uncool.

It makes sense that Three would ask him to act as ambassador. Not only because he's clever enough not to lose an edge to me, but because Gabriel Wellborn doesn't care. About anything, but least of all move-in pranks and the Weston-Winfield rivalry.

Three cares though. Sometimes I think Three cares even more than I do. Which is why his offer to open a dialogue sounds absurd to me. It smells of forfeiture. It reeks of a white flag. A stalemate with no winner.

If there's one thing Three and I agree on, it's that there has to be a winner—and, more importantly, there has to be a loser.

This isn't a war that ends in treaty. Too many Weston girls have worked too hard to see this die in a handshake and admission of equal skill.

Three had to see this coming. Which is why I'm not surprised when I get back to my room with the yogurt I bought at the Brick—I would not let a Winfield boy let me forget what's important—and find a text waiting for me.

SATAN HAS THREE MOUTHS
You'll regret that decision soon.

CHAPTER TWO

He wants to do *what*?"

We're in the Kingdom after curfew, and I'm sprawled in a chair, my feet propped on the ladder of a nearby bunk bed.

I feel the outrage rolling off of Sumi and crack an eye open. "You're even angrier than I was."

"It's appalling!" Sumi thrusts her open bottle into the air for emphasis. Organic peach tea splatters the rest of us.

Gemma shrieks like she's been shot. "Sumitra! This is a brand-new cardigan!"

"Who wears a cardigan in August?" Shawn asks. "I mean, it's balls hot up here."

Jade grimaces. "Please don't say *balls* in this sacred space."

"It just doesn't make sense," I continue. "Three offering to open a dialogue two years ago is weird, but senior year? That's like being in game seven of seven and forfeiting before it starts."

"When did you get into sports metaphors?" Shawn asks.

"*My point is*," I say with a glare in her direction, "why would he even consider it? Three always has an angle."

"Maybe he's just tired," Gemma says. "He's not the only one."

Jade, who's elbow-deep in a bag of popcorn, throws some at her. "Speak for yourself, Dr. Neurotic. Some of us are having a good time."

"I didn't mean me!" Gemma protests, throwing popcorn back.

"The fact remains," Sumi says, "that Three would never go out on a limb unless he knew he'd get what he wanted. And he knows you'd never agree to opening a dialogue without some kind of incentive."

I sit up a little straighter. "You think he wanted me to say no?"

Sumi shrugs. "I'm just hypothesizing."

It's a good hypothesis. But the question remains—*why*?

"We have time to figure it out," Shawn says, giving my elbow a comforting squeeze.

"Not too much time if we want to do something really significant before graduation," says Gemma.

I give her a look. "What a disgusting thought."

Jade grins. "Little Doe not ready to grow up?" She throws an arm around my shoulders and gives me a shake.

My stomach flips. The year has barely even started, and already I'm dreading graduation.

"Never," I say. "Not until I win the war against Winfield."

"That's a war that's been going on for, like, a century," Gemma says. "You really think we'll be the ones to end it?"

Shawn scoffs. "Why shouldn't we be? Who says it can't end with us?"

I nudge her with my elbow, and she bumps her fist against mine.

"I don't care if I have to shave Three's head while he sleeps," I say. "Before we graduate, Winfield will forfeit."

"Strong words," says Sumi.

Shawn grins. "At the very least, we want to end on a note where there's no question who won this year."

I imagine Three begging us to relent, to let him save face in front of his boys, and I smile.

Shawn is right—why shouldn't it be us? From the start, we've been contenders in this war. It was a prank that brought the five of us together in the first place.

When I started at Weston, I knew instantly that the next four years would be nothing like the nine years I'd spent back home at St. Aloysius. The student body was diverse, the girls knowledgeable and worldly, and even though there were cliques—day students sticking together in the dining hall at lunch, the girls who liked to sneak into town on the weekends gossiping in the dorm common rooms, future Ivy Leaguers monopolizing the tables in the library—there was a place for everyone. Weston made St. Aloysius look like the Wild West.

I was desperate to prove myself worthy of my spot at Weston. The upper school girls were practically untouchable, and I was eager to get in their good graces. I needed Weston to be my place. I was out of other options.

Shawn was the only person I knew, the two of us thrust together by our random roommate assignment, so I recruited her to help.

It was supposed to be a low-stakes prank. We planned to sneak out late one night to slip bubble bath into the Winfield fountain.

We didn't anticipate running into Jade and Gemma downstairs. They were headed to see the dorm monitor, a woman named Mrs. Pearson, who we were already terri-fied to cross. Shawn and I froze as soon as they spotted us. Gemma was sniffling, her face flushed from crying. Jade had her arm around Gemma's shoulders, half comforting and half dragging Gemma down the hall.

Jade frowned at us. "What are you two doing?"

It was a fair question, considering we were dressed like cat burglars, and I was carrying a backpack.

"Nothing," I said. "What are you doing?"

Jade eyed us, then glanced at Gemma.

Gemma wiped her nose on the sleeve of her pink polka-dot pajama set. "I'm having an episode."

"I found her in the bathroom," Jade said. "I thought Mrs. Pearson could help."

We learned later about Gemma's "episodes"—bouts of homesickness that usually ended with her sobbing in the bathroom. Those episodes are long over, but she's still prone to crying when her stress levels peak.

A thump sounded from behind Mrs. Pearson's door. I reached for Shawn to shove her behind me right as she tried to shove me behind her, so we ended up locked in a weird half hug.

I would have laughed if I hadn't been so terrified of get-ting caught. My spot at Weston wasn't set in stone, and get-ting caught on even the lowest-risk prank could end with me packing.

Shawn and I shuffled back from the door, and Jade grabbed Gemma, hauling her with us.

When we asked Jade later why she followed us, she didn't have an answer. Gemma couldn't say why she didn't protest. And none of us knew why we decided to run for the common room.

Maybe it's because the light was on.

Inside, Sumi was tinkering with an old radio, static humming low.

She glanced up as we rushed in, looking only mildly interested. "What's up?"

"Oh god, oh god." Gemma ducked immediately behind the armchair while Shawn ran to switch off the light.

As the others hid, I grabbed Sumi and hauled her behind the couch. We bumped into Jade, the three of us shuffling around in the dark until a jaunty little xylophone tune rang out. Shortly after, a tinny, male voice said, "Seven. Four. One. Three. Three."

The light flicked on.

"Seven. Four. One. Three. Three," the man repeated.

The happy little tune played once more. Static followed, swiftly cut off by a click.

"Little slobs," Mrs. Pearson said from across the room. "Refuse to clean up after themselves. Scared the bejesus out of me."

The light clicked off again, but I motioned for Jade and Sumi to wait until I heard, very distantly, Mrs. Pearson's door shut.

I poked my head up to check that we were alone.

Across the room, Shawn peered at me over the top of the armchair.

We grinned at each other.

"Clear," I said to the others as I stood.

"What *was* that?" Shawn asked, glancing toward the radio on the table.

"A numbers station," Sumi said. "I found a thread on a forum that predicted a broadcast tonight. I'm trying to crack the code. What are you guys doing?"

She glanced between the four of us, Jade and Gemma dressed for bed, Shawn and me dressed for something more nefarious.

"We're going to prank Winfield," I said.

Sumi tilted her head, considering this. "What's your plan?"

"Putting bubble bath in the fountain," Shawn said, motioning to my backpack.

Gemma frowned. "They closed their fountain two days ago."

Shawn and I looked at her.

She shrank a little behind Jade once she realized she had our attention. "I, um, saw them?"

"Crap." I let my backpack drop to the floor and slumped into a chair at the table.

The others followed.

"You can always do something else," Gemma said, sounding like she was trying to cheer me up.

I pouted. "I couldn't think of anything else. I'm not trying to get in trouble. I wanted to do something with low risk but big impact."

"Sneaking out is extremely high risk," said Jade. "They have security on both campuses. Even if you avoid Weston's guards, you're bound to run into Winfield's. You'd need a lookout."

"You could do way better than bubbling the fountain," Sumi said. "Something equally low risk but with a live audience."

Shawn pursed her lips. "You know, basketball season starts soon."

We spent the next two hours planning.

Two weeks later at Winfield's first home basketball game, we snuck onto the catwalk of their gym and dumped hundreds of Ping-Pong balls over the side during halftime. Our escape was a less-than-sophisticated mess of running as fast as we could. We only managed to get away because Jade played lookout from the stairwell. She's taken her role of watching our backs very seriously ever since.

For the impact our prank had, it wasn't the best-laid plan. But since we didn't get caught, we made out looking like pranking geniuses.

It didn't take long for word to spread that my friends and I had masterminded the whole thing. "Getting Ping-Ponged" became synonymous with getting humiliated in public. Upper school girls we'd never met knew our names.

Our group came together like a five-part machine. I'd never had friends like that before.

It no longer mattered that the upper school girls respected me as an equal. I didn't need to be taken under anyone's wing. On my own merit, I belonged at Weston.

The day classes start, Weston holds First Assembly. It's like a little welcome home coupled with reminders, mostly for the first years. They're easy to pick out of the crowd; they're the ones clutching campus maps and looking terrified.

Little ducklings, I think, making a point to smile at the ones I pass.

"Ugh, perv alert," Shawn says as we make our way to the nearest open row. Mr. Tully is standing at the end of the aisle, watching as we file into our seats.

I bite back a grimace when I realize I've caught his eye.

He gives me a big wave. "Welcome back, Dorothy."

I clench my teeth in a smile and wave back.

There isn't anything overtly pervy about Mr. Tully. He isn't some middle-aged guy with beady eyes wearing small shorts and always adjusting himself or anything like that. He's pretty young, probably early thirties, and he's got a friendly face. Outside of class, he wears regular teacher clothes—nice slacks and a button-down shirt with a tie. In class, he wears swishy athletic pants and a T-shirt.

But there is something off-putting about him, something that makes us wait for each other if he asks to speak to us after class and watch the younger girls when they're talking to him. My mom always says: where vulnerable people gather, so will predators. I've never told her about Tully. We don't have anything on him except a bad feeling and rumors no one will substantiate. I've heard whispers and warnings—don't go to his office alone, politely decline if he ever offers you his number, and never, under any circumstances, go off campus with him.

When I was first put in Roseland House, where Mr. Tully is an advisor, the upper school girls passed these rules down like sacred bylaws. But when I asked how they knew these things, it was all furtive glances and zipped lips.

"Just trust us, Doe. You don't want to know."

They didn't know me at all if they thought that was true.

"Maybe this is the year we get something real on Mr. Tully," I whisper to Shawn as we slide into our seats.

She hums in agreement.

The others are late, which isn't surprising. Sumi and Jade are notoriously bad about time management, and Gemma is always stuck dragging them wherever they need to be. It stresses Gemma out to no end that she's constantly late by association.

Shawn glances toward the back of the auditorium. "Ten bucks says Jade is still in bed."

"Nah, she'll be out of bed, but I guarantee she's making them wait while she puts on eyeliner."

Shawn looks at me. "Bet?"

I nod. "Bet."

Headmistress Cotesmore takes the stage, and the auditorium doors snap shut behind us. When I glance back, there's no sign of the others.

I chuckle as I slide down in my seat.

"For those of you rejoining us this year," Cotesmore begins, "we're as thrilled to have you back as I'm sure you are to be back."

Pause for light laughter.

"For those of you joining for the first time, we are happy to have you with us on this journey for knowledge and growth. To all of you, returning and new, welcome to The Weston School."

It might seem very uncool from the outside, but this gets a roar of cheers from us. Weston girls love The Weston School. You won't find any eye-rolling here.

My phone buzzes in my pocket, but I ignore it.

"Before we begin our regular assembly, we have a very important announcement to make about the future of Weston," says Cotesmore.

I have her First Assembly speech down to a formula, but she's gone off-script.

I glance at Shawn as my phone buzzes again, three times in quick succession.

"Is your phone going nuts, too?" Shawn whispers to me.

I discreetly slide my phone out of my pocket.

GEMMY

SOS

SOS

WE JUST HEARD

I frown at my screen and then look over at Shawn.

Whatever question I'm forming dies on my lips when

Cotesmore says, "The board of trustees at Weston has decided that this will be the final year of operation for The Weston School."

My stomach bottoms out.

"Next year," Cotesmore says, "we will be merging with Winfield Academy, to become a coeducational institution."

The entire auditorium explodes with noise.

The others are waiting for us in the back row of the auditorium when Cotesmore dismisses us to class.

"This can't be happening," I say, feeling sick. "This is—this goes against *everything* Mallory Weston wanted for this school!"

"At least we're seniors," says Jade. "We won't have to worry about it, because we'll be gone."

"It's called a *legacy*," I say. "We *have* to worry about this, even if we *will* be gone!"

Jade shoots Sumi a look, but Sumi doesn't quite meet her gaze.

My hands are shaking just thinking about Winfield boys roaming our sacred halls. These walls are what keep Winfield boys out, creating the safe space where Weston builds us up. We can't give Winfield boys another place to tear us down.

"We shouldn't talk about it now," I say, backtracking when I notice first years nearby. I put on my best fake smile and lower my voice. "Let's go to the diner after school. I need a large dark chocolate while we unpack this mess."

I turn away from my friends and cup my hands around my mouth. "Hey, first years! I'm headed to McHenry Hall. That's near Ivers, Roche, and Lohmeyer. If you need any of those, follow me."

When I have a decent-sized crowd, I start off.

"Hey, aren't you Doe Saltpeter?" one asks. "I heard you're the one who did the move-in-day prank on Winfield."

I glance at the group, put my finger over my lips, and wink. "Weston girls never tell."

"I saw some of the Winfield boys moving in," another girl says, waggling her eyebrows. "I can't wait to be coed. My mom's going to flip."

I round on the group as they start to titter excitedly. "Hey, rule number one at Weston: we don't idolize Winfield boys. You want to date one? You want to think one's cute? Fine, go ahead. But Weston always comes first. We're sisters—that's bigger than who has a cute butt and who you kissed at Fall Fest."

She grins. "You really think I could get one to kiss me?"

"I'd say your worth isn't decided by whether or not you can get a girl-starved demon from Winfield to lay his nasty fish lips you."

She still looks pleased.

I sigh. "Okay, anyone heading to Ivers"—I motion to the path ahead—"take this straight down the hill, and you'll run right into it."

Thankfully, the girl breaks off from the group, as do a few others.

"I kind of agree with her on some points," another says as she sidles up beside me. She has red hair even curlier than mine and pale skin covered almost completely in freckles. She's older than the rest—definitely not a freshman—but I don't recognize her.

She must see my confusion, because she says, "I'm not with your ducklings. I just happened to be going in the same direction."

"Junior?"

She nods. "Virginia Brinkoff."

I open my mouth to introduce myself, but she laughs and waves me off. "You're Doe Saltpeter. Everyone knows who you are."

I close my mouth.

"I'm just saying, Weston going coed isn't the worst thing ever," she says. "Separating by gender is archaic."

"I disagree. Boys' schools started with keeping girls out. We weren't allowed to be educated—we were supposed to be wives. It's the whole reason Mallory Weston started the school to begin with. Keeping boys out of a space for girls isn't archaic—it gives us a place to develop a sisterhood."

"Like a sorority," Virginia says.

At my horrified look, she shoots me a wry smile.

"I guess we agree to disagree," she says, turning her attention forward. "Weston won't be yours for much longer. You'll be gone, and time will do what time does best—change things."

My stomach ties itself into one million little knots while Virginia turns to face the first years and calls, "I'm heading to Roche. You can come with me if that's where you're going."

A chunk of first years break away from the group and follow Virginia.

I've always been prepared for the war with Winfield, but I never thought I'd find a fight on my home turf—not with Three, or any boy at all, but a Weston girl just like me.

"Guys, I'm really worried about her," Gemma says, putting her head down next to mine on the table. "I don't think she's blinked in, like, over three minutes."

"Come on, Doesy," Shawn says, patting my back. "Your milkshake's here. It'll make you feel better."

I lift my head a little. There's a dent on my face from where my cheek was smashed against part of the diner menu.

Jade grimaces. "I can't believe you put your bare face down like that. Do you know how many people have touched that menu?"

"I don't care." I slide down in the booth until my butt nearly hangs off the seat.

"She's been like this all day," Gemma says.

Sumi drags my milkshake closer to her, scoops some onto a spoon, and motors it toward me. "Open up. I'll spoon-feed you. Like a mommy goat."

"Do goats use spoons?" Jade asks with a laugh.

"Well, I can't exactly feed her milkshake from my nipple," Sumi says.

Gemma shrieks.

"I can't believe I'm going to have a war on two fronts now," I tell them, grabbing my milkshake back. I suck down a long gulp from the straw. There's nothing like a dark chocolate milkshake from Phoebe's Diner to soothe your soul.

Phoebe's Diner is a staple in Delafosse. The whole place is like if old Greece had a baby with a fifties American diner— blue vinyl booths, an old jukebox, a counter with swivel stools coupled with grapevine-decorated white walls, paintings of Greek towns, and small statues of various Greek gods scattered around. It's the reason their dessert case features cheesecake and apple pie next to baklava and kourabiedes, and the menu has sections for burgers, sandwiches, and traditional Mediterranean Greek food.

Even the lettering on the sign outside is done in a Greek style.

We've been coming to Phoebe's forever for their top-quality milkshakes. Plus, there are no Winfield boys, *ever*.

Phoebe's is a Weston girls spot. Winfield boys have Mr. Dino's, the Italian place on the other side of town.

It's not that there are rules, technically. But there's an unspoken understanding that certain places in town belong to Weston girls, and others, to Winfield boys. Sure, there are other places to eat where I might run into Three and Company, like the coffee shop or the sandwich place. Wells tends to hang out at Rotty's Bookstore, and plenty of girls shop there, myself included. He's like a fixture in the highly coveted red armchair at the back of the store. I've been tempted to sneak in early and steal it, just to see what he'd do when he showed up. But Phoebe's is ours, and Mr. Dino's is theirs, and it's always been like that.

Which is why I nearly upend my milkshake when I glance up at the tinkling of the bell over the door and see Three ducking inside with a couple of his boys in tow.

Three looks like he fell out of a J.Crew catalogue, or maybe the brochure of a military school where they show you how they send your delinquent son back looking like a youth group leader. His neatly cut brown hair, golden-tanned skin, and winning smile scream innocence, while his sharp blue eyes scream, *I eat the innocent for dinner.*

I glare with what feels like the heat of a thousand suns. "What. The. Fuck."

Shawn follows my gaze and scowls. "Not allowed," she calls to Three. "This is a breach of territory."

Three grins and heads toward our table.

We're in one of the big circle booths, which can easily fit ten people, so Three wastes no time squeezing in next to Gemma.

Gemma slides over so far and fast, she nearly ends up in Jade's lap.

"May we help you?" Jade asks, leaning around Gemma to get a look at Three's face.

The boys with him, Zamir Salahuddin and Alex Hyun, insert themselves on our side of the booth, pushing Shawn into me until the five of us are smooshed together in the middle, while the boys make themselves comfortable on either end.

Sumi, who's smashed in the middle of us all, looks like she's holding court at the head of the table.

She looks at Three and says, "I'm sorry, I don't believe we invited you to sit."

"No apology necessary." Three flashes her a grin. "Besides, we're about to be one happy family. Better start setting a good example for the kids."

Three leans out of our booth and gives a delicate finger wave to another table.

I haul myself up onto my knees and twist to look. Some younger Weston girls are crowded around a table. Two perk up at his attention while the other ducks her head and blushes.

I point at the first two. "Don't you dare wave back."

They shrink into their seats.

I slide back into the booth and glare at Three. "Don't get any ideas. This merger isn't happening. I don't know what your headmaster told you—"

Three barks out a laugh. "Headmaster Pritchard? Please, Doe. I've known about this for months."

Shawn stiffens beside me. Across the table, Gemma's jaw drops.

I can only imagine what my face must look like for Three's smile to turn so smug.

"I warned you that you'd regret your decision," he says. "We could have made a truce. Maybe I could've helped you stop the whole thing."

Shawn snorts. "You really think we'd buy that?"

"Good point. I honestly don't care about the merger. I'll be gone by then."

I have a hard time reconciling the Three I know with this statement. He cares about Winfield as much as I care about Weston.

I glare at him, unsettled that I can't make sense of it. "You want the same thing we want. To win."

He grabs a fry off Gemma's plate and pops it in his mouth. "You know, I've always liked that about you, Doe—you're always on the same page as me."

"That's why I knew your 'open a dialogue' offer from Wells was bullshit."

"Hey, at least I offered."

"Knowing I'd turn you down!"

He shrugs. "Can't help that I know you well."

"You don't know anything about me."

Three levels me with a look that makes my toes curl in my sneakers.

"This changes nothing," Shawn says. "Phoebe's is still Weston territory, which means you have to go. Now."

On my other side, Sumi grips her fork prongs-side-up and glares at Three.

"I don't think so," Three says, eyeing Sumi, then settling his gaze on me. "We're not abiding by territory rules anymore. This is a fucking free-for-all." He starts to slide out of the booth. "I came to give you a courtesy warning. Next time, we'll be getting menus."

"They won't serve you!" I practically shriek, slamming my hands down on the table.

Three tucks his hands into his front pockets and smirks. "I wouldn't be so sure about that. Everyone in town knows about the merger, and they've been itching for the revenue."

"If you can come to Phoebe's, we can come to Mr. Dino's," Jade says. She's been noticeably quiet during this entire exchange, her expression unreadable.

Three smiles. "You're absolutely right. And the door is always open to Weston girls," he says, raising his voice a bit. He turns toward the younger girls and gives them a little finger-gun move. "Tell your friends."

"Do not!" I shout, coming up over the top of the booth again. "Do not listen to him."

But they're already whispering amongst themselves.

Three backs away and gives me a salute. "See you later, Dorothy."

CHAPTER THREE

Headmistress Cotesmore has always had an open-door policy, so I shouldn't be surprised that every time I've come to see her this week, there's been a long line of girls waiting.

When I first came to Weston, my meetings with Cotesmore were mandatory, part check-in to see how I was settling in, part observation to make sure I wasn't falling into old habits. We've come a long way since then.

When I was twelve, my parents told me they were getting a divorce. The fighting in our house had hit all-time highs that summer, each argument ending in long stretches of aggressive silence. Sometimes at night, it felt like the silence had a hand around my neck. By the time my parents split, it was almost a relief.

It wasn't until the divorce was underway that Mom dropped the bomb: she wanted to leave St. Louis, and she wanted me to go with her.

I sometimes wonder how different things would be if I'd just agreed. But I never could have done that to Dad.

In the end, Mom stayed for me, but the damage was done.

Dad was angry she'd even considered trying to take me away, and Mom resented him for keeping her stuck in the place she so desperately wanted to leave. I wondered if Mom resented me for keeping her there, too.

I wasn't as angry as I was sad. My parents, who for so long had been a single entity to me, were no longer speaking. I was transferred between houses every two weeks, dropped at the curb like a poorly delivered package.

When I was midway through eighth grade, Dad started dating again. He met a man through a friend, and they hit it off. A literature professor named Chris. He used to come over with stacks of essays, and he and Dad would hang out on the couch, Dad clicking through program code on his computer and Chris marking up papers.

Then, one of my classmates saw Dad and Chris out on a date, and suddenly, everyone at St. Aloysius knew my dad is bisexual.

It wasn't a secret, and yet they treated it like something I'd been trying to hide. Something I'd kept from them, as if it had ever been anyone's business.

When kids at school started making jokes about him, the anger I'd tried so hard to stash away during the divorce clawed its way out of me. My reaction was kerosene on an already-burning house. Once they knew they could get a rise out of me, it was like they made a bet to see who could get me to do my worst.

Eventually, a parent meeting was scheduled. I was granted leniency, because the divorce meant I was "going through a tough time." The school turned my parents into the problem, rather than the bullies.

Mom and Dad were suddenly speaking again, part of the same team trying to keep me afloat. And the more trouble

I got in, the more they banded together. So naturally, I got myself in more trouble.

My so-called friends jumped ship almost right away. They couldn't relate to what I was going through. I felt completely alone.

And when a boy called my dad an unforgiveable word in the hall one day, I punched him in the nose.

I was on the verge of expulsion when my parents took me out of school. Mom had to pull every string she knew to get me an interview at Weston. When I finally got my acceptance letter, it felt like a life preserver. I'd been drowning, but now I had something to hold on to. I was getting a chance to rewrite who I was. I could be someone different. I could be a Weston girl.

I can't let Winfield come in and ruin the place that saved me. What if there's another girl out there who needs a life preserver?

So even though I've never, in all my years at Weston, had to *schedule* a meeting with our headmistress, this time I have no choice. Her first opening is a small window on Friday during my free period, and I snatch it up before someone else can.

"I was wondering when you'd be by to see me," Cotesmore says warmly when I step into her office.

"Well, you would've seen me first thing Monday afternoon, but there was a line twenty girls deep when I got here." I drop into one of the chairs in front of her desk and heave a deep sigh. "You can't do this, Headmistress."

Cotesmore smiles. "Oh, Doe. I'm flattered you think I have that much power in what happens here."

"I know it's not your decision. But you're right here with us—you *know* what would happen if we let Winfield boys into this school."

"I'm not sure I do."

I gape at her. "You're a Weston girl! You know what they're like!"

"The rivalry between our schools—"

"*Rivalry?* We're at war!"

Cotesmore turns away, tapping her fingers against her mouth. I get the sense she finds me amusing.

"I understand where you're coming from, Doe," she says, facing me again once she's smoothed out her expression. "I know how much this school means to you, and I value your feelings on this. But this merger works in Weston's favor. Winfield has always had better donors and resources."

"We benefit from that at what cost? You bring in boys, and everything the girls do becomes second. Our rowing team ranked first in the region last year. Our soccer team won state two years ago. Do you think anyone will care about girls' rowing or soccer or anything we do at all, once boys come in? Everything will be about them."

"There would have been challenges without the merger," says Cotesmore. "What if we ran out of money and couldn't fund a rowing team? The fewer donors we have, the less girls will enroll, and Weston would have to close its doors. Maybe not next year, or the year after, but the board is thinking long-term, Doe, and this merger *saves us*. It keeps the doors open for new Weston girls. It gives us money to offer better financial aid and scholarships, to bring in kids who aren't like the majority of students we get here."

I frown, sinking into my chair.

Cotesmore sighs and leans in. "I love your enthusiasm. I always have—you know that. There is no girl at this school who embodies and embraces what a Weston girl should be more than you. You've become a role model to the younger girls. I want to keep our doors open so we can help more girls grow the way we've helped you. Most mergers like this happened in the sixties and seventies. Big-name schools have been coed for decades. It wasn't the end for them, and it won't be the end for us."

"And when there's one school, who do you think's gonna run it? You, or that guy?" I point toward her office windows, which look out at Winfield in the distance.

Cotesmore's smile stills.

I stand up. "Mallory Weston wanted a school for girls so we could have the same opportunities as boys. Once we're coed and we're sharing resources and finances, whose enrollment will benefit? Do you think we'll really end up with the same number of girls? That girls will have room to grow when they're constantly pushing against the glass ceiling? We can grow here because there *is* no ceiling. Bring boys in, and everything we do, everything we want, will never be enough. Girls will get passed over for college acceptances and internships because they can only take a few students from each school. They'll end up at second-rate schools doing second-rate things, and the next thing we know, they'll be married and popping out kids and *what* career? Who cares about a career when a boy bats his eyes at you and says, 'I'll bring the bread, you bring the baby'?"

Only when I stop and my ears are ringing do I realize that I've been yelling. Cotesmore watches me, her eyes tight with worry.

I lick my dry lips and turn away. It's bad form. But I can't stop. I haven't been dismissed. I get the feeling Cotesmore doesn't know what to say.

I don't know what to say, either. There's nothing I haven't already said.

So I leave.

* * *

I ditch the rest of my classes and take an unsanctioned trip off campus. The rebellion makes me jittery with nerves, and I plan to hide out in a booth at Phoebe's sucking down milkshakes until I figure out what to do or die from sugar overload—whichever comes first.

I'm almost there when I see a Delafosse police car turning the corner, and I'm forced to duck into Rotten Row Bookstore.

Delafosse is serious about truancy, with Winfield and Weston so close, on top of their own schools in town. I realize belatedly I'm wearing a bright orange T-shirt from a volunteer event at one of Delafosse's animal shelters last spring. It's eye-catching for its color and the huge dog face on the front. I couldn't be more obvious. Worried I'm already spotted, I stride right past the counter and straight down to the basement.

The basement at Rotty's is reserved for their used items, and always smells a little damp and musty, like old books and mildew. The packed shelves stretch wall to wall. Books are even stacked on the floor. It's probably a massive fire hazard.

I hear footsteps overhead, and my heart jumps into overdrive.

That's it. I'm about to get picked up for truancy the first time I've ever skipped class or gone into town without a pass. It's just my luck.

I duck down an aisle and around the other side, pressing myself against the end of the bookshelf. I smooth my hands over my hair, holding down my curls, making every part of myself small.

But with my hair over my ears, I can't hear any footsteps—only the sound of my heart pounding in my throat.

Someone turns the corner, and before I can scream, a hand clamps over my mouth. I start to thrash him in the chest, freezing when I realize it's Wells.

He puts a finger to his lips and points to the ceiling. I look up, then feel stupid because it's not like I can see anything. I glare at Wells, and he smirks.

Then I hear footsteps—and voices. A radio beeps.

Wells drops his hand from my mouth and grabs my wrist. He drags me to the back of the basement, and I point to a door marked EMPLOYEES ONLY.

He shakes his head.

I try to pull him toward it, but he holds on and hauls me the other way, toward the fire exit.

The sign on the door reads: ALARM WILL SOUND.

"Ready to run?" he asks, putting his hand on the push bar.

"No!" I whisper-yell.

Wells pushes the door open, and the alarm shrieks.

I vaguely feel his fingers slotting between mine as he yanks me out into the parking lot. It's half filled with cars, and a woman leaving the hardware store glances our way.

"Come on," Wells says. "If you keep dragging your feet, I'm leaving you."

So I run.

We end up a few blocks away, in the alley behind the sandwich shop and the fancy Chinese restaurant, next to a dumpster teeming with flies.

I press the back of my hand against my nose. We couldn't have stopped *anywhere else?*

"Why couldn't we use the other door? Hide out there?" I ask, my voice thick as I try not to breathe in the scent of garbage.

Wells grins. "You must be new to this whole ditching

thing. You think they wouldn't check a storage room? They saw you come in."

I frown and look away, feeling dumb. "So, why'd you help me? Why not let me get caught? Three would be beside himself if I got grounded."

Getting grounded at Weston is basically the same as a normal grounding by actual parents—stronger monitoring from the dorm supervisor and restricted off-campus outings. I would've been drinking takeout milkshakes delivered by my friends for weeks.

"You caught me. It was just an elaborate ploy to get you to hold my hand."

"Wha—" I look down. Sure enough, our fingers are still entwined.

I shake him off and cross my arms.

Wells smiles. "You know, this may shock you, but not everything I do is for Three's benefit. I helped you because you looked freaked out. And because you led the cops straight into my hideout. Now, I could've hidden in the storage closet and been fine. But what kind of friend would I be if I let you get caught?"

I scoff. "Hey, delusional? We aren't friends."

"No, but you want to be."

I can hardly hold back my laughter. "Friends? With you?"

Wells turns and walks away.

I stop laughing. "Hey, wait—I was just—"

He peeks around the corner, and when he turns back, he runs right into me.

I stumble back.

Wells tilts his head. "What are you doing?"

"I thought you were leaving."

"Because you said you don't want to be friends with me?"

Wells snorts. "Come on, Doe, I'm a Wellborn. I've got thicker skin than that. Besides, I know it's a lie. I can see it in your eyes."

"The only thing you're seeing in my eyes is a milkshake craving."

He grabs my sleeve and pulls me after him, toward another unknown destination. "I know what I see. I'm the Wellborn you want to befriend, and Three is the Wellborn you want to fu—"

I elbow him hard in the ribs. "*Don't* finish that sentence."

Wells grins.

I huff out an annoyed breath. "Where are we going, anyway?"

"The only place they won't look for a couple of truants," Wells replies.

Which turns out to be the Bellefontaine Cemetery.

Wells and I collapse in the grass behind the big mausoleum. It's hotter here than anywhere else in town, and I try to discreetly dab sweat from my forehead.

"Classes at Delafosse High start letting out soon. We won't be as noticeable then."

"*You* won't be." I motion to my orange eyesore of a shirt. "I don't know about me."

Wells gives me a once-over and shrugs off his hoodie, tossing it into my lap. "You can borrow this."

I stare at him.

The corner of his mouth kicks up in this half smile that's a little amused but also a little exasperated. "It's too hot for it, anyway. I don't need it. You do. Consider it a charitable service."

"Why'd you even wear it when it's so hot out?" I ask, picking up his hoodie and folding it neatly in my lap.

"It's always cold in Rotty's."

"Do you skip class a lot to hang out there?"

He shrugs. "A decent amount, I guess."

"It's only the first week and you're already skipping class?" I catch the glance he gives me. "Don't look at me like that. My skipping is different. It was an extenuating circumstance. I was emotionally distraught."

Wells doesn't ask what about. He'd be stupid not to know—the only thing anyone cares about right now is the merger.

"I feel like an idiot," I say, staring out over the sea of headstones. "I really thought if anyone would be on my side about this merger, it'd be Three."

Wells lets out a breath. "Then you've learned the most valuable lesson. You can't count on Three for anything."

"He's supposed to be the reliable one. Christian Page is richer than a king, the Biermann brothers are the hot-tempered meatheads, Three is reliable, and you're—" I cut myself off.

Wells raises an eyebrow. "And I'm . . . ?" He circles a hand in front of me, prompting me to continue.

"I'm not saying it."

"You have to. I saved your life."

"Hardly!"

"I saved you from getting grounded. It's basically the same thing."

"I didn't ask you to save me."

"Consider this *your* charitable service. Come on, it's so easy. Three is reliable, Biers and Joc are most likely to get in a bar fight before they turn eighteen, Christian is Mr. Moneybags, and I'm . . . ?"

I clench my jaw and grind out the answer from between my teeth. "The pretty one."

Wells makes a startled noise, puts a hand over his heart, and falls back into the grass. "Oh, I've been hit. Dorothy Saltpeter called me *pretty*. Someone get a doctor. It looks bad."

I'm laughing but also kind of panicking because he's fallen out from behind the mausoleum and can probably be seen from the street.

"Shut up, you're so stupid." I grab him by the shirt, hauling him up. "And you're gonna get us caught."

Wells huffs out one final laugh and leans back against the mausoleum. "So, you're mad that Three didn't have your back."

"I wouldn't say *mad*. Just . . . surprised."

"Because he should want the merger stopped as much as you."

"Well, I'd assume. Our end goals have always been the same—to win. If we merge, we both lose, because it's all anyone will care about. It takes the sweetness out of winning. The merger will overshadow everything."

"Except for one thing. If the merger happens, Three technically wins."

I look at Wells. "What does that mean? *How?*"

Wells looks unsure of himself for possibly the first time ever. "I think I've already told you too much."

"But you don't care about this war—you never have," I remind him.

It's the wrong thing to say. His face goes blank.

He pulls his phone out and glances at it. "Almost time. I'm heading back," he says, standing up.

I scramble to my feet and grab his sleeve before he can get too far. "Wait—what about me?"

He motions to his hoodie, which I dropped in my haste to stop him.

I grab it from the grass. By the time I slide it on, he's halfway across the cemetery. When I pull the hood up over my hair and peek around the mausoleum, he's gone.

There is a pile of homework on my desk that I should have started days ago, but I can't find the energy.

It's almost time for dinner, but the sun is still so bright, it's giving the world an unnatural glow, like nothing is real.

Not even Shawn when she pushes my door open and pokes her head in.

"Hey," she says gently, like she's approaching a wounded animal in the woods.

I grunt in response. I'm facedown on my bed, where I've been since I snuck back on campus earlier.

I hear her kicking things aside. We haven't been back long, but my room is already a sty.

"You weren't answering my texts," she says, coming to sit on my bed. "Where were you all afternoon? Everyone said you went to see Cotesmore, but no one saw you after that."

I turn my head to look at her, cheek pressed into my sheets. "I went into town."

She blinks, looking startled. "How? Cotesmore gave you a pass? During school hours?"

I sigh.

Shawn slides off my bed and onto her knees, putting her face right up to mine. "You went into town without a pass? And *skipped class*? Doe, what's going on?"

"What does it look like?"

"Like you're moping."

"I'm in mourning."

Shawn snorts. "For what?"

"A legacy." I push myself up and look down at her. "It's

the end of an era. This merger is going to erase everything that's good about Weston."

"Maybe it won't happen."

It's my turn to snort. "Please. It's happening."

"Maybe we can stop it."

"I wouldn't even know where to start. I thought if enough people were against it, maybe. But—" I shake my head, still reeling at what Wells said earlier.

Shawn starts to climb up next to me, stopping when she ends up on top of a crumpled hoodie. She pulls it out from under her hip and holds it up.

"Uh, what is this?" She sniffs it and turns an accusatory eye on me. "It smells like *boy*."

"I ran into Wells earlier."

She scrunches her nose. "You guys are swapping clothes? What did you give him of yours?" She gives me a quick once-over. "Because I don't think you're missing anything. Unless it's something you wear *under* your clothes."

I roll my eyes and snatch the hoodie from her. I shove it under my pillow and out of sight. "It wasn't an exchange, you pervert. I borrowed it."

"You could do a lot worse than Gabriel Wellborn."

"That goes without saying. Three would definitely be worse."

I collapse against my pillows.

"Do you feel better after your rebellion?" Shawn asks, crawling up beside me.

I put my head on her shoulder. "No. I feel like garbage. Possibly worse than garbage. Definitely worse than I did before."

"What did Cotesmore say?"

"*It's all about the Benjamins, baby*," I sing.

"Weston's broke?"

"No. Not yet, anyway. But the merger is about money for Weston, for sure. I just can't figure out the angle for Winfield. What do they get out of it?"

Shawn leans her head against mine. "If we don't know, how do we find out?"

"Wells knows something." I sigh and sit up, twisting to face her. "I don't know how much, but more than we do. He said Three wants the merger."

"But Three said he doesn't care either way."

"Maybe that's the point. Wells said if the merger goes through, Three wins. But Three could also win without the merger, same as us. Whereas we only win . . ."

"Ah. We only have one winning scenario," Shawn says. "If the merger happens, we lose by default."

"We need to know why Three wins if the merger goes through. If we figure out what Winfield gets out of it, we get that answer, too."

"So we ask Wells, then?"

I shrug. "Maybe. But I barely got this much out of him."

"It's worth a shot," Shawn says. "To save Weston? Just bat those pretty eyes of yours. I bet he melts on the spot."

"Please. You forget he looks at his own reflection every day. He's much prettier than I am."

"Not true," Shawn says, pointing at me. "Besides, I've always thought he liked your attention. Can't hurt to try." She glances at her phone. "So, were you planning on skipping dinner, or . . . ? Because that does not sound like the Doe I know and love."

I groan and slide down the bed until I'm horizontal. "I don't want to draw attention to myself. If I don't go to dinner, I can pretend I was sick this afternoon. Maybe get a retroactive pass for skipping class."

"They're serving lasagna tonight," Shawn says.

I shoot up and swing my legs over the side of my bed. "Okay, well, you didn't mention *that*."

Shawn follows me to the door as I hastily slip on my shoes. "I thought you had the dining schedule memorized."

"I've been slacking off." I glance toward my desk and almost add, *in more ways than one.*

But Shawn is the most organized, levelheaded person I know. She already has her short list of colleges ready and at least one essay draft done. And school *just started*. At this rate, she'll be off at college before I even finish an application.

But I'm not ready to think about that, so I throw my door open and wave her out into the hall.

Better leave the existential dread for another day.

CHAPTER
FOUR

A s I'm climbing off the bus at Parc Provence Assisted Living, I find out that our traditional Weston School Labor Day Volunteer Event is going to be the first Weston-Winfield merger test.

We're split up by house, which means my friends are off on other assignments. Weston doesn't group us by dorm—they like a house system to give us a sense of community, and dorms to get us socializing outside our houses. For study hours, meetings with our advisers, and *fun* little events like Labor Day volunteering, we're separated by house—Jade, Shawn, and Gemma in Ewing, Sumi in Storey, and me in Roseland. None of us are stuck in Belair, thank god, because they really cultivate snobbery in that house.

Still, I'd take a whole day of forced volunteering with Belair House over Winfield. I'd take forced volunteering with a pack of rabid wolves over Winfield.

"This cannot be happening," I say to Shantel Subirana, the Roseland House prefect, as Mrs. Milner and Mr. Tully direct us into a line.

"Don't be so dramatic, Doe," Shantel says as she heads off toward the front of the line.

When she gets there, Mr. Tully says something to her that makes her smile go stiff on her face.

Roseland House is truly blessed to have Mr. Tully as one of our faculty advisors. Like, I feel very blessed to never need advising on anything, ever.

But Tully is the least of my worries today. Because the line he and Mrs. Milner are directing us into forms right beside a line of Winfield boys.

And at the front is Three.

He's with Biers, the older Biermann brother, who towers above the rest of his classmates. He's one of those boys who's always looked about twenty-five, with a thick neck and face that we can attribute to his former pro–football player father. He has the kind of fair skin that splotches up with red when he's angry, which really adds to his look. Biers kind of reminds me of a bull. Like he might charge at you if you get too close.

Not like Three, who looks over the line of Weston girls with this blithe smile while he chats with Shantel. Because of course Three is also his house prefect. Three can't be second at anything—house prefect, rowing team captain. If he doesn't end up valedictorian from sheer force of will, I'll eat my shoe. And if he misses it by a hair and his family doesn't pay for some building expansion to get his GPA up a few hundredths of a point, I'll eat both.

Even being the eldest Wellborn cousin is fitting for Three. Being the third Nathaniel Emeric Wellborn must kill something in his soul. It almost makes calling him Three feel like an insult. He's a walking toothpaste commercial with an inferiority complex.

Three spots me, his smile widening. He must see on my face that I was thinking about him, because he looks smug.

"Gross," I mutter, rolling my eyes and turning away.

"What, you're not into that country club born and bred style?"

I turn around, surprised to find Virginia standing behind me.

"What are you doing here? You're not in Roseland."

She frowns at me. "Uh, yeah I am."

"No, you're not. I know everyone in Roseland House."

"By name?" she says, her brows going up a little. "Really? Are you *sure*?"

"Well, maybe not by *name*," I say, "but I recognize every girl in my house, and you're not one of them."

Virginia rolls her eyes. "Doe, I have no reason to lie. Ask Mrs. Milner. Just because you don't recognize me doesn't mean I haven't been here the whole time."

I turn away from her, unsettled by this, and catch Three's eye.

I give him the finger.

Three pretends to catch it and tuck it into his pocket, grinning. His smile makes him look so much like a portrait of a young senator it pisses me off.

I half turn away in time to catch Virginia's smirk.

"For someone who doesn't want the merger to happen, you sure love to flirt with a Winfield boy."

I gape at her. "*Flirt?* With *whom*?"

She gives me a look.

"I'm not flirting with Three. You better watch what you say—that's practically slander."

She smiles a little. "I don't have to say it when people can see it with their own eyes."

I briefly consider asking the girl in front of me to switch places, but I don't want Virginia to feel like she's won something.

I'm not used to fighting with other Weston girls. My focus has always been elsewhere.

But Virginia clearly takes this fight for the merger seriously, and she isn't backing down. In fact, she hardly seems bothered by me at all.

That worries me almost more than anything else.

I end up in the art class, where the residents are set up with easels like a real art studio. I'm not much of an artist, so I can't really help beyond making sure everyone has enough paint and water to clean their brushes. One woman already upended her water cup three times, so I've been pretty busy.

I also got stuck with Three. So, I've been *keeping* myself pretty busy.

That doesn't stop him from saying something to me every time I drift close enough.

Like when we first arrived and started setting up the easels: "It's weird seeing you without your little girl gang. What do they do when you aren't around to tell them? Just wander aimlessly, hoping someone will give them some direction?"

"Are you asking because that's what your boys do? Unlike your friends, mine have brains of their own."

He snorted. "They hide it well."

At that point, I was filling water cups for the residents, and he was quick to retreat, likely sensing the chances of my throwing water in his face were rapidly increasing.

At the end of the class, I'm dumping the used water in the sink when the door creaks open behind me. I glance back as Wells pokes his head in.

I blink, surprised to see him, and wondering how I didn't notice him outside. I think back on Virginia insisting she's in Roseland House and frown. Am I really that oblivious?

Wells ducks into the room, rubbing the back of his neck. He won't quite look at Three, and he really won't look at me.

"You must be Mrs. Panisello!" he says brightly, putting his back to us as he approaches a woman with baby pink hair. "I'm supposed to escort you to bingo."

Mrs. Panisello positively beams at him. "What a handsome boy you are! I'm honored. Let's get to bingo. That Arthur Knuppel won two days ago and hasn't shut up since." She twists a little in her wheelchair to look up at Wells. "Maybe you should stick around while we play and help me beat him."

"I'd love that. I haven't played enough bingo in my life."

I glance at Three, an idea taking root.

"Hey, Wells," I say as he passes us.

Mrs. Panisello looks over at me, but Wells only nods. "Hi, Doe."

"I still have your hoodie," I say before I can stop myself.

I practically hear Three's neck crack as he whips his head around.

Wells closes his eyes briefly but seems to remember he's pushing an old woman in a wheelchair and opens them again. He's almost past us, so I can't see his expression.

"What does that mean?" Three asks, his voice tight. "Why would—"

"I'll wash it before I give it back," I call after Wells.

He gives a wave over his shoulder.

He hasn't confirmed anything, but his silence only escalates things. If he'd blown it off as nothing, maybe Three wouldn't be turning so red.

Three must know I'm not bluffing. Wells can act like he doesn't care—and maybe he doesn't—but Three cares. Wells isn't one of his boys, but he's family, and that's a significant hit. Wellborn boys don't associate with my friends. Not in a way where we'd end up exchanging clothes.

I start humming, turning back to the sink to take care of the rest of the cups. Three's gaze is burning into the side of my head.

"Why are you breathing like that?" I ask mildly, glancing over at him.

His face is pinched, like he's trying to blank his expression but can't quite get there.

I turn away to hide my smirk. "They probably have some laxatives lying around here somewhere," I tell him. "You look like you could use it."

Three forces out a breath. "He won't date you."

I pause. "Oh?"

"He might be nice to you, but he'll *never* date you."

"Interesting." I start drying the cups. "Thanks for the warning. It's nice to have someone worried I might get my feelings hurt."

Three makes a strangled sound. "I'm not *worried* about you."

I grin. "Okay, Three."

I continue drying while he stands there and seethes.

Later, as I'm heading toward the dining room to help with lunch, I see Wells coming from the other end of the hall.

I grin a little, still riding the high of pissing Three off.

Wells works his jaw as he stares at me, like he's trying to decide something. As soon as he gets close enough, he grabs my arm and hauls me back the way I came.

"What an interesting turn of events," I say with a laugh as he moves his hand from my arm to my back, propelling me forward until we reach a supply closet.

He pulls the door open and motions me inside.

"I don't think Three will like this."

"Get in."

I roll my eyes and step into the closet.

Wells shuts the door behind us.

It's pretty roomy inside, but feels smaller, with an automatic light overhead. Wells looks pale under the bright white glow, and the circles under his eyes go dark purple. I didn't notice those earlier.

"Don't tell me you're mad." I cross my arms and lean back against a shelf. "I only did it to rile Three up. He's so easy."

"I don't want you using me in your games, Doe."

"But you'll let Three use you?"

He's shaking his head before I even finish. "No, no, I don't. I'm either a player or I'm not, but I'm no one's pawn, especially yours."

I roll my eyes.

"I'm serious."

"So don't be a pawn. What I did was a play. You don't have to be a pawn—you can be player two."

"And how would that benefit me?"

I give him a look. "Come on, Wells. We both know you like getting under people's skin as much as Three. And probably getting under his skin more than anyone's."

"I don't mess with Three."

"But you could."

"I *don't* mess with Three," he says.

He says it with such conviction, I almost give up. I don't know what I'm seeing in his face, but there's a hard set to his jaw that makes me feel like I'm pressing a button without knowing what it does.

Instead, I do exactly what I know I shouldn't—I move closer, and press it again.

"Don't you ever get bored?"

"*Get* bored?" he repeats, looking down at me. "I'm *always* bored. That doesn't mean I want to get involved in your weird games with my cousin. That's not my kind of entertainment."

I shrug. "Fine. I mean, I don't get it, but fine."

Wells eyes me. "What were you thinking?"

I purse my lips in a smirk. "You want to know the game, but you don't want to play?"

He reaches for the door. "Never mind."

"Date me."

He stops, his shoulders stiffening. "You know," he says, "I've been asked out by a lot of girls, but you're the first to just come out and say it like that."

I scoff. "I don't mean for real."

"Right."

"It would make Three crazy."

"I'm not interested."

"You are. You'd love a chance to one-up him in something."

"And you and me dating would be me one-upping him?"

"It'd be you doing something he doesn't approve of, which is the same thing."

Wells shakes his head.

"Think about it," I say. "Aren't you tired of always coming in second to him?"

"I don't."

"Maybe not in all categories," I say, because looks-wise, Wells always wins. "But in the ones that matter, right?"

"I still don't see your point."

"Throw him off his game. If all he's thinking about is how furious he is that we're dating, then he knocks himself down a peg. You can pull ahead. Doesn't that sound *fun*?"

He chews his lip, and even though he doesn't answer, I count it a win that he's considering it at all.

"Look, you're not in the big game, but there's always more than one game going at a time. You let him win and you act like you don't care, but you must care a little. You have pride in there somewhere."

He glares at me. "I have pride. That's why I'm *not* agreeing to this."

"How is pretending to date me a blow to your pride?" I jerk back, realization dawning. "Oh. Unless . . ."

"No," he says, pointing at my face. "Don't do that."

"You have high standards," I say, ignoring him. "Three said you'd never date me. He didn't mean because you don't date. He thinks I'm not good enough for you."

"Doe."

I grimace. "That stings more than I expected."

Wells runs a hand over his face. "That's not what I'm talking about."

"Then what's the reason?"

"Because it may shock you, but I *like* dating."

"But you don't date."

He gives me a look.

"Okay, you don't *date*. What, you fool around? You think because you're dating me, you can't fool around with other girls without looking like an asshole, and that's boring?"

He tilts his head a little. "I mean . . ."

"I'm not fooling around with you, so that's off the table."

"Don't sound so disgusted."

"You brought it up."

"I didn't—you—" he splutters, going a little red.

"I guess you have to weigh your options, then." I reach past him for the door. "Is it better to not hook up but win against Three? Or is fooling around with other girls the only thing you actually care about?"

I push the door open and step out into the hall.

Wells grabs at my shirt, trying to pull me back, but I move out of his grasp.

Let him mull it over for a while.

CHAPTER FIVE

I don't tell the others about my proposition to Wells.

Not only because I was immediately rejected, which is one of the purest forms of humiliation.

Or that I'm worried he won't come crawling back—Three has a way of driving people to do their worst.

But because, after everything, I'm not sure they'll get it.

This war is supposed to be about Winfield, not the individual boys who go there.

It's not supposed to be about Three.

But for me, it's always about Three. He's Winfield personified. If ever a boy were going to represent a place, it'd be Three representing Winfield. They're both dull and uptight and pretentious, and they take themselves way too seriously.

A week after Labor Day, I'm in Sumi's room, hanging upside down off her bed. Sumi has the most comfortable bed—fashioned with a three-inch-thick memory foam mattress pad and expensive linen sheets with a plush duvet. She sleeps with exactly three pillows. Sumi is extremely serious about the art of sleeping well. For her last birthday, we pitched in on a set of silk pajamas for her, and it's the closest I've ever seen her come to crying.

Today she sits with her feet propped up on her desk while she knits a new scarf. Over her desk is a picture of her and her parents when they visited the extended Balakrishnan family in Kochi two summers ago. Underneath are posters for her top three workplaces—not even colleges, *workplaces:* an organization based in Sweden that's battling human trafficking, an Australian marine conservation group, and a law firm in Boston that helps exonerate the wrongfully accused. Every time Sumi learns about some new injustice, she develops another career dream, all of them centered around saving the world.

The knitting she does for fun, and to keep her head clear.

I wish I could find a hobby as relaxing as Sumi's. Instead, my hobbies are masterminding a war against Winfield and, when the existential angst sets in, hanging upside down off the bed until the only thing I can think about is how long it will take for my head to explode. Forget my top three workplaces—I can't even figure out where I want to go to college. I don't have any list, let alone a short one. It would help if I knew what I wanted to do with my life. Or had an idea of where I wanted to end up. Or even a slight inkling of anything I care about at all.

I do a quick internal search and come up empty. All I can think about is this stupid merger.

I wonder what I'd be doing right now if the merger weren't a factor. Would I be working on my college applications like my friends?

Blood rushes to my head and my eyes are starting to pulsate when my phone buzzes.

"You're disturbing my vibe," Sumi says.

"Your vibe has been disturbed since the day you were born," I tell her, my voice only a little strained as I struggle to sit up and grab my phone.

She turns around to blink at me through her big, round glasses. "The vibration is upsetting."

"Yet you're not at all annoyed by the clicking of your knitting needles?"

"No," she replies, turning back to her scarf.

I scowl at her back and grab my phone from where it's tucked up against the wall, half falling behind the bed.

UNKNOWN
Tangible reward

I frown at the screen.

ME
Stranger danger

UNKNOWN
You can't stranger danger
someone when you asked them to
date you

My blinks per minute triple as I read and reread the message.

ME
I don't know what you
mean by tangible reward.
I'm not paying you to fake
date me.

UNKNOWN
I don't want money

ME
I'm not letting you see
my tits either so forget it

I'm keying in a name for him when the next text comes through.

PRETTY BOY
You said tits first
I wasn't even thinking tits

ME
You sure?

PRETTY BOY
I mean
It's not that I've NEVER thought
tits

ME
I'm going to sue whoever
gave you my number

PRETTY BOY
I stole it out of Three's phone
At least appreciate the effort

ME
Depends on what you did
with the phone after

PRETTY BOY
Put it back on his desk . . . ?

ME

Weak

Could've put it in the

ceiling

On the roof

Out the window

In a first year's backpack

PRETTY BOY

I get your point

ME

What's YOUR point

My phone starts vibrating in my hand, and I feel Sumi's glare as she twists around in her desk chair.

"I'm going, I'm going," I say, rushing out into the hall.

I answer the call but wait until I'm safely in the stairwell to say, "You're calling me. Why are you calling me?"

"I thought it might be easier to get my point across."

"And you don't want anything in writing?"

"Can't deny there's an added benefit."

I pull my phone from my ear to stare at it, then raise it again and say, "I didn't know this thing made calls."

"Me?"

"No, my phone."

Wells huffs out a small laugh, and I get a rush of gratification.

"So, what is it you *want*, Wells?" I ask, leaning against the rail so I can see up and down the stairwell to make sure I don't have eavesdroppers.

"Let's say it's something mutually beneficial."

"Can we say that?"

I hear his smile through the phone as he says, "I mean, it's something that'll piss Three off more than you could ever imagine."

I grin. "I like the sound of this."

"I figured you would. Only problem is you can't take credit for it."

I frown. "I don't like the sound of this."

"You still get what you want. I pretend to date you, and you get to watch Three's head explode. And you help me pull off something I can't trust anyone else for, getting the added benefit of knowing it'll get under Three's skin more than any prank you could ever pull."

"Is it dangerous?"

"Not exactly."

"That doesn't answer the question."

"It's not exactly *legal*. But it's not dangerous. No one would ever have you arrested for it." He pauses. "Okay, they would probably *try* to have you arrested for it, but I'd cover for you. If we get caught, I'll take the heat. I just need a wingman."

"Do I get to know what this is about?"

"Not before you agree."

I scoff. "You want me to sign a blank check? No way."

"I can't tell you until you've agreed, and we've started this thing. I need leverage. I'm not slipping in fine print here. It's major. But I can't trust you wouldn't use it against me."

The insult whips me in the stomach.

"Wow, glad to know you think so highly of me."

"I don't think anything of you, Doe. I hardly know you. That's the point."

I've never heard Wells sound so serious. He's right, though—we hardly know each other. Wells has always been on the periphery. I know him even less than I know his cousins, or Three's boys. The only one I know anything about is Three.

I think about the look on Three's face when he realized I wasn't bluffing about having Wells's hoodie. About what he'll do when he sees us sharing a milkshake at Phoebe's, or cuddling in a Ferris wheel gondola at Fall Fest, or perched together in the big red chair at Rotty's.

I'm so high on the idea of it, of the way Three's face will turn pink, red, then purple, the way his eyes will bulge and that vein in his forehead will throb and how I'll make a nest right under his skin, that I answer after only a small hesitation.

"I'll do it."

Wells lets out a breath, and I can almost feel the tension release on the other end of the call.

"Okay," he says, sounding a little bit like he can't believe I agreed.

I can't really believe I agreed.

But there's no going back now.

"We need a plan," I tell him. "You figure out the timeline for whatever it is you want. I need a solid ninety days of fake dating to really throw Three off his game. I'll dump you over winter break."

"You'll dump *me*?"

"Well, obviously it can't be the other way around, or Three gets to be smug about it."

He mulls this over. "I'll need my part done before that. At least a month. Thanksgiving feels soon, but it's probably the best option."

"Okay. I . . . I feel like we should shake on it, but that's kind of hard through the phone."

"You could come meet me at your front gate."

"I could?"

"Yeah, we could do a couple's handshake."

"What's a couple's handshake?"

"Where you shake hands but with your mouths."

I bark out a laugh. "You think I'm coming down there to kiss you in front of everyone?"

"I assumed that's part of the deal, isn't it?"

"I'm far more subtle than that, Wells. Besides, I can't start fake dating you without telling my friends."

I'm still not sure how I'm going to explain this to them. But I at least need to prepare them for what they're about to witness.

I can almost feel Wells rolling his eyes. "Whatever you say. Then I guess you need to come up with a plan. Where you want Three to see us for the first time."

I grin, imagining it.

"I can hear your creepy smile right now."

"I don't have a creepy smile."

"You do when it comes to my cousin."

I frown.

"Don't worry, his smile for you is even creepier."

"All his smiles are creepy."

"Sure," Wells says with a laugh, "we'll say you believe that."

A doorway opens below me, and noise bursts into the stairwell.

"I have to go," I whisper, covering my mouth with my hand. "I'll text you."

I hang up and spin around as a gaggle of sophomore girls comes bounding up the stairs.

"Hey, Doe," one says.

I wave, shrinking into the corner to let them pass. When they're gone, I head to Sumi's room.

She's hunched over a tangled knot of yarn, cursing quietly as she picks at it. She looks up as I come into the room and spins in her desk chair to watch me cross over to her bed.

"Who are *you* so popular with today?" she asks.

I shove my phone under her pillow and throw myself down on the mattress. "Oh, you know. Just convincing my mom I'm not going to get myself arrested this year."

Sumi shakes her head. "One near misdemeanor, and our parents just cannot let it go."

"Tell me about it!"

Last fall, we got sloppy doing some light graffiti on the outside wall of Winfield's campus. No one noticed the police car coasting down the street until the lights were flashing.

My parents tightened the reins a little after that, but my mom understands the war with Winfield. All things considered, graffiti was a pretty minor infraction.

I watch Sumi return to her yarn knot and try to imagine what she'd say if I told her about Wells.

Of all my friends, Sumi would probably be the one to see the reason in it.

But I can't imagine telling one without telling the rest. I don't want anyone left out or left behind.

So, I wait, biding my time.

Biding my time for what, though, I can't even begin to guess.

By Saturday, I still haven't found a way to tell my friends, and Wells is getting antsy. He's texted me at least three times a day all week: Have you told them yet?

Not like he's dying to have our relationship out in the

open. He just wants my plan going so he can finally brief me on his. He won't tell me anything until I'm too deep in my scheme to get out of it. This is his collateral.

I don't exactly have collateral in this deal, which worries me less than it probably should.

Jade is craving baklava, so we head to Phoebe's for dinner. I'm feeling some baklava myself, and I'm mentally scanning the Phoebe's menu when we pass the first of the windows and I spy something unseemly.

"*No,*" I whisper, pressing my nose to the glass.

There, at a corner booth, are Three and his boys. And not just Zamir Salahuddin and Alex Hyun, but the Biermann brothers and a skinny, younger boy with light skin and a flop of sandy hair. It's curly and on the longer side, and it mostly hides his eyes, but I recognize the frowny mouth and slightly upturned nose. This must be Baby Page. I have the fleeting thought that I know his real name—Caleb—before filing it away in my Information I Will Never Need folder.

I wonder if all the Pages look like it's hard to make them laugh.

I'm practically vibrating as I turn to my friends. "The audacity."

Gemma's got her thumbnail in her mouth, already chewing it down to nothing.

"I'm starving," Jade says, striding past us. "Let's get this over with so we can eat."

I watch her go, frowning.

"She's had a long week," Shawn says, putting her arm around me.

Sumi yanks Gemma's hand out of her mouth. "Bad for your teeth," she says. "Don't make me get that stuff again."

"No, not the *stuff,*" Gemma whines.

Sophomore year around finals, Sumi got Gemma a bitter-tasting nail-biting deterrent to paint onto her nails. When Gemma tried to bite through the bad taste during her calculus final, it kicked in her gag reflex and she threw up in the classroom garbage can.

Shawn drags me toward the door, and I ignore Three's smug smile as we file into a smaller booth. The other corner booths are taken, and I try really hard not to let it show on my face how much that annoys me.

"Can we have a cease-fire, please?" Jade asks.

I balk. "Why are you only looking at *me*?"

She narrows her eyes.

I hold up my hands. "I'll be good. Just because Three and his boys have totally breached our territory doesn't mean I'm going to blast them into the next century."

Jade makes a noise from the back of her throat that sounds like she doesn't believe me at all.

I grab a menu and hold it up so she can't see my face. Then I crane around in my seat to peek at Three over the top of the booth. He's staring right at me, and when he catches me looking, he smirks like he's won something. I whip back around and slide down in my seat, muttering under my breath.

Shawn elbows me, and when I glance at her, she's smiling behind her menu.

"I'm not doing anything," I whisper.

She just grins.

I slap my menu down. Gemma jumps, banging her knees into the underside of the table. The contraption of silverware and sweetener packets Sumi is building jangles together and collapses.

Sumi jabs her fork at Gemma, but Gem is quick to point at me and shriek, "It was Doe's fault! She's making me jumpy!"

I hold up my hands. "I'm going to the bathroom."

I shove at Shawn until she slides out of the booth.

"Hey," Jade calls before I go too far, "you better not get us kicked out before I get my food."

I put my hands on the edge of the table and hiss, "*I'm behaving!*"

Jade waves me off.

In the bathroom, I tie my hair up, splash cold water on my face, and stare in the mirror, wishing I could dump a strawberry milkshake right over Three's stupid head.

I try some deep-breathing exercises from when my parents first divorced and I had to see an anger management therapist, when screaming "I hate you" and throwing things was the order of the day. Three has always bothered me, but this is an old anger I feel creeping up. The kind of anger that can ruin your life if you let it get the best of you.

I massage my head for about thirty seconds before leaving the bathroom, feeling slightly calmer. The tension comes screaming back when I spot Wells standing at our booth.

Christian Page is a few steps ahead of him, but he glances back when I walk into an empty chair and send it screeching across the floor.

Wells turns, but he doesn't look startled the way his cousin does. Instead, he grins.

"Hey," he says, coming over to move the chair back to its table.

I blink at him. "Hi. What are you—why are you—"

"Don't have a fit," he whispers, his smile sliding into a smirk. "This is perfect timing. Everyone's here."

"Wait, I'm not ready," I tell him.

Wells leans in close, putting his mouth right up to my ear, and says, "If we wait until you're ready, we'll never start. Don't forget this was your idea."

He slides his hand down my arm and twines our fingers together. He gives my hand a squeeze and drags me toward my booth.

With our clasped hands on full display, the noise in the diner ratchets up. By the time we reach my friends, they're staring at us in varying degrees of confusion.

"What—what—what—" Gemma stammers, glancing from me to Wells and back.

Shawn gives me a look like she's expecting an explanation.

Jade stares at our clasped hands with an undercurrent of annoyance, but I can't tell if it's because I'm consorting with a Winfield boy or because we're delaying her meal with our show.

Sumi points at us with one of the forks she's hoarding and says, "So this is why your phone's been going off nonstop."

Wells grins and deposits me on the end of the booth next to Shawn. He leans down next to me, one hand on the back of my neck and the other on the table.

"I'll call you tomorrow," he says.

Then he pops a kiss against my cheek.

It's so brief, I barely feel it. But my whole body goes hot with embarrassment as he says goodbye to our table and heads toward his.

I twist around to watch him go, and past him, Three's got his murder eyes on.

Relief slides through me.

I turn to my friends, and they must mistake what my smile is about, because Shawn says, "Well, I guess if you like him . . ."

"I'm just a little surprised," Jade says, watching me closely.

I clear my throat and shrug, my cheeks aching from smiling. "Me, too. But here we are. I guess I'm kind of . . . talking to Wells."

And I promise myself that eventually, I'm going to tell them the truth.

Just as soon as we're out of Three's earshot.

The inquisition is coming—it's only a matter of how long they'll make me sweat.

We're in the Kingdom after Phoebe's, and I can practically feel the questions building as we rearrange furniture and get comfortable under the stars.

"Anyone else have to unbutton their pants on the walk back? Or was that just me?" Jade asks as she falls into a chair.

"I could go straight to sleep," says Sumi, resting her head on Gemma's shoulder.

Gemma stares at me, looking a little quivery.

Shawn flings her legs across my lap, trapping me in place, and says with a grin, "I'm stuffed. But Doe hardly ate a thing."

"Nervous?" Sumi asks me, her mouth curling up in a smirk.

I roll my eyes. "What would I have to be nervous about?"

"Well, you're dating a Winfield boy, for starters!" Gemma jabs a finger at me.

Jade sighs. "How long you been holding that in, Gemmy?"

Gemma flushes. "I'm just *surprised* is all."

"You, me, and the entire diner," Jade says. She hits me with a look that says *explain yourself.* No one is better than Jade at silent communication.

"I—Look, I was gonna tell you, but I wasn't sure how to explain—I thought you'd be disappointed—"

"As long as you're not going out with him to spite Three, I think it's great," Jade says.

I freeze, but none of them seem to notice.

"I agree," says Shawn. "It sends a message to the other girls that the rivalry is about Winfield, not individual boys.

Some of them have it in their heads that it's a war between you and Three."

"Three isn't that important," I say with the confidence of someone who is absolutely not dating Wells to make Three's head explode.

I didn't expect my friends' reactions, and now I'm not sure how to break the truth to them. I imagine Shawn's expression sliding into disappointment, and it makes my stomach clench.

"I think we sometimes let the rivalry get in the way of us living our lives," Shawn says. "I know it's never stopped us from, like, bringing a Winfield boy to a dance or something, but I'd be hesitant to actually go out with one of them."

Gemma lets out a small, shaky laugh. "I'm glad I don't have to deal with that. I'm having a hard enough time getting a girlfriend in a school *full* of girls. The added stress would send me over the edge."

"I've always told the younger girls they can go out with Winfield boys," I say. "I've never said no to that."

"But Weston comes first," says Gemma.

I nod so fast, I nearly scramble my brain. "Of course! Wells will never come before Weston."

"You say that now," Sumi says, grinning, "but let's see how you feel around Vally's Day when you're making him homemade heart cookies and letting him put his hand—"

"First of all," I say, cutting her off, "I don't know how to bake, and even if I were the type to bake cookies for Valentine's Day, we don't have an oven."

"Fine, bribing the kitchen staff to make him homemade heart cookies," Sumi says, still beaming.

"It's not that serious with Wells," I tell them. "It's not— it's not serious *at all.*"

I'm trying to work my way into the truth, to dig it out and offer it up, because I can't lie about this—I can't lie to my friends.

But Shawn says, "I'm proud of you, Doesy. You're growing up. Putting aside the rivalry to date the cousin of your worst enemy? I mean, we're graduating soon. We have to find more to live for than this war eventually, don't we?"

Jade hums, nodding.

Fire burns in my stomach. *Proud?*

Why does it sound like she's sick of fighting with Winfield?

And why does Jade seem to agree with her?

Sumi sighs and tips her head back. "I don't know," she says. "I've used some of my best work on Winfield. I'm having a pretty good time."

"I'm not saying it's not fun," Shawn says. "I'm just saying, eventually we'll be leaving Weston, and we'll have to pass the torch. I'm all for stopping the merger—let's throw our whole hearts into it. Do it big this year. But also . . . finding other stuff we want to do wouldn't be the worst idea."

"Like . . . hobbies?" Gemma says, looking appalled. "I don't have time for hobbies."

Jade shoots her an incredulous look. "You cross-stitch."

"For my *Etsy* shop," Gemma says. "That's not a hobby—it's a small business."

"Hey, could you cross-stitch something for me?" Sumi asks. "Like the phonetic spelling of my last name? I want to give it to Mr. Auburn so he can hang it next to his desk. I swear the man never calls on me just so he can avoid learning how to say Balakrishnan."

Jade frowns. "Does he not realize your last name is already spelled how it sounds?"

Sumi gives her a look, and Jade snorts.

"Hey, while you're at it," Sumi says, turning back to Gemma, "maybe you could cross-stitch something for Doe? Like Dorothy Wellborn with little red hearts on it?"

I pick up my empty water bottle and throw it at her.

It nails her in the forehead, but that only makes her laugh harder.

It's not a big deal, I tell myself as I settle back into my chair.

They won't get it. They'll think I'm taking things too far. And this thing with Wells will be over practically before it's started. It's already almost Fall Fest, and then midterms. Before we know it, it'll be Thanksgiving, and then winter break. We'll be home for most of December.

It'll be like I never dated Wells at all.

Which will be true, because I'm *not* dating Wells.

One little lie won't hurt.

CHAPTER
SIX

F all Fest is one of the biggest events in Delafosse. It's
like our homecoming, but since we don't have a football
team, Weston throws a big carnival, and all the alumni and
families come to town.

Winfield has their own Fall Fest the week after ours, but
theirs is more formal—a banquet dinner, awards given out,
black-tie dress code, the whole thing.

It marks the End Times before midterms start, before we
really have to buckle down and Get Serious. It's supposed to
be the easiest part of the school year, especially for those of us
not sending in any early decision college applications. Sumi
and I are the only ones not applying early decision somewhere, but whereas she's busy knitting us all new winter hats
and figuring out which college from her short list she wants
to work on first, I spend my time slacking off and thinking
up new pranks against Winfield.

The week before Fall Fest, Headmistress Cotesmore held
an off-script assembly to announce that Winfield will be participating in Fall Fest with us this year. We'll have the whole
street shut down and Fall Fest spanning both campuses. Of

course, Winfield will still hold their alumni banquet—and we are *not* invited.

Things were precarious at the idea of a joint Fall Fest, but the banquet thing put us over the edge.

"Why should we share our Fall Fest, when we don't get to go to their fancy black-tie banquet?" I asked when I was called on.

Cotesmore nodded. "That's a valid question. But the banquet is a Winfield alumni event, not like our Fall Fest. Winfield has always been invited to Fall Fest in the past, like the rest of Delafosse. Now they want to contribute to show the alumni that we make a great team and the integrity of neither school will be lost when we merge."

I wanted to call bullshit, but from Cotesmore's gaze, she wouldn't be engaging me. When it comes to silent communication, she's almost as good as Jade.

I was sliding back into my seat when someone else stood up.

Virginia Brinkoff.

"Winfield participating in Fall Fest is a great idea," she said.

"Suck up," Sumi muttered.

Shawn snorted.

"Volunteering together will be a good way for us to get to know each other before next year," Virginia added. "Assuming Winfield will be volunteering with us?"

"They will, yes," Cotesmore said. "This Fall Fest will be bigger than it's been in the past, so volunteering is mandatory for all students."

She wasn't exaggerating about the size of the Fest.

The carnival company rolled in last night, and by the time I got to class this morning, there was a Ferris wheel in the faculty parking lot, a pendulum pirate ship outside the Winfield front gate, and smaller rides up and down the street.

With so many volunteers, we only have to dedicate a couple of hours to Fall Fest, rather than the usual full day of volunteering offset by two days of fun. And I can't say I'm not excited to have more time to track down the chocolate-covered pumpkin pie on a stick I saw someone carrying earlier.

I'm in a booth making apple cider donuts with Shawn and a couple of Winfield seniors I don't recognize. They don't seem concerned with us, either, so things have worked out better than expected.

Especially when Weston junior Ilana Rotko strolls up carrying two stuffed canvas bags.

Shawn knocks one of the donut baskets, sending donut holes flying.

"Oh no! Cody, Tim, could you help me?" she calls, dropping to her knees to clean them up.

While the boys are distracted, I take the bags from Ilana. I shoulder one. The other is so heavy, I have to let it rest on the ground.

"Raise hell," Ilana says, giving me a salute. Her hands are ink-smudged, but that's nothing out of the ordinary for Ilana, who works on *The Weston Chronicle*.

I stow the bags under the back table where Cody and Tim won't notice them. A half hour later, when Shawn and I are relieved of donut duty, we grab the bags and head out into the crowd.

"Kind of exciting, isn't it?" she says to me, a giddy note in her voice.

I suck at the back of my teeth. "From the girl who *can't wait* to find other hobbies?"

She elbows me. "Not funny. I just meant maybe the thrill of my life shouldn't be crushing Winfield boys." She cracks her knuckles. "But now that I'm here, it sounds fun."

I grin. "That's the adrenaline talking. Don't forget your gloves."

She pulls a pair of black winter gloves out of her dress pocket.

It's not quite cold enough, but nothing would be a dead giveaway like ink-stained hands.

"Watch out for Mr. Tully," Shawn says as she slides on her gloves. "I saw him hanging out at that ring toss booth earlier."

I freeze. "The one the first years are running?"

She scrunches her nose. "Where else?"

I swallow a sick feeling, and we share a grimace.

Shawn shakes her head. "Anyway, be careful. I'll catch up with you later," she says, heading off.

I slide on my gloves and start in the other direction.

Fall Fest is already packed with students from both schools, townies, and alumni, so slipping unseen through the crowd isn't difficult.

I'm about a quarter of the way through my canvas bag when I feel someone behind me, and I whip around in a panic, certain I'm caught.

"Oh, it's only you," I say, breathing out in relief.

Wells scoffs. "What, I don't strike fear in your heart?"

I snort. "Probably not even if you tried."

He grins and falls into step beside me, peeking into my canvas bag as I open it.

"Newspaper?"

"M.Y.O.B."

He rolls his eyes. "So mature."

I slide out a few papers and drop them on the next booth we pass. One of the Weston girls working it moves the stack to the other side of a decorative pumpkin, so the Winfield boys there can't see it.

I wink at her, and she smiles.

"Want to do something fun?" Wells asks.

"I'm having fun right now."

"The kind of fun that'll make Three's head spin?"

I glance into my bag and smile. "I think this'll make his head spin."

"How so?" He reaches for my bag again. "What are you up to?"

I spin out of his grasp. "Sorry, I can't reveal my secrets to the enemy."

"The *enemy*? Hey, are we going out, or what?"

"Or what," I say with a laugh. I link my arm through his and drag him closer to my side. "We can pretend to make out on the Ferris wheel as soon as I'm done."

"Oh, don't do me any favors," he says, putting a hand on his heart. "*You're* the one who benefits from this, not me."

"Does this mean you're finally going to tell me what I agreed to? What's your scheme, Wells?"

I've badgered him since he outed our relationship—or non-relationship—but he's been hedging. I'm high on our next prank, so it's easy to pretend this doesn't irritate me as much as it does. I hate being left in the dark.

Wells sucks in a breath through his nose, his smile faltering. "I'm—"

"You can't put me off forever."

"I'm *not*—"

"Then what's the deal?"

Wells sighs. "There's something Three has that I want."

"Three has so much, everyone probably wants something he's got."

We've stopped walking, and people stream around us. I adjust my bag on my shoulder. I'm eager to get back to work, but I'm too curious about Wells's side of the deal.

"Not this. It's a watch."

"What, like a Rolex?"

He snorts. "No. It's the watch my grandfather bought himself with the first real profit he made off his company."

I don't know much about the Wellborn family business, except that it's a highly successful construction company that's built up half of Cincinnati. It's the reason they're kings of their city.

Which is why I assume the watch is expensive.

"So, it must be worth something, then. Not a Rolex, but . . . ?"

Wells shakes his head. "No, it's not worth anything—not to anyone else, at least. But it's worth everything to me, and that makes it worth something to Three. If it disappeared tomorrow and he knew I didn't have it, he wouldn't care. But he can't let me have it if he knows I want it. That's not how we work."

I watch his face change, the blank expression I'm accustomed to twisting into something almost pained.

When I catch people glancing our way, I realize that we look too intense, especially for two people who just started dating. We're supposed to be in the honeymoon phase. I close the distance between us and put my arms around his waist.

To his credit, Wells doesn't falter. He puts his arms around my shoulders, holding me close.

And in case he still looks pained, I say, "I can see right up your nose."

A laugh splutters out of him, which makes me smile.

"I think you'll be reaping some other rewards from this whole arrangement, too," I tell him, glancing over at a group of girls watching us. "Girls love an unobtainable guy. You'll have your pick as soon as I dump your ass."

"You're enjoying that you get to dump me more than you should. Is there something you're not telling me?" He peers down at my face, squinting. "Have I *scorned* you, Dorothy Saltpeter?"

I bark out a laugh, releasing him. "Oh, that's hilarious!"

He smiles, tucking his hands into his pockets as we start walking again.

"Listen," I say, "why don't I meet you at the Winfield gate in, like, ten minutes?"

"Why?"

"You're kind of cramping my style."

He frowns. "How so?"

"You draw a lot of attention." I nod at the eyes darting his way as we pass by. "You can't help it that you're good-looking, but I'm going for anonymity here."

He slows his pace. "Fine. I'll meet you at the gate in ten. You better not leave me standing there like a chump."

"No one could ever mistake you for a chump," I say, reaching up to pat his cheek.

A spot of ink stays behind.

"Shit," I mutter, rubbing at it with the wrist of my glove. When that doesn't work, I slide my glove off, lick my thumb, and reach back up.

Wells knocks my hand away. "Okay, enough momming me. Jesus, I'll go to the bathroom." He rubs at his cheek, giving me a dark look, and walks off.

I smile a little and turn to move on.

THIS MAY END BADLY

When I've emptied my canvas bag, I slide it off my shoulder, fold it up as small as I can, and pass it off to a girl working the pumpkin sale on the Weston campus. While I slide off my gloves and stuff them in my pocket, a girl behind her unfurls a similar canvas bag, slides two small pumpkins into it, and hands it to a waiting couple.

I grin, but then I realize I'm late to meet Wells. I head into the packed street, where it's all chatter from the crowd and delighted screams from the carnival rides. I have to skirt around the pirate ship ride to get to the Winfield gate, where Wells is leaned up against the brick, waiting for me.

"I was about to leave," he says.

"I'm not that late."

"It's been twenty minutes."

"It has not!"

"Fine, it's been sixteen, but I was rounding up. It's only fair."

He grabs my hand and tugs me through the gate. I glance up at him, checking his face for ink.

"I got it," he says when he notices me looking. "No evidence of your crimes here."

I smile but don't mention they'd suspect him before me.

"Hey, where are we going?" I ask as he leads me toward the big tent, where there are tables set up and hot food being served.

"I've got someone I want to introduce you to."

"What? Who?"

"It's alumni weekend," says Wells. "My uncle wouldn't miss this for anything."

Before I can protest that I haven't had time to prepare, we've reached the table of the most elite family at Winfield.

There's a certain kind of sparkle people as rich as the Wellborns have. It's the shine of someone whose name is probably plastered on a building, who can afford large donations for dorm renovations and will happily foot the bill for an alumni dinner. Like a gold dusting for people who have the money to get what they want. It's the kind of family most people only read about—the ones who can sink their teeth into you. That's probably why their smiles are so perfect.

I spot Three right as the man next to him calls, "Gabriel! We've been waiting for you!"

"Sorry I'm late. You can't rush girls for anything." He squeezes my hand and jerks me a little closer, and when I glance at him, I see a flash of apology on his face.

I clench my jaw a little as I smile, turning to the table. "Well, to be fair, no guy will tell you that you're meant to be somewhere until you're already running late."

Two of the women chuckle, but the woman sitting beside Three only gives me a bland smile. This *has* to be his mother. They clearly have the same sense of humor.

"This is Dorothy Saltpeter," Wells says. "My girlfriend."

Three grips the edge of the table, his knuckles going paper white.

I put on my winningest smile. "Very nice to meet you all."

"Well, Dorothy, have a seat," the woman in front of me says, pulling out the empty chair next to her. She has sandy hair cut in a stylish shag, and I'd bet you can see the diamond on her ring finger from space.

"Don't mind if I do."

"I'm Anne-Marie Page," she says as I slide into the chair.

Ah, the Pages. Now that I look at her, I recognize Christian and Baby Page, although her face has an underlying smile to it that her sons did not inherit. They sit on her other side, not quite frowning, but doing that nearly frowning thing they do when they're in resting mode.

I do a quick head count of adults and realize we must be

missing a few of the older generation Wellborns. The last remaining woman I haven't placed must be the Biermann brothers' mom, the last Wellborn sister. She looks a lot like Mrs. Page. Mr. Biermann, Mr. Page, and both of Wells's parents are missing.

Joc Biermann, a slightly smaller replica of his older brother, is on my other side, but Wells jostles him out of his chair, forcing him to move over. I didn't know the Biermann brothers could be jostled, but Wells makes it look easy.

Maybe they don't want to fight in front of the parents.

"Doe, this is my aunt Bridget," Wells says, motioning to the woman squished between Biers and Joc. She probably wouldn't seem that small next to me, but with her sons on either side, she looks like her chair is swallowing her. Biers has a plate piled almost as tall as she is with food.

"Pleased to meet you," I say, trying to ignore the slurping sound Biers makes with his spaghetti. He has sauce splattered on his cheek.

"And Aunt Jeanie and Uncle Nate," Wells says, nodding to Three's parents.

"You go by Doe?" Mrs. Page asks. "That's adorable."

Three starts humming that inane "doe, a deer, a female deer" song. The Biermann brothers laugh.

"Darling, that's quite rude," Mrs. Wellborn says to him, but it comes out loaded with affection.

"So, you're a Weston girl?" Mrs. Biermann asks.

"Till I die," I say with a grin.

My phone buzzes in my pocket.

"Bridget and I went to Miss Porter's," says Mrs. Page, motioning to Mrs. Biermann. "It's our mother's alma mater. She's from Connecticut."

Mrs. Biermann makes a noise of disgust. "There's nothing good about New England. Everything's old and cold."

I laugh.

"Oh, I don't know," says Mrs. Page. "I do love Nantucket in the summer."

"Dad hates New England, too," Biers says, pausing inhaling his food.

"That's because Dad played for the Colts," Joc replies, reaching over to smack Biers on the back of the head.

"Boys, boys!" Mrs. Biermann shouts as they start to shove at each other over her head.

My phone buzzes again. With everyone sufficiently distracted, I slide it out and glance at the screen.

SHAWN
Where are you???

SUMI
Probably making out with that
pretty Wellborn on the Ferris
wheel

       ME
       Big tent with Wellborn
       fam
       Winfield campus
       Perfect opportunity
       Hurry

I slide my phone back in my pocket, and when I glance up, Wells is looking at me. I shoot him an innocent smile, leaning into him a little so I can put my hand on his forearm.

I don't look at Three, but I see him going red out of the corner of my eye.

Mr. Wellborn is going on about something to the Biermann brothers, but I'm not really paying attention, because I have one eye on the lookout for my friends.

Shawn's voice rings out from behind me, "Doe! We've been looking for you everywhere!"

I drag myself off of Wells's arm and twist around in my seat. They're all here.

Perfect.

"Oh, hey."

"Can you—?" Shawn starts, but she glances quickly at the rest of the table. "I'm sorry to interrupt. Could we just . . . speak to you for one teensy second?"

Gemma, fluttering nervously behind Shawn, beckons me with a discreet little wave.

I make a big show of putting on a concerned face. "Of course. What's going on?"

Gemma beckons me again, this time with more urgency.

One of our group's greatest assets is Gemma's ability to act so convincingly under pressure. Mostly because we use her for a lot of nervous-looking girl bits, and she's usually so nervous to play the part, she pulls it off with Oscar-worthiness.

Behind her, Jade and Sumi are leaning into each other. Jade's expression is totally wooden, but Sumi is trying not to laugh, and Jade is pinching Sumi hard so she'll keep a straight face.

Shawn holds out a newspaper, flapping it at me.

"You won't believe what they did!" Gemma whispers.

"Is everything okay?" Mrs. Page asks.

I look up from the newspaper and shoot her a tight smile. "Oh, sure. It's—it's nothing. Sorry."

Shawn puts a hand on my shoulder and murmurs, "I think we should go."

"Did something happen?" Mrs. Page asks.

"It's—it's the Winfield school paper." I look at Three and put on an innocent face. "I guess you guys put out a special edition."

"We have a school newspaper?" Biers said to Joc, looking confused.

Sumi snorts.

I look at Three and frown. "Aren't you editor in chief?"

Biers looks at Three. "Wait, seriously?"

Three stares at me, saying nothing.

"Can I see that, please?" Mr. Wellborn asks, holding out a hand.

I lean over Wells to pass the paper to Mr. Wellborn. Before I can pull back, Wells leans his shoulder into my stomach, like he wants my attention. I put my hand on his shoulder and squeeze.

"*The Winfield Tribune,* special edition. 'Weston Merger: Ploy by girls' school to harvest more alien hosts?'" Mr. Wellborn reads.

"This weekend is supposed to be about proving we can work together," Jade says. "But Winfield boys clearly can't even be mature for three days."

Sumi, who has produced her copy of the paper, reads, "'One anonymous Weston junior is quoted saying, "I can't wait to see the schools merge. It'll be the best having the boys out with us for our monthly full moon naked dance rituals in the forest."'"

I scoff. "Ridiculous. We haven't done those in years."

Mrs. Page cracks a smile.

I can't help my little smirk, and Three clocks it from across the table. He's still as a block of ice.

Mr. Wellborn scans the paper, flips to the inside page, and closes his eyes briefly.

Behind me, Sumi continues, "'We interviewed top Winfield boys to see how they feel about the merger. The general consensus is Weston girls just aren't up to snuff. "What do they do when you aren't around to tell them? Just wander aimlessly, hoping someone will give them some direction?" one senior mused, drawing into question whether Weston girls have free will, or if they're all mindless alien hosts barely keeping themselves from bumping into furniture.'"

Three's nostrils flare briefly, even as the rest of his expression remains stoic. I wonder if he's thinking whether there's anything else he's said to me recently that's likely to be quoted.

I put my hand behind my back, and Shawn gives it a light low-five.

Putting on my best sad face, I crouch beside Wells. "I should probably go. Clearly Weston girls aren't wanted on the Winfield campus."

And because I can't resist shooting one last arrow in Three's direction, I lean up and kiss Wells on the cheek. "I'll call you tomorrow," I say, in an exact impression of him from the diner a few weeks ago.

He screws his mouth up, trying not to smile.

"It was nice meeting you," I say to the table as I straighten. "Sorry I can't stay."

"You're always welcome at our table, Doe," says Mrs. Page. "Don't let the boys make you think otherwise."

Three makes a strangled noise like he's going to protest, but his dad shoots him a look that could freeze hell over, and he goes silent, sulking in his seat.

"Thank you, Mrs. Page."

I link my arm through Shawn's and let my shoulders droop, my friends ushering me out of the tent.

By now, the newspaper has made the rounds, and nearly everyone we pass is reading it.

If the administration planned to force us to work with Winfield boys, there was no better way to strike back than to pretend Winfield had done the newspaper themselves. No one would ever be able to definitively prove who'd pulled off the prank, and it worked in our favor either way—Winfield printed a newspaper outright insulting Weston girls and the merger, or Weston girls printed the newspaper and framed Winfield for it. No matter which way you spin it, one thing is true: these are two student bodies that cannot mix.

We wait until we're safely off Winfield campus to break into a run, and by the time we make it to the Kingdom, we're falling over each other laughing.

"I have a treat for us!" Sumi calls, pulling a shopping bag out from under one of the beds. "Got it off a townie. Paid a sweet stack for it, but this calls for celebration."

She pulls out two bottles of wine and a corkscrew, and we spend the rest of the night lounging on the furniture, watching Fall Fest below, and passing the bottles between us until we're sufficiently buzzed.

"You can tell the season's turning already. It's freezing."

I glance at my mom as she cups her hands together and blows into them.

Shawn laughs. "Shouldn't you be used to this kind of weather, Mrs. Guidry? It's colder in Chicago."

"He's a bad influence on me," Mom says, nudging Oscar with her elbow. "All that warm-blooded bayou bullshit. He keeps the thermostat set at eighty-two!"

Oscar grins, flashing bright white teeth. He's bundled in a long winter coat, the collar pulled up so it obscures three-quarters of his face. He's just a nose, a bright smile, and warm brown eyes a few shades lighter than his dark skin. Even though he's freezing, he wears only his signature gray tweed flat cap on his closely shaved head.

Shawn laughs again, loving that my mom throws around swear words. Her own parents are pretty stiff-collared.

"Thanks for inviting me to brunch," Shawn says as the host calls in another group ahead of ours.

"Of course," Mom says, putting an arm around Shawn's shoulders and giving her a little shake. "You're always welcome with our family. Your parents must be disappointed they couldn't make it."

Shawn shrugs. "I've gotten them the last three years. It's only fair that Marcus should get them for his first family weekend at college. Plus, they're way closer to Ann Arbor than Delafosse."

"And you get to have the best sugar pearl waffles in town with us," I remind her. "It's not a bad trade-off."

"Guidry, party of four?" the host calls from the front door.

Mom knocks Oscar out of the way to get inside first, and he falls back next to me, laughing.

"She's a monster, your mother," he drawls as we pass the host, who holds the door for us. "Absolutely no decorum."

"Chicago's changed her."

We order coffee for the table then half peruse the menu and half chat, not ready to order until the server has left, come back, left again, and come back a second time.

"Oh, you're here," Mom says, flipping her menu up from the table. "You know what? I've almost decided. Let me go last."

We order, and when it's Mom's turn, she spends another minute or so peppering the server with questions about the big breakfast omelet versus the BLT, and by the end of it, she's somehow convinced him to let her order halves of both.

"She should've been an attorney," Oscar says as soon as the server is gone. "She could convince a leopard to wear stripes."

"In another life, maybe," Mom says with a grin. "I could've saved a fortune on the divorce."

I freeze, my coffee mug halfway to my mouth. The ceramic is so hot, it burns my fingers.

Mom drags her gaze to me, looking a little chagrined. "I'm only kidding."

I take a sip of my coffee so I don't have to answer.

"So, Mr. Guidry, how's work for you?" Shawn asks, jumping in to save me. "Still out every night?"

Oscar nods. "Oh, yeah. Jazz doesn't sleep in Chicago. Everyone needs a horn guy."

"He'd probably be in better shape if there was less work," Mom says, reaching for Oscar's hand. Instead of holding it, she inspects his knuckles. "And the weather doesn't help his arthritis."

"I'm too young for arthritis," Oscar says, sliding his hand back to grab his coffee. "That's just regular musician aches."

I make a thoughtful sound. "What does your doctor say?"

Oscar scoffs. "What do doctors know, anyway?"

I grin, and he shoots me a smile.

We finish lunch without any more hiccups. Later, out on the sidewalk, away from the warmth of the restaurant, I shiver as a sharp wind hits me.

"Told you," Mom says, giving me a look as she buttons up her jacket. "You swore you only needed a sweatshirt, and now look at you."

"Far be it from me to deny you an *I told you so*," I say,

nudging her with my shoulder. Instead of moving away, I burrow under her arm to get warm.

She laughs. "Okay, girls, where to next? I'd love to stop by Rotty's if you're not in a rush to get to Fall Fest."

"We've got all weekend to do Fall Fest. Why don't we hit your favorite haunts, and you can tell us your top ten vintage Weston pranks?"

"*Vintage?*" Mom says. "I'm not *that* old!"

"Okay, fine, *retro.*"

She makes a strangled noise of protest.

"Hey, Wells, aren't you going to say hi to your *girlfriend*?" someone calls as we pass through the crowd of waiting families.

I whip toward the voice. It's Biers, and I can't tell by the red creeping into his face if he's pleased or angry. He's got on one of those expressions that could go either way—I call it the Biermann special. Bully satisfaction mixed with roid rage.

Three leans against a street sign behind him, and there's no mistaking his expression—his self-satisfied smirk says it all.

Oscar notices I've paused, and he touches Mom's arm to get her attention.

Shawn lets out a half-pleased, half-panicked laugh. "Introducing your boy-thing to your mom? *Big* step, Doesy."

I elbow her.

Wells's parents are with them today. There's no question it's them. He looks like his mom—same catlike eyes and messy brown hair. Hers is tied back in a braid, but most of it escapes in unruly curlicues.

His dad looks like Three's dad, except where Three's dad is wearing a Cincinnati Bengals sweatshirt and jeans, like any casual alumni dad, Wells's dad has a history professor vibe—from his elbow-patch cardigan to his wire-rimmed glasses. Like a full-grown nerd.

"Hi," I say, moving in front of my mom like I can block her from view.

"You must be Gabe's girlfriend," his mom says, reaching for me. I expect a handshake, but she envelops me in a hug. She smells like lavender.

When she releases me, Wells's dad reaches out, and I brace for another hug, but he shakes my hand.

I breathe a small sigh of relief.

"Nice to meet you," I say, forcing my voice to remain steady.

"Why are your hands shaking?" Three asks. "Nervous to meet the parents?"

I shoot him a tight smile. "Coffee overload. But thanks for the concern."

His mom gives him a look, and I can't tell if it's in reprimand or solidarity.

"This is my mom and . . . my . . . stepdad," I say, the word still strange in my mouth. I've only had about a year to get used to it.

Oscar is the first to recover, shaking hands and introducing himself. Mom follows quickly after.

"Sorry, I'm just surprised—*boyfriend*," she says to the Wellborns. "Doe didn't mention—I mean, they haven't even been back long—"

"We just found out, too," says Wells's mom. "We got in this morning, and the first thing I hear from my sisters-in-law is how Gabe got himself a girlfriend, and everyone met her yesterday!"

"Right before the newspaper incident," his dad says.

"What newspaper incident?" Mom says, looking at me.

I cringe. "I'll tell you later." I shuffle my feet. "Aren't we going to Rotty's? Shouldn't we hurry? Don't we have—*things*—today? Planned?"

Mom gives me a look like she has no idea what I'm talking about.

That makes two of us.

I look to Wells for help, but he seems as freaked as I am. I don't think either of us anticipated a parent introduction today. I wasn't planning on introducing him to my parents *ever*. Lying to my friends is bad enough. I don't want to start lying to everyone in my life.

My mom looks at Wells, and his cheeks go pink as he seems to realize he hasn't said a word.

"Nice to meet you, Mrs.—" He falters, looking to me for help.

"Guidry," Mom supplies. She looks at his dad and adds, "I think we just missed each other in school. I believe I was a freshman when you were a senior."

"A Weston girl!" His dad grins. "I was class of '87. This old man was '85." He thumps Three's dad on the shoulder.

"I was '90," she says, smiling.

I glance at Shawn. I wonder if one day we'll come back to Weston and reminisce with Winfield boys about how we *just missed each other.*

She hides her face behind Oscar's back and pretends to gag.

I bite my cheeks so I won't laugh.

"We should all meet up at Fall Fest later," Mom says. "If you have time."

"Absolutely," says Wells's mom. "We've never met one of Gabe's girlfriends before."

I try to send Wells a telepathic message that he needs to handle this, but he's too busy giving Three a look that would put a normal human in the ground.

Of course, Three isn't a normal human. I'm not even sure he's human, period.

Still, I'm reminded that even though Wells plays it off a lot and it seems like it doesn't bother him, there's a definite power struggle between the two oldest Wellborn boys.

I grab Mom's hand. "Sure, sure, if we have time, yeah, we should all meet up." I tug her away, knowing I'm never going to let that happen. "We've got a lot to do today, though, so let's get going. Bye, everyone! Great to see you again!" To Wells's parents, I add, "Really glad I got to meet you both."

When we're a safe distance away, I release my mom, who gives me a long look.

"A *boyfriend*? From the girl who could rail about how terrible Winfield boys are for days? Now she's dating one?"

"It's a new thing," I say, not meeting her gaze.

"Don't feel bad, Mrs. Guidry," says Shawn. "I thought they were just talking. She didn't tell me she'd gotten a boyfriend, either."

I choke a little as I try to defend myself. "I didn't—we didn't exactly *talk about it*! He introduced me to his family that way yesterday, and like—it's easier than explaining we're just—I mean, I don't know, maybe he is. We haven't put labels on it yet, or anything. I don't know why he said it."

Shawn looks only marginally less annoyed.

I reach for her hand and squeeze. "You'll be the first to know when it's *official*-official. Not just *parent*-official."

"I'd think parent-official *was* official-official."

"They're simple folk, Shawny. We can't expect them to understand the intricacies of relationships. Their generation was different."

Mom shoots me a twisted look. "You are deranged, my child." She tucks me back under her arm. "I guess I won't be buying you anything at Rotty's after all."

"Okay, fine, but will you still get me ice cream?"

Oscar groans and rubs his stomach. "How could you even think about more food right now?"

"I have a second stomach for dessert."

CHAPTER SEVEN

A boyfriend. A *boyfriend*. I can't believe—"

"This isn't the first time I've dated, Dad."

On the other end of the line, he raspberries his lips together so loudly, it garbles my phone speaker. I pull it away from my ear, and when I return, he's saying, "Yes, but this is the first time your mother or I have met a boyfriend."

"It's not like I meant to introduce them!" I say. "We didn't start going out that long ago."

"It'd have to be not long ago. You just got back."

I make a *wrong-answer* buzzer noise. "It's already midterms, my dear sweet father."

Dad chuckles. "I long for the days when seeing someone for a month and a half qualified as a long-term relationship."

"Please, now isn't the time to reminisce about your glory days."

"I'd hardly call high school my glory days," Dad says. "Especially not my dating glory days, that's for sure. I was stag at every dance."

"And what about now?" I ask. After spending Fall Fest weekend with my mom and Oscar, I'm worried about my dad alone at home, making dinner for one and watching the World Series even though any team he remotely likes got knocked out ages ago. "I thought you said you met a guy at that work happy hour thing."

Dad makes a noncommittal noise. "I haven't talked to him in a while."

"Well, what about what's-her-name from up the street? The one with the big dog. You like dogs."

"I'm not really interested in Regina," Dad says.

"Have you thought about getting a pet?"

Dad laughs. "You don't need to worry about me, Doe. I've got plenty going on. I'm not really ready to jump back into dating yet."

I don't remind him that it doesn't really count as "jumping in" when it's been four years since his last relationship. Mom and Oscar getting married last year really threw Dad off in his divorce recovery. He's been back at the starting line, too nervous to put himself out there.

"I'm gonna look at the Humane Society and send you some contenders."

"I don't need a pet. I'm gone all day."

"Cats are very self-sufficient."

Dad sighs. "If it amuses you to look, fine."

"It amuses me to look," I confirm. "Hey, I'm almost to the bookstore. Can we talk later?"

"Of course," Dad says. "Don't think I forgot about this boyfriend thing. I'm gonna need a lot more details. I hear he's a *Wellborn*."

"You don't even know what that means."

"Mom told me," he says. "Apparently they're quite the family."

"Yeah, sure," I say absently. "They're like the Kennedys

of Winfield. I can't believe you and Mom were gossiping about me."

He lets out a shocked laugh. "Relaying that our daughter has a boyfriend isn't gossiping."

"I fail to see what else we could call it."

I don't hear Dad's response over the rushing in my ears when Wells swings out the front of Rotty's.

"Sorry, Dad, have to go—"

I barely have time to hang up before Wells has his arms at my waist. I let out a surprised squeal as he lifts me off my feet, swinging me around so he can push me up against the bricks on the other side of the bookstore window.

He rests his chin against my jacket collar, and his eyelashes brush my cheek. "Three's inside," he says, his breath warm on my neck. "He followed me all the way to the door saying I need to tell you to go home. I'd bet my Sat Lit grade he's watching."

"Wow, you're good at this," I whisper, tilting my mouth toward his ear.

He nuzzles his nose against my jaw, and I feel the tiniest brush of his smiling mouth on my neck. It sends a jolt through me.

Stupid. But Wells is crazy good-looking, and my body knows what it wants, even as my brain reminds it that this boy is *off-limits*. I can't let myself forget that everything between us is fake and always will be. No matter what I'd do to piss Three off, I'd never *actually* date a Wellborn.

I fist my hands in the back of Wells's jacket and imagine Three's face going so red, his head shoots off into space like a rocket.

I grin, and for a second I'm convinced Wells can hear it, because he pulls back to look at my face.

But then he looks down. I've hooked my leg around his, my knee resting against his hip.

While I was imagining Three, apparently my body had other plans for Wells.

I start to move my leg. "Sorry."

"No, that's good," Wells says, his voice a little hoarse. He leans an arm against the wall, blocking our faces from anyone in the bookstore. "But first, maybe we should have a talk about, you know, what happens to guys when you . . . start . . ." He waves his free hand in a circle, like I'm supposed to connect the dots.

I look down.

He lets out a strangled half laugh. "I'm not—I just meant before something happens, we should—so you aren't surprised—"

I look up again. "We're talking about boners? That's what's happening here?"

He hangs his head, and his hair tickles my chin. I have to really hold in my laughter.

"I was just trying to give you warning," he says to the ground. "So you don't have a heart attack."

"Do I seem that easily shocked? I'm a virgin, not a nun. I can handle it."

He lifts his head and smirks. "I'm not sure you could."

I shove at his chest. "You're stupid."

His grin widens as he takes my hand, dragging me toward the front door.

A few days ago, in the midst of impending midterm madness, Wells informed me that rather than study at the campus library, which is always packed with students crinkling snack bags and whispering, Three likes to retreat to Rotty's to study, because there's less foot traffic and people are more reverent in bookstores.

There are tables in the back near the big red armchair, and when we get inside, Three has his books spread across one of them. Alex Hyun sits across from him, a sketchpad propped up against the edge of the table.

Three doesn't look up when Wells and I arrive, but I see his shoulders tense. I try not to watch him as Wells drops into the red armchair and pulls me down next to him. Technically, it's big enough for two, so I'm not even really in his lap—until he reaches down to grab my ankles and drapes my legs across his thighs.

I hear a low murmur, and when I glance up, Alex is looking at us. Whatever he's saying, Three doesn't acknowledge it.

But his ears are going red. He's more aware of us than he'd like to let on.

When I'm settled with my books in my lap, Wells rests his hand on my knee and opens a copy of *Slaughterhouse-Five* that's stuffed to nearly twice its size with sticky notes crammed with handwriting.

I expect him to have messy chicken scratch, but his letters are small and neat, and he writes in cursive, not print.

"What are you studying for?" he whispers, lifting my textbook to look at the cover.

"American Diplomacy," I say a little too loud.

Three's head swivels toward us, and I smile at him. He clenches his jaw and returns his attention to his notes.

I look at Wells. He wrinkles his nose, like he's trying not to laugh.

I return my attention to my textbook, but I'm not here to study. I knew I wouldn't be able to focus, so I studied for most of the afternoon. I had something entirely different in mind coming to Rotty's tonight.

I get an idea while watching Alex and his sketchpad. He has a case of different pencils, along with some drawing markers.

I snap my book shut loudly enough that Three's entire body flinches, and Wells jumps in surprise.

"Sorry," I half whisper, holding a hand up in apology.

Wells's gaze follows me as I climb out of the chair and head over to Three's table.

"Hey, Alex," I say, crouching next to him.

Three gives me a look that should boil my insides, but I can barely contain my grin.

Alex glances at me, then Three.

"Can I borrow one of these?" I ask, reaching into the case of art supplies.

He gives Three a look like he's asking for permission.

Three nearly snaps his pen in half. "If you're gonna be quiet, you can take the whole fuckin' thing."

I shoot him a wide smile and hold up a black marker. "I only need the one."

To really set him off, I put a hand over his and say with as much sincerity as I can muster, "Study hard."

I salute Alex with the marker. "Thanks."

I return to the big red armchair and swing my legs over Wells's, this time curling into him even more.

"Hey," I say, tugging at his hoodie, "take this off."

He glances at me, his eyebrows shooting way up, but he obeys.

As soon as he slides it off, I drape it over my shoulders and uncap the marker.

He shoots me a sideways look. "Big plans over there?"

"Oh, yeah." I nod and lean in, pressing the marker to his skin.

Wells doesn't protest as I begin to draw. I pause every so often when his bicep flexes as he adjusts the book in his hand and when I have to push the sleeve of his T-shirt up over his shoulder to give me more room.

Even though we're quiet, I get the sense Three is more distracted by this than any sound we've made.

Eventually Wells gets up to use the bathroom, and when he comes back, he's got this look on his face like he can't believe what he just saw.

"*Peanuts?*" he says when he reaches me.

Three's head snaps up.

I laugh. "It's the only thing I know how to draw!"

Wells pulls his sleeve up to show off the different scenes from *It's the Great Pumpkin, Charlie Brown* that I've drawn from his elbow to his shoulder. Among the pumpkin patch are *Peanuts* characters and curving over his shoulder is Linus holding the WELCOME GREAT PUMPKIN sign.

"I've been in the pumpkin spirit with Halloween coming so soon," I say, hanging over the arm of the chair.

Three slams his pen down and twists to face us. "If you two aren't planning to study, could you *please leave?* I actually care about passing my midterms." He looks at Wells and adds, "It's probably a foreign concept for you to care about anything, but try your best to understand."

Wells gives a low whistle and slides his sleeve back down. "Okay, Three. Whatever you say." He keeps it light, but there's tension in his face as he turns his back on his cousin.

I straighten up and glare at Three. "What is your problem?"

He looks up from his notes and stares at me.

I hold up a hand in surrender. "Fine. I'll go. I mean, they invented noise-canceling headphones for a reason, but sure, you should have this entirely public bookstore to yourself for your personal study citadel, and we mere common folk will work around that so we don't disturb you." I hold out the marker like a microphone. "But before we go, please tell us what it's like to be a prince amongst commoners."

He glares at me.

I roll my eyes, drop the marker in Alex's case, and grab my stuff.

Wells takes his hoodie from my shoulders and slides it back on, covering the *Peanuts* drawing.

I grab his hand before he can get too far ahead of me, and as we make our way to the door, I don't know if I'm doing it as a show for Three, or if I think Wells needs it.

But once we're on the sidewalk, he releases me, and any tension I saw in his face is gone.

"Sorry if I messed up your studying plans," I say, motioning to the book clutched in his other hand.

He shrugs. "I'm not worried about it. What do I care how I do on midterms, anyway?"

I frown. "Don't tell me you actually listen to Three when he talks."

"Ah, that's the beauty of it," he says. "I don't have to listen to Three. It's what everyone says."

I remember the day in the cemetery, when "everyone" also included me. A small, sick feeling creeps up from my stomach.

"Well, don't listen to anyone," I say with enough force that Wells looks over at me.

He smiles a little. "Okay, Doe. I won't listen to anyone."

"Oh, except you do have to listen to this," I say, turning to face him. I tap his shoulder where the WELCOME GREAT PUMPKIN sign is drawn. "Don't wash this off. It's good luck."

His smile widens. "Oh, yeah?"

"Yeah. It's the Great Pumpkin, so it only works during October. Keep it for your midterms."

"Okay," he says, still smiling.

I grab his arm before we get too far and tug him across the street. "Come on, let's get ice cream before we head back. My treat."

And even though there's still something bothering him, and it's so close to the surface I can almost see it, Wells crushes down whatever it is and follows me.

I roll over on my beach towel and groan. The sun beats on my face, warming me against the mid-October chill. Tension unfurls from my shoulders as I breathe out the stress of my last midterm.

"I feel like I haven't seen the sun in a year," Gemma says. We're all lying head to head, our towels spread out in a sunburst.

"Longer," says Jade.

"It's been six days since the last full sunshine day in Delafosse," Sumi says with all the authority of a weather forecaster. "So technically—"

I crack one eye open and glance over. Shawn has her hand flung over Sumi's mouth.

"Shh," she says as she pulls her hand back. "Let's just enjoy some peace and quiet."

My phone buzzes in my pocket. Once, twice, three times. Another phone starts to buzz.

"I thought we were enjoying peace and quiet," says Sumi, sounding annoyed.

I sit up and pull my phone out of my pocket.

ILANA ROTKO
You need to get down here
Big field hockey game tonight
It's a disaster

I stand up and walk to the other side of the roof. Clumps of girls are crowded on the lawn, some of them pointing toward the back of campus—the athletic fields.

I glance back at the others. "I think something happened."

"You think right," Jade says, standing up.

She holds out her phone, and we crowd around it to look at the photo someone just sent.

It's a shot of a crowd of girls around our field hockey pitch. A large swath of perfect green not yet yellowed by fall. Branded into it, in lines of dead brown grass, is a giant penis.

I gasp. "No."

It's crudely drawn with lopsided balls and an overly fat head. It's so obscene and yet so particularly unique, I won't forget the details for months.

Sumi scoffs. "Disgusting."

"What do you think they used? Rock salt?" Gemma asks, grabbing for the phone.

"Had to be." I march to the other side of the roof, facing Winfield. I glare at the school across the road, my blood running hotter by the second.

Somewhere in there, Three probably just finished his midterms and is feeling high and mighty.

I do the only thing I can—the only way I know how to hit back.

"Send me that picture," I say to Jade.

"What are you doing?" Shawn asks, peeking over my shoulder.

ME
What's the scale on this?

SATAN HAS THREE MOUTHS
What do you mean?

I send the photo.

> **ME**
> Such unique proportions
> I just assumed it was a
> self-portrait

SATAN HAS THREE MOUTHS
Risky subject for you to be
texting me about
I thought you had a boyfriend
But if you're trying to solicit a dick
pic from me for comparison . . .

I nearly drop my phone.
"Jesus," Shawn breathes.
Backfiring, backfiring, backfiring.

> **ME**
> You wish!
> If you send me a dick pic
> I swear to god I'll show
> your headmaster

SATAN HAS THREE MOUTHS
Seriously Dorothy?
YOU wish

I shove my phone in my pocket, breathing hard, my cheeks burning.

"He's good," Shawn says, looking toward Winfield. "Like, I hate to compliment him, but that was A-game material. He turned that on you so fast, I think I got whip-lash."

"What happened?" Sumi calls from where they're still crowded at the other side of the roof.

"Doe almost got her first dick pic," Shawn says.

Gemma's head nearly shoots off her neck. *"What!"*

"It's fine," I say, returning to my towel. "Nothing happened."

But now it feels too hot to be lying in the sun. Instead I crawl into the lower bunk of one of the beds, the slats springy beneath me.

"Lucky you," Jade says from her towel. "Do you know how many white boys have sent me unsolicited dick pics? Like, *Ha ha, would you ever do a white dude? Here's some incentive.*" She makes a retching noise. "As if their nasty, flaccid dick is really gonna get me going."

Gemma giggles. "Just one of the upsides to being a lesbian."

"What, girls don't send vag pics?" Sumi asks. "I would."

"I have a hard time believing Molly didn't," Jade says, shooting Gemma a look.

Gemma flushes. "Molly and I were hardly—we were *hardly* that involved."

Molly Harding was a girl in the year above us, whom Gemma briefly dated last year. Gemma wasn't really out yet—not officially at school, and definitely not to her family. Molly kind of helped her, I guess. Lent the guidance of an older girl who'd already gone through it.

They weren't together long—maybe two months at most—before Gemma had to end things. Between us and Molly, she was running out of time for schoolwork, and her grades were slipping.

"Your junior year is the most important of your entire high school career," I remember her telling me. "And if having a social life means choosing between you guys and Molly, obviously girlfriends can wait. I'll date in college."

She shoots us a prim look and says, "Besides, sending unsolicited photos of your genitals is a guy thing."

The use of the word *genitals* pushes me right over the edge. "Can we rein it in, please? We need a new plan. Something big."

"The newspaper *was* big," Jade says. "Possibly our biggest prank yet."

"Half their school didn't even know it wasn't their newspaper that published it," I say. "We need something even bigger. Something territorial."

"Like a giant pair of boobs on one of their fields?" Sumi suggests with a grin.

"I don't want to carry that much rock salt," Gemma says. "Seriously, I already have a bad back."

Jade rolls her eyes. "We can do better than that."

"Absolutely," I say. "I'm thinking *bigger*. I'm thinking *inside*."

"You want us to break into Winfield?" Gemma's teeth practically start chattering.

Shawn's lips curl in delight. "I heard they have tile halls."

I grin, knowing exactly where her head is at.

Sumi catches on next. "Oh, I'm in."

"You don't have a choice," I say, laughing.

"We don't?" Gemma asks, sounding terrified.

Jade sighs. "Get ready for Gemmy to teeth-chatter her way into the ground like a cartoon character."

Gemma shoves her. "Guys, this is *serious*!"

"We know," the rest of us answer.

The unison makes us dissolve into laughter, even as Gemma continues to protest and a field-sized penis forces our field hockey team to face our rivals in shame.

And we begin to formulate our biggest prank yet.

CHAPTER EIGHT

There are very few occasions for Weston and Winfield to socialize with students from Delafosse High School. But when it comes to Halloween, there are only two rules: find the Townoween party, and the best costume wins—in that order.

My friends have only been to the party once—last year. First year, we didn't even know about it. As sophomores, we didn't understand the game. But by our third year, we knew what we were looking for, and the magic of being in upper school means seniors will let you in on little secrets, passing on their legacy.

The week of Halloween, a Delafosse High student leaves clues all over town for the biggest party of the year. It always starts with an anonymous social media page under the name Townoween, for which the Delafosse High kids hand the password down from party host to party host. And a riddle.

Who's gonna drive you home?

There's a well-known sign that goes up outside Town Hall every Halloween advertising a number for free rides home on

Halloween night. Naturally, the riddle led us there, where we discovered a little wizard's hat painted on the back of the sign.

From there, it was Mr. Wizard's Ice Cream Shoppe, where we found a flyer tucked under the napkins advertising a secret show for the band Kids Not Kills at a local bar called Third Shift Brew House. The band was fake, but when we went to the guy working the door, he told us we could only buy tickets with pizza slices.

"I can't believe I'm about to set foot in Mr. Dino's," I grumble.

Sumi tosses her arm around my neck and gives me a violent shake. "It's fine, Doe! They keep stinking up Phoebe's. It's about time we return the favor."

"I showered this morning," Shawn says, giving one of her armpits a sniff. "I'm fresh as a cucumber melon. I won't be stinking up anything."

Gemma wrings her hands. "Am I the only one who has a bad feeling about this?"

"You have a bad feeling about everything," Jade says. Then she flings open the front door and steps inside.

The place is packed with Winfield boys. There are a few tables interspersed with Delafosse families, who look spooked either by the volume of the noise or that there's a line spilling out of the men's room that's so long, it nearly reaches the front door.

I turn to Shawn. "This can't be how it always is."

She looks toward the counter, where an older man is taking an order from a group of younger Winfield boys. I recognize Baby Page.

"Crap," I mutter as someone calls, "Dorothy Saltpeter, gracing Mr. Dino's with her presence for the first time in four years?"

The boys fall quiet, and relief creeps into the faces of the families who decided to brave Mr. Dino's. I wonder if they see the dread creeping into mine.

I turn around, bracing myself.

Three hasn't even stood up, but somehow, with the way he's sprawled in his chair, he looks like a boy king on his throne, surrounded by his right-hand advisors and his goon-guards.

Zamir says something to Alex that makes Alex smirk. The Biermann brothers look ready to toss me out the door at the first word from Three.

This is Three's carefully cultivated persona. The oldest son of one of Winfield's most prestigious families. *Of course* he holds court here.

"Hello, Three," I finally say. "Do you all just come here to use the bathroom? None on campus or something?" I motion to the line of boys.

Three smirks. "Only when it suits us."

I nod. "Sure, sure. So, is it a requirement that we speak to you if we want to come in here? Because we don't make you talk to us at Phoebe's. I mean, I'd prefer to never speak to you anywhere at all."

Three motions to the counter. "Carry on."

Jade sighs. "I'm getting a slice. I'm starving."

Sumi jumps into action. "I want garlic knots!"

Gemma hesitates, fidgeting at my side, until Sumi drags her away.

"I'm not hungry," I tell Shawn when I feel her looking at me.

Shawn makes a noise like she doesn't believe me, and who can blame her? I can't remember the last time I said I wasn't hungry, and even then, I had to be lying.

I glance around, wondering where we're going to sit, until Three calls, "Have some manners. Clear a space for the ladies."

A group of younger boys reluctantly abandon their table. I don't want to give Three the satisfaction outright, so I turn to give him an overdramatic curtsy before falling into one of the seats.

"It has to be in there," Shawn murmurs, leaning across the table. "There's no way this is a coincidence."

"You want us to go in the men's bathroom?" Jade says as she sits next to me, holding a plate with an extra-large slice of veggie pizza. "Have you been in a men's bathroom before? It's disgusting."

"Not to mention the crowd." I observe the line, which is moving slowly.

"What if it's in the women's, too?" says Shawn. "And they're too scared to check?"

I brighten.

Jade takes a bite of her pizza. "Too small for all of us. You guys go."

Shawn and I move past the long line of Winfield boys, and their whispers follow us all the way to the women's restroom.

Inside, we do a sweep of the walls and stalls until finally, under the sink, we find an address written on the wall in permanent marker.

16211 FARFIELD LN
$10

"Boom," Shawn says, snapping a picture with her phone. She grins at me as she stuffs it back in her pocket. "Idiots could just walk right in here and have their answer."

I shrug. "Can't knock them for respecting the women's restroom. I can imagine nothing worse than a herd of Winfield boys stampeding through here while I'm trying to pee."

I pull the door open to let her out first, and she's immediately ambushed by Three.

"What'd you find?" he asks, crowding her into the corner next to a stack of old crates.

Shawn grimaces and turns her face away. "None of your business."

"What, you don't want to share with me?" he asks with a smile. "I could make it worth your while."

"You couldn't make anything worth my while," Shawn says primly, stepping around him.

I shoot him a victorious look as she moves past me to the dining room. "What was that, your famous Wellborn charm?"

He rubs his mouth, blue eyes narrowing. "Speaking of the Wellborn charm, where's your boyfriend tonight?"

"Must've forgotten to turn his tracker on," I say, turning away.

"You might want to make this the last time you forget," he calls after me. "Because I heard a rumor, and you're not gonna like it."

I tense up like an idiot, stupidly giving his words merit.

"I don't know why you'd think I'm interested in rumors," I say tightly, twisting to face him. "I'm not worried about what he's up to when I'm not around."

Three smirks. "Wow, Dorothy. I didn't know you were so cool about that kind of stuff."

"Yeah, I'm a real cool girl, *Nathaniel.*"

I'm really getting sick of him using my full name. I'm used to hearing it every once in a while, but he's really amped it up since Fall Fest.

Any humor drops from his face, and he heads back to his table looking pissed off.

When I get back to my friends, Shawn has half a garlic knot in her mouth, and there's a slice of sausage-and-mushroom pizza waiting for me.

"You guys are the best," I say, dropping into my seat.

But I still really don't have an appetite, anxiety souring my stomach.

And even though I don't want to give Three's words merit, I text Wells.

> **ME**
> You better not be
> embarrassing me

PRETTY BOY
???

> **ME**
> Are you with another
> girl?

I watch those three dots appear, disappear, and reappear several times.

"Aren't you gonna eat?" Gemma asks, nudging my foot with hers.

I set my phone down, my mind racing. Is he typing and retyping because he's shocked that he's been caught?

I imagine the humiliation if Three knows Wells is cheating on me—or fake cheating on me, I guess, since we aren't really dating. But it feels like real cheating, because we had a deal. He can't let people, *especially* Three, think he's cheating on me. It would be the height of embarrassment.

We never explicitly agreed on exclusivity. But if I'm not going to let him dump me, I'm certainly not going to let him fool around with other girls behind my back.

My phone buzzes, and I snatch it up like I'm stranded on an island and just discovered the last coconut. And I don't even *like* coconut.

It's a photo from Wells—a white tile bathroom, a small bucket, some squeeze bottles of dark liquid, and, hanging in a shower stall, a pair of tie-dyed bell-bottoms.

PRETTY BOY
Does this answer your question?

I frown.

PRETTY BOY
Do I need to be in the pic for you
to believe me?

                                    ME
                                    Of course not
                                    I believe you

PRETTY BOY
It's an honor

                                    ME
                                    Are you mad?

He doesn't respond.

"Doe, are you okay?" Gemma asks, and I suddenly have the attention of our whole table.

"I'm fine." I set my phone down. "It's fine. It's nothing."

But Wells doesn't text me back for the rest of the night.

*   *   *

16211 Farfield Lane is a big farmhouse on the outskirts of town, with large stretches of land between its nearest neighbors. It's typical for Townoween to be held at one of these houses, so the noise doesn't attract the Delafosse police. We had to call for a car just to get a ride out here. An even smaller number of Weston girls than I heard were coming have actually shown up—we had to sneak out of the dorms, and they've been cracking down on security this year after so many pranks.

I feel a little bad about that.

I sip my watery beer and try not to focus on how I haven't seen Wells yet. We haven't spoken since I texted him from Mr. Dino's last night, and Three showed up with Alex and Zamir ages ago. It was impossible to miss him in his bright yellow raincoat, dressed as Georgie from *It*.

"I swear to god, I'm never buying a costume online again," Shawn says, adjusting her Sailor Moon skirt. It arrived much shorter than she'd anticipated, and the volleyball shorts she borrowed from Jade to wear underneath are almost as short as the skirt itself. "It's thrift stores or bust from now on."

"You cared too much about winning the costume contest," Jade says, gulping down her beer like the only way she'll survive this party is with a buzz. "You know the odds are stacked against you."

It's true—no one from Weston or Winfield ever wins.

"Someone has to be the first."

Jade, who's in a black suit and tie with a homemade earpiece hanging from one ear, says, "Is it really worth the gamble? I spent approximately zero dollars on this costume, and I feel great."

"Well, not all of us are so creative," says Shawn. "Even Sumi had to buy part of her costume."

Sumi pushes her Jason mask up and says, "No, I had this."

"Why am I not surprised?" Gemma says. "Next year, remind me not to wear orange. Velma was a great idea until I realized this outfit makes me look like a giant citrus fruit."

"There is no next year," Jade says.

I gasp. "Jade!"

Gemma's face crumples. "Oh, yeah."

"Don't worry, Gemmy," Shawn says, putting an arm around her. "We'll remind you next year anyway."

"We might not all be together, but we'll still be best friends," Sumi says.

I glare at Jade, who holds her hands up in apology.

"Wow, looks like quite the party over here."

I groan. "What do you want, Three?"

He's flanked by Alex and his sad attempt at a costume—a simple plastic crown on his head—and Zamir, in a dinosaur-costume onesie, his face framed by T. rex jaws.

Three looks over my green army jacket and the purple bandana tied around my head. His gaze lingers on my fake mustache.

"Should I even try?" he asks, mouth curling into a smirk.

I roll my eyes and slide forward the cardboard fish I have slung across my back. Jade and I spent all week painting it; it's rainbow with glitter, which I keep finding in my hair, on my clothes, and stuck to the bottoms of my feet whenever I'm in my room. The place is a glittery wreck.

"Country Joe and the Fish," I explain.

"Ah, makes sense," he says. "I heard you and Wells had matching costumes, but when I saw him earlier, he wasn't dressed." He taps his chin. "In fact, he didn't seem like he was headed anywhere at all."

He glances at Alex and Zamir. "Did he?"

Zamir says, "Not unless his costume is pajamas."

Three looks at me, eyebrows going up in false concern. "He's not coming tonight?"

I turn my nose up. "I'm not his keeper."

Alex snorts. "Trouble in paradise?"

"Can you guys go away, please?" Sumi glowers. "You're fucking up the vibe."

Three holds up his hands, one clutching a red cup. I can't imagine Three drunk, but I wonder how many of those cups it'll take.

"I was just wondering if he was coming. He didn't tell me," he says, a little gentler this time, but he's not fooling me. "Want me to text him for you?"

"Not necessary," I say with a little more force than I intend.

Zamir grins. "I think you might be onto something," he says to Alex.

"I think not," says Jade, nodding to the other side of the room.

Relief floods through me as I turn.

Wells makes his way through the crowd, his mouth set in a grim line. He's decked out in tie-dyed bell-bottoms and a tie-dyed, bell-sleeved shirt, with long necklaces draped around his neck. His hair looks wild, but I'm not sure if that's part of his costume—his hair is always a little wild.

"Janis," I say to him, grinning wide enough for both of us. I set my beer down on the console table behind me, which is already littered with cups.

"Joe," he says, putting a rigid arm around my waist. His hand doesn't quite touch my back.

I lean into him and slide a hand up to his shoulder. "Come with me," I say in his ear.

Three's jaw tightens as I pull Wells away. I lead him through the crowded house to the stairs.

"Where were you?" I ask as we start up. "Three tried to say you weren't coming."

"I considered it."

I stop halfway up and turn to face him. "What?" I can't keep the hurt out of my voice, and that's probably the worst part of all.

Wells frowns. "I can't do this if you aren't gonna trust me, Doe."

A girl coming down glances at us, and even though I don't recognize her, it's enough to make me drag Wells the rest of the way up.

I find a very pink bathroom and pull him inside, locking the door. Wells perches on the counter, leaning his head back against the mirror.

"Look, I trust you."

Wells snorts.

I move to stand in front of him but leave some space so he doesn't feel cornered. "Yesterday was a momentary lapse in judgment. I let Three get to me."

"You always let Three get to you. Have you considered that you'll never be able to win as long as you let him get under your skin?"

"I have considered that, yeah." Just not with as much sincerity as I should.

Wells leans forward, resting his elbows on his thighs. "You're never gonna be able to do as much damage to him as he does to you. Not when we're like this."

"Look, I *do* trust you. But I thought meeting my mom, and me meeting your parents, might have freaked you out a little. I wouldn't blame you if it did."

"That's bullshit."

I jerk back. "Excuse me?"

He slides off the counter and leans back against it, long legs stretched out and crossed at the ankles. He's taking up way more space than I'm entirely comfortable with. Wells isn't big—he's not much taller than me—but it feels like he's eleven feet tall sometimes.

"It didn't freak me out. And you *know* it didn't freak me out. A week ago, you sat in my lap and drew *Peanuts* on my arm. Did I seem freaked out?"

"I wasn't in your lap—"

Wells presses forward. "This doesn't have anything to do with me. It's about you, and it's about Three. As usual. I wasn't freaked out meeting your parents. And I always planned on you meeting mine."

"What do you mean? You planned on me meeting your parents?"

"Well, they come to Thanksgiving," he says. "You were going to meet them at some point, even if it wasn't Fall Fest. Although convincing everyone to let you come to Thanksgiving will be a lot easier now that you have."

My ears feel like they're filled with cotton. "Come to Thanksgiving?"

He looks at me like I'm insane. "That's what we've been talking about this whole time."

"Are you high?"

"Are *you?*"

"How do you expect me to get to your Thanksgiving? I'll be in St. Louis, and I don't have a car. Even if I did, it's not like Cincinnati is a little day trip!"

"It's five hours," says Wells. "But I figured you'd come home with me from school."

I drown on dry land.

"Seriously, Doe? I told you we'd be doing this on Thanksgiving."

"But you never said the watch wasn't here. I figured you meant Thanksgiving as a general time frame, not a set date. I thought we were breaking into his dorm. I didn't know we were breaking into his *house!*"

"We aren't breaking in. We'll be invited. Thanksgiving is always at Three's, and it's smaller than Christmas, so it made the most sense. Plus, we have to get it done before you *dump my ass.*"

"Think about what you're suggesting. If we get caught—"

"If we get caught, I'll take the heat. They won't do anything to you. It'd be too embarrassing for them to admit even the possibility of something underhanded happening with Pop's will. Which it *did,* for the record."

I hesitate. "That doesn't change how serious this is."

"It's not stealing if the watch was supposed to be mine. Pop left it to me. I don't care what my uncle and his attorney say. Three doesn't care about it. That's why it's sitting at his house instead of at school with him. He gets everything—*everything.* Why should he get this, too?"

His mouth pinches. I get the feeling he's said more than he wanted to.

I feel a twist of sympathy, but as I reach to put a hand on his arm, someone bangs on the door.

"Hello? I seriously have to pee!"

I jump, trip over Wells's feet, and fall straight into him. My hand closes around his shirt, pulling his scoop neck down.

"Sorry, sorry!" I apologize, trying to right myself.

Wells shifts, arms going around me. He straightens, pulling me upright.

I step away, then frown at his shirt. "Damn, I'm sorry." I

try to fix it, but I've stretched the collar out so badly, the shirt slips off his shoulder.

He pulls it back up and shrugs. "It's fine."

I pause. "Hold on," I whisper, grabbing his hand before he can reach for the door.

I push him against the wall and shove my hands into his hair, which is sticky with hairspray. I run my fingers through it until it nearly stands on end.

"Better make the most of this, right?" I say as I peel off my mustache and pocket it.

His gaze tracks my hand as I pull out a little capsule of red lip tint. I dab it messily onto my mouth, then reach up and smear it across Wells's lips.

His mouth parts under my fingers, and I think he might be holding his breath.

"I'm not sure this is my color," he says at last.

I try to smile, but it feels flimsy on my face. I focus on smudging my lip tint at the corner of his mouth.

"Perfect."

I grab his hand, and when we step out of the bathroom, there's a line five people deep.

My face heats, even though I wasn't *actually* doing anything. The whole line starts to titter.

When we reach the bottom of the stairs, Wells leans down and whispers in my ear, "We should probably finish that conversation."

"Oh, I know," I say. "I can't believe you sprung that on me. I'm still recovering."

"*Sprung it* on you?" He laughs, but he's unamused. "Are you kidding me, Doe?"

"Hey." I grab him, pulling him close as the crowd surges around us. "We'll talk about it later. Tonight is about this."

"Tonight won't be about anything," he says, sliding his

arms around my waist so I can't step away, "if you're about to bail on my end of the deal."

"I'm not bailing. I just—well, I have to plan!"

"I want your word."

"You already have it."

"I want it again," he says. "With collateral."

I blink at him. "I don't have anything on me. What collateral?"

"You always have something on you, Doe," he says with a wicked smile. "Not all collateral is tangible."

I clench my teeth. "What do you want?"

"A secret. A big one. One even your friends don't know."

"You're the secret my friends don't know."

He raises an eyebrow.

"Fine. *Fine.*" I rack my brain for something—*anything*—other than the first secret that comes to mind.

"You have ten seconds, or I'm walking into that room and dumping you first."

I gape at him. "What the fuck, Wells?"

He shrugs, looking like he couldn't care less what happens.

And maybe he couldn't. For all the time we've spent together, I still don't know a single real thing about him.

Maybe he doesn't know a single real thing about me, either. But he's about to.

I take a deep, steadying breath, push up onto my toes, and press my mouth right to his ear to tell him my most embarrassing secret.

The reason I came to Weston in the first place.

When I settle back on my heels, his expression hasn't changed. But he nods.

Then he takes my hand and leads me down the hall to the

living room, where the majority of people are gathered. My friends are still there, and I see Joc in a baseball uniform and Biers in a Thor costume. There's Christian Page in a scarecrow outfit, face painted, chatting up some girl. I spot Three's yellow raincoat in the crowd, too, with Zamir and Alex.

The gang's all here.

"What are we doing?" I bite out through a big, fake smile so no one can tell how miserable I am.

"You're worried I'm out doing all kinds of who knows what with other girls. You want to stake your claim." He stops and pulls me against him. "There are better ways to do that."

"Like what? Stick a flag with my name on it through your chest?"

He grins. "We can try that next."

And he kisses me.

I'm so mad at him, I could scream, but goddamn, Wells knows how to kiss. My legs go a little weak as he slides one hand up to cup my cheek, tilting my head the way he wants me. I press against him, my body knowing what to do even as my brain reels from the contact.

He pulls away slowly, pressing one, two, three tiny kisses against my mouth as he does.

I try to reach for the fury that was boiling through me a few seconds ago, but kissing him burned it all away. "You're an asshole," I say without conviction.

He grins. "Maybe. But Three looks like he wants to put someone's head through a wall. So, isn't it worth it?"

I don't turn around to look, instead watching Wells's face as he glances over my shoulder at his cousin. The corners of his mouth curl in satisfaction.

Whatever he said about not messing with Three is bullshit. Maybe he doesn't want to, but he likes to.

Wells returns his gaze to my face and reaches up to tap my nose. "You better figure out what you're gonna do. I already told my parents you're coming." His smile widens. "Should I let you tell Three?"

At that, I have to smile. "Oh, please, yes. Let me."

He squeezes my waist. "Anything for you."

He leads me away from the center of the living room and deposits me back with my friends while he goes off to get a drink. I lean into Shawn, still feeling a little dazed, and also a bit intimidated by the number of heads turning my way.

"Hot damn," Sumi says, fanning herself. "If I ever get kissed like that, I might drop dead on the spot."

Gemma glances the way Wells went and adds, "He is *very* pretty. I might even let him kiss me, just to see what it's like."

Shawn laughs. "Should he add *even tempting to lesbians* to his résumé?"

Jade downs her drink. "What'd you two do upstairs?" she asks, waggling her eyebrows.

"M.Y.O.B.," I tell her.

She scrunches her brows together. "Is that a new position I haven't heard of?"

And they all scream with laughter.

CHAPTER
NINE

I feel bad for anyone who needs to make a cake this week," Sumi whispers as we crouch in Winfield's perfectly manicured hedges.

"Their fault," Gemma says, her voice shaking. "They should be using something with more flavor than vegetable oil."

"Okay, *The Great British Bake Off*," Jade says from my earbud. "Alright, they just rounded the building. You've got three minutes to get in."

I heft the canvas bag higher on my shoulder as we creep out from the hedges and to the front door.

Shawn darts ahead, swipes our stolen keycard over the reader, and yanks the door open. Jade lifted the keycard off a Winfield boy last night at Hot Cup. We've been tracking the upper school boys for weeks trying to find a weak link. It didn't take long to find one with a perpetually unzipped backpack.

"Nice," Jade says in my ear. "Keep me posted on your progress. No lights on any floors—everyone's asleep."

Sumi leans the generic WET FLOOR sign she carried over

from Weston up against the wall, ready to place in front of the dorm monitor's door on our way out. We don't need a Winfield faculty member breaking a hip.

We creep up the stairs to the fourth floor, planning to work our way down. Even though it's riskier to get caught that high up, we don't want to have to run for it while our escape path is a minefield of vegetable oil puddles.

Shawn and I put our bags on the floor, and the four of us begin pulling out bottles of vegetable oil.

I grin as I crack open the first bottle. Shawn, Gemma, and I work on oiling the floor in front of each door and down the center of the hall. Sumi cordons off the stairs, our handmade signs hanging from each rope. They say BAD IDEA in huge letters, and beneath is a mangled stick figure with a broken neck at the bottom of a stairwell. Sumi spent about twenty minutes making them this morning. She's very proud.

I catch her admiring her handiwork as we start on the third floor.

"Sumi," I whisper, motioning for her to grab a bottle and get to work.

Gemma freezes in front of a door. "Guys," she whispers.

We go still as the door she's standing in front of rattles.

Shawn grabs Gemma and drags her flat against the wall while I duck around the corner with Sumi. We peek out and watch as a Winfield boy in just his boxers steps out of his room, rubbing his eyes. He shuffles across the unoiled floor to the bathroom, leaving his door open behind him.

"Oh, fuck," I breathe. "Oh, *fuck.*"

It's Biers.

"What's going on?" Jade demands from my earbud. "What happened?"

While he's in the bathroom, Shawn peeks into his dorm,

and I see her brace herself as she reaches for Gemma. They sprint past the open door to us, and we all press against the wall, breathing hard.

I can see the shine of oil on the floor just beyond Biers's room. If he takes one wrong step—wanders a little too far—we are so screwed.

"Guys, what's happening?" Jade asks.

"We gotta get out of here," Gemma whispers.

I put my finger over my lips, silently shushing her.

A flush sounds from the bathroom, and I tense as I peek out to watch Biers heading back to his room.

That's when I see it—the bag of oil bottles on the floor. I glance at Shawn, eyes wide.

Biers has one foot across the threshold of his room, and I'm about to breathe a sigh of relief when he pauses.

He steps back out and turns toward the bag. He leans down and picks it up, peering inside.

I point my friends toward the stairs. But someone— Gemma, *it has to be Gemma*—gets nervous, jumps straight into action, and runs directly into Sumi.

Sumi lets out an *oof*, clutching her stomach where Gemma hit her.

Biers whips around and looks right at me.

"Run," I whisper, at the same time he roars, *"WESTON GIRLS!"*

We clamber down the stairs, no longer attempting stealth.

"Holy shit, holy shit," Jade says in my ear. "What the hell, what the *fuck*."

"Are we clear?" I ask.

"You are so not clear," she says. "You are *so far* from clear."

Above us, the entire hall has sprung into action, and a chorus of shouts and thumps ring out as boys hit the floor. It gets louder as the boys above them start to wake, and we're halfway down the hall of the first floor when doors start flinging open.

"East door, east door," Jade says.

"Which way is east?" I ask.

"Left, left!" she shrieks.

Sumi grabs Gemma's arm and swings her left, and we follow. We tear out the doors and spill out onto the lawn.

I can hear shouts from security on the other side of the building as we sprint for the front gate.

A security guard yells behind us, but I can't hear what he's saying over the rushing in my ears.

"Back door," Jade says.

We race under the Weston gate and around the side of Walsh. Jade has the back door open for us.

We run all the way up to the roof, where we arrive panting and exhausted. I creep to the ledge and crouch behind the bricks, watching the lights in the boys' dorm flick on.

"Holy shit," Shawn says, grabbing onto me.

"We gotta get back to our rooms, *now*," Jade says, and her voice echoes in my earbud.

I tear it out and shove it in my pocket. "I know. Go fast."

They still have to make it across the lawn to Halcomb and Itaska without being seen. Gemma looks like she's going to have a nervous breakdown right here in the Kingdom.

Sumi takes her hand. "It's okay, Gemmy. I'll get you there."

Gemma, Sumi, and Jade leave, but Shawn and I linger on the roof, watching Winfield. Within ten minutes, most of the school looks to be awake, and a shadow stalks out the front doors of the upper school dorm, heading straight toward the gates.

"Their headmaster," I say to Shawn.

She looks at me. "I think we got his attention."

I grab Shawn's hand and squeeze. "I think we're about to have a lot more attention than we bet on."

I wake abruptly to pounding on my door. I stumble out of bed and flip the lock, and Shawn sweeps into my room in her pajamas.

"Winfield hit back," she says, going to my window, which overlooks the commons. "Small, but effective."

It's been three days since the oiling incident, and even though we've heard whispers of the Winfield headmaster storming over to our campus and demanding to see Cotesmore in the middle of the night, Cotesmore never said one word to the student body.

I grab my toiletry basket and head for the bathroom. "Tell me."

While I brush my teeth, Shawn talks.

"I woke up to a million texts," she says. "They took Mallory."

"What!" Toothpaste splatters across the mirror.

A girl a few sinks down frowns at me.

I shove my toothbrush back in my mouth and scrub furiously at my teeth.

"They must have come last night," Shawn continues. "I don't know—I don't understand how they got her off the base. They seriously de-welded her from the metal."

I wash my face and slather on some moisturizer.

"I need pants," I say, heading back to my room.

"Cotesmore just announced an emergency assembly," Shawn says, following me. "We're supposed to be down there at ten."

I grimace. A Saturday assembly is never good.

"I need food," I say.

"I'm going to get dressed," she says, heading for her room. "I'll text everyone to meet in the dining hall."

The others are there when we arrive, holding our place at a round table. The dining hall is packed, everyone talking about the missing Mallory Weston statue and the emergency assembly.

"What are we supposed to do?" Gemma asks when Shawn and I join the table with our breakfast. "If we get busted, it could mess up our college admissions."

Shawn puts an arm around her. "They can't prove anything, Gem. Besides, this is about Mallory. Otherwise we would've been doing this the morning after the oiling."

I point my fork at her. "True. I agree."

Gemma looks at me. "Do we maybe need to cool it for a while?"

I glare at her. "*Cool* it? They stole our school symbol— the woman we've modeled ourselves after. Further proving that Weston girls and Winfield boys do *not* mix well. We're getting exactly what we wanted—proof this merger will be a disaster."

Jade snorts. "Right, until they figure out a bunch of seniors are responsible and their problems will be solved by graduation."

"It's not just a bunch of seniors," says Sumi. "Plenty of juniors and lower school girls have helped us."

Jade takes a bite of her veggie omelet and shrugs.

"I hope you all are pleased with yourselves."

I nearly choke on my oatmeal. Virginia Brinkoff stands behind Gemma, and even though she says "you all," she's glaring at me.

I take it upon myself to respond. "We have no idea what you're talking about."

"Sure, you don't," she says, crossing her arms.

The three girls behind her are just as smug, and I want to knock their heads off their necks—Virginia's first.

"You're really starting to irritate me," I tell her, pushing back my chair and standing up. "Are you that hard up to get boys in this school that you have to pick a fight with me? We're not the only ones who hate the idea of this merger."

"Yeah, but you're the only ones who snuck into a Winfield dorm and oiled their hallways. Do you just love wasting money? Olive oil isn't cheap."

"It was vegetable oil!"

Shawn grabs my wrist and gives it a warning tug, but Virginia's mouth has already curled into a satisfied smile.

"I guess we know who to thank for Mallory going missing," she says, glancing back at her friends.

"Mallory didn't 'go missing,'" Shawn says, standing up beside me. "She was stolen."

"And who would bother to steal our school symbol unprovoked?" Virginia asks. "Aren't you *tired*?"

"No," Sumi says with a blithe smile. "We're just getting started."

"You're naïve if you think Winfield boys wouldn't hit this school unprovoked," I say, putting my hands flat on the table. "Either that, or you haven't been paying attention. This war has been going on longer than any of us have been alive—longer than our parents have even been alive. Winfield couldn't stand it when Weston became an academic rival—when the curtain dropped, and they realized we weren't learning china patterns and place settings. They hit us *first*. Learn your history before you try to come at girls who've been here longer than you."

"What do you even think you're fighting for, Doe?"

Virginia asks, putting her hands on the back of Gemma's chair.

Gemma stiffens. "Weston pride," she says, twisting to look up at Virginia. "Now, get your hands off my chair."

It's the most solid I've heard Gemma's voice sound since the oiling incident.

Virginia releases the chair and lifts her chin at me. "Whatever happens at assembly, know you're all to blame. The rest of us suffer for what you and a handful of other girls do."

"Collective punishment is a war crime," I tell her. "Feel free to take it up with Cotesmore. That's not on us—that's on the administration."

Virginia backs up into her group, and they leave, no longer smug, but not exactly retreating with their tails between their legs, either.

I sit back down and clench my fists in my lap.

Sumi smacks Gemma on the shoulder. "That was badass."

Gemma puts her fingers in her mouth and starts to chatter on her nails.

Sumi drops her hand and sighs. "For a second, anyway."

Gemma glares at her.

"Do you think we're really getting the whole school in trouble?" Jade asks.

I shrug and glance at the clock over the door. "In about an hour, we'll know for sure."

The noise level in the auditorium is almost deafening as we file in. I glance at Shawn, brows arching way up, until a hand settles on my shoulder.

I jerk around and nearly trip back into my friends when I find Mr. Tully standing there, mouth set in a grim line.

"Take a seat," he says, motioning me into the row. "Try to keep the chitchat to a minimum."

I resist the urge to motion to the rest of the auditorium, where the other girls talk without restraint.

"What's his problem?" I grumble to Shawn as we slide into our seats.

"You'd think he'd be thrilled for the opportunity to perv on us on a weekend," she says.

I snort, and on her other side, Sumi laughs.

"What?" Jade asks, leaning around Sumi. "What's funny?"

Gemma slides into her seat and shushes us. "If we make a scene, he'll come over here."

"He'll do that anyway, just hoping Doe pops a button on that flannel," Sumi mutters.

The button over my cleavage does look a bit strained. When I notice Tully glancing my way, I cross my arms.

When everyone finally settles, Cotesmore approaches the podium. She has on that no-nonsense face of hers, and I sink a little farther into my seat.

"Quiet, please," she says into the microphone, and the auditorium goes dead silent in seconds.

I glance at Shawn, eyes wide. She bounces her eyebrows at me like she's just as surprised.

"It has recently come to the attention of this administration that our longtime rivalry with Winfield Academy has spiraled out of control," Cotesmore begins.

I fidget in my seat as attention swivels our way.

Sumi clears her throat. "Uncomf," she murmurs.

"Next year, our two schools will be one," Cotesmore continues. "This rivalry will no longer matter, because we will be one student body. I know some of you are pleased with this and others are not. But the fact remains that this will be the last year Weston is run as an all-girls' school."

I reach over and take Shawn's hand, and she squeezes.

"I expect perfect conduct from *all* of you"—I know I'm

not hallucinating when her gaze lingers on me—"as we welcome Headmaster Pritchard and Winfield Academy to our assembly this morning."

The auditorium erupts with noise as the back doors are flung open and Winfield boys stream in on both sides.

The auditorium is the largest hall on campus, big enough to host graduation every spring with friends and family in attendance. Our student body doesn't even fill it halfway. It can fit an entire second student body, with room to spare.

I stare in horror as the Winfield boys are directed into the empty seats behind us. I manage to spot Three in a small bout of bad luck, and when he catches my eye, he grins.

I pretend to throw up over the back of my seat, and the younger girl sitting behind me shrieks in protest. I apologize while my friends laugh, and when I look up again, I spot Wells coming in, almost the last to arrive.

My stomach drops and then crawls back up. Now I might really throw up.

I haven't seen Wells since Halloween, but I've stupidly, idiotically been thinking about that kiss all week.

He texted me after the oiling incident to say, Thanks for the bruise on my ass. A little warning would've been appreciated.

But we haven't talked about anything real. I'm still shaken after giving him my secret, something I've gone to great lengths to keep separate from my life here. Wells having that in his back pocket is unsettling in the worst way.

Not to mention that I'll soon have to bake up a lie good enough to convince each of my parents that I'll be with the other for Thanksgiving. And I can't decide if I'm mad at Wells for that.

Would I have asked him to do this, and agreed to his terms, if I'd known this was the blank check I was signing?

Headmaster Pritchard joins Headmistress Cotesmore on stage, and she shakes his hand, motioning him to the podium.

He takes her place at the microphone.

"Hello," he says, "I'm Headmaster Pritchard. It's nice to meet you all."

The auditorium goes silent. Down our row, I hear Sumi snort.

Pritchard clears his throat. "Next year, our schools will merge into one coeducational institution. To celebrate that, our administrations have developed a plan for the rest of the year to help ease in some of our students more reluctant to change."

Cotesmore joins him at the podium. "After today, we will be holding weekly merger tests with different years and houses within both schools. It may be volunteer work, clubs we have in common, or school events. No student is exempt, and all years are included."

Now I know I'm not imagining it when she meets my gaze and adds, "Even seniors."

I grind my teeth together. More forced time with Winfield—it's a living nightmare.

"And to end the semester, Winfield will host a dance for both schools," Pritchard says, "in lieu of our usual celebrations. Only Weston and Winfield students will be permitted to attend."

Cotesmore smiles. "We suggest you begin making friends."

Never has the idea of making friends felt more threatening.

I glance over my shoulder at Wells, who looks like he might be sleeping with his eyes open.

At least I have a fake boyfriend to drag to the dance with me.

And then I start to wonder—what trouble could we get up to at a Weston-Winfield dance? I glance at Shawn, and she's already smiling.

Gemma mutters, "Don't look too pleased. Cotesmore has her eye on us."

"She better put both on us, fast," says Jade.

"Her nightmares should run wild with the possibilities of what we'll do," Sumi says, a grin in her voice.

Shawn glances at me. "She'll be watching us like a hawk."

"Let her," I reply. "I do love a challenge."

CHAPTER
TEN

This is seriously disgusting," I say to Gemma from where I'm perched on her window ledge, looking out over the commons.

"Just stop looking," Gemma says. "That's what I do when—Oh! You *motherfucker*, I swear to—"

I glance over at the screen where Gemma is demolishing a dilapidated room full of zombies. The room on screen is a stark contrast to Gemma's dorm, which is decorated in pastels, fake flowers in delicate glass vases, and vintage-looking pictures hanging on the walls. She has framed photos of her with Polly and May, her older sisters, lined up across her desk. Her bedspread is lavender and ruffled, and there's a pearl-framed mirror standing up beside her dresser. She even swapped out the drawer handles for faux-crystal knobs. The whole room smells citrusy and sweet.

Gemma makes a low growling noise as she jabs at the controller in her hands, and explosions erupt onscreen.

I sigh and turn back to the window. With the merging of so many clubs, our campus is crawling with Winfield boys. They've joined clumps of Weston girls, and my stomach roils with annoyance when I see them laughing and smiling together.

"It kills me to see Winfield boys looking this happy," I tell her. "And to see Weston girls this happy with Winfield boys. It's unnatural."

"Aren't you dating a Winfield boy?" she says. "If he's not making you happy, you probably want to find a new boyfriend."

I frown. "That's different."

She lets out a frustrated scream and throws aside the controller as her character dies. She shoves her feet against the floor, and her gaming chair rolls onto its back. She looks at me upside down, her hair splayed around her in a tangled mess.

"What's really bothering you?" she asks. "It can't just be the boys on campus."

"Says who?"

She rolls off the chair and sits up on her knees. "What's on your mind?"

I hunch my shoulders and turn back to the window. I hate that Gemma can see straight into my brain sometimes. I'm used to her momming Sumi, and even Jade, but I've always been the self-sufficient one.

And I've always had Shawn to lean on.

But things are different now that my stress revolves around Wells and Thanksgiving, and how I'm going to pull this off.

I've caught myself wondering more than once if it's worth it, but I always remember Three's twisted, angry face when he looks at us, and I feel a rush of satisfaction that reminds me I *am* winning something.

"You don't have to tell me," Gemma says. "But tell someone, okay? Tell Shawn."

I turn to Gemma. She tries to stow the sad look on her face before I catch it, but she's a second too late.

I climb down from the window and sit next to her on the floor. "It's about Thanksgiving," I say before I can think better of it.

Her brow creases. "What's up? Is it your parents?"

I shrug. "Kind of. It's more . . . about Wells."

She waits, not urging me to continue, but clearly hoping I will.

"He wants me to come to his family's Thanksgiving."

Gemma's mouth drops open. "In *Ohio*? You guys have only been dating for, like, a minute!"

"I know. I—I kind of promised him." I rub my forehead, pain pricking between my eyes. "He asked me to come home with him, and I said I would, but I didn't realize how hard it would be. My parents will never go for it, and I always spend Thanksgiving with my dad."

"So tell Wells you can't go."

"That's not really an option at this point."

"Why?"

I wince, suspecting this may have been a bad idea. "I just can't. I made a promise."

Gemma tilts her head, watching my face.

"You really like him," she says, surprised.

I twist away, afraid of her seeing everything I'm hiding. "I hate lying to my parents. Especially my dad. And what do I even say? If I say I'm going to my mom's, he'll be crushed. And we know they still talk, because she told him about Wells. So—"

"Tell him you're coming to my house."

I whip around to look at her. "What?"

She shrugs. "Tell him I invited you. Tell him . . . I'm

having a hard time this year, and you want me to be with a friend on Thanksgiving."

I shuffle closer, until our knees are pressed together. "Gemmy . . ."

"I kind of wish you were coming, now that I say it," she says with a watery laugh.

I put my arms around her. "Do you want me to? Say the word, and I'll cancel everything. I'll tell Wells exactly where he can shove it if he has a problem."

She wraps her arms around me and squeezes so tight, I can tell she's holding her breath.

When she finally replies, her voice wobbles. "It's okay. I'll be fine. I mean, I was fine all summer, right?" She pulls back and gives me a weak smile. "But my first Thanksgiving after coming out to my family? I hate to exploit your dad's empathy, but I don't think he'd fight you on it."

I brush my hands over her hair, pushing it back from her face. "We haven't really talked about it. Your summer."

"I haven't wanted to," Gemma admits.

According to Gemma, the Honeychurches are simple folk—they have fried chicken every Friday, church every Sunday, and on Thursday nights, no matter what, they watch the long-running show *Our Family* together, even long distance. More than once, I've had to lend Gemma my phone so she could stream the episode while on her phone with her family.

Needless to say, having a gay daughter probably wasn't on the agenda, and Gemma was nervous about disrupting their neatly ordered lives.

"My parents were fine, though," Gemma continues. "My sisters, too. Great, actually. But you know how it is in the Midwest. It's not like I was running to the neighborhood pool to scope out a summer girlfriend with Polly and May."

I think of St. Louis, and my years at St. Aloysius, and all the things people said about my dad when they learned he isn't straight.

It sometimes feels like we live in a bubble at Weston, because the school philosophy is so forward-thinking, and there's a zero-tolerance policy for hate. I try to imagine St. Aloysius enforcing a zero-tolerance policy. They'd have to halve the student body.

"Tell your dad you're coming to Thanksgiving with me," Gemma says, taking my hands in hers. "I'll cover for you."

I watch her face, waiting for a crack in her calm façade.

She smiles. "Stop looking at me like that. I'm fine. I'll *be* fine. You always feel like you have to mastermind our plans. Let me mastermind yours for once."

"If you have a hard time," I say, holding on tight to her hands when she tries to pull away, "call me right away. I'll— I'll buy a plane ticket if I have to."

Her eyes go watery, and she sniffles. "Yeah. Okay. I will."

"Promise?"

She nods. "I promise."

I put my hands on her cheeks and squeeze until her mouth puckers like a fish. "I love you. And this offer stands no matter what or when. You can always call me, and I'll be there. I'll drop whatever I'm doing. In fifty years, I'd drop a grandkid to be there for you."

Gemma laughs and pulls away. "Please don't drop any children for me."

"I would," I say. "Seriously."

She crawls over to her gaming console and grabs the second controller. "For now, I'll be satisfied if you play a few rounds with me. You look like you could use the stress relief."

I take the controller and climb up onto her bed. "You know games don't relieve my stress."

"Only because you're bad at them," she says as she rights her chair. "You'll get better with practice."

I die within minutes of the first round. But it makes Gemma laugh, and that's all that matters.

I put off calling my dad as long as I can, until Thanksgiving is looming around the corner and bailing on him is almost unreasonable.

I head up to the Kingdom alone, bundled in my winter coat, wondering where fall went. The trees are almost completely bare.

I climb into a lower bunk and dial my dad with trembling hands.

He answers almost instantly, which makes me wonder what he's doing tonight. Sitting on the couch, eating leftovers while he watches TV?

I don't ask, ignoring the ache in my stomach.

In this moment, I hate Wells. I hate him so much I can barely see straight. I hate him more than Three. I hate him even knowing it's my actions that led me here. And I hate that he has my secret because of it, and that for the rest of my life, he'll have my secret, and I don't have one single thing of his.

I sniffle, and Dad stops talking about the promotion his boss was given this week and asks, "What's wrong, Dorothy Ann?"

I swipe at my eyes, even though I'm not crying yet. "What makes you think something's wrong?"

"I can hear it in your breathing," he says. "I could hear it from the second I picked up the phone. I was hoping you'd tell me on your own, but now I'm asking."

I take in a deep breath and let it out, grimacing when it shakes.

"It's about Thanksgiving," I say, my voice small.

"What's the matter? You want to spend it with Mom?"

I can hear the disappointment fighting its way through the phone. He doesn't want me to, but he can't keep it out of his voice.

"No! I don't want to spend it with Mom. It's—it's about Gemma."

Guilt tightens my throat until I can barely force a breath, let alone words.

"What's going on with Gemma?" Dad asks, his voice hitching up in concern.

"She's just having a tough time after coming out," I say, and my free hand curls in self-loathing.

"Oh, my," Dad says.

No going back now.

"She wants me to come home with her for Thanksgiving. She said her parents and sisters have been great, but she's worried about the rest of the family now that they all know. She's afraid to do it alone."

"Of course, Doe," Dad says. "I understand. You can absolutely go with her."

Relief and shame flood through me at the same time, a combustible combination.

"Hey, Dad?"

"Hmm?"

"Have I told you lately that you're the best? And not just the best dad, but like, the best person?"

He chuckles. "I'm glad you think so."

"I'll miss you." This, at least, isn't a lie. "I wish I could be in two places at once."

"We have the rest of our lives full of Thanksgivings together," Dad says, but there's some conviction missing from his voice.

After my half summer in Chicago, he's feeling my absence. I'm feeling his, too.

"But Gemma only gets to do her first out Thanksgiving once," Dad continues. "And it's important that she asked you to come. Doe—I'm proud of you for going."

My throat is so tight, I can hardly speak. I try to swallow against it, too aware of the silence. Tears wet my cheeks, turning the cold air icy on my face. "I love you," I say at last, because over everything else, this is true. "I love you the *most*. Don't tell Mom."

He gives a small laugh. "I won't, but you shouldn't rank your parents, Doe."

"Can't help it. You've pulled ahead of the pack on your own. The judges have taken note."

I manage to calm down over the next few minutes, easing back into work-school-friends chitchat, until Dad asks the thing that makes my entire body freeze over.

"And how's the boyfriend?"

I close my eyes. "He's great," I lie with a perfect smile on my face, hoping he can hear it through the phone. "I couldn't be happier."

I'm still sporting my fake smile when we hang up a while later. I sit in the cold, shivering, until I've taken enough deep breaths to calm my roiling emotions.

Downstairs, I pause at Shawn's open door, surprised to see everyone gathered.

"We texted you," Shawn says as I step inside. "You didn't answer."

I glance down at my phone. Sure enough, I have twelve texts in our group chat, and—my heart thumps—one from Wells.

I shove my phone in my pocket and take a seat between Gemma and Shawn.

Gemma reaches over and squeezes my hand. "You okay?"

I nod.

Jade looks between us, then at Shawn.

Sumi is busy unwrapping a granola bar stolen from the stash I keep in Shawn's room. I make it a point to have a snack stash in all of their rooms, just in case.

"What happened?" Shawn asks me.

I hesitate, but I know it's stupid—I can't lie to my friends about everything. It's bad enough I'm lying to them about one thing.

"I'm going to Cincinnati with Wells for Thanksgiving."

Shawn gasps like she's starring in a period drama and I admitted I'm dying of consumption.

"He asked me, and I agreed, but convincing my dad took some . . . delicate wording."

"You mean lies," Jade says flatly. "What did you tell him?"

I glance at Gemma.

Sumi finally gets the bar unwrapped, and her attention returns.

"You can say you're coming to my house," she says around a mouthful of granola bar.

"She already said she's coming to mine," Gemma says. "I told her to."

Jade makes a strangled sound. "What's so important about going to his house for Thanksgiving that you have to lie to your parents?"

"Not both. Just my dad."

"Who will tell your mom," Jade points out, rotating a hand in the air, "which is, in result, lying to your *parents,* plural. How did you even convince him to let you go—" Jade's gaze swings to Gemma, her jaw dropping.

Gemma goes red. "I offered."

Jade looks at me. "Tell me you didn't."

I hesitate.

"Tell me you *did not* exploit Gemma's and your dad's sexualities to get what you want."

"Hey," Gemma says sharply, red splotching her cheeks. "She didn't exploit my sexuality. I told her to do it."

"So just your dad's then?" Jade says to me, her lip curling.

I put my hands on my knees and stare at the floor, unable to look her in the eyes. Shame courses through me, turning my insides sick.

Jade scoffs. "Jesus Christ, Doe. Is it that important for you to get laid?"

My head whips up. "*Excuse me?* That's not what this is about at all!"

Shawn puts a hand on my arm, making soothing noises, but I jerk away from her and scramble up.

"Then what are you going for?" Jade asks, standing. "What's so important?"

"I made him a promise."

"For what?" Jade shouts, throwing her hands up. "This is fucked up, Doe. You don't do stuff like this!"

"What are you so mad about?" I ask. "It doesn't have anything to do with you!"

"I can be mad on someone else's behalf," Jade says.

"I don't want you to get mad for me!" says Gemma, lurching to her feet.

Shawn jumps up and grabs Gemma's arm.

Sumi leans back on her elbows, watching us while she chews.

"Maybe I'm not getting mad for *you*," Jade says, baring her teeth. "Maybe I'm getting mad for Doe's dad, who you've now played a part in hurting!"

Gemma's face crumples, and her eyes fill instantly.

"I don't have to listen to this," I say, storming to the door.

"Doe, don't leave!" Shawn says, coming after me.

Out in the hall, other girls are leaning out their doors, unabashedly eavesdropping.

I ignore Shawn, flying into the stairwell and all the way down. I rush out onto the front lawn and let the door slam behind me.

I don't have a pass, but I walk right off campus and don't stop. I head straight into town, past Hot Cup and Phoebe's, and when I spot him through the window of Mr. Wizard's, sitting alone at a table with a huge waffle cone, I fling the door open and step inside. It's otherwise deserted, which isn't surprising in the current weather. A cold drizzle was starting on my way into town.

My jaw is clenched so tight, I can barely force out the words, "Go fuck yourself," as I march past him to the counter.

Three's eyebrows arch way up, and his chair scrapes as he pushes away from the table.

"What's your problem?" he asks without venom.

There's so much rage coursing through me, I'm practically levitating. But I can't tell him what my problem is, or who I'm really mad at. It's easier to take my anger out on him. Even if I'm being marginally unfair.

Three follows me down the ice cream case as I choose a scoop of chocolate-bourbon brown sugar and espresso chocolate chip in a chocolate-dipped waffle cone. When I get to the register, I hold out my hand to him.

He blinks at me.

"I forgot my wallet," I say. "Can you please pay for my ice cream before I put my head through the wall?"

He glowers at me, handing his card over to the girl at the register.

"You have serious issues," he says, following me to the table against the window. I climb up onto a high stool, and Three settles on the one beside me.

"Thanks for the ice cream," I say, not looking at him.

He swivels toward me and leans an elbow on the table, his gaze burning into the side of my face as he finishes off his own cone.

When he's done, I motion to the door. "Aren't you going?"

"No," he says. "I'm really actually curious what you're so mad about."

I look over at him.

He shrugs. "I know. I'm surprised, too."

"Don't act human. It freaks me out."

"Well, I'd hate to do that," he says. "What should I do instead? Push you off your chair? Knock your ice cream out of your hand?"

"You could leave."

"I'd rather see what you're planning to do next."

"I'm not planning anything. I'm going with the flow."

"Is the flow going to take you to my cousin? I know you're great at sneaking into dorms."

I chuckle, pride swelling.

"You know," Three says quietly, "that was a pretty dangerous prank. I almost cracked my head open."

"You could probably use a concussion to rattle your brain into something resembling a human's."

"You're pretty convinced I'm not human. But, you know, I've never met someone else who was so like me."

I spin to face him. "We're nothing alike."

He shrugs. "Agree to disagree."

"Don't we always?"

He grins, then glances out at the street. The rain has picked up.

"Do you have an umbrella?" he asks.

"Of course not." I shoot him a sidelong glance.

He snorts. "I'm not *offering*. I don't, either."

"What were you going to do? Ask to borrow mine?"

He laughs as he slides off his stool and pushes it under the counter like the rest of the unoccupied seats.

I hate when he proves he has manners. It's unnerving.

"Wells is at Rotty's. I'm sure you already know."

"Isn't he always?"

He shrugs. "Guess so."

"Why are you telling me? Don't you hate seeing us together?"

"I won't have to see you together if you go there," he says, heading for the door. "Besides, I can't tell you my reasons, or I might seem human to you, and I know how much you hate that."

The door swings shut behind him, and I watch as he pulls up the hood of his coat and heads back toward campus, a shadow shrinking into the dark.

CHAPTER
ELEVEN

Jade always needs a cooling-off period after a fight, so I wait a few days before I finally drag myself to her dorm. When Jade thinks she's right, she almost never breaks her silent treatment unless you come to her first.

Itaska is one of the older dorms, and I huddle into my sweatshirt as I push out from the drafty stairwell into the frigid hall.

Every door is shut.

Jade's is one of the more decorated doors, which shouldn't surprise me. While I gather myself, I look over the magazine cutouts, printed-out poems by Nayyirah Waheed and Lang Leav, and carefully rolled flowers made from junk mail. There's a cheery little sticker that says DON'T TOUCH MY HAIR with a smiley face.

I'm still looking when the door swings open.

I jerk back. "Oh. Hey."

Jade narrows her eyes. "Are you planning to stand out there all day?"

I frown. "How'd you even know I was here?"

She gives me a look like I shouldn't have to ask, and I wonder if she has a camera planted in the hall. She must see the gears turning inside my head, because she says, "I recognized your footsteps."

I wonder if I could recognize *anyone's* footsteps. Doubt it.

"Come in, I guess," she says, stepping out of the way. "You're letting all the warm air out."

Her room is at least ten degrees warmer than the hall, and when she shuts her door, she shoves a towel up against the crack at the bottom. Jade's room is a study in hygge—something she learned about when she visited her dad in Denmark over Christmas a few years ago. Her dorm has a thick, faux-fur rug layered over a threadbare Persian rug, and her bed is piled in blankets—one fuzzy, a thick cable knit, a flannel-Sherpa combo with an *S* for Solheim monogrammed on the corner.

She has three lamps—on her desk, on her nightstand, and on her dresser. She doesn't use the overhead light, and the lamps give the room a warm glow.

On her walls are star maps and tarot cards, more magazine flowers, and a moon phase tapestry. There's a hand on her desk with palm-reading guides on it, and each finger is stacked with Jade's rings. Above her bed is a whimsical-looking poster that reads BLACK GIRL MAGIC. Under the window, the radiator clicks and hums.

She climbs up onto her bed, which is lofted over her desk, and I suddenly feel like a commoner coming to pay respects to a queen.

"So, what do you want?"

Clearly the few days I gave her to cool off wasn't enough.

"I don't want you to be mad at me."

She narrows her eyes. "Interesting phrasing. Not *I don't want to do things that make you mad at me*. Implying you aren't upset about what you're doing—only that someone called you out on it."

I glare at her, my shoulders tensing. "That's mean."

"You need someone to be a little mean to you," she says. "You're making bad decisions, Doe. It's hard to watch."

"I've made *one* bad decision."

Two, technically. But if she knew I was lying about Wells, I'm not sure what would happen.

As if she can read my mind, Jade says, "I don't know if that's entirely true."

"Look, I just want to get through this Thanksgiving thing. I promised something I couldn't deliver on without lying to my parents, and Gemma gave me a way out. It's messed up. I knew it was messed up as I was doing it. It was hard enough just to *do it.* I know actions have consequences, but can't you give me a break? *Please?*"

Jade watches me, her expression stony. "That's not what friends do. Friends don't give each other breaks on the big stuff. I let you have your morally gray area all the time and never say a word. Like with Wells."

I freeze. "What's that supposed to mean?"

"You think I can't tell you're with Wells just to make Three go insane?"

I hold my breath.

"I'm not entirely convinced he isn't with you for the same reason," she adds. "He kissed you on Halloween, but do you know who he was looking at? Do you *want* to date someone who's looking over your shoulder all the time, making sure he's hurting someone else?"

"Hurting is a strong word. Three doesn't get hurt. He gets mad."

Her jaw goes slack. "Oh my *god,* it really is true. You're dating Wells to make Three mad. Does Wells know?"

"That's not why I'm dating Wells," I lie like an absolute

idiot. But now is not the time to admit it. I'm trying to repair something, not damage it further.

"You said yourself it's not about sex. What did you promise him?"

"It's none of your business what goes on between me and my boyfriend, Jade!"

She sits back, her expression cooling.

I clasp both hands around the back of my neck, bracketing my face in my arms, trying to rein in my temper.

"When you do things that hurt other people, it's my job to call you out," Jade says.

I lift my head.

She works her jaw, looking uncomfortable. "But even if it's my job to call you out, it's not my job to tell you what to do. You're perfectly able to figure it out for yourself, just like I have. And I can't be complicit in something like this. *That's* why I get mad. When you hurt other people and I sit there and do nothing, I feel like I'm hurting them, too."

"I'm not trying to hurt anyone." My voice cracks, and I know what she's going to say, because I'm already thinking it.

"Sometimes you don't have to try."

I cross my arms, curling in on myself. "Okay. Cool. Well, I guess I don't know what else there is to say." I start for the door but stop when I hear her bed creak.

Jade slides to the edge. "I don't want to fight with you, either, Doe."

I wait, but she doesn't say anything else.

Finding a place in Delafosse where we won't be overheard is nearly impossible, so Wells borrows Christian Page's car and drives us two towns over to a highway diner where the only people who might be listening are just passing through.

Even with an off-campus pass, leaving Delafosse is strictly against the rules, but I'm caring less about consequences these days. Plus, our administrations are busy dealing with a problem of their own creation right now—making sure Weston girls and Winfield boys aren't sneaking into dorm rooms and isolated corners and abandoned classrooms to feel each other up.

"Why are we acting like we're starring in a spy movie?" I ask Wells as I slide into a corner booth. It's an odd time of the afternoon for a meal, but that hasn't diminished the crowd.

Wells glances around us. For all his paranoia, I'm surprised he isn't wearing dark sunglasses and a hat.

"I told you this is a big deal," he says when he finally sits across from me. "If someone overhears and it gets back to Three, I'm dead. And I'll never—"

He stops short as the server approaches. She takes our drink order and disappears again.

"I'll never get another chance like this," Wells finishes.

"So, what are we doing?"

He motions to my menu. "Figure out what you want first."

"What are you getting?" I ask, flipping the menu open.

"Coffee."

"And?"

"Coffee."

I peek under the table at his bouncing leg. "Maybe you need something other than caffeine."

"I'm not hungry."

"Well, what makes you think I'm hungry?"

He raises an eyebrow at me.

I roll my eyes. "Okay, fine, I'm hungry. What do you want from me?"

The server returns with coffee for Wells and water for

me, and I order a breakfast skillet. There's something about eating breakfast at three in the afternoon that always feels special.

I glance at my phone, frowning at my blank screen. I told my friends I was going to be gone in the afternoon, but it's strange not to have a single text in our group chat. Normally it runs all day long, conversations stopping and starting throughout the day. But it's been quiet since my fight with Jade.

We don't know how to act when there's tension in the group. It's not like we never fight or anything. But every time, this is how it happens—a blowup, then tense silence until apologies are made.

"Hello?" Wells says, waving a hand in front of my face. "Are you listening to me?"

I blink myself back to the table. "Sorry. What'd you say?"

His brow creases. "Are you okay?"

I wave him off. "I'm fine."

"You don't seem fine. You keep looking at your phone."

"I'm looking at you."

"You said you weren't busy today."

"I'm *not*, Wells." I shove my phone into my purse. "Is that better?"

I can't imagine what he's read off my face when he asks, "You haven't made up yet?"

I knew I'd regret going to see him at Rotty's after I ran into Three at Mr. Wizard's. I stupidly told him I'd had a fight with Jade, even though I sensed I was looking for comfort in the wrong place. But he didn't ask me a bunch of questions. He just slid over in the chair and let me sit with him for a while.

I still haven't told him what the fight was about, and I'm definitely not telling him about the conversation in her room yesterday. Some things he doesn't need to know.

"This is normal," I tell him, and even though it's not exactly a lie, it doesn't feel like the whole truth, either.

Wells tilts his head. "Okay," he says, but it comes out like he knows better.

I take a deep breath. "Isn't today about our Thanksgiving plan?"

"You don't seem like you're in the mindset to plan."

I fold my hands on the table. "I'm in the perfect mindset to plan. Don't act like you know what's happening inside my head."

"You could tell me what's happening inside your head." He stirs his coffee, the spoon clinking lightly against the mug. "Then I wouldn't have to guess."

"We had a fight. I told you already. It's going on a little longer than usual, but it was also a bigger fight than usual. Everything's fine. We'll get over it."

He takes a sip of his coffee. "This year's weird, isn't it?"

I jerk back, startled. "Yeah. Super weird. It's felt different from the jump, you know? As soon as they announced the merger."

"I've been wondering if that's it, or if this is how everyone feels their senior year."

I lean forward, mesmerized as he pulls each thought so perfectly from my brain. I've spent the last few months thinking the weirdness was in my head, a by-product of knowing the Weston legacy is about to be destroyed. But maybe Wells is right—maybe it's natural for us, in our final year of school, to feel strange in our own skin.

"It's the end of an era no matter how you spin it," he says. "I can't pretend I'm as attached to Winfield as you are to Weston. But this has been my home. It's weird to think that in a year, the places I've known so well could be different. And in twenty years, I could come back to campus without a clue what or where everything is. Like how my dad needs me to name the new buildings for him whenever he visits. If the merger happens, Weston and Winfield could be completely unrecognizable."

I scoop an ice cube from my water into my mouth and crunch on it. Dread skewers my insides.

"Sorry," Wells says. "I shouldn't have—"

"It's fine." I slouch in my seat. "That might be the first thing you've ever said to me that means anything."

His stare hits me with a force that makes my breath catch, and I'm floundering for something to say when our server returns with my skillet—eggs, bacon, and home fries with extra seasoning. My mouth waters.

I thank her with a touch too much enthusiasm, and when I glance at Wells, he has a small, amused smile on his face.

"So, Thanksgiving?" I prompt as I mix the contents of my plate together.

Wells opens his mouth, then closes it, watching my hands. "Why do you do that?"

"It tastes better," I reply.

His face twists.

"Don't give me that look. Here, try it." I push my plate across the table.

Wells plucks my fork out of my hand and takes a bite. As he chews, he hands my fork back and slides my plate over.

I try not to look stunned that he used my fork. It's not *that* weird. I'd share a fork with any of my friends. Plus, we've already—

My brain goes haywire when I remember kissing him.

"I guess it's not bad," Wells says at last, sounding like he'd rather admit anything else other than I'm right. It reminds me of Three, which is a sobering thought.

I roll my eyes.

"So, Thanksgiving," Wells says at last.

I wave my fork in a circle, urging him to continue.

"We'll have to do it during dinner—it's the only time Three won't be able to follow you without being noticed. I'll keep him occupied at the table. But you have to be the one to take it—if I'm out of my uncle's sight, they'll know I have it."

"And they won't assume you sent me?"

"Three will. But Uncle Nate will assume you wouldn't have the balls to steal from him in his own house. And he'd never admit it, even if he knew you pulled it off."

"The balls," I mutter. I take a deep breath and let it out through my nose. "So, I pull the whole thing off during dinner. I have, what, fifteen minutes to get it done before I lose my window for blaming it on diarrhea or something?"

"Fifteen is pushing it," says Wells. "I'd say ten. He doesn't have a ton of stuff, and he keeps his room neat. You won't have a problem finding something in there."

I hesitate. "This is, like, *real* stealing, Wells."

"I told you what it was already. I said it's not exactly legal." I don't know what my face must look like to cause him to add, "You can't back out—I have collateral."

"I wasn't talking about *backing out*," I say, slamming my fork down. "Don't think you get to use that collateral to get whatever you want out of me. After this, I'll have your secret, too."

A muscle jumps in his jaw, and he picks up his coffee, his gaze turning toward the window.

I take another bite of my skillet, but it's tasteless in my mouth. I push my plate away and cross my arms.

Wells sets his coffee down. "This would work better if we could agree to act like a team, instead of two people dead set on blackmailing each other."

"Should I remind you that *you* asked for collateral first?"

"Should I remind *you* that you're the one who wanted to bail?"

"I never said I wanted to bail!"

He motions for me to be quiet.

"Don't *shush* me!"

He sits back and pinches the bridge of his nose.

I rein in my temper. "I never said I wanted to bail. You assumed and started making demands."

"I'm not gonna apologize for it, so you can kiss that dream goodbye."

I glare at him. "I see the Wellborn charm really is a family trait."

"You can leave if you don't like it, but I don't think you'll enjoy the consequences."

I lean forward, hands gripping the edge of the table. "You're acting more like Three every day. Would it really make you happy to tell everyone the most embarrassing thing about me? Would humiliating me get you off?"

"Why? Are you interested in what gets me off?"

I make a face and reel back in my seat. "That's it—I'm leaving."

He grabs my hand. "Hey—don't. I was kidding."

"You weren't."

"Okay, sorry. I wasn't kidding, but that got out of hand."

I settle back in my seat.

"You really know how to ramp up a situation, don't you?" he says with a tentative smile.

I shoot him a cool look.

He pushes my plate back toward me. "Keep eating."

I pick up my fork but pause to ask, "What's the point of getting this watch if you can never wear it or display it or anything?"

"It's mine," Wells says with a fierceness I've never heard from me before. "He—I don't—" He sighs and shakes his head. "It doesn't matter. You don't need to know. Plausible deniability is your best friend in this scenario."

"For when Three interrogates me later?"

"Or if you get caught."

I scowl. "I won't get caught. And even if I do, I'm the queen of improvising."

"Yeah? Like running screaming through our dorm when you got caught oiling the floors?"

"I don't know what you're talking about."

He gives me a look.

I turn up my nose. "And I wasn't screaming."

He grins. "I'm still mad you didn't give me a heads-up."

"Consider that my payback for you getting my secret."

"This bruise might not heal until New Year's."

"You deserved it."

He licks his lips, watching me. "Yeah. I guess I did."

I squirm, uncomfortable with the sincerity in his voice.

"So, when do I get to tell Three?"

"We leave Wednesday morning. I don't think I mentioned this, but we, uh, carpool."

I blink at him.

"I don't have a car," he says, "and Aunt Bridget won't let Biers have a car because she doesn't trust him. Joc doesn't have his license. It's just Christian and Three."

"I'm not riding all the way to Cincinnati with Three."

"Not even to torture him?"

"I'd kill him first."

He chuckles. "I figured, so I told Christian you're coming. He won't say anything to Three. I know you want to do the honors."

"I think I'd like to spring it on him in the parking lot Wednesday morning. He'll shit twice and die when he sees me with my suitcase."

CHAPTER
TWELVE

have to pee."

Baby Page groans, tipping his head back against the front passenger seat. "Again?"

"I have a small bladder!"

Christian reaches over and smacks his brother in the stomach. "Manners."

"I wouldn't mind stretching my legs," Wells says from next to me in the back seat.

I jump. I thought he was asleep.

When I glance over, he's leaning against the window with his eyes cracked open, watching me.

Christian dials Three through the car, and Three's voice fills the speakers.

"Let me guess," he says, voice like molasses. "Doe has to pee again."

"I drink a lot of water!"

"There's an exit coming up," Christian says.

I glance at the sign. "No, not there!"

"I forgot Princess has her thing about the bathrooms," says Three.

Christian sighs.

"Hey, when you have to actually sit on a public toilet to pee, you get to have an opinion," I say.

"There's a Love's coming up in a few miles," Wells says, tapping at his phone.

"I see it," says one of the Biermann brothers. They're in Three's car, and I can only imagine what it smells like in there after three hours of driving.

We still have two to go. At least the Page brothers are mostly hygienic, although Baby Page's sad, sparse goatee suggests otherwise.

Three took the whole thing surprisingly well when I showed up this morning, lugging my suitcase across the street. I'd said goodbye to my friends the night before—mostly in person, but in the group text for Jade, who I still haven't repaired things with. The boys wanted to get on the road early, but it ended up being an hour later than they planned. They were too busy fighting over how to pack their luggage in the cars.

Three did a double take when he saw me.

"Oh, what the *fuck*!" he roared, whirling on Wells. "You're bringing your girlfriend to Thanksgiving?"

"Chill out," Wells said, clapping Three on the back. "It's not like she's going in your car."

"She's coming to my house!" Three said, his whole face going red.

I grinned. "What, worried I'll find your secret fetish porn stash and tell everyone about your anime bondage tentacle kink?"

He took in a breath so long I was surprised his lungs could handle it.

"Better hide your dirty laundry," I told him. "Both figurative and literal."

Wells gave me a look, and I eased off the gas.

Three slammed his trunk shut, surprising Joc, who jumped back just in time to spare his hands from being smashed.

"Dude, what the hell!" Joc shoved Three, and then Biers shoved Joc, and then the brothers descended into chaotic shoving and hitting while the rest of us watched, including Three, who'd kind of started the whole thing.

My confidence that I'd survive five days with them waned with every passing second, until my only sliver of hope was that I wouldn't have to put up with them at Wells's house.

Except the stress of being alone with Wells at his house is about to put my head through the stratosphere.

At least being stuck in the tiny back seat with him for five hours is good practice.

Christian pulls off the highway and into the Love's, where he parks at a gas pump.

"May as well fill up," he says to Three, who has stopped at the pump next to ours.

As I jump out of the car, I can hear the Biermann brothers arguing inside Three's car. Three looks like he's contemplating leaving them both here.

His undisguised misery makes me smile.

We reach Cincinnati in the early afternoon, and as Christian's car climbs the steep hill to Wells's house, I marvel at the view of the river below. The Wellborns all live in Mount Adams, like kings atop the throne of the city.

"We don't have much of a view from our house," Wells says, and it comes out like an apology. "But you'll like Three's place. You can see everything from there."

Wells's house is narrow and pale yellow with a red front door and white shutters. The street reminds me of an old colonial city with the houses densely packed together and right on the sidewalk—no front yards, and rare front porches.

Wells takes my suitcase out of the trunk, and I'm struck again by the reality of the situation.

Five days.

Five days in this house with Wells and his parents.

An entire evening with the Wellborn family for Thanksgiving dinner tomorrow.

And the deal we discussed at length all week. A plan I didn't mastermind, which makes me feel itchy.

Wells's parents aren't home yet. We pull our bags up the front steps, and Wells unlocks the door. The car pulls away from the curb.

Wells shuts the door behind us, and we're alone.

I can't remember the last time I was alone in a house with a boy. Two years ago? More?

Wells's house looks so lived in. Coats crowd each rung on the rack by the door, and it looks in danger of toppling at the lightest addition. Pictures hang in a gallery wall going all the way up the stairs, some listing slightly to the side. There's a bowl on the entryway table filled with change, extra keys, and few little lollipops.

"You can leave your suitcase down here," Wells says. "I'll bring it up."

"That's okay, I can—"

"It's fine, Doe. The stairs are narrow. I'd rather you not put a hole in the wall."

I glare at him, and he grins.

"Come on." He takes my wrist and tugs me up the stairs, which are even narrower than they looked from the bottom.

On the way up, I survey the photos, which I can tell stresses Wells out. There are school photos from when he was younger—one where he's missing both front teeth, and another where he clearly has a self-done haircut. The family photos are all candids—nothing posed. There's a shot of a very young Wells and his mom on the Dumbo ride at Disney World, mouths open in screams of delight. There's another of him, maybe middle school–age, and both parents in helmets and life vests, climbing into a raft on a river.

I try to get a closer look, but they blur by as Wells pulls me along.

On the second floor, he takes me into the first bedroom on the left and flips on the light.

"You're in here," he says.

It's small, dominated by a bed pushed up against the wall, under windows overlooking the small courtyard behind the house next door. The bedding is simple, neutral colors, and paired with a short wooden frame, no headboard. There's a desk by the door with a single lamp and a TV on the dresser at the end of the bed.

I'm thinking it's a guest room when I notice the squat bookshelf beside the desk. It's so packed with books they spill out onto the floor. As I step inside, I see stacks of them under the desk.

The farther I go, the more I notice—the artsy prints of figures done in looping, unbroken lines hanging on the wall by the door, a baseball bat with a glove on top leaning in a corner, and an old-looking world map tacked up above the desk, stuck with so many pins, there's no way they're marking travel.

There's a familiar scent underneath it all, like the outdoors in autumn. A scent I know well by now.

"This is your room," I say at last, turning to him.

He nods. "I'll stay downstairs."

"I can stay in the guest room."

The corner of his mouth twitches, amused. "There is no guest room. I'll be on the couch."

I should apologize for being presumptuous, but I can tell Wells doesn't want me to by the way he plows ahead.

"My parents are really loud in the morning, but it gets hot in here at night if the door is closed, so you'll have to pick the lesser evil. The bathroom is across the hall." He moves out of the room, and in two steps, he's in the bathroom.

"This is the only shower," he says, jerking his thumb over his shoulder. "But my parents have a half bath in their room if this one's occupied. Sometimes my dad likes to use this one instead. He says it's a change of scenery."

I fight a smile.

"I know." He blows out a breath, rubbing the back of his neck. "He's weird. But I told him to behave while you're here."

"Worried I'll start to think badly of you?"

He leans a shoulder against the doorjamb, the bathroom light casting a halo around his hair. "Nah, worried about the opposite."

My breath goes short.

He flips the light off and heads for the stairs. "We have a while before they get home. You can eat whatever you want in the kitchen, and the TV in my room gets everything we have." He hesitates halfway down and turns back around. "Or you can hang out with me. Up to you."

I swallow. "Oh—I could eat."

Wells grins. "Why am I not surprised?"

We end up on the couch, Wells with his feet propped on the coffee table while he flips through channels, me hunched over a plate of sliced apples and peanut butter. I felt like a trespassing scavenger digging through the kitchen, but I really am starving.

Wells stops flipping channels when he lands on HGTV, and I pause.

"Don't look at me like that," he says.

"I wasn't even looking at you." I twist to face him.

"You were thinking it." He turns his head toward me, mussing his hair against the back of the couch. "You were looking at me with your mind."

"I'm just surprised."

"I contain multitudes, Doe." He returns his attention to the TV. "And I like watching couples fight over backsplash. Sue me."

"Do you have HGTV nights with your dorm?" I ask, sliding my plate onto the table and easing down against the throw pillows on my side of the couch. I cricket my legs together for a little warmth. "Gather 'round the TV to watch *First Time Flippers.*"

"That's on DIY," Wells says.

I splutter out a laugh. "I guess everyone has their guilty pleasures. Shawn's watched *The Office* at least fourteen times all the way through. And Jade loves those—"

I falter, and he looks over.

"Those high-drama shows about teenagers played by twenty-five-year-olds," I finish, my voice strained.

Wells reaches over the arm of the couch, drags a fuzzy red throw into his lap, and tosses it over my legs.

"Are you guys still fighting?" he asks, tucking it around my feet.

I shrug. "I don't know. I've seen her a few times. Things are just . . . weird."

He nods, his gaze straying to the TV. "Well, you can unwind here. I know how therapeutic you find it to piss Three off. And maybe being away for a while will be good. Hey, watch the Realtor's face when these people list their must-haves and then tell him their budget. Priceless."

I watch him instead, and the lazy smile invading his usually blank expression. I can't help but wonder if it's HGTV that relaxes him like this, or just being home.

I wonder how different I am at home, too.

I wake on the couch, the dark living room lit blue by the TV, and soft yellow filtering in from the hall.

". . . inside voice. You're gonna wake her up."

Wells.

"Why is she so tired?" a woman whispers back, although *whisper* isn't exactly it. It's more like a whisper-yell. "Is she feeling okay?"

"It was a long drive," Wells says.

I try to squirm into a sitting position, but Wells has his hands on my ankles. I somehow managed to slide down the couch in my sleep, my legs curled in his lap. I can only imagine what my hair looks like.

"Never mind," Wells says, huffing out a laugh. "She's awake."

"Hi, Doe! How was your nap?"

Wells releases me, and I sit up, trying to seem alert as my senses rush back to me. "Hi—I'm—Sorry, I didn't mean to fall asleep."

"You must have been exhausted!"

"I guess so." I rub a hand over my face and try to discreetly smack my tongue against the roof of my mouth to get rid of my sleep breath. "Sorry. Hi, Mrs. Wellborn."

She fluffs up the throw pillows and drops onto the cushion next to me. "Mrs. Wellborn," she repeats, smile widening to an alarming degree. "You're so polite. You're a guest here—you don't have to call me Mrs. Wellborn. You can call me Winona."

"Winona," I say, testing it out. It feels weird to call a parent by her first name. My cheeks burn.

Winona smiles at me. "I called my friends' parents by their first names when we were in school," she says. "If I didn't call them Mom and Dad outright. I want you to feel at home here. It was so nice of your parents to let you come visit us."

She glances at her son and raises an eyebrow in an expression that is *so* Wells. "Now if only my darling son had thought to tell me you were home, we could have taken you out to dinner."

It dawns on me that the reason Wells looks nothing like Three is because of his mom. Wells and Winona are a study in similarities.

Wells sighs. "She ate before she fell asleep. She's like a baby. I'll take her to get something in a little bit."

"Not my point, Gabriel." Her voice turns stern, no longer my friend Winona but Wells's mom. "We might have to lay some ground rules while your girlfriend is visiting. I'm sure you were very eager to have some time alone—"

Wells sits straight up, his expression panicked. "Mom, don't—"

"I know what high school relationships are like," she continues. "Especially at boarding school, when you're always surrounded by other people. It's only natural to want to explore your relationship."

Wells groans and sinks into the couch like he's hoping he can go straight through it. "That's not what's happening here."

It takes me a minute to realize they're talking about sex, and my face burns red-hot.

"We—we didn't—we aren't—that's not—" I splutter.

"I'm not trying to police your relationship," Winona says, patting my knee. Then she looks at Wells. "But we aren't sending anyone back to school pregnant, okay?"

Wells puts his hands over his face and groans so loudly that his dad comes in.

"Oh, good, you're awake," he says when he sees me.

I jump up, my legs tangling in the blanket. I almost topple over onto the coffee table, but Winona catches me.

"Hi, Mr. Wellborn. I'm sorry I was—I was just tired—*We didn't do anything!*"

He sighs and looks at his wife. "Winona. You couldn't have waited fifteen minutes for her to get her head on straight?"

Winona puts an arm around my shoulders and gives me a squeeze, and I can almost feel her laughing. "I'm sorry, Doe. Come on, let's get you some dinner."

"I said I'd take her to get something," says Wells, his voice muffled by his hands. I can't even look at him.

"She spends all year at school *getting something*. She deserves a home-cooked meal." She peeks around me at Wells. "And I am inclined to remind you that she'd have had one at a reasonable hour if you hadn't neglected to tell me you were here."

She leads me into the kitchen, and while Mr. Wellborn gets me set up at the table, we have the whole *call me Jeff* conversation. Wells slinks in after a few minutes, looking both chastised and embarrassed. He sits down next to me.

It's drafty in the kitchen, and I resist the urge to scoot closer to him. Instead I rub my hands together in my lap, then tuck them between my legs for warmth.

"So, is everyone done embarrassing my girlfriend?" Wells asks.

"Probably," Winona says. "But I can't guarantee we're done embarrassing you."

"I figured that was your ongoing mission in life."

Jeff laughs.

"We don't have any meat in the house," Winona says from where she's disappeared into the walk-in pantry. "I forgot to go to the store today."

"It's fine, Mom," Wells says. "Doe eats anything."

Winona leans out of the pantry, eyes narrowed. "Would you like to let her speak for herself, my son? Or have you forgotten that women are autonomous?"

I grin, shooting Wells a smug look. My embarrassment has melted away entirely. "I'm okay with anything," I tell her. "Although I hate to admit when he's right."

"Veggie fajitas?" Jeff suggests.

Winona snaps her fingers and points at him. "You are a genius amongst mortals."

"They're vegetarian," Wells says. "I am not."

"How'd that happen?"

"We always cooked meat for him growing up," Winona says, reappearing. "It's a lifestyle choice, like anything else. He should get to choose for himself. Besides, I was still getting my masters when he was living here full-time, and with both of us so busy, he ended up with his cousins a lot."

"I really love burgers," Wells admits to me.

"And we really love him," Winona says, the stove clicking and bursting to life under the pan. "So, we cater to him a bit."

Jeff gets up and starts washing vegetables in the sink while Winona chops up an onion. My eyes start to water, while hers fill and spill over.

"I got it," Wells says, getting up to replace her at the cutting board. She goes to the freezer and sticks her head in.

Watching a family interact and move around each other so effortlessly is almost surreal. It makes me envious. I think of Dad and me in his house, always stepping on each other's toes, never quite getting the rhythm right after the divorce. About how I feel as out of place in Mom's new Chicago house as I do here with Wells—maybe less so here.

Wells must sense my mood, because after dinner, he brings my suitcase up to his room but doesn't leave right away.

"If you need anything and you're afraid to ask or something, you can text me," he says. He leans against the doorframe while I slide my suitcase in front of the bookshelf and unzip it.

"I have manners, Wells. I know how to ask for things when I'm a guest."

He puts his hands up. "Okay. I was just offering. I don't want you to be freaked out that my mom thought we were in here hooking up all afternoon. You could barely look her in the eye."

"Like you could!"

He rumples his hair, looking embarrassed and tired.

I stand up, pajamas clutched in my hands. "I'll be fine. Go to sleep."

"It's, like, nine o'clock."

"And yet, you look like death on legs."

He gives me a flat look. "Wow, kill me with compliments. Please."

I grab my toiletry bag and shoulder past him into the hall. His shirt is super soft but his chest is solid against my arm, and my mouth goes dry.

I stop at the bathroom and twist around to face him. He's turning toward the stairs but pauses.

"Do you want to watch a movie or something?" I ask, motioning to his bedroom.

He looks from me to the bedroom and back. "Do you think you'll survive my mom coming in to remind me we have an open-door policy in this house?"

"After this afternoon? I could probably survive anything."

He grins. "I'll remember that when we're at Three's tomorrow."

I grimace. "Please don't say his name this close to my bedtime. I'll have nightmares."

"Oh, those are the dreams you have about him? I would've guessed a different kind."

I throw my toothpaste at him, and he catches it.

"Sure, I'll watch a movie with you, Doe."

"I take back the invitation."

He moves across the hall so we're almost touching and holds the toothpaste out to me.

"Sorry," he says as my fingers close around it. But instead of letting go, he gives it a tug, reeling me in. "No take backs."

Then he leaves me standing there, my heart beating fast, wondering how I'm going to survive sitting on a bed with him for a whole movie.

I shut myself in the bathroom and convince myself that I don't need to invite Winona up to play chaperone.

I can handle a Wellborn.

Even this one.

When I come out, Wells is waiting in his room. He occupies it with the comfort of someone who lives there, sprawled on his stomach across the bed. He's scrolling through movies on the TV, a pillow bunched up between his elbows and his feet propped against the wall.

"Is this how we're sitting? Are you that worried about your mom?" I joke as I prop myself up against the pillows at the head of the bed.

Wells glances back at me, his mouth kicked up in a smirk. "I thought this would appeal to your foot fetish."

I scoff and smack him on the leg. "I don't have a foot fetish. Don't be gross."

He rolls onto his back, propping himself up on one elbow and offering me the remote. "What do you want to watch?"

I put a hand on my chest. "I get a choice? But I'm—oh, I'm just a *girl*."

He rolls his eyes, falling back against the pillow. The remote drops onto the bed. "Should I thank my mom for this?" he asks the ceiling.

"What do *I* know about *films*? Why don't you choose, darling?"

I've slipped into a terrible Southern accent, which makes Wells smile.

"Are we doing pet names now?" he asks, pushing up onto his elbows. "Sweetheart?"

I pull a face. "How do you manage to make that sound so condescending?"

He chokes out a laugh. "I didn't!"

"You did."

"Wait, let me try again," he says, sitting up. He hits me with a look, but even before he says it, that dumb smile is pulling at his mouth. "Angel face."

I put my foot on his chest and push him onto his back. "Ew."

He laughs. "What? What's wrong with that?"

"You can't even take yourself seriously. Let's watch something before you embarrass yourself."

He pushes my foot away and sits up. "You couldn't do any better."

I fix him with a flat look. "Babe."

"That doesn't count. That's easy." He leans up, bracing a hand against the bed, right between our knees. "Babe."

I put a hand on his shin, because it feels like the safest part of his leg. I'm sure as hell not touching his feet after the foot fetish joke.

"Honeybun," I say, almost imploringly, "let's just watch a movie."

He blinks at me. "How are you so good at that?"

"You have to pick the right nickname. Do I look like an angel face to you?"

He scoffs. "And I look like a *honeybun*?"

I eye him. "I mean, yeah. Definitely."

He grabs the remote and lobs it into my lap.

"Don't pout," I say as he settles beside me, making a big show of fluffing the pillow before he slumps against it.

"I'm not," he says, but his pouty lower lip tells a different story.

I bite back a smile as I turn my attention to the TV and finally settle on *Beetlejuice*. Restless energy rolls off of Wells, but eventually he relaxes into his loss. We share his bed like we share the big red chair at Rotty's—comfortably, without any awkward apologies or *where do I put my arm*. When his hand brushes mine, I don't jump out of my skin.

Until Wells turns to me halfway through the movie and says, "Hey. Gorgeous."

And my stomach dips like he pushed me off the bed.

I whip my head toward him. "What?" I ask, but it comes out kind of like a hiccup: *wha-AT?*

He smiles. "You do look like an angel face, for the record."

I try to swallow, but my mouth has gone desert dry.

"Wow," I croak. "Don't ever let anyone accuse you of being a slow learner."

He huffs out a laugh.

Winona chooses this moment to wander past and poke her head in. "Hey, how's the movie?"

"Mom," Wells says, his voice cracking.

I jerk back against the pillow, forcing my gaze to the TV. It takes me a second to even remember what we're watching.

"Okay, okay," Winona says. But before she leaves, she gives the door a little tap, pushing it open another inch.

Wells groans, and Winona puts her hands up, retreating.

As soon as she's gone, I sag in relief. Laughter bubbles up, and I have to cover my mouth to stifle it.

"I'm glad you're amused," Wells says.

More like panicked.

With the moment shattered, it should be easier to focus on the movie, but I've completely lost the threads of the plot. I watch it without really seeing it.

All I can think about is how long Wells's eyelashes are, and that little indent in his lower lip, and the way one of his eyebrows curves a little higher than the other.

Somehow I think "angel face" might fit him better.

But I can't deny it felt nice to hear him say it.

CHAPTER THIRTEEN

'm not surprised that Three lives in the biggest house I've seen in Mount Adams so far. It hangs over a cliff, the last lot on the street, with big windows and a cylindrical glass tower on one corner with panoramic views of the city.

What does surprise me is that instead of a floppy-eared golden retriever trotting out to greet us, there's a fluffy gray cat that winds its way around my legs while I shrug off my coat in the foyer.

I did not take the Wellborns for cat people.

Winona coos at the cat and crouches to scoop it up.

Okay—I didn't take *Three's* family for cat people. I wouldn't be surprised to find out Winona and Jeff raise baby goats in their courtyard.

"I hope you're not allergic," Mrs. Wellborn says to me. It's very clear I will never be on a first-name basis with Three's parents. I'll probably call them Mr. and Mrs. Wellborn when I'm thirty. "I didn't even think to ask."

"No, I love cats!"

I want to smack myself for my enthusiasm, especially when I hear an amused snort from Wells as he takes my coat.

Mr. Wellborn hangs the coats in the front closet. "She's a Siberian forest cat," he says like I should be impressed, which I'm not, or should know what it means, which I don't.

I look at the cat.

"Wow," I say at last, attempting a fraction of my earlier enthusiasm.

Wells freezes behind me, and I feel him shaking. He leans down, letting out a soft laugh against my shoulder.

I elbow him.

He slides his hand into mine and pulls me behind the parents as they start toward the back of the house. Straight ahead is a wide, winding staircase that goes up to the second floor and down to a floor below. We move past it through a small hallway that opens up into a large living room and kitchen. Various members of the Wellborn-Biermann-Page families are scattered throughout, and I hear noise from a room beyond the kitchen, where I glimpse a chair and the edge of a dining table.

Winona takes her sweet potato casserole into the kitchen. "We'll probably need to warm this up right before dinner," she says to a large man checking the oven. He looks like an older version of the Biermann brothers, so he can only be their father, Dermod Biermann. Being a former offensive lineman for the Indianapolis Colts, he's the most google-able of the Wellborns. And I should know. I've googled the hell out of this family.

I'm surprised to see him in the kitchen, when I was sure this would be the kind of Thanksgiving with a staff.

Until a man, dark hair smoothed back in a neat ducktail, calls from the living room, "Dermod, you're going to give Chef Nusbaum a heart attack if you don't stop opening the oven."

Winona was actually speaking to a man *behind* Mr. Biermann, a small wisp of a chef in a pristine white coat.

Everything clicks into place when I register the sounds from the dining room aren't the Wellborn family—it's the catering staff.

Of course Winona brought a sweet potato casserole to a catered Thanksgiving.

It makes sense. Thanksgiving with Dad and our family is pretty casual. I usually wear leggings for the necessary stretch. But this isn't a leggings Thanksgiving. I knew earlier when Wells came downstairs wearing a tie. It made me glad I'd thought to bring one of my nicer dresses.

Wells must see this in my face, because he leans in and whispers, "Welcome to the Stepford House."

He takes me around for introductions to Mr. Biermann and Mr. Page, the man with the slick hair. Mr. Biermann barely glances at me as he grunts hello. He returns to the TV when a commercial break ends on the football game. By the time I'm shaking his meaty hand, his attention is back on the screen.

Mrs. Page introduces me to her twins, eight-year-old girls named Adele and Ariana in matching dresses. I immediately forget which is which. Christian and Baby ignore me, tapping away at their phones on the other end of the sectional.

While I say hello to Mrs. Biermann, Joc and Biers demonstrate a tackle in the middle of the living room, which Wells quickly helps me sidestep.

Three leans against the wall, glaring at me. I'm so distracted, I almost overlook the girl perched on an armchair in the corner. She has brown hair pulled into a neat French braid and a dress that, although cute, looks like it's meant for someone much younger. It's sleeveless and tight across her chest, pinching around her armpits. Her cheeks, still round with baby fat, go splotchy red when she catches me assessing her. She looks away as I draw closer.

Three intercepts me. "Doe."

"Three."

"Mer, this is Doe," Wells says.

"I know," the girl replies. "I know *all about* Doe Saltpeter."

Three gives her a deadly look. "Meredith."

She sniffs primly and looks at Wells. "Your girlfriend."

Wells smiles. "Doe, this is Meredith. Three's sister."

The cat wanders in and hops up onto her lap. "Nice to meet you," she says to me, her voice polite even though she won't meet my eyes.

"I see you've been slandering me," I say to Three.

He scoffs. "I don't talk about you enough to slander you."

Meredith makes a noise. "But you were just saying—"

Three gives his sister a look that freezes her mouth in a pucker. She idly runs her fingers through the cat's fur, and I realize I've found the cat person in the family. It sure isn't Three, who eyes the cat with thinly veiled disdain. Kind of like the look he tends to give me, only those aren't veiled at all, even thinly.

"And who's this?" I ask her, motioning to the cat.

"Dick," says Three.

Meredith shoots him a glare that could melt ice. "Emily Dickinson," she says through clenched teeth.

"That's funny," I tell her. "Hope really is the thing with feathers for a cat."

Meredith's eyes widen. "That's what I said! *Hoping* to get that bird!"

Three groans, rubbing a hand over his face. "Please don't tell me you guys have the same sense of humor."

I glance at him. "How fast would it kill you if we did?"

Meredith giggles.

Wells slides his arm around my waist, resting his hand on my hip. I want to applaud myself for not jumping out of my skin—especially since Three clocked the move. I lean into Wells and put my hand on his stomach. His muscles tense under my fingers.

I wonder if he can feel the lines of my underwear through my dress.

"What grade are you in?" I ask Meredith.

"Eighth. I'm going to The Weston School next year."

I almost sing with glee. "A *Weston* girl! In this very home!"

She opens her mouth to respond, but someone cuts her off.

"A Weston-Winfield girl."

I turn to find Mr. Wellborn standing behind the sectional, watching us. He gives me a bland smile.

Wells squeezes my hip, and I'm no longer worried about him feeling my underwear lines.

"Right, well, it's more about the Weston spirit. No merger could kill that."

"You're warming up to the idea, then," Mr. Wellborn says.

I give a soft laugh. "I wouldn't say that much. I like things the way they are."

"A lot of people think it's long past due," Mr. Wellborn says.

"Everyone's entitled to an opinion."

Wells slides his hand up to my waist and squeezes again. This one feels like a warning.

I take the hint and turn toward the TV. "Do you mind if I . . . ?" I ask Joc and Biers, disengaging from Wells's side to sit between them on the couch.

Mr. Biermann gives me a sideways look from Joc's other side. "You're a football fan?"

"I'm a fan of watching the Rams lose."

He snorts. "You from St. Louis?"

And that's how I end up talking to Mr. Biermann for the next twenty minutes while the catering team finishes up the last touches on Thanksgiving dinner.

Then we're ushered into the dining room, and Wells motions me to a seat next to him and pulls my chair out for me. Mr. Wellborn sits at the head of the table, and the catering staff hustles out of the dining room, leaving us with the image of a home-cooked Thanksgiving meal.

"Jeff, why don't you start us off this year?" Mr. Wellborn says, and they may not have cooked this meal, but they are apparently one of those families that likes to go around the table and say what they're thankful for.

Jeff sits to Mr. Wellborn's right, and he gives a big smile, like he's glad to go first.

"I'm thankful that we get to spend this Thanksgiving with Doe," Jeff says, leaning around Winona and Wells to smile at me.

I smile back, my cheeks tight.

"Oh, I have to second that," says Winona. "I'm also thankful they're reopening the winter farmer's market."

Mortification seeps into my bones when I realize I'll have to say something, too.

Wells rests his hand on my knee, which I know is supposed to be comforting, but instead sends my heart into overdrive. I put my hand over his to move it, but we are so not on the same page, because he threads his fingers through mine.

I blank out as everyone else speaks, smile frozen on my face.

I don't hear what Wells says, but I know it's my turn because he squeezes my hand.

"I'm just super thankful you've all welcomed me to your Thanksgiving," I say, feeling like the world's biggest ass.

Wells lets go of my hand. I feel a rush of relief, like I gave a class presentation and now I get to relax knowing my part is done.

"I'm thankful to be done with my college apps," Three says when it's his turn.

Mrs. Wellborn *tsks*. "Nathaniel, you can do better than that."

"Should I also talk about how thankful I am to have Doe at our Thanksgiving?"

"Should we talk about how thankful we are you've been so quiet tonight?" Wells shoots back.

Three glares at him.

"Enough," says Mr. Wellborn with finality.

Tension settles over the table.

But it makes for the perfect excuse when we finish going around the table, because when I excuse myself to go to the bathroom, no one bats an eye.

They all think I'm uncomfortable.

Which I sort of am.

I follow the directions Wells made me memorize—back to the small hallway off the foyer, where I flip on the light in the half bath and shut the door. Then to the stairs and straight up to the second floor.

I move as fast as I can without running, keeping my footsteps light as I slip into the last room on the right. There are no sentimental photos or items of interest. Everything looks professionally decorated and un-lived-in. There is zero personality in here, and yet it is so clearly Three's bedroom. I want to throw up just looking at it.

I step around his pristine bed and into his walk-in closet, which is neatly stocked with expensive dress shirts, polos, and racks of polished shoes. There's a case on the dresser filled with shiny watches, and I pick through them for the right one—checking and rechecking, until I'm sweating with the knowledge that time is passing, clocked right here on two dozen watches.

Then I hear footsteps thundering up the stairs.

I make it out of his closet right as Three bursts in, Wells behind him.

"I knew it!" Three shouts, pointing at me.

"I told you I would," I say with a breeziness I am sure not feeling. "I said to hide your dirty laundry. It's not my fault you don't take me seriously."

"You have a lot of nerve coming to my house and doing this."

I roll my eyes. "You're so dramatic."

Wells gives Three a little shoulder shove. "Don't make a big deal out of this. You're not kicking my girlfriend out of your house. Besides, your dad's already had enough with all the merger talk."

Three shoots Wells a warning look.

"What?" Wells says, holding his arms out at his sides.

I glance between them, something niggling at me.

Wells grabs my hand. "Come on, let's go."

"I want something," Three says.

When I turn back to him, his usual smug expression has returned.

"For my silence," he adds.

"Go fuck yourself," Wells replies.

Three smirks. "You're refusing? Interesting."

"I told her to meet me up here," Wells says, backpedaling.

"You want to tell your dad I was trying to hook up with my girlfriend in your room—be my guest."

I tug on his arm. "Wells."

"I guess I will," Three says, sounding gleeful.

I want to hit him, but I also need him to turn around, just for a second—less than a second.

But he isn't letting us out of his sight.

Oh, screw it.

I throw my arms around Wells's neck like a hug and press my mouth right to his ear. "I didn't get it."

His hands tighten on my lower back.

"Get out," Three growls.

I pull away, but Wells catches my wrist, jaw tight.

"I'll meet you downstairs," he says to me. He looks at Three. "You stay."

"Don't order me around," Three replies.

I get that glimpse of the power struggle between them, like a game of tug-of-war. Tonight, Wells has loosened his grip, and Three has the rope wrapped around his wrist. It takes almost no effort to pull the power to his side.

I clutch my hands to my chest as I move out into the hall.

Three shuts the door behind me, and when I put my ear up to it, he bangs a fist against the other side.

I jerk back, holding my ear, and retreat to the dining room.

Whatever it is, Wells will tell me. We're a team.

I think about our impending New Year's breakup and wonder how I'm going to repay him now that I couldn't get this done.

I sit down at the table, feigning confusion when I catch curious glances in my direction.

A few minutes later, Wells and Three return.

The look on Wells's face makes my entire body go rigid. Whatever happened upstairs, it wasn't good.

Three flashes me a satisfied grin. He's won something big tonight.

The next day, Wells avoids being alone with me. At breakfast, lunch, and dinner, Winona dominates the conversation, and even quiet, introspective Jeff comes in second. While we explore the city with his parents, Wells finds a way to walk next to one of them, or alone, rather than beside me.

In an antique mall in one of the northern Kentucky suburbs across the river, I try to drag him into a display of Greek busts, but he pretends to be fascinated by some old candle holders and takes off to get a price. They end up being so appallingly cheap, he can't get away with refusing, and he winds up with four antique candle holders.

We haven't talked about what happened, and I know that's the reason for his weirdness. Whatever went down with Three after I left the room, Wells gave up something he's either upset or embarrassed to have lost.

Or he's really angry with me for not pulling off my end of the deal, and he's ready to end the whole thing between us.

When he disappears into the bathroom to shower, I station myself in his bedroom doorway and wait.

But I'm not prepared when the door swings open and he steps out in a pair of low-slung black sweatpants and only halfway into his shirt. My gaze snags on all that bare skin.

"Jesus! What are you doing?" He stumbles back in surprise, yanking the shirt down over his stomach.

I drag my eyes up to his face. His cheeks are tinged pink.

"I was waiting for you."

He blinks at me, and I can't tell which of us is more surprised by my honesty. It definitely wasn't what I was planning to say. But my brain has deflated like a soufflé.

His wet hair hangs in his eyes, and I notice he's missing his usual dark circles. He appears well-rested, and his skin has a warm, healthy glow to it.

Once again, Wells's stupid good looks have reduced me to a drooling zombie. I want to take a bite out of him.

"I wish you were a little uglier," I tell him, trying to shake off the lingering lust.

Wells makes a noise from the back of his throat, like a hiccup. "Is that what you were waiting for? To tell me that?"

"No, that just occurred to me. I was waiting to ask you what happened with Three."

He darts across the hall to herd me into his bedroom, shutting the door behind us.

"No closed doors," I remind him.

"I'd rather take the heat than have my parents find out I tried to steal from Three."

I sit down on the edge of the bed and pat the spot next to me.

Wells hesitates.

"I'm not looking up at you the whole time."

"You're the one who sat down."

"I'm tired. We walked all day."

His expression softens, and he sits next to me. Despite having room to sit a safe distance away, he ends up right up against me, our legs pressed together.

I can't decide if it's a strategic move to turn my brain to Jell-O, or if he really is oblivious.

"I gave him what he wanted," he says. "It sucks losing to Three, but that's life. I always lose to him. It doesn't matter."

"You don't lose to Three in everything. You said so yourself."

"Oh, yeah? In your opinion, how do I win?"

"You're way better looking, for one."

His head swivels in my direction, and I force myself to act casual.

I can't believe I just said that.

"Okay," Wells says slowly, like he can't believe it, either. "So, I win against Three in looks. According to you."

I roll my eyes and lie back on the bed. "It's not only according to me, Wells. You know how people look at you. I told you you're the pretty one. I'm not the only one who knows it."

Wells leans back beside me, propping himself up on his elbow. "You don't win by being better looking. All you're saying is I win with something that requires no effort whatsoever, and Three wins in everything that matters."

"I didn't say that's the only way you win. You're also funnier than Three."

"Three has no sense of humor. Emily Dickinson is funnier than Three."

"The poet, or the cat?"

"I meant the cat, but I'm sure both apply," he says.

"You're also nicer than Three."

He scoffs. "I'm not that nice."

"True. You did practically blackmail me into coming here." I'm still mad about it, but I somehow manage to make this sound teasing.

Wells collapses onto his back. "I got scared."

"Scared?"

"That you would bail. I'm not great at on-the-spot problem solving. I did the first thing I could think of."

"You did what Three would do."

He sits up on his elbow again and looks at me.

"You're surprised to hear that?" I ask. "I would've thought it was obvious."

"I'm sorry," he says.

I blink at him. "Oh."

The corner of his mouth twitches. "You're surprised to hear that? I would've thought you saw it coming."

"I didn't know Wellborn boys knew how to apologize."

"I'm not Three."

"I know that."

He drops onto his back again and sighs.

"Where does he keep it?" I wonder. "If not with the others, where could it be?"

"No idea."

"Probably in his super-secret lair where he summons the demon that is a parasite on his soul."

"That's generous of you, assuming Three has a soul."

I laugh.

"I guess we'll be dating a few months longer," he says.

My laugh dies a swift death. "Excuse me?"

"We'll need to try again at Three's birthday."

I sit up, twisting around to face him. He has his eyes closed, but he cracks them open.

"What are you talking about?"

He props himself up on his elbows. "Three's eighteenth birthday. It's January twentieth. They're planning some huge party to celebrate. He's officially set to inherit the company once he turns eighteen."

"How are we supposed to try again? You said it yourself—you'll never get another opportunity like that. I got caught. He won't let me out of his sight."

"He won't have a choice. There's a big speech he has to give, and the whole thing will be way less structured than

Thanksgiving. We'll have no problem sneaking out to find it. And I have all winter break to figure out where he's keeping it."

"How am I supposed to get back here again? It was hard enough—I had to lie to my *parents*, Wells!"

"Can you please learn how to whisper?" He sits up, facing me. "It'll be fine. It's not that much longer than we planned."

"I thought you were dying to get back to hooking up with other girls," I say.

"I've figured out my priorities." He gives me a once-over. "Unless you're into it."

I shove him, and he falls back on the bed, laughing.

The door flies open, and Winona's petite form fills the doorway. Her braided hair is loose and the baby hairs around her face have frizzed up.

"Door open," she reminds us.

Wells's shirt rode up a bit when he fell back, and the way he adjusts it as he sits up makes us look incredibly guilty.

I scoot toward the corner of the bed, distancing myself from him. "Sorry," I say to Winona. "We forgot. We were just talking and didn't want to be loud."

She smiles at me, but when she turns it on Wells, her gaze hardens. "Don't forget again."

Wells holds up his hands, playing innocent.

When she walks away—leaving the door wide open behind her—Wells turns to me and whispers, "We need to have a safe distance between getting the watch and our breakup. Late February only makes sense."

An extra two months. Going into the new year with a fake boyfriend. Continuing to lie to my friends and parents.

I put my hands over my face. "I don't know if I can do that, Wells."

He stills beside me.

I drop my hands and turn to face him. "Is there nothing else you want? Nothing else I can give you? Test answers, or forged weekend passes, or *anything*?"

He rubs the back of his neck, looking away. "Nothing I want more than this."

I let out a shaky breath.

Wells sighs and stands up. "It's fine, Doe. Don't worry about it. I'll—I don't need anything. I'll let you off the hook. We don't have to wait for New Year's. Dump me when we get back to school. You don't have to worry about your secret—I won't tell anyone."

I watch him, my heart squeezing at the empty expression on his face. I try to catch his hand, but he untangles our fingers.

"Go to sleep," he says. "I'll see you in the morning."

I should feel free. I've won here—I got a fake boyfriend for nothing in return, and Wells is going to keep my secret. No one else will ever know how messy my life got after my parents' divorce. I can go back to letting it stress me out only when I'm home for school breaks. This secret dies with me, Wells, my whole family, both schools, and my transcripts.

I can dump Wells as soon as we get back to school, and that's fine—I've already done the most damage possible with this relationship.

I've gotten everything I wanted.

But as I lay in Wells's bed hours later, sleep hovers out of reach. I can't stop picturing that look on his face, the blank expression, how his eyes shuttered.

Something twists inside me—something like guilt.

I climb out of bed and creep down the stairs, wincing at each creak and groan of the old wood.

The TV is on in the living room, a low drone in the silence of the house. Blue light shines out into the hall.

Wells is sprawled on the couch, one arm slung over his head and his legs twisted in one of the throws. I'm surprised he's not freezing; it feels ten degrees colder down here. I shiver in my thin T-shirt.

Wells turns his head toward me, and I jump.

"You're awake," I whisper, stepping around the coffee table.

Wells starts to sit up, but I perch on the edge of the couch and put a hand on his chest to stop him.

He freezes under my touch.

I hesitate, my fingers curling in the front of his shirt.

"Doe—"

"I'll do it."

His brow creases. "You don't have to—"

"I do, though. It's only fair. I shouldn't get everything I wanted while you get nothing."

"I got to watch Three squirm; that's enough for me."

"No, it isn't. I know it isn't."

He doesn't object, but he does put his hand over mine on his chest.

I give a hesitant smile. "What's a few more weeks, right?"

He sits up, and I let him, my hand dropping. He catches it and twines his fingers through mine.

"Thank you," he says.

I smile.

"Seriously, I mean it," he adds, his gaze catching mine. The blue light casts shadows across his face, making his expression more severe and desperate than I've ever imagined it could be.

I cup his jaw with my free hand and stroke my thumb over his cheek.

Wells leans into it, and that strange, buzzing energy of a late night when you're overtired washes over me.

If I kissed him right now, he would let me. And it wouldn't be for the satisfaction of pissing off Three, or to stake claim on him in front of everyone at Halloween. It would be for the simple pleasure of kissing him.

I pull away, and he lets me do that, too.

And in place of a kiss, he gives me something else.

"Uncle Nate is spearheading the merger."

CHAPTER
FOURTEEN

Campus is abuzz the day after we return from Thanksgiving break. Overnight, Mallory Weston reappeared,
welded back to her base, but this time upside down, in a
long skirt that hangs over her head to show off a pair of big,
polka-dotted underwear. Right side up, she had a wide, pow-
erful stance. Upside down, she's spread-eagle. It's completely
degrading.

In retaliation, Cotesmore announces that we are now required to submit to our head of house a log of at least three
hours a week spent in a volunteer group, club, or tutoring
session with a minimum of two Winfield students, signed by
a faculty member. For me, that means more interactions with
Tully, which is the last thing I need.

It also means I've been roped into helping the joint-school
dance committee, along with the rest of my friends and a
handful of Winfield seniors.

"It's worked out kind of perfectly," Sumi says when we
gather in the Kingdom after our first meeting. "If we want to
pull something off, we'll need to know what to expect behind
the scenes."

"What are we thinking, anyway?" Shawn asks. "It's not like they're naming a king and queen and we can just do a *Carrie*."

I scoff. "What is this, amateur hour? We wouldn't do a *Carrie* even if they were naming a king."

She tosses the cap from her drink at me, and it bounces off my forehead.

"What do you have in mind?" Jade asks me.

It's the first time she's spoken to me directly since our argument. I hope this is a sign she's ready to put it behind us.

Judging by how Gemma's expression has brightened, she's hoping the same thing.

Shawn and Sumi exchange a glance.

"I'm still thinking on it," I say. "But it needs to be big. It'll be our last prank before winter break, and it's the first big merger test since Fall Fest. I bet Winfield will be planning something, too."

"Of course they will," says Shawn. "They're a bunch of asses."

I pause, slowly turning to look at her.

"Doe's got that face on," says Gemma.

Jade leans in. "Care to share with the class?"

"Okay, this might sound crazy—"

"She says that like she's ever had a single sane idea in her life," Shawn says.

"But if we can scrape together two hundred bucks, it's totally doable," I add, pulling my phone out and doing a quick search. I turn the screen toward them and smile.

We delve into the planning, and when we've got a solid foundation, I drop the bomb I've been holding since Friday night.

"So, there's something else," I say. "Something I found

out over Thanksgiving. It's about the merger, and the Well-borns."

I tell them what Wells revealed, and what became clear the more I thought about it.

"Three has a sister. Eighth grade," I say. "She told me she's coming to Weston next year. I guarantee the merger has something to do with that."

"They don't think Weston is good enough," Shawn says. "If she can't go to Winfield outright, the Wellborns will bring Winfield to her. Simple."

"That's what I think, too. Wells wouldn't tell me specifics. I barely got this out of him."

"And how'd you pull that off?" Sumi teases.

I pick up Shawn's bottle cap and lob it at Sumi. She ducks, and it sails over her head.

"That would explain why he seemed so mad about the newspaper," Gemma says. "Three's dad, I mean."

"And that's why Three wins either way," says Shawn.

I point at her. "Exactly. He can win the traditional way, in our war that's been going on forever. And if the merger happens, we lose by default, because we don't want it, but his family does."

Gemma sighs. "So, we have to stop the merger, or we lose."

"Seems like it. And Three's dad is super smug about the whole thing. At Thanksgiving, he came at me a little when I brought it up."

Jade makes a disgusted noise. "Imagine being so imma-ture you have to argue with a teenager about your agenda. Get a life, dude."

I smile at her. It feels good to have Jade back in my corner.

Later, as we head back to our rooms, Jade hangs back, and I follow her lead.

"I take it you aren't mad at me anymore?" I ask her.

She sighs. "I wasn't *mad*, Doe. I was disappointed. Friends are supposed to push each other to be better."

"I didn't like lying to my dad, either. But I had to go; I didn't have a choice."

"You could've come up with a better way of doing it." She looks over at me. "But I don't need you to apologize to me, or to absolve yourself. I'm just looking for some acknowledgment that you get what I'm saying."

"I do. I get it. I really do."

She slings her arm across my shoulders and pulls me in. "Good. It was weird for too long, right?"

"I should've tried harder."

"I could've, too." She leans her head against mine as we walk. "So, how was it in Cincy with your boyfriend? Did you guys sneak around in the dead of night to touch each other below the waist?"

I shove her away, shrieking in protest, which only makes her laugh.

"Hey, quiet," Shawn calls from the stairs. "I know we were gone for a few days, but curfew is still a very real thing."

"Talk to Doe," Jade says, pushing me toward her. "That was her natural reaction to the thought of putting her hands on her boyfriend's—"

"Jade!"

She laughs, slipping past Shawn into the stairwell.

Shawn looks at me. "You and Wells . . . ?"

"Nothing happened," I reply, following her down to our floor as the others head for the exit. "We were highly chaperoned the whole time. It was all very Victorian England."

Her phone buzzes in her hand, and she glances down, frowns, and shoves it in her pocket.

"What's wrong?"

She shakes her head. "Nothing. Stupid spam texts. Some-one must have put my number somewhere. It goes off all day long."

"Annoying. Did you call your carrier?"

"I'll tell my dad," she says, heading for her room. "He'll take care of it."

"Hey, we'll need to get a sheet to make a banner," I tell her. "Should we run to the thrift store this week? And paint. We should get that before it gets too close to the dance, oth-erwise it'll look suspicious."

"At least that's less suspicious than four dozen bottles of vegetable oil," she says.

I laugh.

"Hey, Doe?" she says before I reach my door.

I turn back.

She smiles. "I'm glad you and Jade are good again."

I grin back. "Me, too. You have no idea."

And truly, for the first time in days, I feel real relief.

"Can we have some quiet in here, please? We're trying to provide direction."

I glance over my shoulder at Virginia Brinkoff, roll my eyes, and return to separating a chair from its stack. Accord-ing to the Winfield senior helping me, it's been so long since they've used these, they're practically glued together.

It shouldn't surprise me that Virginia volunteered for the dance committee. Her friends make up the majority of Weston girls participating in the planning, and my friends make up the majority of girls getting bossed around in the Winfield banquet hall.

It doesn't help that the other committee head is Three, and he is dead set on making my life hell during this whole thing.

I wonder how Wells got out of it. It's not like he's in clubs or plays a sport. Even Gemma and Sumi couldn't eke out enough time for their logs in board game club—Gemma—and knitting—Sumi. Most of the athletes were able to weasel out of it with "joint practices" that involve running around a field in the vicinity of Winfield boys, which really irked Shawn, who doesn't have softball until spring.

Jade and I are the only ones not really involved in anything, so no one should be surprised to find us here.

My chair comes loose without warning, and I let out a yelp of surprise as I stumble back and hit the floor.

Three sighs. "Doe, please, we're trying to plan here."

I shove the chair off of me and climb to my feet. "Oh, sorry, did my being injured interrupt? Next time I'll make sure I only get hurt on my own free time."

"It's the least you could do," Three replies smoothly, returning his attention to Virginia.

I resist the urge to flip him off.

It's helpful to be in these meetings for prank purposes, but listening to Three talk is melting my brain. It doesn't help that Virginia hangs on his every word.

"How does it feel being a traitor to your school?" I ask Virginia when she drifts close enough. Jade and I are arranging chairs around a table, and I have a feeling Virginia is coming to criticize, so I want to beat her to the punch.

She sighs. "You really want to do this right now?"

"Should we get you a bib for when Three talks? You've got drool down your chin."

"You're disgusting."

"Doe," Jade says, "let her walk away. She clearly doesn't get it."

"True. I guess you can't force people to understand something when they don't want to."

Virginia glares at me. "You're right—I don't want to understand you. You think it's all about boys for me, but *you're* the one who doesn't want to understand. These schools are running on archaic tradition. Gender is a social construct. What about people who are nonbinary, or transgender? Where do our separated student bodies leave them? It's like the bathrooms thing all over again."

"We have a trans girl at Weston," I tell her.

"I know. But a lot of transgender people don't feel safe enough to come out until they're in their teens or even later in life. So, we have one girl who lived in a safe home and could come out in middle school, and she has supportive parents, and Weston accepted her. But not everyone and everywhere is like that."

"But if someone were to come out as trans while at Weston, he'd already be one of us. We wouldn't kick him out for that."

"And then technically we'd be coed," Virginia says. "And you haven't even touched on the nonbinary aspect of it."

I freeze, caught off guard. I think of Parker from my art elective last year, who came back from winter break and asked us to start using they/them pronouns. No one gave them a hard time—the students or the administration.

But would Parker have gotten into Weston as a little eighth grader using they/them pronouns?

And I think of Mia, a trans girl in the sophomore class whose enrollment caused a stir amongst parents last year. Weston was firm on their decision to allow her to enroll, and I know more than a couple of girls were pulled out of school when it happened. After what I saw at St. Aloysius, I watched her like a hawk those first few weeks, worried she'd be bullied.

But she fell right in with the theater crowd, and she's always surrounded by friends.

I steel myself and say to Virginia, "We have room for everyone at Weston."

"Just not boys?"

"Just not *Winfield* boys."

From across the hall, Three calls, "Doe, do you ever stop talking? Get to work."

This time, I do flip him off.

"Dorothy Saltpeter!" Mrs. McNabb appears at my elbow.

I almost forgot she was here. She's been so quiet. I don't think she expected being the dance committee advisor to be such a challenge. She's one of the oldest teachers at Weston, and she tends to take it easy. I have her for World Governments, and it's the only class I can confidently say I've been coasting through this year.

"I'll need to note your rude gesture on your log," she says, holding out a hand. "You can discuss it with Mr. Tully. Right now. You can make up your lost time tomorrow."

I suck in a breath, but the damage is done.

It was bad enough knowing I'd have to see Tully to sign off on my hours. Now we'll be having a *discussion*.

Shawn appears at my side as Mrs. McNabb hands back my log and returns to her seat.

"I'll go with you," she says.

"Me, too," Jade adds.

Even Virginia looks worried, because no matter how she acts, she's a Weston girl. We all have the same feeling about Tully. It's probably the only thing we'll all ever agree on.

"I'll be fine," I tell them. I glance over at Three. He's clocked the response, and I can see the wheels turning as he tries to figure out what's happening.

I tuck my log back into my pocket. "I can go alone."

"You shouldn't," Jade says.

"He won't do anything. You won't be able to get out of this, anyway." I pat the back of the chair in front of me. "Now make sure these are six inches apart, because Virginia will be coming around with a ruler later."

Virginia rolls her eyes and stalks off.

I feel a small rush of victory.

But dread quashes it as I head across the street to Weston, my feet on the path to Tully's office.

When I get there, he's with another girl. I can see the back of her head through the dusty window—lank black hair, skinny shoulders, light brown skin. Tully isn't behind his desk, but sitting in the chair beside her, his body angled toward her even though she's facing straight ahead.

I lean against the wall and strain to hear what he's saying, but the door blocks all noise.

Cold seeps into my stomach.

When the door opens and the girl steps out, her eyes are red-rimmed.

"Dorothy," Mr. Tully calls, "you can come in."

I ignore him, grabbing the girl by her elbow. She's so thin, my fingers circle it. My mind races. "Are you okay?"

She nods, sniffling. "Yeah, I'm fine."

I glance toward the door. I can hear Tully getting up.

I pull her down the hall, whispering fast, "Don't see him alone again if you can help it. Always bring a friend. If you can't get someone, call me. Give me your phone."

She fumbles for it, pressing it into my hands.

I type in my number and dial, so she'll have a record of mine—and I'll have one of hers. My phone buzzes in my pocket.

I end the call and hand it back to her.

Tully leans out of his office. "Dorothy."

I put my back to him. "What's your name?"

"Noelle," she whispers, her voice shaking.

"I'm Doe. Call me anytime, okay? Whatever you need."

Her eyes fill.

I squeeze her hand, and it's so bony, so frail, I worry I may have hurt her.

"Dorothy," Tully repeats, warning in his voice.

I turn to him while Noelle shuffles toward the stairs.

"Hi, Mr. Tully," I say brightly. I wait for him to move back into his office, but he doesn't.

He waves me in. "After you."

I have to squeeze past him in the open doorway. I make myself as small as possible and sidestep past him with my arms crossed over my chest, so the only thing that touches him is my elbow as I graze by.

Tully follows me into his office and shuts the door. "Log, please," he says, holding out his hand as he moves behind his desk.

I hand it over and slump in the chair.

"I see Mrs. McNabb sent you," he says, scanning the log.

"I flipped off a Winfield student. It was impulsive and immature. I reflected on the walk over here, and I regret my actions."

Mr. Tully's gaze flicks up, watching me over the top of my weekly log.

He sets the paper on his desk and folds his hands. "I think I get what happened here."

"You do?"

"You're very against the merger. I understand. I am, too. I'd hate to see our girls swept under the wave of male achievement."

I hate that I agree with him.

"But you're a leader at this school," he says, getting to his feet. He comes around his desk and sits in the chair beside me. I bristle, knowing this is exactly what he did with No-elle, and wondering if this is how he does it. Does he start by breaking that desk barrier between himself and whoever's sitting here?

"The younger girls look up to you," he continues, turning toward me.

I put my hands on the arms of my chair and wrench it around to face him completely.

He jerks back in surprise as I fling one leg over the other and cross my arms. My foot keeps him a safe distance away, poised very close to his knee.

His gaze flits over my legs, and my muscles tense in response.

In control, you are in control here, don't let him see you sweat.

"Mr. Tully," I say at last, "the example I want to set isn't one that rolls over and plays dead for this merger. I'm going to fight it with everything I have. So, if you're planning to let me off with a warning if I agree to set a more docile example for the younger girls, with all due respect, I'd rather take the demerit."

His eyebrows arch up. "Okay," he says, getting to his feet. He returns to the other side of the desk and sits down.

I turn the chair back around as he clicks away at his computer, pulling up my record.

"You've earned yourself a demerit."

I smile at him. "Thank you for understanding."

I get up to leave, but his next words stop me cold.

"I'm also adding a demerit for back talk." He gives me a bland smile from the other side of his desk. "I'm sorry, Dorothy. This semester you're exhibiting a real disrespect for authority. That's two demerits today, and it looks like you got yourself one for being late to class a few weeks ago."

My stomach drops. "Mr. Tully—"

"I'll see you in detention," he says. "Wednesday afternoon in the Wellness Center."

I fall into the big red armchair next to Wells, barely missing his thigh as I settle in.

"What happened to you?" he asks, adjusting to make room for me.

I put my head on his shoulder and sigh. "I got detention. Wednesday afternoon. With the biggest perv at Weston."

He stiffens. "What?"

"I got detention—"

"I heard that part. What about a perv at Weston?"

"My house head, our wellness teacher. He's . . . I don't know. There's something about him. Nothing's been substantiated or anything. It's just a feeling that, like, *everyone* has about him."

"And you have detention with him on Wednesday? Alone?"

"He won't do anything. Not to me. Predators go for people who are isolated, who won't talk. I'd be too much of a risk."

"Or he'd consider you a huge score," Wells says, turning to face me. "Why can't you report him? Tell your headmistress he makes you uncomfortable and you want to serve your detention with a female faculty member."

"Because he'll know he got to me, and if I can't be around him, I can't protect other girls from him. He won't do anything to me, but there are other vulnerable girls who need me."

Wells shakes his head. "You can't always be the hero, Doe. You have to take care of yourself first."

"I *can* take care of myself. That's my point. Can we just be quiet for a while? Finals are coming—I need to study."

It's weird hanging out with Wells when no one else is

around to witness it—not because I feel weird about it, but because I don't. After spending Thanksgiving together, it feels like we're friends. And I want to see him, not because I have something to gain, but because I like having him around.

I can't tell if he feels the same, but when I asked to see him tonight, he told me where to find him. That has to count for something.

"Hey, I did want to ask—"

"Aren't you the one who just asked if we can be quiet for a while? Is *a while* really only two minutes for you?"

I elbow him. "*I wanted to ask,* how did you get out of setting up for the dance? Are you secretly super involved in a bunch of clubs or something?"

He snorts. "No. I just didn't go."

My brow furrows. "Won't you get in trouble?"

He shrugs. "Probably. But it'd take a lot more than that to get a Wellborn kicked out of Winfield—trust me."

I scoff and settle back in the chair. "Must be nice to be you. I've been stuck with Three and Virginia Brinkoff. It's like someone reached into my nightmares and created my own personal hellscape."

"You can just say you miss having me around. It's okay, Doe."

I roll my eyes. "You're so full of yourself. You are coming to the dance though, right?"

"I assumed I was going with you." He shoots me a sideways look. "Unless you got another fake boyfriend—"

I cover his mouth with my hand, glancing around quickly.

He breathes out against my fingers, and I drag my gaze to his face. His eyes are heavy lidded and focused on me, and I realize I've pressed close to him, my other hand on his thigh.

I pull back, swallowing hard. Then, to expel the weird energy running between us, I smack him the chest and whisper, "Anyone could be listening!"

He catches my hand and holds it, and suddenly we're back in his living room in the middle of the night, and everything feels warm and heavy with tension.

I yank my hand back. "Stop looking at me like that."

"Like what?" he asks, and his hoarse voice sends a little zing through me.

I pick up my book. "You know like what."

He grabs my waist and pulls me against him, hard enough that I land in the crook of his arm.

"Wells—!"

His mouth touches the shell of my ear. "Zamir."

Sure enough, Zamir comes around one of the shelves a few seconds later, stopping when he sees us. He looks from Wells to me, the arms around my waist, Wells's mouth hovering near my jaw, and sighs heavily.

"Are you two planning to be here all night? Because I have a date, and I don't want you hovering."

Wells eyes him. "I'm always here."

"Then can she go?"

I glare at him. "It's not like you have to speak to us. Who has a date at a bookstore anyway?"

Wells looks at me. "Are we not on a date right now?"

"That's different."

Zamir sighs. "This is cute, but I'm serious. I don't want drama. He goes to Delafosse—he won't get it."

Wells slides his hand up my thigh. "We could go downstairs," he says low in my ear.

Zamir watches Wells's hand, then looks at our faces, grimacing. "Do I have to witness this?"

"You could turn around," I tell him, willing my voice not to quiver.

"Are you with her because she's *so* funny?" Zamir asks Wells.

Wells ignores him and gives me a light push. I climb out of the chair, my whole body feeling shaky and hot. He takes my hand and leads me toward the basement stairs.

"Good luck on your date," I call back to Zamir, my voice only a little taunting.

He scowls. "Keep it. I don't want your luck."

I shrug and follow Wells into the stairwell.

As soon as we're out of sight, he lets go of my hand. Cold seeps into me the farther down we go. Wells falls onto the plush, green velvet couch, and instead of following him, I perch in the matching armchair. It's only big enough for one.

He glances at me as I do, but I can't read anything in his expression. He has his usual Wells blank face.

"Zamir couldn't have his date down here?" I complain, dragging my books back out of my bag.

Wells leans against the arm of the couch. "What's wrong with the basement?"

"It's cold." I slip my coat back on, burrowing into the warmth.

Wells picks up his coat and drapes it over my legs.

"There," he says, settling back in his seat. "Now you're warm."

I slump a little and set my books in my lap. Whatever was happening between us upstairs, the cold has delivered it a swift death.

CHAPTER FIFTEEN

On Wednesday after classes end, Shawn walks me to detention with the air of my last ally escorting me to my execution.

"I don't like this," she says when we reach the Wellness Center. "You shouldn't provoke him, Doe. I'm serious."

"I wasn't trying to provoke him."

"Sometimes provoking people doesn't take effort for you."

"Do you worry at all about my self-esteem?"

She gives me a small smile, grabbing my arm when I reach for the door. "I'm only trying to make you aware of yourself. Hold back tonight. Be quiet and obedient and then get the hell out of there."

"Quiet and obedient aren't exactly in my repertoire."

"Well, learn them fast. When you think about mouthing off, ask yourself what Shawn would do."

"Shawn wouldn't roll over and show her belly."

"No, but she'd bite her tongue for the sake of self-preservation."

"I'm gonna be late." I squeeze her arm and give her a smile. "It'll be fine. Don't worry about me. I'll see you at dinner."

But as I head into the Wellness Center, my bravado falters. I glance over my shoulder at Shawn's retreating back.

Inside, it smells like sweat and gym mats. The track above the basketball court is empty, and the hoops have been retracted out of view. Mr. Tully waits on the bottom bleacher, a clipboard propped against his knee.

He looks up at the sound of my shoes squeaking on the gym floor.

Normally Tully is cheerful and overly friendly, even when he has to discipline us, like he can trick us into trusting him. *Our friend Mr. Tully.* I'm so surprised to see him looking outwardly irritated, I check my phone to make sure I'm not late.

Two minutes early. What's the deal, then?

I slide my phone back in my pocket. I should be happy to see him look so annoyed, but it puts me on edge.

"Hi, Mr. Tully," I say when I reach him, grasping for the formality that's been drilled into me for the last three and a half years. "Where should I start?" I set my bag down on the bleachers.

"We have another person joining us," he says, standing. He's white-knuckling his clipboard.

I frown. "Someone from Roseland?"

"The administration has decided that detentions earned from merger-related infractions will be served jointly."

I don't get what he means until the door to the gym swings open, and two people step inside.

"Wells?"

He gives me a lazy, two-fingered salute. The woman behind him grimaces and says something I can't hear, but it makes Wells grin. She looks to be about my mom's age, and she radiates that deadly mixture of maternal exhaustion and disappointment—like she's just come home from work and found out we forgot to thaw the chicken like she asked.

"Brian," she says when she reaches us, addressing Mr. Tully like he's a student, rather than one of the faculty.

I feel a rush of satisfaction until she looks at me, and I get the full force of her weary stare. "Dorothy Saltpeter, I presume. I'm Mrs. Meintz. I see you know your fellow offender. Brian—Mr. Tully, this is Gabriel Wellborn."

Wells grins at Mr. Tully. He's absolutely brazen, and I can tell it makes Mr. Tully want to knock his head off his neck. Mrs. Meintz doesn't bat an eye, and Mr. Tully doesn't seem to have much love to spare for her, either.

"You'll be cleaning the floors and setting up the nets for tonight's volleyball practice," Mr. Tully says. "There are cleaning supplies in the janitorial closet in the lobby, and the practice nets are in storage."

Mr. Tully escorts us to the janitorial closet while Mrs. Meintz perches on the bleachers with a tablet and stylus. I get a sense Mr. Tully isn't keen on leaving Wells and me alone. I get an even greater sense that Mrs. Meintz would rather be literally anywhere else. She'd probably let us off the hook early if she were the only detention monitor.

Wells and I move into the closet to gather cleaning supplies, and I whisper, "What the hell are you doing here?"

"I got detention. Hey, grab that solution above you. The blue one—yeah. We'll need that."

I make a thoughtful sound. "You know a lot about cleaning gym floors?"

He chuckles. "I've done it once or twice."

"Wow, no one told me I'm dating the Winfield rebel."

"Really? You had to be told?"

I hand him two of the special gym floor mops and slide two buckets over to the spigot and drain.

Mr. Tully leans around the door and says, "Detention isn't for socializing. Get what you need, and let's move."

Wells glances back at him, an insolent smirk on his face.

Tully's mouth settles into a flat line. "You have one minute."

"We're at the mercy of the water, Mr. Tully." I look at Wells. "How much blue should I add?"

"One part blue to ten parts water," Wells replies.

I stare at him.

He grins. "Just dump some in—it'll be fine."

When I finish filling one, I slide it to Wells. He pushes his bucket out of the closet, and Tully has to jump back before his toes get run over.

As soon as Wells vacates the closet, Tully takes his place.

I take in a sharp breath, moving farther into the corner with the spigot.

"There should be a measuring cup on it," Mr. Tully says, reaching for the cleaning solution in my hand.

"She already dumped it in," Wells says, squeezing in next to him. He reaches out and puts his hand on the shelf next to Tully, effectively trapping him in here with us.

But Mr. Tully no longer looks in control of the situation. It occurs to me that Wells is bigger than Mr. Tully and takes up much more space in the closet.

"Let me see it," Wells says to me, motioning for the solution.

Tully's gaze swings toward him.

Wells uncaps the solution and nods. "Huh. Look at that. There is a measuring cup." He slides the solution back onto the shelf and shrugs at Mr. Tully. "Guess I'll remember that for next time."

"You find yourself in detention a lot, Mr. Wellborn?" Tully asks, crossing his arms.

I turn off the water, looking between them as I roll my bucket out from under the spigot.

Wells shrugs. "I'm trying to behave nowadays. Detention impedes on my time with my girlfriend."

I roll my bucket toward them, and when Tully doesn't move, Wells motions for him to go. "After you, sir."

Mr. Tully is really starting to come undone. He levels Wells with a glare as he turns and stalks out of the closet.

Wells takes the mop handle from me and rolls my bucket out.

Mr. Tully has us start at opposite ends of the gym, so I don't get to talk to him until we meet in the middle.

"I don't need a male savior," I tell him. "I can take care of myself."

He frowns, leaning on his mop. "I'm not trying—"

"No socializing!" Mr. Tully barks.

I turn away and start back the way I came.

When we meet in the middle again, Wells says, "I know you can take care of yourself. But you also don't have to."

I feel like two dance partners at a Regency-era ball trying to have a conversation during the quadrille.

"How'd you pull this off, anyway?" I ask when he reaches me again.

He grins. "I might've turned myself in for not doing my logs."

We separate and meet again.

"But how did you know about the joint detention thing?"

He flushes, looking like I've caught him off guard, and turns away without answering. The next time I make it to the middle, he's already moving back toward the other side of the room, and he keeps our tempo off as we finish cleaning the floor.

Mr. Tully hovers over us while we empty our buckets in the janitorial closet and bosses us around the equipment storage area while we extract the practice nets for volleyball.

"Okay, don't be mad," Wells says finally as we secure the nets. "But I might've pulled some strings."

"*Which* strings?"

He winces. "I may have suggested that joint detention would be a good way to force time together for the people who are most resistant to the merger."

"Suggested to *whom*?" I ask.

"Less talking," Mr. Tully calls.

I ignore him. "Tell me."

"I called Uncle Nate and asked for a favor. He saw the logic and made it happen."

I put my hands on my hips. "Just so you could come here and throw your weight around in front of Mr. Tully? What exactly do you think that's gonna do? I'm dumping you in a few months, anyway."

He narrows his eyes and threads his fingers through the net. "I don't care. We're friends. And I'm not letting my friend ride out detention with a pervert by herself. It's not because I don't think you can take care of yourself, or to throw my weight around. I'm here because it puts two extra pairs of eyes on him. Any of your friends would do the same."

It's true, but since I'm the only one in Roseland House, my friends would've ended up in detention with their heads of house, likely doing something else. We're in the Wellness Center because this is Mr. Tully's domain.

"This is completely unproductive," Mr. Tully says, stalking toward us from the bleachers.

Wells ducks under the net, putting me behind him. "Sorry, sir. Doe was catching me up on the plans for the winter dance. I was drafted to help the committee, but I haven't been to any meetings yet."

"That's why he's in detention, Brian. He's been slacking

on his logs," Mrs. Meintz calls. "Just let them finish so we can get out of here."

"Detention isn't for socializing," Tully says over his shoulder.

Mrs. Meintz rolls her eyes. He doesn't see it, and Wells is too focused on Mr. Tully, but I'm looking right at her.

I move toward the other net. "We're almost done." And then, imagining what Shawn would do, I add, "Sorry, Mr. Tully. I thought when you said detentions would be served jointly, you meant we're supposed to learn to get along. I was trying to extend the old olive branch, you know?"

Tully stares at me like he doesn't believe a word coming out of my mouth, but I put on my best innocent face and get back to work.

Later, the four of us leave the Wellness Center together, and when I move to break off from the group, I discreetly reach for Wells's hand and squeeze.

He squeezes back.

"We didn't do half bad in here," Jade admits as we step into the Winfield banquet hall. It helps that it's one of the nicer facilities on their campus; it's where they host their annual banquet every fall. Can't have the alumni thinking donations are going to waste.

"The balloons look good," I agree. "Even if I still have a headache from blowing them up all afternoon."

"That's because you kept sucking the helium so you could yell 'stranger danger' in that voice every time Three came near you," Gemma says.

I chuckle, remembering the look on his face. "Worth it."

"Isn't he a bit overdressed?" Sumi asks, nodding toward Three, who is checking the wiring on a speaker at the edge of the stage. He's in a suit and tie, although I have a feeling it's the least formal of his formalwear.

I glance at Sumi's knit, rainbow-colored sweater dress. It hangs off one shoulder and looks like something you'd find at a craft fair. Which is exactly where she found it.

Shawn puts an arm around Sumi. "Do you think maybe you're just a bit underdressed?" she asks gently.

Sumi snorts. "I don't care about me. It's only embarrassing to be *over*dressed at a school dance. Hasn't he ever seen a movie?"

She flounces off toward the buffet, which hasn't even opened yet—not that that stops Sumi from peeking under the lids and stealing a plate for a scoop of pasta.

Gemma sighs, starting after her. "We can't take her anywhere."

"Boyfriend alert," Jade says, looking past me.

I turn, and my stomach drops. I told myself I wouldn't do this—I would not let the sight of Wells in formalwear get to me. I am not a cliché. Besides, I already saw him in a suit at Thanksgiving.

But man, he looks really good. I start to sweat and immediately regret my choice to wear velvet. It's too warm in here.

"Hey," he says when he reaches me, sliding his arms around my waist. He leans down and nuzzles into my hair to whisper, "Better put on a good show. Your perv is watching."

"So's yours," I whisper back, allowing myself a quick glance in Three's direction. Sure enough, his gaze flickers away from us.

Wells pulls back to give me a look. "Not the same thing."

"Hi, we're here, too," Jade says, holding up a hand.

Wells chuckles. "Sorry—hi. You guys look nice."

Jade gives her dress a little swish. "Thank you. Very kind." She looks at me. "Don't forget . . ."

"I won't."

Shawn smiles, looping her arm through Jade's. "We'll go claim a table."

Wells eyes me as they walk off. "What are you guys up to?"

"Us? Up to something?" I fling my arms around his neck. "We're just innocent girls, Gabriel."

Something changes in his expression, and he goes still.

I frown. "What's wrong?"

He blows out a breath, a smile pulling at the corner of his lips. "Nothing. I just—the last time you said my name, it was all . . . derisive. Like an insult."

"You remember the last time I said your name?" I let my arms slide down, my hands flattening against his chest.

Two spots of pink appear on his cheeks. I'm too stunned to speak.

"Yeah," he says, his voice hoarse.

"And how did I say it this time?" I ask when I finally find a sliver of my voice. It comes out a breathless whisper.

He works his jaw, and I can't tell if he doesn't know how to describe it, or just doesn't want to.

The noise picks up around us, and I step back, remembering where we are. I smooth my hands down the front of my skirt and then slip them into my pockets—*pockets*! I'm even more grateful for dresses with pockets. I need somewhere to safely put my hands.

"Um, I don't know where you're sitting, but if you want—I mean, you should probably sit with us. Right?" I glance at the dance floor. "Are we gonna have to slow dance?"

Wells clears his throat. "I doubt it."

"Take a seat, please, you two."

I look up, surprised to find Mr. Tully hovering, a tight smile on his face.

Wells puts his hand on my back and steers me away. With his other hand, he pulls at his collar, like it's too tight.

"He really doesn't like you," I say to Wells when we're a safe distance away.

"Just how I want it," Wells replies.

When we reach my friends, Wells pulls out my chair and then drops into the seat next to me.

The next fifteen minutes consist of an opening speech from Headmistress Cotesmore and Headmaster Pritchard about the integrity of our schools, the importance of team-work, blah blah blah—I blank out about halfway through. There's only so much merger talk I can take in one week, and it's been all anyone has talked about since the dance commit-tee started planning.

After the speech finally ends, the buffet opens. Sumi and Jade finish eating quickly and head off under the guise of using the bathroom. Wells watches them go and glances at me while I try to stuff my face to look innocent.

"What are you guys planning?"

I look at him, mouth full of penne, and blink innocently.

He nods. "Uh-huh. Sure."

A few minutes later, the doors creak, and a man in a trucker hat props them wide open so he can lead two don-keys into the banquet hall.

The whole place explodes with noise as faculty members rush to stop him and students start screeching with laughter and taking pictures.

And for the second time this year, a banner unfurls, this time over the banquet hall doors, displaying the words we painstakingly painted two nights ago in my dorm room.

ALL ASSES WELCOME AT WINFIELD

The man argues with Mrs. Meintz, who motions for him to take the donkeys back out. Mr. Tully stares at our table while we shriek with laughter. Sumi and Jade return from the "bathroom," feigning shock as they skirt around the donkeys and their handler.

"I've been paid for the hour," he's saying.

But his words are drowned out as a great cacophony fills the banquet hall—fiddles, bagpipes, accordions, and some kind of handheld drum. The band filed onstage while no one was watching, and judging by the look on Headmaster Pritchard's face, they are not what he was imagining.

Chaos erupts.

I look at Wells and shout over the music, "So, no slow dances?"

He grins. "Do you think the donkeys would let us double up for a ride instead?"

Mrs. Meintz finally convinces the handler to go, and he takes the donkeys with him, but the band is harder to quiet. They're enthusiastic and committed, and even as a few teachers try to wave them off, they only play louder.

Wells takes my hand and pulls me toward the dance floor. "Do you know how to dance to this stuff?" he shouts to me.

I laugh. "No! Am I supposed to?"

He starts jumping wildly, and it's insane and uncoordinated and so, so stupid—but I start jumping with him.

And weirdly enough, we aren't the only ones. People start streaming onto the dance floor, and eventually the teachers stop trying to quiet the band. I look around as I jump-dance with Wells, sweating, panting, exhausted, and having the time of my life—and realize I'm surrounded by Winfield boys and Weston girls alike.

But what shocks me more than anything is that rather than slouching and pouting at a table, Three is right in the thick of it, as unkempt and happy as I've ever seen him.

It's about the craziest thing I've ever seen happen. And for the first time, I'm not itching to get away from Winfield. Because as absurd as it feels, I'm happy, too.

It's the exact opposite feeling from what I should be having, when we worked so hard on this prank to prove that Weston girls don't want to merge with Winfield. And the Winfield boys, hiring this band, clearly wanted to make a farce of this dance as much as we did.

And yet, I'm having fun.

It's good we're heading home for winter break. Because feeling any kind of camaraderie with Winfield boys is about as dangerous as it gets.

CHAPTER SIXTEEN

Dad saved all of my favorite ornaments for me to put on the tree when I got home, but things were so busy the first few days of break—last-minute holiday shopping, seeing my grandparents, and eating at my favorite local spots—I haven't gotten a chance to put them up until tonight. I feel bad that Christmas Eve is tomorrow, and our best ornaments will only be up for a short bit before Dad takes them down again.

Dad waits until I'm holding a very delicate crystal ballerina that I got from my grandparents a million years ago to say, "You're being careful with this boyfriend of yours, right?"

I nearly fumble the ballerina but manage to catch her. The house is old, and even though Dad has these plush Moroccan rugs in every room, the ballerina would be toast if she fell.

Hanging ornaments is half getting them on the tree, half the adrenaline rush when you nearly drop one you love.

"Dad," I say sharply. "Could you please not bring up the sex talk when I'm holding something breakable? You almost gave me two heart attacks."

He sighs, head lolling back against the arm of the couch. He's been sprawled there since we finished eating, laptop perched on his knees. He's wearing two pairs of fuzzy socks, and his feet stick out a little from under a throw blanket.

"I know you don't need the sex talk," he says. "I mean . . . I assume you don't. Your mother said—"

"Not to worry, Father dearest. Mom and I shared that particular humiliation a *long* time ago. Also, I read a lot."

He snorts. "Speaking of—Gen found a box of your paperbacks in your room when she was looking for a dress for homecoming."

I spin to face him, clutching a sparkly snail ornament to my chest. "You let her in my closet?"

He holds his hands up, and his laptop nearly slides off the couch. He catches it at the last second. "She needed a dress! She's about your size."

My cousin Genevieve has about four inches of leg on me, two fewer cup sizes, and zero waist definition. The only size we share is probably in shoes.

"I can say goodbye to whatever dress she took." I turn back to the tree. "Aunt Cecily probably had to have it altered beyond recognition."

"I told her she could keep the dress—"

I whip back around. "Dad!"

"And borrow some of the books if she wanted."

"She's too young to be reading those!"

He narrows his eyes at me. "I'm sorry—are those not your stash from *middle school*?"

"That's different. I come from a broken home."

He rolls his eyes. "Well, I might've picked one up myself."

"You *didn't*."

He grins in a way that tells me he absolutely *did*.

I throw a balled-up piece of tissue paper at him. "It's embarrassing enough that Gen knows. You realize if Aunt Cecily finds those, we're in deep trouble, right? She'll have

Genevieve at church saying the rosary fifty times in penance."

"Cecily isn't that straitlaced," Dad replies. "I'll keep her in line. I have tons of blackmail on her from high school."

"Oh, she'll love having you manage her like that."

Dad laughs. "So, the boyfriend . . ."

"I'm not doing that kind of stuff, Dad. We barely even see each other"—lie—"and when we do, we're more focused on just talking." The truth, unfortunately.

"Well, that's a relief. But I'm also not naïve. I talked to your mother about it—"

"God, you two just *love* to talk these days, don't you?"

"When it comes to our daughter, yes. You're the most important thing in the world to us."

I pick up another ornament and turn away.

"We would rather you be safe if the situation arises," Dad continues. "So, I got you some condoms to take back to school."

I drop the seashell ornament I'm holding, and it hits the rug with a thud.

"Dad!"

He holds up his hands. "And Mom made you an appointment with a gynecologist in Chicago for when you get up there. Which she should have done a long time ago, in my opinion."

"Oh, you're an expert on vaginas now?"

He gives me a flat look. "You should see a gynecologist once a year from the time you get your first period. I read up on it."

"Well, good news for you, which Mom must have neglected to share: I *do* see a gynecologist every year. We have one in the clinic."

"Mom did share. But she wants you to see this one. She thinks you'll be more honest with a doctor who isn't associated with your school." He eyes me. "I told her I think you'd be perfectly honest with me, too."

Guilt shoots through me. I am perfectly honest with my dad—*always*. Except for now. About my fake boyfriend, about what I did over Thanksgiving. I hate keeping secrets from him.

"I am being honest with you," I say at last. "I can buy condoms if I need them. And also, don't those things come in . . . like . . ." I wave a hand around, embarrassment flashing through me. "Sizes?"

"I got a variety pack."

"For all the boys I'm sleeping with?" I shriek.

Dad covers one ear, wincing. "You can give some to your friends. Everyone should be practicing safe sex."

"My friends—my friends are not having sex, Dad. That's not the kind of stuff we get up to."

There are girls, though, who have boyfriends at Winfield or Delafosse High or even who visit on the weekends from other schools or college, and they're sleeping together for sure. Maybe having a variety pack of condoms wouldn't be the worst thing. It could help someone else.

I sure won't be using them with Wells. It's something I actively try not to think about, for my own sanity's sake.

But when I'm in bed later, I can't resist prodding him.

ME

My dad wants to know
what size condoms you
need

The three dots appear, disappear, then reappear, probably five or six times before my phone rings.

I jolt up in bed.

"Hello?"

"Uh, your dad wants to know what now? Should I assume you mistyped the words *Christmas sweater*? I get it if condoms are all that's on your mind when you think of me, but—"

"Oh, don't worry. You took so long to respond, he bought a variety pack."

"You're kidding."

"A little," I say, settling back into bed. "But only about you taking too long to respond. He really bought a variety pack. I hope they have glow in the dark in there."

Wells makes a little choking noise.

I smirk. "Have I offended your delicate sensibilities?"

"No, I love talking about glow in the dark dicks before bed. It cools me right off."

"Oh, good to know."

I'm starting to feel a little warm, too, and I don't know if it's my imagination running wild or the sound of his voice in my ear. I imagine him lounging in bed in the dim light, a book clutched in one hand, the rest of the house quiet and asleep.

"So, is that all you wanted?" he asks, his voice a low rumble.

I pull the phone away from my ear, take a deep breath, then put it back. "Um, you called me, remember?"

"You texted me first."

"I was making a joke. Wow, you *really* wanted to hear my voice, didn't you? You wanted to hear me say the word *condoms* out loud."

"Trust me," he says, his voice strained, "if I'd known, I probably wouldn't have called."

"That's rude. Hey, I'll wrap the condoms in really nice

Christmas paper, okay? You can open them when we get back to school."

"If your dad got you a variety pack, it sounds like they're more for you than me. I can really only use the one . . . size."

Embarrassment has crept into his voice, with an undercurrent of something else I can't place, and I wonder if it's anything like the warmth buzzing through me.

"Can't wait to get back to school for all my sex marathoning, then. I better start stretching now."

"Jesus, Doe," Wells says, huffing out a laugh. "Listen, we gotta change the subject. I can't talk this much about sex right before bed."

"Worried about ruining your sheets?"

"Hey, do you employ your brain-to-mouth filter at all, or is that just for decoration?"

"I definitely don't have one of those, even for decoration. But okay, fine, I'll let you go."

He makes a noise of protest. "You can't go! You have to talk me back down."

I freeze. "I'm sorry—did I talk you . . . *up*?"

Wells doesn't say anything right away, but I can hear sputtering sounds from the other end of the line. "I—that—it's just—a figure of speech."

"Okay."

"Don't say it like that."

"Okay!"

"Now you sound like one of those Delafosse spirit squad people. Can you just be normal?"

"I'm panicking a little, so no."

"You can joke all night about condoms, but you can't talk about nonexistent erections?"

"Don't be so hard on yourself—I'm sure it's a perfectly

reasonable size. Oh—*hard on yourself.* That was like a two-for-one special."

"*Doe.*"

"Okay, fine. What do you want to talk about?"

My brain has broken from the pack and sprints ahead, tearing around the track at breakneck speed. It leaves me behind, practically drooling and incoherent.

I think all my jokes may have worked though, because Wells sounds a lot more settled when he answers, "How's St. Louis? Did you guys get snow today?"

"We're talking about the weather?"

"It's called a segue. I'm trying to move the conversation elsewhere."

"Oh. Well, the weather's fine. It's supposed to snow tonight. My dad's been wearing two pairs of socks to work. Oh, and my cousin found my dirty romance novels in my closet, so they've both been reading them. Not together—separately. Ew, *together.* Imagine. Never mind, don't imagine."

"Can you take a breath?"

I shut my mouth and breathe in through my nose.

"What dirty romance novels? I ask, knowing we're veering directly back into a subject I was trying to avoid."

"Oh, I like to read those—you know, those, like—on second thought, I don't want to talk about this."

What am I doing?

"Tell me."

And I don't know if it's the quiet authority in his voice, or just that it's Wells and he never judges me, but I blurt out, "Bodice rippers!"

He goes quiet on the other end of the line, and I wait, wait, wait until I realize the muffled noise that I'm hearing is laughter.

"It's not funny!"

"You read the grocery store romance novels?"

I sniff, turning my nose up. "I have very high standards."

"Sounds like it."

"Don't be dismissive. Romance novels are important to a lot of people."

"I'm not being dismissive. Tell me about one."

"Absolutely not."

"Go in your closet right now and pick one up and read the synopsis to me."

"I will not."

"Doe."

I climb out of bed and go to the closet. "Fine—okay. Here's one."

I'm still sitting in here an hour later, only I've sorted picks from my box into two piles.

"Bring those back to school with you," Wells says about the smaller of the piles—his favorites. "I want to try one."

"Seriously?"

"Why not? You read them. I can't read them?"

"I just—I'm—I've never heard of a boy reading romance novels, *sorry*, I know that's messed up."

He chuckles. "Well, now you'll have heard of it, and it won't be so weird to you."

"I have better ones on my e-reader. These are old."

"I don't care. I want these. You better not forget them."

"I'll put them in my suitcase right next to the condom variety pack."

"Okay, now I'm really going."

I sit there for a second after he hangs up, still clutching my phone.

Then it buzzes in my hand—he's calling back.

"Hello?"

"Good night," he says.

I smile so wide my cheeks start to hurt. "Good night."

Christmas Eve with my family is not a quiet affair, despite how our group keeps getting smaller, now that Dad and my cousin Gordon are both divorced. My grandparents host, and Aunt Cecily tries to force my grandparents to let her help with the cooking, which they adamantly refuse. Grandpa is a retired chef, and Grandma made me teach her how to watch test kitchen shows on "the tube"—YouTube—so it's probably best that Aunt Cecily stays out of it.

The last time she cooked a meal for us, I had diarrhea all night. That was two years ago, and I don't have much faith that she's improved. Mostly due to the wild-eyed, panicked look on Uncle Lawrence's face as he tries to steer her out of the kitchen.

I think he does most of the cooking at home.

"Mom does fine," Gordon says to me as we set the table, "as long as it's a raw meal. Salads, sandwiches—you know."

"Please don't say the word *raw*," I plead, my brain cycling me back to that terrible chicken dinner. A heavy feeling creeps up my throat.

"Our Doezer—she loves to cause a scene," says Genevieve, waltzing into the room in one of my nicer middle school dresses. She's so tall, she has to hold it down when she bends over. But other than the length, it fits her like a glove.

Definitely altered.

"I'm not causing a scene," I grumble, still feeling nauseous.

"She's a casual vomiter," says Gordon. "Super-sensitive gag reflex."

Gen hits me with a look. "Must be a bummer for your new boyfriend."

Gordon nearly fumbles the plate he's holding.

"Genevieve!" I protest, glancing toward the kitchen. Grandpa hasn't overheard anything in a decade—a side effect of constantly turning off his hearing aids because he enjoys the quiet—but Grandma is always listening. Even when she's not around. Sometimes when I'm at school and I say something bad, she'll call me. *Just to chat.*

"Did I hear Doe has a boyfriend?" Grandma says, sweeping into the room with a covered casserole dish in her hands. She sets it on the table and slides off her oven mitts, tucking them under her arm.

"Does Grandpa need help with the ham?" I ask, heading toward the kitchen.

Grandma catches me by the back of my dress. "I don't think so, baby."

Gordon laughs, heading for the kitchen. "I'll check on him."

"What do I have to do to get a little privacy in this family?" I complain as Grandma steers me to the table and sits me down.

Genevieve perches on the chair across from me, like a circling vulture waiting for me to die.

"Disown us," Dad calls from the living room, where he's helping Lawrence fix the tree. It's been leaning to the left.

Grandpa swears he doesn't know what happened, but *Grandma* swears Grandpa bumped into it and knocked it into the wall. She knows because she has three ornaments missing and found shards on the floor. She also knows one of those ornaments was her favorite, even though when I asked her about it, she couldn't describe it. Then she got mad and told me to stop bothering her.

"I have a boyfriend," I say at last. "It's not that serious. We barely get to see each other between school and volunteering and stuff. So, it's still early days, technically—emotionally."

"Physically?" Genevieve asks.

I want to tell her the only *physically* I'm doing is physically holding myself in my chair to keep from launching across the table at her.

"Yes," I say instead. "Of course."

Grandma *harrumphs*. "I don't know that I like you being up there with all those boys."

"It's an all-girls' school," Uncle Lawrence says.

"I heard they're merging with that boys' school," Grandma replies. "I don't like it. Boys and girls together. If Genevieve's school were going to merge, I'd say pull her out."

"And we would!" says Aunt Cecily. "It's not like there's a lack of options for girls' schools in St. Louis."

Genevieve attends a very prestigious private Catholic girls' school not far from Aunt Cecily and Uncle Lawrence's house in Frontenac.

"That's true," Grandma says thoughtfully, looking at Dad.

They all blame my mom for sending me away. Grandma wants me closer to home. Aunt Cecily hates that Genevieve goes to one of the best schools in the city, but everyone gets hooked on the words *boarding school* when I'm around.

"Ham time, ham time," Grandpa sings, waltzing into the room with the ham on a platter.

Gordon hovers behind him, looking ready to act if disaster strikes. Which is good, because Grandpa has an extension cord running across the dining room floor to light up a reindeer in the corner that bows its head every thirty seconds, its nose glowing red.

"Watch the—" Gordon starts, but Grandpa steps right over it without missing a beat.

I breathe out a sigh of relief.

We sit and pray, and I'm sure we're about to move on to a new topic when Aunt Cecily says, "I guess that school of yours isn't so great after all, if they have to merge with a boys' school."

I bristle. "The merger isn't set in stone."

"Oh, isn't it?"

I grip my fork. "There are a lot of girls who are against it—some boys, too. The administration is taking that into account."

"I'm sure you're all over the situation," Genevieve says, smirking as she spears a long green bean.

"Of course. I don't want our school merged with Winfield."

"Isn't Winfield Academy one of the best schools in the country?" asks Uncle Lawrence.

Gordon makes a shushing noise, like he can feel the situation beginning to boil.

"It is," I say to Uncle Lawrence. "But The Weston School is also highly ranked. We can stand on our own."

"Shouldn't you let it go, Doe?" Aunt Cecily asks. "You're graduating soon. Focusing all your energy on a merger for a school you won't be attending in a few months—well, seems like a waste of time, doesn't it?"

"No," I answer without hesitation.

Dad clears his throat. "I—"

"Isn't it time to grow up?" Aunt Cecily says. "Instead, you've got your headmistress calling your father with concerns about your behavior—"

Dad makes a short noise of protest, batting his hand at the air like he can knock her words away.

My head jerks toward him so fast, my neck twinges. "She did what?"

Dad clenches his jaw and looks at Grandma. "I asked you not to say anything."

"I didn't—she was eavesdropping!"

"We haven't talked about it yet," Dad says to Aunt Cecily. "Not that it's your business, Cee."

"You only sent her to that school because of Mary," Aunt Cecily says. "She was always uppity about the schools here, but look at Genevieve—she's getting a fine education in a respectable, prestigious school. We'll never have to worry about some rivalry overtaking her life, or the school going coed, because they have principles."

"Didn't a private school just close a few years ago?" I ask.

"That was an archdiocese school," Aunt Cecily says with disdain. "That's practically public school."

"Oh, the horror," I deadpan.

She fixes me with a look. "From the girl who goes to boarding school, I don't think you have room to talk. You're almost an adult, Doe. Your life shouldn't be about rivalries and stopping this merger and troubling your father. You need to be worrying about college applications. Where have you even applied?"

"It's still early."

She scoffs. "It isn't—and you know it isn't. I remember when Gordon was applying—"

"That was a hundred years ago, Mom," says Gordon. "Can we eat and enjoy Christmas Eve already?"

"I'd just like to know what you plan to do with all the time and money spent on your education," Aunt Cecily says to me. "Where do you want to go? What do you want to do, Dorothy?"

A panicky feeling fills my chest. Even Genevieve, smug as she was a few minutes ago, looks worried.

I set my fork down and push back my chair.

"Doe," Dad says, reaching for me.

I step around him, the noise behind me muffled under the blood rushing in my ears. I stalk across the living room and walk out the front door.

My grandparents live on a quiet, tree-lined street, the houses set close together. They're finely decorated and lit up. One of their neighbors has a large, blow-up menorah in the yard, the tops of three of the candles burning gold.

I fumble for the phone in my dress pocket, but I find myself hesitating. When I pulled it out, I knew who I was calling, but I waver as I think of him now.

I shake my head. *What am I doing?*

I dial a different person instead.

"Doesy! Merry Christmas Eve!"

I smile. My face feels stiff, and I realize I've been crying. The cold has frozen the tears on my cheeks.

"Happy third night of Hanukkah," I say.

"Uh-oh," Shawn says. "What happened? You sound sad. Do I need to come beat someone up?"

She's slurring a little.

"Are you—have you been drinking?" I ask, surprised.

She giggles. "My uncle got bottles of this super-fancy kosher wine and is making everyone drink it, so we stole the Manischewitz my grandparents brought."

"We" must mean her and her brother, Marcus. Their cousins are all much younger.

"Is Marcus glad to be home?" I ask.

"He's more glad to be heading back to school a week earlier than me," Shawn says with a laugh. "He's in a fraternity—can you believe that? Marcus, in a frat."

"It's one of those nerd frats," Marcus says in the background. "Stop making fun of me."

I smile. "You guys sound like you're having fun."

"But you don't," she says. "Tell me what happened."

"That's okay—I'm fine. You should get back to your family. Enjoy the time with them. *Someone* should enjoy their time with their family tonight."

"Oh no," Shawn says. "No, don't go. I'll sober up. I can talk."

I laugh. "Honestly, hearing you sound so happy has cheered me up enough."

"No, Doe, I'm good—Marcus, take the bottle—I'm here. Tell me what happened."

"Just my aunt being . . . my aunt."

Shawn waits. Even wine tipsy, she won't push. It makes me want to cry again.

"She asked me what I'm doing with my life, and I realized—"

"No."

"I realized I have no fucking idea, Shawn."

"Doe," she says, sounding straight-line sober now, "that's bullshit. You're seventeen years old. None of us know what we're doing with our lives."

"That's not true. Sumi knows. Gemma knows—"

"Gemma knows where she wants to go to school—not what she wants to do. Sumi is an outlier, and knowing her, she'll change her mind after a few years and decide on something else. And you know what? You're not supposed to know yet."

"I should probably start applying to colleges, at least."

Shawn goes quiet. "You didn't tell me you hadn't."

"I haven't narrowed down my options."

"That's okay, too. Deadlines for a lot of schools are the first of the year, and even into February. And some schools have really late deadlines! We'll work on them together—you and me."

"She said this rivalry dominates my life."

"So what? We're seniors, Doe! We're supposed to let our lives be dominated by stupid stuff. It's called having fun, before we head off to college and the workforce and have to be adults about everything."

I sniffle. "I don't want life to suck the fun out of me."

"Listen, right now. You have me. You have me *forever*. I will never let you have the fun sucked out of you, and I will never let you fall—not without being there to pick you back up. Okay?"

"Okay."

"Promise me you won't let your stupid aunt get to you. She's just mad that Genevieve gets overshadowed by you. Not only because of your education—but because you're cooler, Doe. You're the cool one. You're smart and funny and badass. You're the girl everyone wants to be best friends with, and guess what! They can't have you, because you're mine!"

I laugh, swiping at my eyes. My teeth chatter a little as I say, "I like what the Manischewitz has done for you."

She giggles. "I'm going to have the mother of all headaches tomorrow. But hey, listen."

"I'm listening."

"I love you, and you're amazing, and Aunt Cecily can eat my ass."

"Oh, god, no."

"Okay, maybe not."

"Bad choice of words."

I've circled the block, and as I come upon my grandparents' house, Dad is waiting outside.

"I should go," I tell her, still smiling. "And let you go."

"You don't have to," she says.

"My dad's waiting."

"Tell him hi for me. Hey—I love you."

"I love you, too."

I come up the front steps, and Dad drapes my coat over my shoulders and puts his arm around me. "Are you okay?"

I nod. "Yeah . . . I mean, I will be."

"I was going to tell you about your headmistress calling. Your mom and I wanted to talk to you together at some point."

"Great—can't wait."

"We're just worried about you. Including Headmistress Cotesmore. She says you're acting out."

"I hate this merger, Dad. *Hate* it. I'm protecting a legacy. It's important to me."

"I know. But Doe, you can't let it take over your life, either."

"I'm not!"

"You are a little." He squeezes me. "But that's why I'm glad to hear you have a boyfriend. You're enjoying your senior year. That's what it's all about—enjoying it."

"Really?"

"And your college applications." He gives me a look. "Which your mother and I will be monitoring much more closely."

I grimace. "Yeah, so will Shawn."

"Well, she is your third parent."

I laugh.

"Speaking of, didn't you text me that you needed money to send in your college apps a few weeks ago?"

I clear my throat. "Oh. Um. I'm not sure—"

"Please tell me you didn't put the college application money toward renting two donkeys for that dance."

"Cotesmore told you about the donkeys?"

Dad groans.

CHAPTER SEVENTEEN

I'll catch up with you guys later," I say to my friends as we head home from Phoebe's the first night back at school.

"What? Why?" Gemma whines. "Campus is scary now—you shouldn't go back alone."

I snort. "It's not *scary*. They're not actually gonna do anything. It just *looks* scary."

And it does—there's no denying that. We returned to campus to find it thoroughly vandalized—the Winfield *W* painted in red on the front lawn, a big red Winfield flag flying from our flagpole, and all the windows at Mallory Hall painted red. But what we didn't find out until sundown was that the outdoor light bulbs had been replaced, too, casting the entire campus in a chilling red glow.

That red glow is one of the reasons we hustled off campus. It felt like we were starring in a horror movie from the lighting alone. Maybe if Winfield was blue instead of red, it would feel a little less threatening to have their school color all over campus.

At least the administration finally managed to de-weld Mallory Weston again, fix the damage to her head, and right her on her base. One less indignity on our campus.

"Besides, I'm meeting someone."

I nod to Rotty's as we pass it, and between the shelves, in the very back, I spy a familiar mess of dark hair in the big red chair.

Sumi snorts. "She's done with us. She's gotta get her hands on her man."

I let out a squeak of outrage. "Hey! Not fair."

"I hope you brought your condoms with you," Jade says, patting my shoulder.

"I regret telling you guys about that."

"You can't keep secrets from us, Doesy," Shawn says, tossing her arm around my shoulder to give me a shake.

My stomach drops. *Right,* I think, *no secrets—except for that boy right there.*

"Have fun," Gemma says, pouting a little.

I put my hand on her arm. "Hey, I can stay. I just need to give him something."

"He's that fast?" Sumi asks, a calm curiosity in her voice— the Sumi special when she's making a dirty joke.

I give an exaggerated guffaw, pulling a face at her.

She grins.

"No, go," Gemma says, pushing me toward the door. "I'm only joking. I just missed you guys."

I frown. "Gemmy—"

"Text us when you're done," Sumi says, tossing an arm around Gemma's shoulders. "Maybe we'll still be in the Kingdom."

"I will. I won't stay long."

"Don't do us any favors," Jade says, giving me a playful elbow to the ribs.

"I'm not! It's a favor to me that you guys let me hang out with you at all."

Sumi blows a raspberry. "Suck up!"

They start to walk off, but Shawn lingers.

"Are you okay?" she asks, squeezing my hand.

"Yeah, I'm—"

The door to Rotty's swings open, jingling merrily as it deposits Three on the sidewalk.

"Oh, good. I was hoping I'd get to see a few Weston girls tonight."

"I'm sure," I deadpan.

He grins at Shawn. "Hey."

She makes a grossed-out noise, her nose scrunching. She turns to me, shaking it off, and says, "I'm going. The air quality here just went down. Breathe through your mouth." She walks off, leaving Three and me standing on the sidewalk together.

I glance at him. "Don't bother my friends."

"Your friends bothered me first."

"How so?"

"Existing."

I scoff. "You're so dramatic. Can you move, please? You're blocking the door."

"And oiling the floor in my hall."

"I don't have any idea what you're talking about."

I reach around him and yank the door open. He jumps out of the way, narrowly avoiding getting clipped in the shoulder.

"You're a menace," he calls after me.

"Ah, the cry that follows my girlfriend wherever she goes," Wells says without looking up from his book. I'm still half obscured by the shelves.

The guy behind the counter chuckles.

"That's not funny," I say to Wells when I reach him. "You're giving me a bad reputation."

He glances up from his book, quirking an eyebrow at me. "You earned your reputation all on your own."

I suck my teeth, grimacing at him.

He slides over in the chair and pats the small spot next to him.

I settle in, and even though I feel like I've done this a hundred times, when my thigh presses against his, want rushes through me.

Whoa, down, girl.

I glance at Wells, and the way he's gone still makes me wonder if he's feeling the same thing.

I clear my throat. "I have something for you."

He shoots me a sideways glance. "It better be—"

"It is."

"And *not*—"

"It's not!"

I open my tote bag and pull out the bundle of paperbacks I've been carrying around, wrapped in a reusable shopping bag. It's purple with a berry parfait on it.

"Sorry about the bag," I mutter.

Wells unfurls it so he can see the full picture and grins. "Why? I like it. It's making me hungry, though." He peeks into the bag. "This is all of them?"

"It's half. I didn't want to carry that many books around! I'll give you the rest later. After you finish these."

He sighs. "I'm disappointed. I wanted to have all my options."

"Don't be disappointed. I gave you a free bookmark."

Which I am now regretting. Why did I bring it up? Why? To torture myself?

Wells picks up the top book and flips it open.

A condom slides out into his lap.

"Jesus," he mutters, shoving the condom back into the book and dropping it into the bag. He glares at me.

That, at least, makes me laugh.

He rolls the books back up in their bag and wedges the bundle under his elbow. "You really are a menace." He glances at me. "Unless this is your way of making a pass at me?"

"Oh my god—all aboard, next stop, Delusional City." I make a train-whistle sound and pretend to wave a hat in the air.

He tilts his head, his tongue sweeping over his bottom lip.

I get an instant head rush.

"Okay, fine, I'm bad at jokes," I say, looking away. "You win. How was your Christmas?"

Wells tips his head back, and for a second I'm distracted by his neck—the muscles, his prominent Adam's apple, how it looks almost graceful, a thing I've never thought about a neck before. His skin looks soft and inviting, like you could nuzzle into it and—

"It was about as good as can be expected with my family," he says, and I force myself to focus on his face—which honestly, isn't much of an improvement for my mental state. "A lot of subtle jabs. A feeling like we all hate each other but still show up for the pretense. To prove to my grandfather's siblings that we get along and everything's great. Uncle Nate has this idea that they're all circling vultures just waiting for us to fall apart so they can snatch up my grandfather's legacy."

"Do you have a big Christmas?"

"Christmas Eve, yeah," he says. "The whole Wellborn clan has Christmas Eve at the Stadler."

The Stadler is one of the many hotels owned by Carey Page, Christian and Baby's father. Winona and Jeff pointed it out to me on our tour of Cincinnati. It's one of those luxurious boutique hotels.

"Christmas Day isn't much better," Wells admits. "But Anne-Marie hosts at their house, so it's a little more relaxed."

"You'd think the hotel family would be the high-strung one," I murmur, leaning my head on his shoulder.

He chuckles. "They used to be. The twins mellowed them out. Although no one's ever been as high-strung as Uncle Nate and Aunt Jeanie. How was—"

"How was your Christmas-Christmas? With your parents?"

"It was fine. We're pretty mellow. My parents are late sleepers, so I hung out for a while and watched TV. Did you—"

"Get anything good?"

"Not a variety pack of condoms, but yeah."

I elbow him, and he laughs.

"Tell me what you got."

"Why do I get the feeling you don't want me to ask how your Christmas was?"

"Mine? It was fine," I squeak. "My dad and I did what we always do—opened gifts under the tree at midnight, drank hot chocolate with a ton of marshmallows, and watched some cheesy action movie until we fell asleep. Then he took me to my grandparents' house to have Christmas morning with my mom."

We went back to Chicago the next day, and other than my trip to the gynecologist, the rest of my winter break was pretty bleak. Just a montage of being cold on different curbs in Chicago while I waited for a car to pick me up, over and over, until I finally got to come back to school.

"Get anything good?"

"Yeah, a variety pack of condoms."

"This joke really needs to die already."

I laugh.

"What about your family?" he asks. "What do you guys do for Christmas? Big family thing?"

Isn't it about time to grow up?

I let out a breath, wincing when I hear how shaky it sounds.

Wells frowns. "What's wrong?"

"Nothing. Christmas with my family is . . ."

What are you doing with your life?

"Normal," I finish at last. I shift so I'm facing forward, hoping I can hide behind my hair. "Boring, mostly."

"Doe."

"Hmm?"

He leans forward so I have no choice but to look at him. "You don't have to tell me if you don't want to," he says. "But trust me, I get complicated family stuff. You've met my family. It wasn't exactly a Norman Rockwell Thanksgiving. I promise Christmas is worse. You're looking at the family screwup—and that's from someone sitting at the same table as Joc and Biers."

I let out a small laugh.

"So, if you're looking for empathy," he says, "I'm sure I can scrounge some up."

"Well, thank you. From one family screwup to another."

"No way," he says, shaking his head. "There's no way."

"What?"

"That you're the family screwup. How high are their standards?"

"Oh, not very. But I've dedicated my entire high school career to a prank war with a rival school, haven't applied to a single college yet, and have no idea what I want to do with my life. Apparently, that's not something to brag about. Who knew?"

I glance away, afraid of what I might see in his expression.

"Hey," he says, tugging my elbow. "Come here."

He puts his arms around me, pulling me into his side as he sinks back into the chair. I curl toward him instinctively, resting my hand on his chest.

He makes a small sound and puts his hand over mine. "You should move that. I don't want you to feel how fast my heart's beating."

I laugh, turning my face into his shirt to muffle the sound. I move my hand down and rest it on his stomach, and his muscles tense under my fingers.

"Worse, worse, definitely worse," he says, picking my hand up and resting it on his shoulder.

"Worse? Most boyfriends would say better."

He shoots me a sideways look. "Only if they could do something about it."

"We could do something about it."

I'm only kidding a little bit—only as much as I think he might say no. But my heart is racing, too, and I'm coming up empty on reasons why we shouldn't.

He groans and sits up, pulling me with him. My heart jumps into overdrive. Blood starts hitting my brain so fast, I feel light-headed.

"Where are we going?" I ask him, my voice shaking. He tucks the bundle of romance novels and his beat-up paperback under one arm.

"Basement." He reaches for my hand. "You're better behaved down there. That chair is a bad influence on you."

I deflate as he leads me toward the stairs.

"Don't look so disappointed," he says as we descend into the cold. Whatever warm feelings I was having upstairs literally disintegrate as we hit the cement floor. "You laid the ground rules, and we still have a few weeks left to go."

"Ground rules? What ground rules?"

He deposits me in the armchair and drops onto the couch. "You said you wouldn't fool around with me. With a tone of *disgust*."

I scoff. "God, you're not talking about Labor Day!"

He holds up his hands. "I remember the terms."

"We didn't draw up a contract. There aren't *terms*."

"Still, better not complicate things this close to the finish line—don't pout."

"I'm not pouting."

"I didn't realize you wanted it that bad."

I kick him in the thigh, which only makes him laugh.

"I wouldn't touch you with a ten-foot pole, Gabriel Wellborn."

"Ah, there's that touch of disdain I love so much."

I laugh.

"Hey, Doe?"

"Hmm?"

He leans forward, resting his elbows on his knees. "You're not a screwup for all that stuff. You know that, right?"

I sober, my shoulders drooping.

"Seriously. No one around here actually knows what they want. And the ones who do—ninety percent of them will end up changing their minds or miserable. Focus on figuring out the where. The what can come later. As for the rivalry, I don't see how that weighs against you at all. You've spent the last four years dedicated to one long-term goal. Isn't that a good thing?"

I smile a little. "You sure know how to spin it, don't you?"

He grins. "It's a skill I'd recommend developing. It'll be great for your college essays."

I roll my eyes. "If I ever get around to applying."

"You will."

"I'll have to now. My parents have involved themselves."
I screw up my face in disgust, remembering the lecture I got
from Mom. It felt like it lasted the whole ride to Chicago.

"No, not *parents*," Wells deadpans.

I shove his thigh with my foot again, but he catches my
ankle.

"Hey," he says, his voice serious. "Don't let anyone make
you feel like a screwup. I can't think of someone who's *less* of
a screwup. I think—I think you're—"

My heart pounds, my skin turning hot.

Wells's cheeks go pink. "You're, like, the best person I've
ever met."

And even though we're barely touching, I kind of feel
like—I don't know—like I've been kissed within an inch of
my life.

The newsletter hits campus a week into second semester. I
don't know who found it first, but by the time I get to physics
with Mrs. Meyer, there's a copy circulating the room.

I catch a small glimpse as someone passes it over my shoulder to another girl, and the words I see make me freeze.

THE DAYS OF SINGLE-GENDER
EDUCATION ARE THROUGH

"Let me see that," I say, reaching for it.

The girl in front of me snatches it before I can get my hands
on it.

I lean up, reading over her shoulder.

"You're breathing down my neck," she mutters, trying to
shoulder me away.

"With your GPA, you should probably focus on what's

going on up there." I point toward the board, and when she looks up, I grab the paper out of her hand.

HEY WESTON GIRLS

ARE YOU TIRED OF SOME GIRLS ACTING LIKE THEY KNOW WHAT'S BEST FOR OUR SCHOOL?

ARE YOU SICK OF **SOME GIRLS** ACTING LIKE THEY REPRESENT THE UNANIMOUS VIEW OF THE ENTIRE STUDENT BODY?

WE DIDN'T ELECT THESE GIRLS.

WE DIDN'T CHOOSE THESE GIRLS.

AND WE DON'T AGREE WITH THESE GIRLS.

SINGLE-GENDER EDUCATION IS A THING OF THE PAST.

IT'S TIME TO STAND UP AGAINST THE SINGLE-GENDER EDUCATION THAT DENIES TRANSGENDER AND NONBINARY STUDENTS THEIR RIGHT TO A WESTON EXPERIENCE.

IT'S TIME TO MAKE WESTON AN INCLUSIVE SPACE FOR PEOPLE OF EVERY WALK OF LIFE.

TO SHOW YOU STAND WITH US AND WITH THOSE EXCLUDED BY A SINGLE-GENDER EDUCATION SYSTEM, DRAW A CIRCLE ON YOUR HAND AND SUPPORT EDUCATION FOR ANY GENDER.

THE WESTON EXPERIENCE IS FOR EVERYONE.

"What the *fuck*," I whisper.

I look over and catch Shawn's eye, holding up the newsletter.

Mrs. Meyer stalks by and plucks it out of my hand. "I'll be taking this, Dorothy. Now, eyes forward, or you might be looking at a demerit."

I stand up. "Mrs. Meyer, I don't feel well. I feel faint."

Mrs. Meyer glances at me. "You look fine to me."

I pretend to sway.

She narrows her eyes. Mrs. Meyer might be a new teacher this year, but she has two daughters who are current day students at Weston and another who graduated a few years ago. It's not easy to pull one over on her.

Luckily, I got really good at this a few years ago.

"I don't . . ." I roll my eyes back and tilt, grabbing onto the nearest desk. I end up pulling Rebecca Wilson halfway into the aisle as I go down. My ass will bruise, but it's worth it.

"Oh my god, Doe!" Mrs. Meyer rushes forward to help me up.

"I'm okay," I say, holding up a hand. "I'm just a little dizzy."

Mrs. Meyer helps me to my feet.

"Okay," she says, "we'll get you to the clinic."

"I'll take her," Shawn pipes up.

Mrs. Meyer glances from me to Shawn and back.

I put on an innocent half smile. "It's probably best I don't go alone."

Mrs. Meyer writes us both a pass. On our way out of the room, Shawn has her arm around me, but as soon as the door shuts and we're a safe distance away, she drops it and stretches.

"You're getting really good at that," she says. "I think your eyes went all the way back this time."

I grin. "I've been practicing."

We pause at the exit to slip on our coats and scarves. It's so cold outside, I can feel it through the glass doors. While Shawn tucks her hands into her gloves, I dig the folded newsletter out of my pocket. I swiped it off Mrs. Meyer's desk on my way out. I'm really hoping she assumes she misplaced it after I fell.

"Have you seen this yet?"

Shawn takes it, using a shoulder to push open the door. Icy wind blasts us. The ground is crunchy with leftover ice and snow from the storm that came through over the weekend.

While Shawn reads, we take the long way to the clinic, not far from our dorm.

"This is intense," she says, handing it back. I don't know what my face must look like—other than frozen from the wind—because she adds, "What's going on in that head of yours?"

"What makes you think something's going on in my head? It's just one tiny pea brain pinging around like a pinball."

Shawn laughs. "Yeah, *okay.*"

I fold the newsletter up. "Nothing. Something. I don't know."

Virginia has me second-guessing myself. Is fighting against the merger transphobic?

I look at Shawn. "What are you thinking?"

"Well, it's put a solid line between us," Shawn says. "Virginia set the stakes. We're the exclusionary side. Which doesn't feel good."

Worse than that—it makes me question what exactly we're fighting for, which isn't something I'm used to. I'm no longer unquestionably confident in what we're doing. We need to regroup. But it's not clear how we do that without our message being, "We saw the newsletter. We just don't care about it."

Because that's not true. I don't want Weston to be the kind of place that shuts out trans and nonbinary kids. But can this school be a place for everyone without going coed?

"Maybe we'll get lucky," I try, my voice thin. "Maybe no one will be talking about it."

The next day, there are circles everywhere I look.

"I don't know what you're thinking, doing this," I say to Virginia when I find her at the dirty dish station in the crowded dining hall at lunch. It's a bad idea, but I can't stop myself.

Virginia glances up from her tray as she dumps her flatware into the bin. "Doing what?"

"Your little newsletter. You're really gonna frame me as some kind of intolerant asshole?"

She puts on a bland smile. "I have no idea what you're talking about." She sets her tray down and clasps her hands in front of her. "But bravo to whoever put out the zine. It really highlights the problems with your cause."

I bristle. "The *what*?"

"Problems."

"No—Jesus—the zine? What's a zine?"

She sighs. "Why don't you look it up? I'm not Google."

When I get back to my table, I flop down into my chair and reach over to grab Shawn's phone from her hands.

"Can I borrow that? I have to look something up."

She snatches it back. "No!"

I blink at her. "What? What's wrong with you?"

She lets out a breath. "Nothing. You just surprised me."

"What, are you looking at porn?" I tease, grinning. I reach for her phone again. "A little lunchtime delight?"

She scoffs. "You're disgusting. Use your own phone."

"I forgot it in my room."

"How nineties of you. I'm busy. Borrow Sumi's."

Sumi slides her phone to me. "But I'm warning you—I've definitely been looking at porn."

"Sumi!" Gemma protests while Jade tosses her head back and laughs.

Sumi shrugs. "What? I have a hot spot. The administration can't track me if I'm not on their Wi-Fi."

"I'm so glad you clarified what you meant by hot spot," Shawn says without looking up from her phone.

"Oh," says Sumi. "Well, I've got another hot spot for sure."

Gemma squeals.

"'A zine is a self-published work with a small circulation,'" I read off. I glance up at my friends. "I seriously thought she was just shortening the word *magazine*. Like *zine*. Like slang. I thought I was out. But I get it now—I'm still in."

"You've never heard of a zine before?" Jade asks, squinting at me.

I shrug. "Should I have?"

Jade shrugs back. "I don't know. Yes?"

I hand Sumi her phone and glance at Shawn as she locks her phone and shoves it into her bag. Technically Weston has a no-phones policy during class hours, but almost everyone breaks that rule in the dining hall. One of those *they can't stop all of us* kind of things.

"Everything okay?" I ask her.

"Oh, yeah, everything's fine," Shawn answers a little too brightly. "So, what'd Virginia say when you cornered her?"

"I didn't *corner her*."

Shawn gives me a look.

"She won't admit it was her, but you can tell she's happy about it."

"She should be," says Jade. "There are a lot of circles around here."

I sigh. It's a strange experience for me seeing so many of the other Weston girls in solidarity against us.

"We need an angle," Shawn says. "We can't just be the side that says 'girls only' anymore. Virginia makes a good point."

"But we have a trans girl at Weston," I say. "And there are people in this school who are, like, gender fluid, right? We wouldn't kick out a trans boy when he came out because he was, you know, a boy."

"Wouldn't we?" Jade asks. "How do we know for sure? It isn't our decision, and we don't know what the administration would do."

"Or has already done," Sumi points out.

I frown, thinking back on the girls who have left over the years, and wondering if I've been missing something.

Then I start to worry.

I look back at my friends. "I don't have a solution."

"You don't have to solve everything," Gemma says.

"There also might not *be* a solution," says Jade. "Maybe we lost. She Trojan-horsed us. We spent all this time so worried about the merger, we never considered people around here might actually want it."

I slide down in my seat and look around. Considering the number of circles that I count at the tables around us, Jade may have a point.

CHAPTER EIGHTEEN

For our next merger test, we're all volunteered to help out at the Delafosse Winter Celebration. It's a two-day affair with an outdoor ice rink, a carousel, sleigh rides down Big Hill, booths with food and crafts, an ice sculpture competition, and a coronation for the Winter King and Queen, which is apparently a big deal for the locals.

I end up stuck at a hot chocolate booth with one of Virginia Brinkoff's friends, Beth Liebowitz. She's an insufferable sophomore with a perpetual sneer and a voice that's somehow both squeaky and husky. She's about six inches shorter than me, but she manages to look down her nose anyway.

We spend most of our time not speaking, unless Beth is snapping at me about something I've done wrong, which I'm generously taking on the chin. I don't want to risk another detention with Tully.

When there's a lull in the rush during a staged dance for the current Winter King and Queen, Beth turns to me.

I bristle in anticipation.

"I saw a lot of circles on hands last week," she says. "You should probably reconsider your stance on the merger. Your popularity is dropping rapidly."

I give her a cool look. "I can't be bullied."

She scoffs. "Who's bullying you? I'm giving you a warning. I bet you never considered how many people want Weston to go coed. Our numbers are closing in on yours fast, if we haven't got you beat already. You're in a dangerous position. I know you love to be liked."

"Clearly not that much, because you don't seem to like me at all, and I couldn't care less."

She smirks. "I should rephrase. You love to be *adored*. You love to be *followed*. You don't necessarily care when a few people break rank. But like any dictator, you hate to see a real uprising."

"Did you seriously just call me a dictator?"

Beth shrugs. "Well, it's not like we voted you in before you started acting in the Weston name."

My hands curl into fists, my fingernails digging into my palms. "You—*ha!*—You're a bitch. I'm leaving."

Beth cackles. "What a stellar argument, Doe. You would've done great on the debate team."

I ignore her as I storm out of the booth and push through the crowd.

A *dictator*?

I think of the little first years I showed to their classes when school started, and the younger girls in my house who I chat with in the bathroom and the dining hall line. Noelle from Mr. Tully's office. I feel a sick, creeping feeling that maybe Beth is right. Maybe they don't want this. Does it make me a dictator to think I know what's best for them?

I'm shaking as I search for my friends, but I can't remember their assignments, or if I even knew them, so I end up wandering. When I start to feel a tightness in my chest, I duck behind the coronation stage to gulp down air in peace.

But I'm not alone. It shouldn't surprise me that some handsy couple is back here. I lean against the wall, catching my breath, feeling hot with embarrassment and envy.

Until he turns his head, and as I squint into the shadows, I feel another swell of panic.

But it's not Wells, I realize. It's Three.

I'm breathing a sigh of relief when the girl pulls back.

My stomach drops, and I move my mouth to speak, but nothing comes out—only wheezing, wordless air.

"Doe," Shawn says, flushing such a bright red, I can see it staining her cheeks even in the dark.

I stumble back, trip over a cord, and go down hard on my ass. It'd be funny if it didn't hurt so bad.

"Oh my god, Doe!"

She rushes forward to help me, but I scramble back, climb to my feet, and walk away.

Shawn and Three.

I shove through the crowd, my chest tightening to an almost unmanageable degree. *Shawn and Three.* Making out behind the coronation stage. His hand up the back of her sweater. Her fingers curled into his hair.

I'm walking back toward school before I realize it, knowing I'll get detention for leaving early and not really caring. What does it matter?

What does it matter when you catch your best friend making out with your worst enemy?

Three might have displayed some moments of humanity, but he's *still* the enemy.

I pound up the stairs and burst out into the Kingdom, gasping for breath.

It doesn't take long for the others to find me. Shawn must have called them, because they arrive together. I'm sitting on the ground with my head between my knees when they come through the door, but I scramble to my feet when Shawn approaches me.

"Doe . . ."

I hold up a hand. "Don't come near me."

Her face falls. "I know you're upset. Listen, I didn't exactly see this coming. I didn't—I didn't think he'd be—that he could—but he approached me, and—"

"I don't want to hear this."

"Doe, *I like him.* Can't you understand that?"

"I understand it. I just hate everything about it."

Behind her, Gemma clutches Sumi's arm, blinking rapidly and chewing her lips. Even Sumi's brow is pinched with worry. Jade stands off to the side, her expression unreadable.

"How can you say that?" Shawn asks me. "You're dating Wells. How is this different?"

"Well, for one, he isn't Three, the person we've been fighting since day one, and two, *I'm not actually dating Wells!*"

Shawn steps back, confusion screwing up her face. "What?"

"I'm *not dating* Wells. We have a mutually beneficial agreement."

"What, like sex?" she asks. "Then why call him your boyfriend?"

"No, like I wanted to piss Three off, and Wells needed something from me. It's an agreement. It's *fake.*"

Shawn covers her mouth.

"Jesus, fuck, Doe," Jade snaps. "What the hell is wrong with you? You lied right to my face. I *asked* you if you were dating him to make Three mad, and you said no!"

I swallow.

Jade laughs—a horrible sound. "My god, you are a hypocrite. You're mad at Shawn for hooking up with Three, but you've been lying to us the whole time! Well, guess what, Doe? You're not the only one who can lie."

She pulls her sleeve back and holds up her hand, flashing the inside of her wrist at us. And drawn there in thick, black ink is a circle.

She pulls her sleeve back down. "So, there you go. Tit for tat, huh?"

"Jade," Gemma says, reaching for her as she storms toward the door.

Jade steps out of her reach but swings back around, leveling me with a glare. "You think this school is so perfect, and maybe it's perfect for *you*. But just because you like it the way it is, doesn't mean it can't be better for someone else. You don't know what it's like here for people who aren't like you. Who don't live like you. Or look like you."

I feel a jolt in my stomach like I've been hit.

"A place can always be better," Jade continues. "Who are we to say everything should stay exactly the way it is, just because it was always perfect for you?"

Jade storms across the rooftop and disappears into the stairwell, her footsteps banging all the way down. Far below us, a door slams shut.

Sumi looks at me and swallows. "I don't know what to say to you right now," she says, sounding as serious as I've ever heard her.

She takes Gemma's hand, and Gemma lets her lead the way to the door, leaving me with Shawn.

I want to sit down and cry, but Shawn is standing there, and I'm still angry. The type of all-consuming anger that landed me in therapy. I could smash everything in sight. I could eat the world. I'm so angry, I want to tear my hair out. But more than anything, I hate myself. I hate myself so much, I want to sink into it.

Shawn sniffles, her mouth pulling into a deep frown.

"I really thought—" Her voice breaks, and she looks away, covering her eyes. "I really thought you were making progress."

She scrubs at her eyes and drops her hands, facing me. "But it turns out you haven't grown up at all. Everything is about this merger to you. Everything is about Weston, and the rivalry, and getting your way. You'll do anything, won't you?"

"I guess so," I bite back. "But at least I didn't hook up with Three behind your back."

She glares at me, wiping her nose on her sleeve. "That's not how it works. You're not entitled to know everything I do, and everyone I talk to, and every boy I might like. I'm allowed to have privacy. I'm allowed to tell you in my own time. But what you did? It was outright lying. There's no getting around it."

I cross my arms, giving nothing.

Shawn scoffs in disbelief. "You really—you really are the worst sometimes, you know that?"

"I guess I'll have to *grow up*."

"Yeah, I guess you will, Doe. And you'll have to do it while staying the hell away from me."

She turns and stalks to the door. It closes behind her with a snick.

I wait, practicing my breathing until my heart rate returns to normal. I try to focus on something that makes me happy, but looking around at the abandoned Kingdom, all I feel is miserable.

I wait until my nose turns so cold, it's numb, until my fingers are so frozen, they're stiff. I wait a long time while I count my anger down to a low thrum.

No one comes back.

* * *

On Monday, we all have detention, and even worse, so does Three.

I can't imagine how Three landed himself here. I thought he was untouchable. But when Mrs. McNabb escorts us across the street to the Winfield dining hall for our detention—dinner cleanup—he's there waiting with a handful of other Winfield boys. He looks pretty pleased when he sees us come through the door. For a second, I mistake his smile for smug, but it broadens when he sees Shawn.

He's happy to see her. It makes me want to scream.

No one has to worry about extracurricular conversation this detention. Gemma and Sumi stick close together, but Jade keeps her distance. Shawn goes straight to Three, and I end up stuck with one of the guys from my Fall Fest booth. Cody or Tim, I can't remember which.

We're tasked with stacking chairs on the tables while Jade and two other Winfield boys sweep, and Sumi and Gemma mop. Shawn and Three work on the other side of the room, talking too low for me to hear.

I wonder if she's told him about Wells and me yet. The thought makes my stomach hurt.

All that work for nothing.

And Wells gets nothing out of it.

I watch them while I work, trying to read their lips.

"Hey, stalker, could you focus?" Cody-or-Tim says to me. "I get you're obsessed with Three, but I don't want to be in detention all night."

"I'm not obsessed with Three, you imbecile," I snap at him. "I'm trying to make sure he isn't jerking her around."

Cody-or-Tim rolls his eyes. "I doubt Three would bother with a girl just to jerk her around. It'd be a waste of time. It's not like he lacks options."

"Are you friends with him or something?"

"I know him," Cody-or-Tim says. "You don't have to know Three well to know what type of guy he is."

"Clearly you don't know him well at all, considering he's the devil incarnate, and you're ready to give him a free pass."

"Funny, most people say the same thing about you."

"Can you go back to being silent?"

"Work, and I will."

I make a big show of picking up the next chair, twinge my lower back, and drop it. It hits the floor with such a horrendous bang, everyone stops working to look at me.

I clutch my lower back, grimacing. "Ow."

Cody-or-Tim gives a long-suffering sigh, picks up the chair, and stacks it on the table.

"Do you need to go to the clinic?" Mrs. McNabb asks, approaching us.

I shake my head. "I'm fine."

Clearly Mrs. McNabb only believes me enough to let me get through the rest of detention, because on the way back to Weston, she sends me to the clinic.

"Gemma, please escort her, won't you?" she says. "Check in with me when you get back to Halcomb."

Gemma hesitates, and Sumi clutches her arm.

"I can take her," Sumi says.

"I said Gemma," Mrs. McNabb replies. "But thank you, Sumitra."

Sumi looks from Gemma to me and back.

"I really don't need to—"

Mrs. McNabb gives me a look, and I shut my mouth.

I'm still furious with Shawn and Jade, but Sumi and Gemma haven't done anything. Especially Gemma, who seems more hurt than any of us.

Guilt swarms me on the way to the clinic.

"How mad are you?" I ask at last.

Gemma sighs. "I lied for you, Doe. Do you understand that?"

"Yes."

"Do you really? You said you wanted to go with him, and I offered you an excuse. Like an absolute idiot."

"You're not an idiot."

"You *made me* an idiot." She sniffles, her voice wavering. "And a jerk. I used the worst thing I could against your dad to help you lie. If I'd known it was about beating Three, I never would have done it. But I thought—I thought—"

"Gem—"

"You should be ashamed of yourself."

My eyes burn.

"I thought you were falling in love. I wanted you to go to Cincinnati because I thought maybe—finally—you'd found something you cared about more than winning this war."

"When did beating Winfield become so despicable to all of you?" I demand. "When did it become something I want, not something *we* want?"

"I never cared about winning," Gemma says. "I cared about being with my friends. I cared about having fun. And even if I was scared to death ninety percent of the time, I *was* having fun."

We reach the clinic, and she stops walking.

"I was having fun until it started to feel like real warfare," she says. "Until you were sacrificing so much of your morality, you're no longer just the gray area."

"Wells agreed—"

"It's not about Wells. It's about us. We don't lie to each other."

"Shawn lied!"

"Shawn never lied. We never gave her a chance to lie. She got found out before she could. Easing into something isn't the same as lying, Doe. I don't know why you don't understand that."

"Jade lied."

"Jade's heart hasn't been in this for a long time," says Gemma. "You'd know that if you could see three feet in front of you."

"What are you saying? I'm self-centered?"

Gemma stares at me so steadily, I almost don't notice her shaking hands.

"Okay. Cool. I'm a self-centered, morally unsound liar. And since everyone keeps insisting that I haven't changed, I guess that's how I've always been. So, why are you even friends with me?"

Gemma's eyes start to fill, but she blinks the tears away, swallowing audibly. "Because we loved you anyway, even when you were bad."

"And now?"

I don't know what I expect her to say, but I imagine she'll at least say *something*.

Which is why I'm so surprised when she turns and walks off without another word.

"Hey, what's—*oof*!"

I've fallen straight into the big red armchair without waiting for Wells to move, and I end up half in his lap with my arms around his neck and my body curled into his.

"Hey," he says, softer. He slides his hand under my coat and settles it between my shoulder blades. I bury my face in his shoulder as he rubs my back.

"What's wrong?" he asks, his voice a low rumble.

I shake my head. I'm afraid to tell him. I know he heard about Shawn and Three, because he texted me on Sunday to ask if I was okay.

I didn't respond. I haven't responded to him all week.

He's taken it surprisingly well.

I pull back to look at his face. We're so close, I can count his eyelashes.

"I think—" I take a deep breath and steady myself, my hands on his shoulders. "I think Three might know. About us."

Wells's eyebrows arch way up. He glances around, then gives me a little nudge.

"I wasn't even flirting with you," I say as he gets up and leads me toward the basement. "I don't need the cool-down room."

He huffs out a small laugh. "Yeah, but we're more likely to be overheard up here."

"At this point, I'm not sure it matters," I say as we make our way downstairs. I burrow into my coat as the temperature drops.

Wells takes me to our usual couch and chair, but he doesn't sit, so I don't, either.

"What makes you think he knows?"

"Shawn knows."

He winces. "And you're fighting."

"She lied to me."

"Did she?"

I narrow my eyes. "I don't need a lesson in what lying is. What she did feels like a lie. It was a betrayal either way."

"You lied to her, too."

"Then I guess we've both got a reason to be mad. At least

I lied for a good cause. Everything I've done, I've done for them."

Wells doesn't respond, but his expression is so carefully blank, I can only surmise that he doesn't agree.

I bristle.

"Don't," he says, pointing at me. "Don't start."

"I'm not doing anything."

He steers us back. "Why do you think Three knows? He hasn't said anything to me."

"Would he? Or would he wait for you to walk into a trap?"

Wells frowns, looking unsure.

"See, you don't know—"

"Go out with me."

I freeze. "What?"

"Go out with me," he repeats, taking a step closer. A flush works its way up from his neck, staining his cheeks. But his eyes are clear. "Go out with me for real. Then it's not a lie."

"I don't see how that solves our problem, Wells."

"Maybe it doesn't. But go out with me anyway."

I stare at him, my mouth going dry. "What—I don't understand," I croak. "If he knows we lied, it doesn't matter if—Why would we—Why would he believe us?"

"I don't really care if he believes us, Doe." He reaches for me, sliding his hands up to cup my cheeks. "Forget the stupid plan."

"It's not stupid."

His mouth curls into a soft smile. "I'm gonna kiss you right now. And then I'm gonna ask you out again, and you're gonna say yes."

He gives me a second to pull away. He watches my face, presumably waiting for some kind of hint that I don't want it.

But the truth is, I've been dying to kiss him for months. So, when he presses his lips to mine, I lean right into it.

He moves a hand inside my coat and around to my back, pulling me flush with him. I wrap my arms around his neck and open my mouth against his, my hands sliding into his hair. It's so soft—much softer than I thought, and I can't remember the last time I touched his hair and really felt it.

I push against him, trying to get closer, to crush out every tiny slip of air between us, and Wells grunts in surprise as he loses his balance and falls back onto the couch. I land half on top of him, and we're fumbling to reconnect, stealing fast, breathless kisses as I struggle out of my coat. As soon as I'm free, my hands are back in his hair, and when he moves his mouth to my neck and up to my ear, I clutch at his collar, trying to anchor myself to this dimension.

Wells pulls back, breathing hard. "Wait—this isn't—"

I kiss him again, pressing him back into the couch.

"Okay," Wells says, coming up for air, "I really appreciate the enthusiasm, but—"

"Hey, what the hell, dude?"

I sit back, stunned. Somehow the creakiest stairs in all of Delafosse didn't alert us to the college-aged guy who works the register coming down to check on us.

Wells scrambles out from under me, grabbing my coat from the floor and clutching it in front of him.

I sink into the couch, dazed.

"Sorry, Jesse," he says. "Seriously, that wasn't—"

Jesse jerks his thumb over his shoulder. "Out."

I startle, jolting to my feet. *"Forever?"*

Jesse looks surprised. "What? No. You can go do that"—he waves a hand at us vaguely—"wherever you want, just not here. Come back when you're ready to appreciate a book."

I move to take my coat from Wells, but he grips it tight, his cheeks going bright red.

"Oh," I say like an idiot.

He clears his throat and heads for the stairs. "Sorry," he says to Jesse as he passes.

Jesse waves him along.

I follow, my head hanging.

Wells moves faster than I do, and when I reach the top of the stairs, he's gone.

I find him waiting outside, leaning against the wall. His breath leaves his mouth in puffs of white.

As soon as I move toward him, he holds up my coat to help me into it.

"Sorry I abandoned you," he says, laughing. "I needed to—um—get into the cold."

I slide my arms into my coat, and as soon as I have it on, Wells puts his arms around me and twists me so my back is against the wall. He leans his weight into me, holding me there.

"So," he says, grinning as he nudges his cold nose against mine, "that wasn't really what I had in mind—not that I'm complaining."

"Uh-huh." I tilt my head to pick up where we left off, but Wells pulls back slightly.

"Go out with me, Doe," he says, giving me a little squeeze.

I frown at him. "I really don't get what you're doing here."

"Yes, you do. I'm asking you out." He grins. "Come on, don't tell me you aren't into it, because—"

"To what end, though?"

"What do you mean?"

"It doesn't help with Three. He'll know we're up to

something—it's not like we can be retroactively dating for real."

"Why are we talking about Three? I'm talking about *us*."

"I just don't get the point, I guess."

He pulls back. "What do you mean?"

"I mean . . . Why would we date for real?"

His grip on me loosens and falls away as he takes a step back. "Gee, I don't know, Doe. Maybe because that's what people do when they like each other."

I blink at him. "What?"

"I'm confused. You come in here and climb in my lap, and flirt with me, and *make out with me in the basement*, and—are you telling me it's all in my head?"

I've thought about kissing Wells—about doing so much more than just kissing Wells—but dating him for real always seemed outside the bounds of reality. I've never even let myself consider it.

"But you don't date."

"What are you *talking* about?"

"I—I don't know what's happening here. You don't date. You *fool around*, remember? Why would you date me? You don't care about that kind of stuff."

He stills. "Oh, I don't? What do I care about, then?"

"I don't know. Hooking up? I thought—I thought that's what we were . . ."

He rubs a hand over his face. "Jesus, Doe. What do you really think of me? Honestly?"

"You just caught me off guard! What do you want me to say?"

"I want you to say you'll go out with me!"

I clutch the front of my coat closed, shivering. "You haven't even given me time to think about it."

"It shouldn't take that much thought to know if you like someone or not."

"Well, I guess I don't! If that's your theory, then I must not, because I have no idea!"

He blows out a breath and takes a step back. "Cool. Good to know."

"Is it?"

"No, Doe. It's not." He turns away and pulls up his hood. "You're off the hook, though. Whether Three knows or not, it's my problem."

I don't know what he means, but I don't get a chance to ask. He walks away before I can say another word, leaving me standing outside Rotty's with the cold wind blowing straight through me.

CHAPTER NINETEEN

I don't know how to fix things with Wells, so on Friday I do the only thing I know how to do: get up, pack my bags, and turn in my forged weekend pass for our trip to Cincinnati.

When I show up, rolling my little suitcase across the street, the boys are almost finished packing up the cars.

Three spots me first and frowns. "What are you doing here?"

"What do you mean?" I ask, stopping at the back of Christian's car. I knock lightly on the trunk. "I was invited."

"Wells told us you weren't coming," says Biers, leaning against Three's car.

I glance up as Wells climbs out of Christian's car. He comes around to the back, frowning at me.

"What's happening here?" he asks me.

"I'm trying to put my suitcase away," I say. "If Christian wouldn't mind popping the trunk."

The trunk clicks open.

"Thank you," I call to Christian. I can see his reflection in the side mirror, and he gives me a little salute.

Before I can lift my suitcase, Wells snaps the trunk shut.

I glare at him. "What are you doing?"

Wells shoots Three and Biers a look. "Can you give us a minute?"

Three holds up his hands and backs away. Biers takes a little longer but eventually lumbers off.

"I said you're off the hook," Wells says, his voice so low it's nearly carried off on the wind. "You don't need to be here."

"I never needed to be here," I remind him. "You tried to let me off the hook a long time ago. But we have a deal. I intend on seeing it through."

I knock on the trunk again, and Christian pops it once more.

This time, when Wells tries to shut it on me, I catch it. He jerks back, startled.

"Are you insane?" he says. "I could've crushed your hand!"

I shrug, hefting my suitcase up into the trunk.

Wells sighs. "I can't do this with you all weekend, Doe," he says, leaning in so his cousins won't overhear. "I'm done faking it."

"You don't have to be convincing," I reply, shutting the trunk and turning to him. "You just have to get me there. I'll do the rest."

I can't read his expression. Frustration? Regret? Resentment? Some unholy mixture of all three? Whatever it is, it makes my heart clench uncomfortably.

"I want to finish what we started," I tell him. "You—you deserve to get what you want, too."

His Adam's apple bobs as he swallows, his mouth pinching into a grim line. He turns and heads around the side of the car, where he pulls open the back door. He waves a hand inside.

I manage a small smile. "Okay. Let's do this."

But he doesn't smile back.

Jeff and Winona can sense something's off. I feel their hesitance whenever they have to ask us both a question, like what we want for breakfast, or if the drive from school was okay. Luckily, we got into Cincinnati pretty late and ate dinner on the road, so we've had one less awkward meal between the four of us.

Wells skipped breakfast to shower, leaving me at the table with his parents, feeling like I've invaded their home even though they've been nothing but kind.

"Every couple fights," Winona said to me, patting my hand.

"Not that it's our business," Jeff added, giving Winona a look.

She made a face back.

I dug into my eggs and tried to eat as quickly as possible so I could leave the table under the guise of getting ready for the day.

I didn't realize what a bad idea it might have been to come until we got to Wells's house and the awkwardness really set in. He's barely looked me in the eye since we arrived, and forget about the car—he didn't even sit next to me. I was relegated to the back seat with Baby.

But I told him I don't need him to fake it, and it's true—I can handle this on my own.

The party at Three's starts in the early evening, and the sun is already setting when we arrive, casting the whole mountain in bright, golden light. It reflects off Three's house in shafts of brilliance that nearly blind me as we hand over the car to the valet.

Because of course Three has a valet at his *house* for his *birthday party*.

It's clear this isn't a normal birthday party, though. Other than his cousins and sister, I don't see anyone else our age in attendance. This reminds me more of some kind of stockholders' meeting. There are mostly older couples seated at the round tables set up on the lower level. I imagine this is the family's entertaining area, because there's a bar along one wall and even a small second kitchen with a back staircase leading up to the main floor.

While we eat—a set meal, like we're at a wedding or something—I try not to seem obvious as I peer into the kitchen, watching the catering staff hustle up and down the stairs.

At least I know how I'll get upstairs without being noticed.

Wells leans over, resting his arm along the back of my chair so he can murmur in my ear, "You don't have to do this. Let's just leave it."

I shake my head.

He sighs, his breath stirring my hair. "Doe, it's not worth it."

I turn to him, and he stiffens, pulling back slightly.

"When does the speech start?"

"Right after dinner."

I glance around. Most people are finishing up, and the catering staff is starting to collect plates.

"I'm going," I tell him. "He can't leave with his speech coming up."

Wells frowns. "I don't think you should do this."

"I have to."

"No, you don—"

I start coughing a little, waving off the looks from Winona and Jeff, and Anne-Marie and Carey. Christian and Baby don't even look up—Christian from his phone, Baby from his plate.

Wells puts his hand on my arm, even though it looks like it pains him.

I give his hand a single pat as I slide out of my chair and weave through the tables, coughing lightly into my hand until I'm around the corner in the small kitchen.

I glance up the steps, see the coast is clear, and dash up to the main floor. I make it up to Three's room faster than I did the last time.

Unfortunately, I'm not alone. I'm not sure how quickly he left the table after me, but before I even hit the landing, Wells is beside me.

"What are you doing?" I whisper, pushing him back toward the stairs. "This is way too obvious. You're gonna get us caught."

He ignores me and pushes into Three's room.

"Wells—"

"Let's just get this over with," he says, heading for the closet. "We have five minutes, max. If we don't find it this time, it's over."

I let out a little huff.

"Promise me," he says.

"You're the one who asked me to do this!"

He turns away. "I also told you to forget it, and you showed up anyway. We're wasting time."

Wells and I rifle through the closet, dresser drawers, and shoeboxes. I double-check the watch collection, to make sure it hasn't appeared since.

When we've exhausted the closet, I step back out into the

bedroom and glance around. Where would I keep a family heirloom if it were mine?

The obvious answer is with my fancy watch collection.

Wells goes to the desk and starts pulling open drawers, but I've got eyes on the nightstand.

I have never willingly looked in a boy's nightstand. I don't need to know what they keep in there—especially not Three.

But when I slide open Three's nightstand, the top drawer is empty but for two things: a collection of antique baseball cards and a black leather box.

I pull the box out and pop it open.

The watch is exactly as Wells described it: black leather strap, silver with gold hands, and only three numbers labeled—12, 3, and 6—with the name GRUEN right at the top center of the face. It's nothing much to look at. It isn't a shiny, head-turning Rolex or Blancpain. It's a normal watch, maybe even something my grandfather would have.

"Wells."

Wells freezes, looking up from the desk.

I take the watch out of the case and hold it up.

He rushes to me, his expression caught somewhere between elated and anguished. He takes the watch and runs his thumb over the face.

I swallow hard, glancing away. This feels like a private moment. I busy myself returning the box to its place.

Maybe Three will never check. Maybe he'll never even know it's missing.

But I have a strange, sinking feeling that there's a reason he has it in his bedside drawer. This clearly isn't a junk drawer to him.

The door flies open, and I grab the watch from Wells and

spin around to shove it into my bra. When I turn back, Three stands in the doorway, red-faced and breathing hard.

"I knew you'd try this again," he says, and even though he looks angry enough to slam it, he shuts the door quietly.

I put on an innocent look. "Try what?"

"Give it back."

I tilt my head, feigning confusion. "Did you hit your head on your way up here? How many fingers am I holding up?"

And for good measure, I flip him off.

Three advances on us so fast, I actually step back.

But it's not like he's going to hit me. He's evil, but he isn't *evil*-evil.

Instead, he stops in front of Wells and addresses him instead. "Give it back."

Wells's jaw tightens, his gaze hardening.

But instead of biting back, he flicks a hand at me and says, "Give it to him."

I drown on dry land. "What—I—*Wells.*"

"Enough," he says, turning his head to look at me. "It's over. Give it back."

I work my jaw, sighing. I turn away to reach into my bra.

I hold it out, and Three snatches it from me, grimacing when it touches his skin—probably because it's still warm from the boob hug.

He closes his fist around it and lifts his gaze to Wells's face. "You know, if you had just asked, I would've given it to you. If you even hinted a little bit that you wanted it, I would've given it to you. But you never tell anyone anything!"

Wells clenches his jaw. "I shouldn't have had to," he says. "It was *mine*. I don't know what your dad did to get it for you, but that was supposed to be mine."

"And this feels better? Stealing it from me? Is that what

Pop would have wanted you to do? You're so *proud* of how you knew him better than the rest of us, so why don't you tell me!"

Wells grabs Three by the collar and hauls him forward. Three tries to shove him off, and they both tumble sideways. I cry out in surprise, jumping out of the way. They crash into Three's desk.

"Stop! What are you *doing*?" I whisper-yell, mindful of the thirty or so people just two floors below. I wonder what they're hearing.

Wells throws the first punch. It hits Three right in the mouth, and blood pours down his chin.

"Oh my god! Stop it!"

Three throws the next punch, catching Wells in the eye. He stumbles back, and there's a sickening crunch of glass as he catches himself on the wall.

"Enough!" I shout, jumping between them before Wells can come back at him. But Wells has stopped. He's staring at the floor, the glass, and the watch. The one he stepped on. The one they shattered.

I rush to Three's bathroom and run a hand towel under cold water. Three has blood on his collar, and when I return, I start to dab at it, trying to work away the stain.

"I'm fine—" Three says.

I shush him. "You're covered in blood."

"I guess I should've expected this," Wells says from where he's crouched on the floor, gathering the broken watch into his hand. "It's him you've wanted since the beginning, isn't it?"

I pause to give him a withering look. "Are you kidding me? After what he did with Shawn, you really honestly think—" I break off, scoffing in disbelief. "If he goes back down there covered in blood, who do you think is getting in trouble? I'm not doing this for him—I'm doing it for you!"

"Don't do him any favors," Three says, wiping the blood from his mouth with the back of his hand. "He's the one who gave me Shawn's number to begin with."

I freeze. "What?"

Wells gets to his feet, his expression blank. His eye is starting to swell.

"It was right here, wasn't it, Wells?" Three says, his teeth stained red like a devil. "We struck a deal. I'd let your girl-friend off the hook for snooping if you did me one little favor. Get me Shawn Aronson's number out of Doe's phone and run defense while I win her over."

I look from Wells to Three, unsure of where to focus my anger.

"You *are* jerking her around," I say, narrowing my eyes at Three.

"I was for a second," he says, grinning. "But she's a real good kisser."

"I'm telling her—"

"She knows."

I frown at him.

"She figured me out from the start," he says, shrugging. "Turns out she was kind of into it anyway. Who could've seen that coming?"

I turn to Wells, but he's a million miles away. With the broken watch clenched in one hand and that blank expression on his face, it's like I'm not even here—like none of us are.

I shove the damp towel into Three's hands.

Then I turn and walk out.

Wells and I hardly speak the rest of the weekend. Our easy conversations and jokes have been reduced to short questions and one-word answers, and only those that are most neces-sary, like "What time are we leaving?" and "Noon."

I don't know what happened between Wells and Three after I left the room last night, but other than his black eye—"I was trying to open a jar for one of the catering staff and my hand slipped" was the excuse he gave his parents—neither seemed worse for wear. Three's lip was a little swollen, but manageably so.

Still, I don't think either of them fooled anyone, and my work with the hand towel was pointless. When Three reappeared, he was wearing a new—albeit nearly identical—shirt. But everyone seemed happy to let them work it out on their own.

If Genevieve and I came in with a black eye and a swollen lip, our parents would start the next Inquisition. But all families are different, I guess.

In the car on the way back to school, we're all silent except for Baby, who tries to bully Christian into letting him control the music because, "These two are killing me. I need something to occupy my brain."

"Read," Christian grunts from the driver's seat.

"I'll get carsick."

"Then roll down a window."

Baby glares at the back of Christian's seat. "You really want to chance it?"

And that's how we spend the rest of the car ride listening to southern gothic rock. It's comforting to know that after everything, I can still be surprised. I'd been expecting frat house rap.

When we get back to campus, I'm the first one out of the car. But Christian doesn't pop the trunk until he's at the back of the car with me. He reaches in and extracts my suitcase.

"I can—"

He jerks his head toward Weston and starts walking, rolling my suitcase beside him.

I hurry to catch up, throwing a confused glance over my shoulder.

If Wells cares, he doesn't show it. He isn't even looking at us.

"I should probably tell you not to waste your time with my family," Christian says as we make our way down to the street, "but Wells is good."

I frown. "I don't know about that. He insisted he isn't as kind as I think he is, and I'm starting to believe him."

"He's been through a lot," Christian replies. "I'm not excusing anything he's done, but—"

"So you know? What he's done?"

Christian's mouth curls up in a half smile. "Yeah, Doe. I know everything everyone's done. Honestly, if you wanted a fake boyfriend, I would've been your best bet. No one hides anything from me."

I stare at him. "What— You knew?"

He glances at me, grinning. "Wells and Three have been fighting since the second we realized this family fosters competition, not affection."

"Wells's parents seem pretty affectionate."

"They are. Mine are, too." He hesitates. "Well, my mom is, at least. But that's not what I mean. As long as there's something to inherit, we'll always be fighting each other. You know Wells and my grandfather were close, right?"

"I've heard."

"Wells grew up closest to him. Aunt Win and Uncle Jeff were in school still, and they were broke—I mean *broke*-broke, not Wellborn broke, which would just mean they only had two cars, one house in Mount Adams, and a country club membership. I mean, Uncle Jeff had lost everything. It's why he went back to school."

I frown. "Should you be telling me this? It doesn't sound like it's my business."

"It's not a secret," says Christian. He rolls my suitcase to a stop at the Weston gate. "Uncle Jeff had a bad gambling problem. He lost everything, and Pop wouldn't help him except for two things: he'd pay for him to go back to school, and he'd take care of Wells. He was retired by then, and my grandma passed away pretty young, so he didn't have much going on. Pop—he wasn't really a warm and fuzzy guy. He loved us in his own way, but I think Win and Jeff have spent a lot of time trying to undo the damage Pop did to Wells."

I frown, thinking of my own grandfather. He's the warmest, fuzziest man I've ever met. My dad says I was late learning to walk because he'd never put me down long enough for me to try. I can't imagine ever being damaged by him, or Grandma. Or anyone, really. Except for Aunt Cecily, who damages my ego constantly.

"Wells is really smart, you know. Like, genius smart. Almost mad scientist smart."

"Okay . . . I've never said he wasn't smart."

"He hides it well, though, don't you think? He doesn't really study, doesn't try. He could blow the whole curve to hell, but you know what he does instead? He skips class, and he reads whatever he wants as long as it's not for school, and if he shows up to take the test at all, he throws it. I've watched him do it. I've watched him get *every question wrong*. Did you know that's as hard as getting every question right?"

"I don't get what this has to do with anything."

"I'm getting there," Christian says, waving me down. "So, Pop spent a lot of time with Wells, and when he saw how smart he was, he kind of started . . . pitting them against each other. Wells and Three. They're only a few months apart, so everything they learned, they learned at the same time. And Win and Jeff weren't there to say no, and you've met Nate and Jeanie—they wanted it as bad as Pop did. They let him do what he wanted. Races, competitions, tests, punishments, and rewards like you wouldn't believe. One time Three lost this toy boat race—they'd built the boats themselves, and his sank. I remember it—I was there, but I'm a year younger, so I couldn't play, which was probably a blessing, even though I was mad about it at the time. I was eight, and they were nine. Three lost, and he cried, and Pop smacked him. Right across the mouth. He said being a man isn't about crying when you lose. It's about figuring out how to win next time."

I feel a rush of sympathy I never thought Three could inspire from me.

"So, the next time they went up against each other, Wells did what he does best—he threw it. Three had worked for weeks on it—whose model plane could fly the farthest. Wells was a whiz at this stuff. He just *got it*. When it happened, even I knew he'd done it on purpose. To his credit, he really did try to make it seem like he'd just missed something. But Pop knew. So he taught them a lesson. He lived in this really old house in Mount Adams, and everyone said it was haunted—especially the basement. We were all terrified of it. You know what he did? He hid a key to the door down there, and he tossed Wells and Three in, and he told them only one of them could come out. Whoever found it first. And the other would sleep there."

I wince. "What happened?"

"What do you think? They beat the hell out of each other trying to get out."

"And . . . ?"

"And Wells won."

I grimace. "That's fucked up."

"It is. But as soon as Wells got out, Pop let Three up, too. And he sat them down, and he told them that's what life is like. Winning by any means necessary is how you survive."

"How do you know all of this?"

"Wells and Three told me. They tell me everything. From the start, they've tried to shield me from it. They didn't want me to grow up hating Biers and Joc and even the two of them and my brother the way they've grown up hating each other."

"I didn't know it ran that deep."

"They do a good job hiding it. It's a weird relationship. It's like they hate each other so much they love each other? Does that make sense?"

I shake my head. "Not at all."

Christian laughs. "Well, you've seen them together. They love to push each other's buttons. But Three would've given Wells the watch if he'd just asked."

"You know about yesterday?"

"I told you," he says, grinning, "they tell me everything."

"So, you knew we weren't really dating. From the start, I mean."

He nods. "But I also knew he liked you."

"Don't tell me that."

He shrugs. "It's true. Not right away, not from the start. But on that first drive? I've spent my whole life watching Wells feel nothing. Or pretending to feel nothing. So, it was pretty obvious the second he started to actually feel something. He couldn't keep it off his face."

I swallow and look away, my stomach turning.

"I know he's messed up with you, and I know you're mad. But have you been perfect?"

I glare at him. "Of course," I answer snottily. "I'm always perfect."

He laughs. "I'm just trying to give you some perspective. On Wells *and* Three. I don't know what your childhood was like, but they are not well-adjusted guys. We're all a little worse for wear growing up the way we did. Wells has this simultaneous love and hate for Pop. He hates the way he was treated, but he hates the idea that he wasn't Pop's favorite more. Three didn't start winning until they got older, and that's the situation everyone runs with. Three always wins. But only because Wells has been throwing the game the whole time."

He slides my suitcase to me and tucks his hands into his pockets.

"It's not an excuse for anything. And he owes you explanations I can't give you. Apologies, too, I imagine. But Wells has never pretended he doesn't care about you. I imagine it's the one game he isn't willing to throw."

"There's no game, though. I've never looked at anyone but him."

Christian shrugs. "When you set up the whole scheme to get to Three, it doesn't matter what the truth is—only what it looks like."

And that's what he leaves me with. He turns and walks off, kicking a stray pebble across the road. Giving me a salute as he goes.

I roll my suitcase up onto campus, my head spinning.

But I don't have much time to mull everything over. I'm almost to Walsh when my dorm monitor appears ahead of me on the walkway and points.

"You," she says. "To the headmistress's office. Now."

I've been found out. It was a really stupid idea to forge a weekend pass, but I was feeling reckless.

Cotesmore is going to be pissed.

But what I don't expect, what catches me off guard more than anything today, is finding my parents sitting at her desk, side by side, a matching set with matching frowns.

"Dorothy Ann Saltpeter," Mom growls, getting to her feet, "you are in *so much trouble*."

CHAPTER TWENTY

Forging a pass!" Mom roars. "Sneaking off with a boy *for the whole weekend*! Dragging your father and me here to deal with it all! What were you *thinking*?"

I clear my throat. "In my defense, I didn't drag you and Dad—"

"Doe," Dad says, a warning in his voice.

I shut my mouth.

Headmistress Cotesmore sits on the other side of her desk, watching us with her hands folded under her chin and her mouth cut in a grim line.

"The only reason we even knew you were alive this morning was because Headmistress Cotesmore managed to get in touch with the boy's parents through his headmaster. Why weren't you answering your phone?" Mom demands.

"I guess I didn't hear it," I say sheepishly. "I don't know. I don't go on my phone in the car because it makes me sick, and I slept the whole way here, and then—and then we were back!"

I don't admit that I stuffed my phone into the bottom of my bag to keep myself from texting one of my friends in my panic over what happened last night. Especially Shawn, to make sure Three wasn't lying that she knew what he was up to.

I'm mad at her, but I don't want to see her hurt.

"We've given you a lot of chances here, Doe," Cotesmore says. She looks from Mom to Dad and back. "We went out on a limb taking you in the first place."

My stomach turns. "Has it been so bad that we have to bring *that* up?"

"This year has been a challenge with you," Cotesmore says. "You've operated with astounding single-mindedness."

It smacks of Gemma calling me self-centered. Saying I can't see three feet in front of me. Of Aunt Cecily telling me to grow up. Of everyone saying my whole life revolves around this rivalry and stopping the merger.

"Your college advisor tells me you've only finished a few applications, and you've had two detentions in as many months, both related to the merger. Not to mention your grades. Your finals scores from last semester are the lowest you've ever received."

I bite my lip and stare down at my hands.

"We had no idea it had gotten this bad," Mom says to Cotesmore. "We found out about her college applications over winter break—we're working on that. But her grades . . ." Mom sighs, and when I look up, she's rubbing her forehead.

"We let Doe into this school on contingency," Cotesmore reminds Mom, as if any of us could forget.

Beside me, Dad straightens. "This is the first trouble she's caused since she started here."

"That's not necessarily true," Cotesmore says. "She's been a major player in this war with Winfield Academy since she was a sophomore."

"That war has been going on since before even I was a student here," Mom says. "The administration has always looked the other way, unless someone was hurt."

"The pranks have escalated," Cotesmore says. She leans back in her chair and rests her hands on her stomach. "And coupled with the other issues Doe is having . . ." She lets out a heavy sigh and straightens again. "I don't like this conversation any more than you do. But perhaps her maturity isn't developing the way we hoped it would."

"Wait, you think I'm immature?" I ask, astounded.

Cotesmore winces. "You've displayed great maturity in some respects. The way you help the younger girls, for instance. Prior to this incident, I would have referenced your academic achievements. But this year has not done you any favors."

"What are you saying?" Mom asks, sounding almost as shocked as I am. "You're expelling her? I didn't realize a contingency set three and a half years ago would extend this long."

Dad shifts in the chair next to me. "That wouldn't be entirely fair, would it? After one bad spell? Were this her first year, I'd fold. We'd take her home today. But this school has been her second home. She has roots here."

Cotesmore frowns. "I'm hesitant to say expulsion. There are certain members of the administration who are pushing for it, but I've been given the final say."

"Then say I don't have to go!" I jump out of my chair, panicked that this could be it. Everything could be ending. Blood rushes in my ears. "Tell me I can stay! I'll do whatever I have to."

"You said that when you first came here," Cotesmore says. "I believed you then."

"So, believe me now," I say. "I'm not immature, Headmistress. I might be self-centered, and I might be obsessive, but I love this school. More than anything."

Cotesmore's gaze softens. "See, Doe, that's what worries me. I don't want to see you leave here and end up adrift. You shouldn't love a place more than anything."

Mom puts her hand on my shoulder, urging me back into my seat.

"Headmistress," she says, "please. It's the middle of her senior year. Expulsion would be a little high-handed, don't you think?"

Cotesmore's expression hardens. "I have to think of the other students, Mrs. Guidry. If she's a distraction, and a danger, that has to be considered."

"I'm not dangerous!"

Dad puts his hand on my arm.

"Please," he tries, "punish her, but do it here. We'll keep a closer eye on her. We'll check in frequently."

Cotesmore considers this. "If you stay," she says to me, "you will be under extreme restrictions."

My throat tightens, but I swallow against it. "I can handle it."

Cotesmore nods. "Detention twice a week with your head of house. Tutoring three times a week in the library, with signed logs. And no more off-campus passes, except for spring break, and we will require you to be signed out by a parent in person."

There are four months of school left. She can't mean that long. The idea of being stuck on campus for four straight months makes me want to cry. Detention twice a week with Mr. Tully makes me want to scream.

The tutoring I could probably use.

"I'll do it," I tell her.

"One more infraction, and that's it," Cotesmore says. "I won't be able to save you."

I nod, swallowing against my aching throat. I can feel the tears coming, but I don't want to cry here.

"While we're in town," says Mom, "we can take her off campus, correct? She won't be out of our sight."

Cotesmore hesitates.

"We're her *parents*," Dad says, bristling.

Cotesmore nods. "You can take her off campus. Of course."

I leave Cotesmore's office feeling like I've gotten a stay of execution.

But it only lasts as long as it takes to get outside with my parents, where Mom really lets loose.

"What were you *thinking*?" she says as we head to the parking lot, my suitcase clacking on the pavement. "You have behaved abhorrently."

I wince. "I'm sorry."

"You've risked your entire life at Weston, and for what?"

"Nothing that important," I say.

Dad sighs. "Can we do this back at the hotel, please, Mary?"

Mom glares at him. "You had an awful lot of nothing to say in there, Russell."

Dad's mouth pinches up, but he doesn't argue, even though he said quite a bit. He at least made some sound arguments.

"Where's Oscar?" I ask, trying to steer the subject to safer ground.

"He's at home," Mom says, pulling out her car keys and handing them to Dad. "I'm not driving like this."

Dad obliges.

In the car, Mom twists around in the passenger seat to

glare at me. "He's at home *where he should be*. Where we should all be right now."

I slump in my seat.

"Don't pout," she says, pointing at me. "You have no right to pout."

I make my expression as blank as Wells's ever was, and it must satisfy her, because she turns around and settles in her seat.

Dad drives us to a hotel in town, where he and Mom are staying. Mom leads us to her room, and while Dad sits at the desk, Mom perches on the edge of the bed, making it seem like a throne.

I stand in the middle of the room, unsure what I'm supposed to do.

"We worked very hard to get you into this school, Doe," Mom says, her voice gentler. "You worked very hard to get *yourself* in. They were so hesitant to take you."

"I haven't forgotten."

"I know you trust your boyfriend," Mom says.

I grimace. "He's not—we aren't—"

Dad frowns. "Did something happen?"

I shake my head. "No. I mean—yeah, I trust him."

"But we know nothing about him, or his family," Mom finishes.

"They're nice people, Mom. I wouldn't have gone if I felt uncomfortable."

"You're not the one who gets to decide that yet, Doe," Mom says. "You're seventeen years old. And I'd like to think you'd consult us even when you're in college."

"His family is perfectly normal."

"That's not what I've heard," Mom says. "When I was in school, there were all sorts of rumors about that family. And from what I know about Jeffrey Wellborn, there might be some other issues, too."

Dad holds up his hands. "We're not here to discuss rumors."

"He lost everything to gambling," Mom says. "That's not rumor—it's fact!"

"A long time ago," Dad says. "And a recovering addict shouldn't have that held against them."

"I'm not sending our daughter to the home of a gambling addict!" Mom shrieks.

Dad winces.

I bristle. "It's not like I would've gone back if they were dangerous!"

"What do you mean, gone back?" Mom asks.

I hesitate, then try to deflect. "What do you mean, what do I mean? I'm just saying, I'm a good judge of character on my own."

"I'm not sure you are a good judge of anything on your own, Dorothy Ann," Mom replies, her words dripping acid.

"Thanksgiving," Dad says quietly.

I sag. "Dad—"

He sighs and stands up, smacking his hands on his thighs a few times. "I'm going to my room for a while."

Mom looks from Dad to me and back. "What's happening here? What did I miss?"

"Dad—"

"You can't just leave while we're in the middle of reprimanding our daughter, Russ!"

He ignores her, brushing past me to the door. "I'm not ready to talk to you right now, Doe."

The door clicks shut behind him, and I slump against the desk.

Mom looks up at me. "What just happened? What's he talking about?"

"He let me go to Gemma's for Thanksgiving . . ."

"I know that," Mom says. "What's he so mad about?"

I chew my lip, grimacing. "I may not have . . . actually . . . gone to Gemma's."

"Well," Mom says stiffly, her expression hardening, "one more infraction to add to your growing list. I don't see why I have to be the one left to deal with it."

"I told him Gemma was having a hard time," I admit, burning with shame. "After coming out this summer. And that she wanted me there . . . for support."

Mom lets out a measured breath. "Oh, Doe."

I cover my face with my hands. "I'm so lost, Mom. Every time I think I can't dig myself any deeper into this hole, I manage to find an even bigger shovel. And I'm worried I won't ever be able to climb out of it."

The sheets rustle, and then fingers close around my wrists, dragging my hands from my face.

Mom's expression has softened. "Doe," she says, pulling me into her arms, "my girl. I promise you, there are very few holes you can't climb out of if you work hard enough. But digging is easy. Climbing is the real challenge."

I wrap my arms around her. "Does Dad hate me?"

She chuckles. "Your dad couldn't hate his worst enemy, least of all his daughter. He's the kindest man I've ever met."

I pull back. "Then why'd you leave him?"

Mom frowns, reaching one hand up to smooth my hair back from my face. "I never left. We both wanted this. He's kind, but he has faults—the same as anyone. Sometimes you're like two puzzle pieces that fit perfectly. And sometimes you never fit to begin with, but anything can fit for a little while when forced. And other times you fit but then life happens, and like waterlogged puzzle pieces, we change, and fitting together gets harder, and sometimes it becomes impossible."

"Which one were you and Dad?"

"I like to think we fit together once," Mom says. "We were very happy for a while. Especially when we had you." She smiles and gives me a squeeze. "Even though you've given us a lot of trouble since then."

"Not always on purpose," I say, leaning into her.

"I'd hope never on purpose," she says, giving me a look.

I pretend to be very interested in a button on my shirt. "So how do you know if you fit for real? How do you know you aren't forcing it?"

I try not to think of Wells.

"Sometimes you don't," Mom says. "People aren't that simple. There are no sure things in life—not when it comes to the stuff that matters."

"That's kind of a bummer."

"Sure. But sometimes it can be fun. I had a lot of fun with your father when we were together."

"The end wasn't so fun."

"No, it wasn't," Mom says. "But I got a lot out of our marriage. The biggest loss was how you felt after the divorce. And during. We never wanted to hurt you."

"Yeah, I'm learning that lesson, too." I pick at some lint on my jeans so I don't have to look at her. "That we can end up doing damage even if we don't intend to."

Mom's expression creases with concern. "I am sorry we put you through that."

I look away. "I thought you were mad at me. For making you stay."

"Dorothy," Mom says, "I was never mad at you. Not once.

I should have talked to you more. I shouldn't have tried to leave. The thing is, sometimes you get so unhappy, all you can see is yourself. And I have a tendency to get a bit single-minded in my mission. You come by that naturally."

I sniffle, shooting her a watery smile.

Mom brushes a hand over my hair. "But my unhappiness wasn't about you—that was about me. I was only ever worried about you. Everything that happened at that school . . . We should have pulled you out sooner. You were dealing with the consequences of our actions."

"I don't think how people acted at school was a consequence," I say, shaking my head. "Some people are just mean. If they'd found out Dad is bisexual while you were still together, they would have bullied me then, too. It wasn't the divorce, and Dad's sexuality isn't an action. It's a state of being. If they'd bullied someone for their skin color, we wouldn't call it an action and consequence. We'd call it hate. That's what this was, too."

Mom smiles a little. "A mature answer."

"From an immature baby," I say.

Mom laughs, pulling me in for a hug. "You are capable of maturity, Doe." She squeezes me tight, resting her chin atop my head, buried in my curls. "You just have to find a way to work through that tunnel vision of yours."

"I know."

Mom pulls back. "Give your father some time. He'll warm up, and then you can apologize."

I nod.

"But don't think you won't be punished," she says, her voice turning stern. "You lied twice."

"I know. But I have detention twice a week and can't leave campus for the foreseeable future. So, maybe that's all the grounding I need?"

Mom hums. "Maybe, but I think we'll come up with something else anyway, to really exert our parental power."

I groan. "Mom, please."

"Oh, Doe, don't whine. You were doing so well."

I huff and flop onto the bed.

"No pouting, either."

I put on a bland, empty smile. Like I've been lobotomized.

"Much better."

My parents aren't staying long and plan to leave tomorrow morning before my classes start. My window to apologize to Dad is closing rapidly, so after a dinner of Chinese takeout with Mom, I head down to Dad's room to see him.

He looks tired when he answers the door. He doesn't open it wide enough for me to come in, and he crowds the doorway like I'm not welcome.

"Doe," he says.

"Dad," I say with a tight, apologetic smile. "Can I come in?"

He hesitates—not long, but long enough that I notice. It stings, but I deserve it.

"Okay," he says, stepping aside to let me in.

His room is messier than Mom's—his bed unmade, clothes spilling out of his suitcase, nightstand cluttered with bottles of water, electronics, and tangled cords.

"I know you probably need a little more time and space," I tell him, wringing my hands. "But we don't really have time, and we'll have nothing but space once you're gone."

He sits heavily on the edge of the bed, like it's taken all his strength to stand until now.

Unlike Mom's room, which had one big bed, Dad's room has two smaller beds, so I sit on the one that's still made across from him. It gives a feeling of two players standing on either side of a tennis net, but I don't know where else to go.

I've never felt this awkward with my dad.

"I'm sorry I lied," I say, because it's what needs to come first.

Dad's mouth tightens into a thin line.

"I know apologizing when I've been caught doesn't hold a lot of weight. I hated lying to you in the first place—I want you to know that."

"Then why did you, Doe? Why not ask?"

"Because you would've said no?"

"Probably. But what was so important that you needed to be with your boyfriend instead of your family? Why would it have been so bad not to go?"

"It's a long story."

"You'll have to explain it to me," he says. "So I can understand."

"I don't think there's any excuse good enough for lying," I reply. "Not for the lie I chose. I used something against you that I knew would work because I needed a sure thing."

"*Why*, though?"

"Because I promised I'd be there. And I thought if I didn't go, everyone would find out my secret. And in the moment, that seemed more important than being honest with you."

Dad frowns. "Your secret? What—" He stops, realization dawning. "Your extra year?"

It's funny that he calls it that. It's the most diplomatic way of saying that I failed eighth grade. That after they pulled me out of St. Aloysius, my grades weren't salvageable.

I spent the next year being homeschooled and going to therapy. Retaking my eighth grade classes. Learning coping mechanisms for my anger.

The divorce was not easy on me, and my classmates were even worse. I was fighting for what I thought were all the right reasons.

And maybe they were. The kids at St. Aloysius weren't kind. It wasn't uncommon to hear a racial slur in the halls, and even less uncommon to hear a homophobic slur aimed at my dad.

But then fighting was all I could think about, and my grades slipped, and suddenly the only blessing I had was that I'd been bumped into kindergarten early, so redoing a year wouldn't put me behind my peers. I'd start high school with other kids my age.

I was held back a year, but no one would ever know.

Especially not when Weston agreed to take me, and I wouldn't have to start high school with any kids who knew me.

It's the one thing my friends don't know—the one thing that now, other than my family and the administration, only Wells knows.

But even though it's no secret with my parents, it's still embarrassing to talk about.

"Yeah." I nod. "My extra year."

"Why would you think that? Are you being blackmailed?"

I wave him off. "No, no, nothing like that."

Although I did accuse Wells of the same thing. But I know Wells better now. He wouldn't have told. Even if he thought he would have, when it came down to it, he wouldn't have gone through with it.

"Doe," Dad says, leaning forward to rest his elbows on his knees. "What's going on?"

"This year kind of got away from me," I say, my throat tightening. "I didn't mean to make so many wrong choices, or to hurt so many people. It's just—Weston has been such a haven for me. I don't want to see it change. I don't want it to be so different that it can't be for some other girl what it's been for me."

Dad gets up to come sit beside me. My throat feels swollen with the effort I've made holding back tears, but when he puts his arm around me, it all spills out. I grab onto him with both arms and cry.

"I've really messed up, Dad," I say through my tears. "With my friends, with Wells, with school, and you."

Dad hushes me, rubbing my back. "You haven't messed things up with me, Doe. I'm your father. I'm here no matter how bad your mistakes are. That's what family is."

I sniffle. "Even though I did something terrible?"

"You apologized," he says. "I believe you're sorry."

"I was sorry as soon as I did it." I swipe at my cheeks. "Even before I did it, I was sorry I did it."

He smiles a little, smoothing his hand down my back. "I forgive you."

I bury my face against his shoulder, crying harder.

Dad pulls some tissues from the box on the nightstand and presses them into my hand.

"Do you want to sleep here tonight?" he asks.

"I don't know if that's allowed."

He gives me a look. "Doe, I'm your father. What I say goes."

I give a little laugh. "I don't know if I should. I'm on thin ice. I don't want Cotesmore to change her mind."

Dad sighs. "We'll talk to her. It sounds like some time with your parents could be just what you need."

Dad makes a call, but it's not to school—instead it's to Mom, who shows up at the door a few minutes later in her pajamas and a fluffy robe, and my suitcase in hand.

"Well, hello," she says, parking my suitcase inside the door.

Dad goes back to his bed and takes a seat while Mom comes over and puts an arm around me, pulling me into her side.

"I spoke to your headmistress," she says. "You can stay the night with us as long as you're on time for class tomorrow."

I wrap my arms around her and squeeze. "Thank you."

I go into the bathroom to change into my pajamas, and when I come back, Mom has settled under the covers in the second bed.

"Are we . . . all staying in here?" I ask in surprise.

Mom gives me a look. "You think I'm gonna be the odd man out in my room by myself? I don't think so." She pats the spot beside her. "Get in here."

I pretend to hate it for a second, but I can't even make it convincing. There's something super comforting about climbing into bed next to my mom.

She wraps me up in her arms. Dad crunches on a snack bag of chips and flips through the channels.

And for one night, even though my parents are still divorced, and my friends are mad at me, and I've probably screwed up everything with Wells forever—not to mention my probationary status at school—things feel almost normal.

CHAPTER
TWENTY-ONE

As it turns out, leaving campus isn't much of a problem. With Wells and me not speaking, and my friends and me not speaking, my schedule is pretty clear. It gives me a lot of time to catch up on my classes.

Tutoring isn't so bad, either.

The only real problem is detention. Mr. Tully seems too pleased to have free rein over me for two hours a week.

Our first two detention sessions, he had me cleaning in the Wellness Center. The first day, I mopped the track. The second day, I put away all the aerobics platforms and got the locker rooms ready for an upcoming basketball game.

Tully is back to being overly friendly.

"I want you to know," he said to me in the locker room on that second day, "I think this is a little extreme. Keeping you on campus would be enough. Even one detention a week. But twice a week is a bit much." He glanced at me with a conspiratorial smile. "Although I'll deny saying that if you mention it to anyone."

I gave him a tight smile, thinking he'd probably deny a lot of things he's said to girls in this school if they ever repeated them.

I see my friends in class, and I catch glimpses of the Well-born boys on social media. Tonight, after my fifth detention and my third week back after the forged pass debacle, I lie in bed and scroll through their accounts on my phone. Alex puts up a video of Three eating a massive slice of pizza at Mr. Dino's; Three records a short clip of Biers cracking a hard-boiled egg on his forehead at breakfast; Christian posts a picture of Wells looking back at him over the top of a paperback copy of *The Hobbit*.

I imagine my romance novels, still wrapped in their bag, tucked away somewhere secret—the bottom of his closet, or under his bed.

Somewhere he won't even think about them.

And I wonder if that's where he's tucked all thoughts of me, too.

"So, this is where you're spending your time these days."

I look up from my notes and frown.

Virginia stands over my table in the library, holding a stack of books.

"Mind if I sit?" she asks, motioning to the empty spot beside me.

I blink at her. "Are you on glue?"

She grins and drops into the seat next to me. "No."

"I saw your new zine. Nice one."

It went out last week. Luckily, I emerged unscathed. After my friend group imploded, there hasn't been much for Virginia to attack.

Especially now that Jade occasionally sits with Virginia's friends in the dining hall.

Shawn, Sumi, and Gemma are still a unit of sorts, although sometimes I see Shawn hanging with girls from the softball team instead.

It's hard to think about, so I try not to. Too weird. Too unreal.

I mostly sit alone, which should shock no one.

Virginia flips open one of her books and pulls her laptop out of her bag. "I'm not going to admit to that, no matter how many times you suggest it."

"Smart." I turn back to my work. I'm not supposed to be socializing. The librarian has her eye on me. Since my tutor had to bail this afternoon, I'm doing supervised studying.

"I wanted to apologize to you," Virginia says as she boots up her computer, her gaze focused on the screen.

I swivel to face her. "Excuse me?"

She smiles a little. "Surprised? I heard about your"—she pauses, weighing her options—"conversation with Beth. She's . . . not the easiest."

"She's a bitch."

Virginia shoots me a reproachful look. "I don't like that word."

"I like it when it fits."

"Beth is intense. She's extremely loyal to her friends and her cause. And she's protective of me."

"It doesn't seem like you need protecting."

She smiles. "I don't. But neither do you, and yet your friends are—well, were—" She winces, and I hate the pity I see there. "Your friends take care of each other, too."

I shrug. I guess it's true, but I'm not a part of that anymore.

"Anyway, I heard what she called you."

"A dictator?"

Virginia nods. "And I don't think that, for the record. I get why you did what you did. And why you feel the way you feel."

I set down my pen, done even pretending like I'm studying. "Awfully big of you. Do you expect me to apologize back?"

"You haven't done anything to me," Virginia replies.

"I've been a little mean."

Virginia shrugs. "So have I. But I don't want your apology if you aren't sorry."

"And I don't want yours," I say. "Not on Beth's account. She probably isn't sorry."

"Maybe *apology* was the wrong word," says Virginia. "I just wanted to make it clear that, for what it's worth, I respect you."

I shoot her a look of utter disbelief. "You've got a funny way of showing it."

She has the decency to look sheepish. "Maybe I didn't at first. And maybe I needed to take a step back and consider every side before I spoke and acted. But maybe you did, too."

"Wow, *apology* really was the wrong word."

She cracks a smile. "I think you and I are more similar than we might have expected in the beginning. And whatever the zine says—and whoever wrote it—I'm sure they didn't mean you're a dictator. Just that there are a lot of perspectives to consider, and we might not all agree with each other. Whoever wrote it must have wanted to make sure that the girls who want the school to go coed know they aren't alone, even if this hasn't been the side that's yelling the loudest."

"You're yelling louder now."

Virginia smiles. "I guess so. But Weston is important to me, too, you know. I won't act like I understand what it means to you, but I know you want what's best for us. And even if we don't agree on what that is, I hope you realize that's all I want, too. I want anyone who comes to Weston to feel happy and safe. The same way I do. The same way you do."

I won't lie and say I enjoy feeling seen like this by Virginia. But it's weirdly comforting to have someone understand me, even if it's her.

Even if we don't agree.

I hesitate, then pull back my shoulders and say, "I guess I'm sorry, too."

Virginia chuckles. "You guess?"

"Well, I am sorry about some stuff and not about other stuff. Mostly I'm sorry if I made anyone think that I don't want Weston to be a place for everyone. I should have considered all sides. I got hung up on the students we have here who don't identify as a single gender, or who didn't always identify as the one they are now, and I thought that meant we were doing it right."

Virginia hums. "Some single-gender schools are trying to create new policies to be more open. But why should anyone have to wait for that?"

I think of what Jade said, the words that roll around inside my head anytime things get even a little bit quiet.

Who am I to say everything should stay exactly the way it is just because it was always perfect for me?

"I never wanted Weston to be exclusionary." I wince at the look Virginia shoots my way. "Okay, I did, but not like that. I wanted Weston to be for everyone. Everyone except . . . Winfield boys."

Virginia nods. "I know."

"You do?"

"Yeah. I get who you are at the center. It might've taken me a minute to figure you out completely—"

"I doubt you've figured me out completely. Even I haven't figured me out completely."

She smiles. "Well, I'm making progress."

I can't decide if I like that or not.

She clicks at her laptop and pulls up a blank document. "So, is it okay if I sit here?"

I glance toward the librarian's desk. She looks up at the same time, and her gaze flicks from me to Virginia and back.

I hold up my notebook and mime zipping my lips.

She smiles a little and nods, giving me the okay.

"My warden says yes," I tell Virginia, turning back to my work.

Virginia, who watched the whole exchange go down, lets out a low chuckle. "Wow, the rumors weren't exaggerated. You really are on house arrest."

"Major," I say.

"How's your boyfriend taking that?"

I clear my throat and duck my head. "Fine, since I don't have a boyfriend."

I can practically feel her choosing her next words, and sure enough, it isn't long before she speaks.

"Doe, is everything . . . okay? With you?"

I don't look up. "I really shouldn't be talking."

And Virginia, thankfully, lets it drop.

Even though I've buckled down and turned in a few college applications, I'm required to attend Weston's annual college information event. For most seniors, it's a way to narrow down their options once their acceptance letters start rolling in—if they haven't already.

But for someone like me, it's a way to figure out if there are any colleges left that I can apply to—rolling admissions and late-deadline schools I haven't found yet. I'm like the juniors, here to find my future.

To make matters slightly more uncomfortable, the college

information event is another merger test, this time held on the Winfield campus.

It's the first time I've left my campus in weeks, and it feels strange to do it only to cross the few hundred feet between our schools.

Their version of our Wellness Center is called a Sports Complex. There's a weight room; treadmills, ellipticals, stationary bikes, and rowing machines; an ice arena for the Winfield hockey team; and an indoor track similar to ours running around the perimeter of the basketball court. Even their bleachers are nicer.

I feel a small swell of anger imagining how much money must be poured into Winfield sports programs every year, and how little our donations are likely to compare. It reminds me of what Cotesmore said at the beginning of the year—could Weston survive without Winfield's money?

Will the Weston girls have access to this facility next year?

I shouldn't care. It's not my problem. Yet, I can't seem to let go of my sour feelings.

The college booths are set up on the basketball court, and the nets have been folded up overhead.

I'm alone, as usual, and I'm not expecting to see anyone I know—or at least not anyone I'm trying to avoid.

Which is why I'm so surprised when I turn away from the Clemson setup and spot Wells standing a few booths away.

He's with Christian, which makes sense, because Christian is a junior. But he's also holding a stack of pamphlets, which doesn't track. Wells finished applying to college ages ago. He only had a handful of schools he was even interested in.

Whether he's gotten any acceptances back, I wouldn't know. I'm no longer privileged to those details.

Christian glances over and spots me. He opens his mouth,

but I turn away. I hear my name over the noise and pick up my pace. I step around a group of girls, turn the corner, and try to lose myself in the crowd.

"Stupid, stupid, stupid," I scold myself as I make my way to the other end of the gym and duck around the line of booths.

How am I supposed to focus now?

And why does my stupid heart clench when I see his face?

I'm supposed to hate him. He wronged me. He wronged *Shawn*.

But I can't stop thinking about what Christian told me about the way Wells was raised, and how that might hurt a person, fundamentally so.

"Doe?"

I look over. Christian stands there, smiling.

"Nice try running," he says, slapping a stack of pamphlets against his palm.

"I wasn't running," I lie.

His smile widens. He holds up the pamphlets. "These are for you."

I frown as I take them from him. "What . . . ?"

"Every college here with a late admissions deadline," he says.

I flip through the stack. There aren't many options, but there are enough. Some I've already applied to.

I glance at Christian. "Thanks?"

"Oh, don't thank me. Wells did it."

I glower at him. "Don't tell me that."

"Why?"

I sigh and shrug on my coat. "Because now I have to go give them back."

Christian's face falls. "Don't do that."

But I'm already gone, weaving through the crowd. I head

for the exit, knowing he wouldn't have sent Christian to me without making an escape first.

I feel that rush of satisfaction from being right when I get outside and spot Wells ahead of me on the path.

"Hey!" I call.

He doesn't turn—doesn't even hesitate. It's almost like he didn't hear me at all.

"Seriously?" I mutter. Then, raising my voice, I yell, "Don't make me chase you, Gabriel Wellborn! You know I will!"

His step falters, and he stops.

I jog to him, and my labored breath clouds the air with white when I reach him.

"You didn't have to run," he says, his gaze darting away. "I would've waited."

"There are no guarantees with you."

Now he does look at me. "That's a little harsh, don't you think?"

"I don't know. As it turns out, I know even less about you than I thought. And that wasn't much to begin with."

He licks his lips and huffs out a breath. "Did you chase me down just to tell me off?" I start to answer, but he cuts me off. "By the way, you aren't my mother. You don't get to use my full name like I'm in trouble."

"I'll use your full name whenever I want," I say. "Gabriel, Gabriel, Gabriel, Gabriel."

He gives me a tight smile. "Okay, Dorothy. Whatever you want."

I glare at him. "Well, I can tell you what I don't want," I say, slapping the brochures in my hand against his chest. "You can keep those. And don't do me any more favors."

He puts his hands over mine, catching me there. I can feel his heart pounding through the stack. I try to pull back, but he doesn't let me.

"Don't try to be cute," I tell him. "You're the one who gave Shawn's number to Three."

"I didn't have a choice," he says, squeezing my hand. "It was the only way to stop him from telling his dad you were in his room."

"You went in my phone!"

"I didn't go in your phone. I already had Shawn's number. He just didn't know that, and I wasn't gonna let him know it was that easy."

"Well, you should have warned me!" I frown, pulling again for him to release my hand. He doesn't budge.

"I didn't need to warn you. I warned Shawn."

I freeze, blinking. "What?"

"His deal was that I give him Shawn's number and run defense, so you didn't find out. He didn't say I couldn't tell Shawn. I was good on my end of the deal."

"So Shawn *did* know he was playing her."

He slowly releases my hand, and the pamphlets litter the sidewalk between us.

"I made sure she did," he says, crouching to pick them up. "But it's not like I could stop her from liking him anyway."

He straightens, tapping the brochures together in his hand, and then grabs me by the front of my coat, pulling me closer.

"Wells—"

"Just look at them," he says, tucking the stack into the inside pocket of my coat. "Pretend someone else gave them to you."

I bite my lip.

Wells sighs and puts his hands on my cheeks. "And try not to hate me too much."

"I thought *you* hated *me*."

He frowns. "Why would you think that?"

"Outside Rotty's," I say. "And you—you said I wanted Three from the start."

He huffs out a small laugh, hanging his head. "Jeez, Doe. I didn't know I'd need to teach you the difference between hate and hurt."

He moves his hands down to my shoulders but freezes, his gaze moving past me.

"Dorothy!"

I turn, Wells's hands falling away.

Mr. Tully stands outside the doors of the Sports Complex, his expression hard. "You're supposed to be inside."

Wells lets out a measured breath behind me. "I really hate this guy."

"Yeah, well," I say, "I've got detention with him twice a week until further notice. So, I'd better stay on his good side."

Wells sucks in a breath. "You have what?"

I glance back at him briefly, surprised to find his face twisted in outrage.

I put my hand on his arm. "Maybe I can catch you up sometime."

"Meet me at Rotty's."

"Ah." I shoot him a rueful smile, backing away. "I'm grounded."

He shakes his head. "I don't—"

"Dorothy," Mr. Tully repeats, warning in his voice.

"I'm glad you don't hate me," I say to Wells.

His expression softens. "You've never been further off the mark than you were with that."

I feel a fluttering in my stomach. Clearing my throat, I tell him, "Yeah, well. Me, too. To you."

"What—?"

"Doe, I'm not gonna say it again," Mr. Tully calls.

I wince. "I have to go."

"Wait, I'll—" He starts to follow, but Mr. Tully puts out a hand.

"On your way," he says to Wells. "You were leaving, correct?"

I glance over my shoulder at Wells. He pulls his shoulders back and lifts his chin.

"I don't think you work here, correct?" Wells says.

Mr. Tully smiles, and it's the most horrible I've ever seen him look. Like he's seen a challenge he doesn't like. Like maybe strangling Wells would give him a certain kind of peace.

"On second thought," Tully says, turning to me, "we'll head back to campus. Since you've decided you're finished here. It'll be good for you to have some time to work on your college applications." He herds me down the sidewalk, back toward Wells, careful not to touch me.

Not here, where someone could see.

And when we get close enough to Wells, Tully adds, "In my office, where you can be supervised."

I take one last peek over my shoulder as we walk away.

Wells stands in the middle of the sidewalk, right where we left him—jaw clenched, eyes hard, fists curled at his sides.

I feel my nails biting into my palms, my fists squeezed tight.

And I wonder how long it will be before Tully makes a move on me.

CHAPTER
TWENTY-TWO

A late snow hits the week before spring break. The maintenance staff works hard to keep the walkways clean, but by the time I slug back to my dorm after my last class, there's snow gathered on the tops of my boots and leaking into my socks, and my face feels chapped from the wind.

I haven't braved the dorm common room in weeks, but the fireplace is roaring inside and it's almost impossible to pull myself away.

I'll only dry off for a few minutes, then I'll leave.

There are a few junior girls at a table, studying. They look up when I enter, and even though I've gotten the feeling recently that people are done talking about me, they start whispering.

I ignore them.

I strip off my coat and kick off my shoes, carrying both to the fireplace.

As soon as I come around the back of the couch, I understand the whispering. Shawn is curled up there, asleep.

I freeze.

I should leave.

But as I start to turn, she opens her eyes.

I hesitate, then put my back to her and start arranging my clothes in front of the fire. I lay my coat on the hearth, set my boots beside it, and peel off my socks. I sit on the floor and hold my socks toward the flames.

I have a million things I want to ask and tell her. It's strange, fighting with your best friend. Once the initial anger fades, all that's left is longing.

I'm too tired to be angry. I've been fighting so many battles for so long, I feel like a seasoned warrior ready to retire into obscurity in the mountains somewhere.

The truth is, I miss my friends. But I don't know where to start—who do I apologize to first? And how? And will I resent them if I don't hear an apology back?

Or am I just scared they won't accept mine?

"I heard Wells warned you. About Three."

I don't realize I'm planning to speak until I'm already doing it.

A long silence stretches out afterward, and I want to kick myself for not choosing my words more carefully. Why does it always come back to Three?

"Yeah," Shawn says at last. "He did."

I hear caution in her voice, like she's afraid a wrong word might start an argument.

"I'm not here to fight," I tell her. "I'm just curious, I guess. Why you'd give him the time of day, knowing what he was doing? Or why you didn't tell me what he was planning?"

Shawn doesn't answer right away.

I test my socks for dampness and, finding none, slide them back on my cold feet. They're warm on my skin, and even though the rest of me is damp with melted snow, my feet feel cozy.

"I know I'm not privileged to every detail of your life," I add in her silence. "I wish you would have told me, but I get why you didn't. I guess I don't get how it started, if you knew what he was doing."

There's a rustling behind me as Shawn moves, but I don't look back to see what she's doing.

"I was curious," she says. "I wanted to see what he'd try. And I wanted to get the chance to knock him down a peg myself. I never get to do that, you know? Three hardly ever looked at me when you were around."

I frown at the fire. "What?"

"You dominate every room you walk into. *Everyone* looks at you. Three was never exempt from that. I don't know if it was some weird hate-lust or what—and maybe I don't want to know if my boyfriend was into my best friend."

My heart sails. *Best friend.* Maybe all hope isn't lost.

"But I liked being in your shoes," she continues. "Getting Three's attention, stomping on his ego a little bit. It was fun. I knew what he was up to, so he could never pull one over on me." She pauses, and I can almost hear her smiling when she adds, "I guess he did in the end, though. I never would've guessed I'd end up falling for him."

I pick up my coat and shake it out. It's mostly dry.

"I'm glad you're happy," I reply. "Even if he did get the better of you in the end. I guess you got the better of him, too. I'm sure he didn't see it coming, either."

Shawn doesn't respond.

I slide my feet into my boots and shuffle away from the fire without lacing them.

"I'm sorry I didn't tell you about Wells," I say, stopping at the end of the couch. "That was a bad decision on my part. I convinced myself no one would understand why I was doing it, when the truth is, I knew everyone would understand why—you just wouldn't approve. And being right was more important to me than being honest, I guess. Even if I was the most wrong that I've maybe ever been."

Shawn blinks at me, looking stunned.

I grab my bag from the floor and heft it onto my shoulder. I'm almost to the door when my phone buzzes in my pocket.

I pause with my shoulder against the door and pull my phone out, frowning when I see the name on my screen.

"Noelle? Is everything okay?"

The sound of a soft sniffle makes every hair on the back of my neck stand on end.

"You said—you said," she says, her voice small and wobbly, "I could call you if—if—"

I stiffen. "Where are you?"

She starts crying, and I push out into the hall, making quiet, soothing noises.

"Shh, shh, it's okay. I'm coming to you, but you have to tell me where you are."

"My d-d-dorm," she says. "I came st-straight here."

There are only two lower school girls' dorms—luckily right next to each other.

I'm almost to the exit when a hand catches my elbow.

I turn, surprised to find Shawn standing behind me. She's got her coat on, and when she sees she has my attention, she smashes a wool hat down over her hair.

I give her a small nod and push out into the cold.

"Eichelberger or Bishop?" I ask Noelle.

"Bishop," says Noelle.

"Stay on the phone, okay?" I glance over at Shawn as we make our way down the walkway. "We're coming."

* * *

As it turns out, I wasn't next on Tully's list.

Noelle was.

I stayed on the phone with her the whole way to her dorm, listening to her cry while Shawn and I trekked through the snow.

Now we're sitting on her floor, drinking hot chocolate her roommate, Simone, made for us in their common room. Simone hasn't taken a sip. She has her mug clutched in one pale hand, the other twisting her long, black ponytail.

"So, he called you to his office," I repeat. "He didn't say why?"

Noelle shakes her head, clutching her mug so it half conceals her face. "He said it was—casual. A standard . . . um . . . check-in."

Shawn shakes her head. "That's bullshit."

Noelle's face darkens with a blush. "I didn't—I didn't know."

Shawn's expression softens. "*No.* No, no, no. I didn't mean you. I meant him. You aren't—you guys don't *need* to know that stuff. You haven't been here long enough to know what's normal and what isn't."

"And Tully isn't normal," I tell Noelle. "He operates differently than the other house heads. You couldn't have known. What did he say when you got there?"

Noelle swallows. "When I got there, he was, um, at his desk. And he, well, you know it's been cold, so he wears that one jacket a lot? But his office was hot. Like, *really* hot. So, he asked if I'd be uncomfortable if he took it off, and I—well, I didn't want to be rude, so I said . . . okay? But he was wearing a—you know—a tank top thing underneath. I didn't—I didn't expect that. I know arms are just arms, but—"

Shawn shakes her head. "Not on a teacher, they aren't."

"I don't know why a few extra inches of shoulder made me so . . . uncomfortable?"

I rub my forehead. "Because *he* made you uncomfortable. You didn't happen upon a teacher with his shoulders exposed. He asked if he could take his jacket off, knowing what he was wearing underneath. What did he do after that?"

"Well, I didn't want to take my coat off since he'd taken his off, but he insisted—he could tell I was hot. But I took so long putting it off, he came to my side of his desk to help me out of it. Like, if I'd just done it myself, would he have bothered?"

"Yes," Shawn and I answer in unison.

We exchange a glance, and she reaches over and squeezes my hand.

Noelle's expression tightens with anxiety.

"This is as far as we got," Simone says to me, putting an arm around Noelle's shoulders.

Noelle's tears start again, and she covers her face with her hands.

"You don't have to tell us," I say. "Not right now—not ever, if you don't want to."

Noelle lets out a pained, keening noise that makes every hair on my body stand up straight.

I clench my fists, my nails digging sharply into my palms.

"I want to," Noelle says. "I promised myself I would, as soon as it happened. I ran all the way back here, and I swore I'd tell everyone, but I just—I just—" She whimpers, leaning into Simone. "I feel so *stupid*."

"No," we all say at once.

Simone looks at Shawn and me with a small, relieved smile.

"You're not stupid," Shawn says. "He's a teacher. He's in a place of authority over you. Whatever he did, and whatever you did or didn't do, it doesn't matter. You didn't do anything wrong."

Noelle is trembling.

"We should stop," I say. "You can always tell us later."

"No!" Noelle wails, dropping her hands. "No, I told myself I'd do it. I can *do this.*"

I slide across the floor and put my hands over hers in her lap. "Noelle. You don't have to prove anything to anyone right now. Not even yourself. If it's too hard, that's okay. We have time to hear this story."

"But you knew," Noelle says, blinking up at me with big, watery eyes, pupils blown wide. "When you saw me in his office. You warned me. That means I'm not the first person he's hurt. Right?"

I hesitate, glancing at Shawn.

Shawn sighs. "No one has ever really come forward. All we've heard are rumors."

"I don't want there to be another girl after me," Noelle says. "I don't want someone to go through this, or worse. When he took off my coat, he put his hand on the back of my neck—"

She breaks off with a shudder.

Simone reaches out, placing her hand palm up on the floor near Noelle's knee. Noelle takes it and squeezes until her knuckles go white.

She drags in a breath. "He slid his hand down my back. And then he touched my face and said I'm so—so—*pretty.* And mature for my age."

I grimace.

"And he asked me if I know how pretty I am, and I didn't know what to say—I didn't know how to answer. And he told me if I don't believe how pretty I am to look down, and I'm an idiot—a stupid, *stupid* idiot who did what he said, and he—he had—he was—he had a boner. And he said—he said—'I wouldn't be like this if you weren't so beautiful.'"

I put my head in my hands. "Jesus. *Jesus.*"

"He didn't—he didn't make you—you didn't—" Shawn stops and starts, stops. She lets out a long breath.

"No," Noelle says, answering Shawn's unasked question. "He didn't do anything else. He went back behind his desk. And he asked me how things are going. Told me to come to his office anytime I need something. That we're friends. And . . . he'd see me soon." She shudders. "Like a promise. Like he'd be watching me. Like he's *been* watching me."

"That sick fuck," Simone says.

I glance at her in surprise.

She shrugs at me like, *What?*

I smile at her.

Shawn takes a deep breath. "Okay. We need to go to Cotesmore about this."

"Won't she want proof?" Noelle asks, her voice small.

Simone gives her a reassuring squeeze.

"That's not your job to provide," Shawn says. "He's a teacher. Your word should be enough to launch an official investigation, at which point I bet girls will start coming out of the woodwork to speak against him."

"What if we spread the word?" says Simone. "Start getting it around to the other girls that we need people to come forward with their stories?"

I consider it. "We could get statements. They don't have to tell their stories in person, or even put their names to them.

They can just write them out if they want to, and we'll hand them over to the administration."

"Do we trust the administration to handle it?" Simone asks. "Y'all have been here way longer than we have. Noelle can't be the first girl to come forward like this."

Shawn and I exchange a glance. We're thinking the same thing. The number of girls we've heard whispers about. The ones still here, the ones who graduated. The ones who lasted the rest of that year, or who transferred. The girls who were here one day and gone the next.

Does Cotesmore know?

Simone sits up on her knees. "Is there anyone at this school who knows how to make a scene better than you do?" she asks me. "We don't want to waste this by handing Noelle's story over and hoping for the best. Clearly that hasn't worked so far."

"I want to make it something they can't ignore," Noelle says, swiping her fingers over her tearstained cheeks. "We can't let another girl get swept under the rug."

Shawn takes a deep breath. "Okay. What do you have in mind?"

Noelle and Simone look at me.

And I realize Shawn is asking *me*.

What do I have in mind?

"Well," I say, "we're gonna need help."

I double wrap my scarf as I pace from one end of the rooftop to the other, hands stuffed deep in the pockets of my heavy coat.

We've been known to visit the Kingdom in winter, but not often. There seems to be nowhere on campus colder than this rooftop, even with the furniture acting as a buffer.

The snow hasn't melted yet, and I crunch through it in my boots, trying not to let my anxiety get the best of me.

They'll come. They have to come.

The door creaks open, and Shawn pokes her head out.

I stop pacing and stare at her.

She shoots me a relieved smile and pushes out onto the rooftop.

Gemma, Sumi, and Jade file out behind her.

Some more reluctantly than others. For instance, Jade stops very close to the door, like she's ready to bolt if she needs to.

"I know you probably don't want to see me," I say, wringing my hands together. "I've messed up big-time. I owe you a lot of apologies for the things I've done and how I've acted this year. Whether you forgive me or not is your choice, and I'll respect it. But our feelings aside, I need your help, because . . ." I glance at Shawn.

She nods, turning to the others. "Something more important is going on."

"So, you two . . ." Sumi points a finger between Shawn and me. "You're good?"

Shawn hesitates.

My stomach twists in the silence. "I'm . . . trying. I deserve everything I'm getting, but . . . you guys are my best friends. Everything I fought for this year, and all the stuff I did—I said it was for Weston. But Weston isn't anything without you. You're what made it what it is for me. I've been fighting all this time to keep it exactly how it is, not realizing that as soon as we graduate, there's no going back to how it was for me. It'll only be that for some other girl if she finds friends like you."

Gemma sniffles, turning her head away, like I won't know she's crying if I can't see her tears.

I blink against the wetness in my own eyes and let out a shuddering breath. "But Weston also needs to be safe. For the girls coming in, and the ones already here. Whether the merger happens or not, this thing with Tully has gone on too long."

Jade edges closer. "What brought this on? You just *decided* you want to take down Tully? Out of nowhere?"

"No," I say. "He came on to a freshman. She told me—us"—I motion to Shawn—"everything tonight."

Sumi swears.

"I'm sorry," I say to Jade. "I'm sorry I put you in a position you didn't want to be in, fighting for something you didn't believe in."

Jade frowns. "I did believe in it. I didn't want the merger. Until I did."

I nod. "Well, I'm sorry I made myself a person you felt like you couldn't be honest with once your feelings changed. Maybe it was because I wasn't honest, either, and you could feel that."

I glance at Gemma, who watches me from under her hair.

"I'm sorry that I tricked you into lying for me, about things that should never be lied about," I tell her. "I took advantage of you, and I'm sorry. For what it's worth, I told my dad everything. I mean, I got caught, so don't give me too much credit. I *had* to tell him everything."

Her mouth pulls in a soft smile.

"But I apologized to him, too."

Gemma gives a small nod.

"I'm sorry for hurting all of you. I'm sorry for lying. I held you to a standard I could never have met and got mad at you if you didn't meet it, either. I didn't give you enough credit."

Jade takes a deep breath and sweeps around Sumi and

Gemma, moving closer to me than anyone else has—even Shawn.

"So, what do you need from us?"

For the first time in hours, I feel like I can take a full breath.

"The girl he went after, Noelle, doesn't want to go to the administration," I say. "She doesn't trust that they'll do what needs to be done."

"She thinks they've been cleaning up after him?" Jade asks.

I nod.

"Even Cotesmore?" says Gemma.

I hesitate. "I mean, if it was the administration, she'd be included. Right?"

Gemma's expression crumples. "Why would she do that?"

"We don't know anything for sure," Shawn says. "But Noelle won't go to Cotesmore with what happened. She asked us to help." She glances at me and smiles. "To do what we do best."

"What, make a scene?" Sumi jokes.

I smile.

"Oh, shit," Sumi says, laughing. "For real?"

"It can't be a setup," I say. "They have to take us seriously, so it can't look like we tricked him."

"Then what do we do?" Jade asks. "How do you prove a creep's a creep without having him caught in the act?"

"Well, we need to get the word out to the rest of the girls," I say. "Get written statements from anyone who had a bad experience with Tully. They don't have to sign it if they don't want to. But we need as many accounts as we can get to prove we aren't making it up."

"How's that different from taking it to the administration?" asks Jade.

Shawn smiles. "Well, we'd discussed something. But I had a thought."

I glance at her. "Okay . . . ?"

"It'll be here any minute," she says, glancing at her phone.

"Your thought?" Sumi asks.

Shawn elbows her, and Sumi laughs.

Down below, someone whistles.

Shawn heads for the door. "I'll be right back."

"What—"

"This is sus," Sumi says, creeping to the edge of the roof to peek over.

"Extremely," Gemma says.

Shawn returns a few minutes later, pulling the rooftop door open wide.

And for the first time in any history I know, Winfield boys spill out onto the rooftop, invading the Kingdom. Christian Page, the Biermann brothers, Alex Hyun, and Zamir Salahuddin.

Wells.

And of course—Three, leading the pack. He grins at me and holds up a large bundle of cloth.

"I heard you might be needing this back."

CHAPTER
TWENTY-THREE

Even with help, this is the largest-scale plan we've ever made, and it takes a few days to get things in order—time we don't really have with spring break looming.

We manage to drone through the days without alerting the administration, all while plans are whispered between classes and over meals, notes slipped between textbook pages in the library and pressed into hands in the halls.

There are carpools to the closest bulk store, which I watch caravan out from my dorm window. We hold meetings in the Kingdom, with Winfield boys phoned in from their campus.

My nerves build until I'm left pacing in my dorm with only seven hours to go.

There is no way I'll sleep tonight.

A soft, quick knock at my door startles me, and I lunge for it. I expect Shawn, or even Jade or Gemma or Sumi, maybe one of the younger girls with a question about tomorrow.

Which is why I gasp when I open my door to a hooded figure in all black. I feel a rush of fear that quickly ebbs when I notice the casual way he's leaning against my doorframe.

He pushes his hood back a little and grins at me.

"Oh my god, you idiot!" I hiss.

I grab Wells by the front of his jacket and haul him into my room, peeking out into the hall to make sure he wasn't spotted.

Then I shut my door quickly but quietly and double-check the lock.

When I turn around, he's lounging against my desk, idly poking through the stack of homework next to my computer.

"Hey, stop it!" I rush over and smack his hand. "That's nosy."

"So this is the Museum of Doe," he says, turning away from the papers to pick through my cup of pens and pull open one of my desk drawers. I reach out to stop him, but he gives me a look. "I know you snooped in my room. This is only fair, don't you think?"

I hesitate, then retreat, glowering at him. He's right. Like I could have resisted poking through his stuff while unsupervised.

But I feel exposed with him seeing my room for what it is—messy, with dishes stolen from the dining hall stacked up by my bed and my shoe collection spilling haphazardly out of my closet. My bed is unmade, and my cheap but cute peach-printed sheets are fraying at the edges. My bed frame is strung with battery-powered twinkle lights. It used to look like some kind of deranged, glowing beast, but most of the batteries have died, and I haven't gotten around to changing them.

The wall above my desk is plastered with printouts of my favorite news articles, like a lost dog finding its way home after eight months, a man exonerated by DNA after being in prison for fourteen years for a murder he didn't commit, and a girl who started making feminine-hygiene bags for homeless shelters.

"What'd you find out about me?" he asks, tossing me a lopsided smile. "From my room."

"You like to read," I reply dully.

He shoots me a dissatisfied look. "Boring. What else?"

"You have, like, the most Counting Crows shirts I've ever seen in one closet."

He lets out a sharp laugh, and I rush forward to cover his mouth.

"You're gonna get us caught, and then we'll both be expelled."

He puts his hand over mine and drags it down to his chest. His heart thumps steadily under my palm.

"You don't seem nervous," I say, tugging my hand back.

"Only that you'll throw me out before morning," he says.

I freeze, my heart rate kicking up. His gaze flicks over my face, and anticipation zings through me.

"You owe me the rest of your books," Wells says at last, and the tension cracks.

My face scrunches. "What?"

"You said you only gave me half of the books I wanted, and I could have the other half when I finished. I finished. You owe me the rest."

"You—I'm sorry, you read them?"

"You're forgiven," he says with a grin. "And yes."

I scowl at him. "Are you five?"

He chuckles, and somehow my insult works as an invitation, because he slides off his coat and tosses it over the back of my desk chair.

"If I'm five, I probably shouldn't have read those books to begin with." He drops his chin and gives me a look from under his lashes. "There's some pretty sexy stuff in there."

My mouth goes desert dry.

He smirks. "I didn't know you were reading so much porn."

My jaw drops. "It's not *porn*." I reach out and smack him in the chest. "They're novels that happen to contain some smut."

"Smut," he repeats like he's testing the word out.

I shake my head. "I'm not—I'm *not* having this conversation with you."

He shrugs, going to lean against the wall so we're facing each other from opposite sides of the room.

My brain cannot compute that he's here, in my dorm. A place where no boy has ever been. With his flushed cheeks and cold-pink nose, messy hair damp with melted frost, looking like a goddamn winter prince who walked straight out of a novel.

"So," he says, looking a little less sure of himself, "can I stay?"

I don't want him to go, no matter how nervous I am.

I nod.

He hesitates. "Could you say it? Out loud?"

I look at him. "Yes. You can stay."

He beams at me. Then he leans down to slide off his shoes.

"What are you doing?" I ask, feeling panicky again.

"Getting comfortable?" he says. He kicks his shoes aside and crosses the room to me. "What are you doing?"

"Getting nervous?"

He flinches. "Because I'm here?"

"Because I like it."

His expression softens, and he takes a small step back. "I promise I'll keep my hands to myself."

I reach out and fist my hands in his sweater. "What if I don't want you to?"

He tilts his head, watching my face.

I lean forward and kiss him.

It's a soft, slow, barely there kiss. My nose nudges against his, and our breaths mingle, and my open mouth brushes his lips. But there's too much distance between us, and I fall against him.

Wells catches me, his back hitting the wall. His arms go around my waist, and I reach up to slide a hand into his hair. I press my mouth right against his throat and feel his pulse racing under my lips.

He nudges his chin into my hair, so I pull back, and he kisses me. It's no halfway kiss. His tongue slides against mine, and his hands dip under my shirt, pressing into the small of my back. I pull at his sweater, breaking away to take in a gasping breath, and then we're kissing again, all the way across the room, until we reach my bed.

I slide back against the pillows, tugging at Wells's sweater until it's over his head, half dragging his T-shirt with it. I run my hands up his bare stomach and under his shirt until Wells sits up on his knees and pulls it off.

"Oh," I squeak.

He pauses, shirt clutched in his hands. "Should I . . . put it back on?"

I shake my head, reaching for him. "Definitely not."

He grins, tossing his shirt aside as he leans back down to kiss me. His weight settling on top of me steals my breath, and I arch my neck, pulling away to take a gulp of air. But it leaves me in a rush when Wells kisses my jaw and drags his mouth down to the curve of my shoulder.

I must stop breathing altogether, because Wells pushes up onto his forearms.

"You okay?" he whispers, brushing the backs of his fingers against my cheek.

I nod slowly, reaching up to take his hand. I hold it against my cheek and close my eyes.

He rolls off me, our fingers still tangled together. I follow, turning onto my side so we're facing each other. Wells lowers his head onto the pillow beside mine. We're so close, I can only focus on one feature at a time—a freckle I've never noticed, the curve of his eyebrow, the pout of his mouth.

And the thing that's been bothering me the most rears up, begging to be set free.

"I never wanted Three."

He lowers his gaze and shifts onto his back with a sigh. "We don't have to talk about it now."

I frown and sit up, leaning over him. He won't meet my gaze.

"You caught me off guard at Rotty's," I say.

His brow pinches, and his throat moves as he swallows.

"In my head, from the start, you were someone I couldn't have. You always seemed untouchable, but Three said it first—you'd never date me. And you kind of confirmed it that first day."

He meets my gaze, his expression hard. He pushes up onto his elbows. "You know that's not what I meant."

"I do now," I say. "But this whole time, I felt safe doing and saying whatever I wanted because I knew, in the end, it wouldn't matter. Because I couldn't ruin something that would never happen anyway. I'm realistic—I don't get my hopes up for things I know I can't have."

Wells sits up, biting his lip.

"When you asked me out—outside Rotty's—I just . . . It upended everything I knew about who we were to each other. I couldn't give you an answer right away, because I'd spent months telling myself something else. That I didn't want to be with you anyway, so it didn't matter if you didn't like me back."

"Doe—"

"So to hear you say I wanted Three all along"—I huff out a sharp laugh—"no, you big idiot. I wanted *you*. Maybe not from the start, but there was never anyone else I wanted. It was no one, and then it was you."

He looks like I've knocked him sideways, mouth parted and gaze intense on my face. "And now?"

I shrug, mustering a small, nervous smile. "I let you stay, didn't I?"

Wells nods slowly, reaching out to touch my face. But he hesitates, changes direction, and reaches for my hand instead.

"What . . . ?" I ask when he clasps my hand like a hand-shake.

"Hi," he says, smiling. "I'm Gabriel Wellborn. I turn eighteen in two weeks. I like reading, chess, and baseball. I'm going to Oberlin in the fall, and I haven't declared a major yet, but I'm thinking history. I have a truly insane family and a weird upbringing that I'm still working through. And I hope none of that scares you off, because I have a feeling you might be the best person I've ever met."

"Gabriel," I repeat, biting back a grin.

"Most people call me Wells. But I don't think I'd mind if you called me Gabriel once in a while." His smile widens. "In fact, I might like it a little too much, so maybe you should only do it on special occasions."

"Like when you're in trouble?"

"Sure, or like"—he slides closer and puts his hand on the back of my neck, stopping only when we're centimeters apart—"now."

I nudge my nose against his. "Okay . . . Gabriel."

He kisses me, long and slow and smiling. His teeth drag at my lower lip until I whimper, pushing myself closer.

We collapse against my pillows again, the frenzy from earlier drained away. It's lazy and unhurried, like we just realized we have all night.

All night.

Wells props himself up on his elbow, studying my face as he brushes his fingers over the sliver of skin below my belly button.

"I hope this isn't too forward," he says as he drags his fingertips up over my waist, pushing my shirt higher as he skims across my stomach and into the dip of my belly button.

I giggle, squirming. "No, it's okay," I answer breathlessly. "Plus, I have a jumbo box of condoms just in case."

Wells stills, then drops his head into the curve of my shoulder.

"I'm only kind of joking," I say.

He huffs out a laugh against my neck. "I was curious what you did with them," he says, lifting his head to look at me.

I roll onto my side and slide open my bedside drawer. Wells peers over my shoulder.

The box takes up most of the space inside the drawer, along with a lip balm, two paperback romance novels, and a small candle that is definitely against the dorm fire code.

Wells groans, falling back against my pillows. "*Why* do you have them right there?"

"I don't know." I slide the drawer closed and roll over to face him. "I guess I couldn't think of where else you're supposed to keep your jumbo box of condoms."

"It probably depends if you're using them or not."

I swallow and shoot him a quick glance from under my lashes.

He takes in a slow breath. "Come here," he says, pulling me into his arms.

I settle in, his arm around my shoulders and mine draped across his waist.

"We can stay like this," he whispers. "You should sleep."

"You come in here and kiss me within an inch of my life and now you want me to sleep?" I look up at him, resting my chin on his shoulder.

"Within an inch of your life?" He grins down at me. "Wow, I'm good."

I dig my knuckle into his side, and he laughs.

I settle back down beside him, and he reaches over me to turn off my bedside lamp.

"Sleep," he says.

"Hey, Gabriel?"

He groans. "Wow, I really like that too much."

I laugh into his shoulder.

"Yes?" he says.

"I'm Dorothy," I whisper, tracing the lines of his collarbone with my fingers. "You can call me Doe. Pretty much always."

He chuckles.

"I like strategy games, my friends, and not much else. I have no idea where I'm going to school, or what I want to do with my life. I'm seventeen, but I was held back in eighth grade. And no one knows but you—and well, my parents and the administration, but like, that's it. The thing is, what I didn't tell you, is my dad is bi. So, like, after my parents got divorced, he started dating a man, and word got around, and suddenly this thing that had been a part of my life forever was a huge deal to all these other people."

Wells lets out a long breath. "They gave you a hard time?"

"Yeah, but I think I gave them a harder time back. I was so angry. All the time. If someone even looked at me wrong, I'd be up in their face, you know? I got in a lot of fights."

"I wouldn't have told anyone," he says. "Even before this or knowing why. I talk a big game, but I couldn't have done that to you."

"I know." I flatten my hand against his chest, over his heart, and feel it thump against my palm. "As it turns out, I know exactly who you are, Gabriel Wellborn."

"Oh, yeah?"

"Yeah. That's why I'm dead sure I'm in love with you."

Wells freezes, the fingers stroking my back stilling. But his heart beats wildly under my hand.

"Yeah, well. Me, too," he says, and I can hear a smile in his voice. "To you."

I smack his chest. "Don't make fun of me."

He laughs. "I'm not—it was cute. Even though I had no idea what you meant."

"Well, now you do."

"And you know what I meant?" He rolls to face me, curling his arm around me so I'm flush against him. "That I'm dead sure I'm in love with you, too?"

"Are you?"

He rolls his head back and groans. "Completely."

"Okay," I say, grinning. "Good to know."

I kiss under his jaw, crawling up until I can reach his mouth.

"We're supposed to be sleeping," he whispers between kisses.

"It's okay," I reply, tugging my shirt over my head. "We have all night."

* * *

"I think that's everyone."

I look up at the sound of Shawn's voice, breathless and excited.

"More than we expected, too," Jade says, leaning up against the wall beside me.

Gemma crouches to tear open a box of granola bars. "I don't know how long this food will last us," she says.

"Don't be negative," Sumi says, checking her hip into Gemma's shoulder.

Gemma teeters sideways and falls on her butt. "Hey!"

Sumi grins. "Get excited, Gemmy. Look *around*!"

She motions to the gym, which is packed with girls. The floors are littered with big blue mats, sleeping bags, and dorm bedding. I spot Virginia and her friends, huddled together in the middle of the basketball court. Virginia has her duvet around her shoulders and her mouth open in a laugh.

Noelle and Simone sit nearby with a group of younger girls, and on the bleachers with their laptops are the school newspaper staffers, including Ilana Rotko.

The house prefects who showed up—admittedly only a few, but Shantel from Roseland House among them—are taking their duties seriously, making their way through the crowd of girls and passing out granola bars and prepackaged pastries.

"Wouldn't complain about some coffee," Jade says, rolling her shoulders and stretching her neck.

I groan in agreement. "I barely slept last night."

They all go still.

I glance up from the box of granola bars.

"What?" I ask when I notice Shawn's all-knowing smile.

"You barely slept," she singsongs.

Sumi smirks, tossing an arm around my shoulders. "Finally put those condoms to good use?"

I shove her away. "You're ridiculous!"

"Are we?" Jade asks dryly.

I look to Gemma for help, but she's smug and pink-cheeked.

"Just tell us," says Sumi, "above or below the waist action?"

"How do you even know I was with him last night?" I whisper-yell.

Shawn scrunches her nose. "How do you think he got in the building?"

"You let him in?"

"I might've given him my key," she says with a grin.

I cover my face with my hands and moan in embarrassment.

"That means below the waist," Sumi says to the others.

I drop my hands. "I did not!"

She sighs, shaking her head. "You got the finest Wellborn up in your dorm room for the whole night, and you didn't get below the waist action? Now I'm just disappointed in you."

She's kidding, but the word draws up a whole slew of guilt and shame.

"Hey, listen," I say to them. "I probably have a lot more I need to apologize for—maybe even stuff I haven't realized yet. But I'm really . . . grateful to you guys. For being here. For trusting me enough to do this."

Gemma gives me a smile. "You don't have to apologize forever, Doe. Your actions say more than enough."

Sumi gives me a quick squeeze. "Right," she says. "But speaking of action—"

"Let's not," I cut in, glancing at her. "Speak of action."

Sumi releases me, holding up her hands innocently.

I glance up at Shawn, and she grins.

Jade crouches beside me and grabs a granola bar. "For the record," she murmurs, tearing her granola bar open, "I love doing this shit with you."

I look over at her and smile. "Yeah?"

She tips her granola bar at me and takes a bite. "Yeah," she says as she chews. She jerks her chin toward the rest of the gym. "This is your brainchild."

I turn and survey the room. Morning light filters in through the high windows, turning the dust in the air to sparkles.

We've got about three quarters of the Weston student body in here. Not everyone was as willing to join us—the perpetual rule-followers, and the ones afraid of how it might look if their future colleges found out.

But our numbers are good. And our message is clear.

And in a little while, everyone will know it.

I grab Sumi's wrist and check her watch. "Almost time." I glance up at Shawn. "Any word from—?"

She holds up her phone. "They're starting the stream at eight."

I nod and turn to the gym.

"Jade," I say over my shoulder, "could you get their attention, please?"

Jade sticks her fingers in her mouth and lets out a long, piercing whistle.

The room quiets, heads swiveling toward us.

I cup my hands around my mouth. "The stream is starting in twenty minutes," I shout to them. "If you don't have the link, get it from a friend."

"Won't this hurt the fight against the merger?" one girl calls. "Teaming up with Winfield boys . . ." She frowns, looking unsure.

I nod. "Yeah, it probably will," I admit. "But some things are more important than stopping the merger."

Shawn reaches over and takes my hand. I squeeze hers back and smile.

"So, let's show the administration what's *really* important to us today," Shawn calls, holding my hand up in the air.

The gym explodes with cheers.

By the time everyone settles down and my friends and I find our empty spots near the doors to the lobby, the stream is starting.

Christian's face fills my screen.

"Oh," he says, grinning his million-dollar smile, "it's up."

He turns the camera away from his face and onto Three as they make their way through a building.

"Where are we headed, Three?" Christian asks.

Three smiles. "To class, of course."

"What do we have first period?"

Three checks a paper clutched in his hand. "Looks like . . . World Governments." He glances at the camera and smirks. "Sounds like a real party."

"Hey, me, too," comes a voice from off camera. My body has an instant reaction—warmth spreads through me, and my legs go all jelly-like. Thank god I'm sitting down.

Christian pans to Wells, who has dark under-eye circles and messy hair and looks completely, hopelessly blissed out.

"What a small world," Wells says to the camera, his mouth quirked in a lazy smile.

Three ducks into a classroom, and Christian and Wells follow. Wells stays slightly off camera.

"Boys, boys," my World Governments teacher, Mrs. Mc-Nabb, shouts as they invade her classroom. Desks screech as they slide into seats, calm and relaxed as though they are right where they belong.

"What are you doing here?" Mrs. McNabb demands. "This is—this is unprecedented!"

"Oh, don't worry," Three says from his spot at the front of the room. "We're supposed to be here."

"What—I don't—I don't understand," Mrs. McNabb splutters.

"Well, until this school is safe for girls, they've decided to take their classes by proxy." He pulls out a textbook for good measure—Shawn's, of course—and cracks it open on his desk. "So, where should we start?"

I push open the glass doors of the Wellness Center and step out into the cold, crisp, early-spring morning.

Down the walkway, Headmistress Cotesmore and a few members of the administration march toward us, with security bringing up the rear.

Shawn holds up her phone, filming them coming.

"Are you ready to hear our demands?" I call out to their group.

Cotesmore's mouth twists into a frown. "Doe, what is this about?" she asks, and even though she slows, no one else does. She gets caught up in the group, disappearing in their midst.

I notice Tully then, pulling ahead.

I point at him. "You better not take one more step."

He doesn't falter, which means he must know. And rather than hide away, he's made a strategic move in showing up here to face us. Like a man who has nothing to fear.

One who's done nothing wrong.

"Doe," he says, like he can reason with me—like we're pals.

"Don't you dare," I say.

Their group fans out, releasing Cotesmore. She stands beside Tully, then takes one step closer.

I steel myself against my frayed nerves. Maybe getting some sleep last night wouldn't have been such a bad idea.

"We took a vote," I say to Cotesmore. "As it turns out, we're done living our lives scared of what some *predator* might do to us next. We're tired of seeing girls hurt, ignored, and lied to. We want Mr. Tully gone."

"Doe," Cotesmore says gently, drawing closer, "let's talk about this."

"We have," I say. "*We've* talked about it." I gesture at myself, my friends, the whole crowded Wellness Center behind us. "We don't need to talk to anyone else. Enough girls have been hurt by this sick monster."

Mr. Tully's face goes red, but whether it's anger or embarrassment, I can't tell. Maybe it's both.

"That's a serious allegation," he says to me, his voice low.

I keep my eyes on Cotesmore. "I won't speak with him here."

"Mr. Tully," Cotesmore says without looking at him, "please give us a minute."

I look at him and raise my chin. The red in his face is pure anger.

"This is *slander*," he says, pointing a finger in my face.

"Mr. Tully," Cotesmore says, her tone sharp. "Now, please."

When he's gone, slinking away with tight shoulders and his hands stuffed in his pockets, Cotesmore returns her attention to me.

"We want a meeting," I tell her. "With you, the president of the board of trustees, the head of the Parents' Association, and the members of the school's faculty disciplinary committee."

Cotesmore takes a deep breath. "Okay, I'll see what I

can do. I'm sure Headmaster Pritchard would also like to be there, now that his students are involved."

"That's a great idea."

"So, I've agreed to your meeting," Cotesmore says. "Will you all come out now? And get to class?"

I laugh. "No. Why would we do that?"

"Doe, this kind of coordination will take time."

"That's fine," I reply. "We have enough food and water to last us *quite* a while in there."

"Doe—"

"Hey, Mr. Tully!" I shout, cupping my hands around my mouth.

Shawn steps back, filming me and my friends behind me.

When I see I have Tully's attention, I say, "This one's for you."

Sumi and Jade pull the strings hanging down behind us, releasing the rolled-up sheet strung between the building's drainpipe and a nearby tree. Above our heads, our banner unfurls, big and beautiful and painted red.

WESTON GIRLS TAKE NO PRISONERS

CHAPTER
TWENTY-FOUR

We meet in a faculty conference room, but there aren't enough chairs for everyone to sit. Aside from my friends, we brought Virginia. Not only because she's been vital to the plan so far, but because we took a vote of the girls in the Wellness Center, and they picked her to speak on their behalf.

We've taken up all the seats available to us, so Three, Christian, and Wells stand against the back wall. It's strange to have them at our backs instead of facing off against them, but it feels good to have them there.

Headmaster Pritchard looks exhausted. Apparently, it's been chaos on their campus, too.

Not surprising, since they took over eight hours to pull this meeting together. Even the girls in the Wellness Center are getting rowdy. We have plenty of granola bars left, but I heard there was a bidding war over a bag of M&Ms this afternoon.

It's safe to say Weston girls are not ready for a hunger strike.

"Thank you all for coming," I say once everyone is settled.

This was Virginia's idea—start off with a power move, making it sound like we summoned them here.

A few of them bristle, but none more than Roger Kresge, the president of the board of trustees. He's an average-sized, middle-aged man with a large forehead, heavy-lidded eyes, and a perpetually pink tint to his white skin.

"The behavior you girls have exhibited is appalling," he says. "The only reason I'm here is because you essentially took yourselves hostage and disrupted the educations of your classmates who did not participate, as well as our neighbors." He motions to Headmaster Pritchard.

I clear my throat. "Thank you for your input, Mr. Kresge. Jade, could you tell me, how long has Mr. Kresge been the president of the board here at Weston?"

"Five years and eight months," Jade answers without missing a beat.

I fold my hands on the table, smiling at Mr. Kresge. "And how long are terms for board members, Jade?"

"Three years," she replies. "With an option for one consecutive reelection, followed by one mandatory year off the board."

I nod, my eyes on Mr. Kresge's face. "Interesting. Looks like you'll have some free time on your hands next year, Mr. Kresge. I hear there are some great sensitivity classes out there. And lots of articles on the warning signs of sexual misconduct."

"Sexual misconduct," Mr. Kresge splutters, his pink face reddening.

"Oh, I guess you aren't actually sure why you're here," I say mildly. "You think you're here because we locked ourselves in the Wellness Center and said we wouldn't come out until you showed up. Well, thank you for joining us, Mr. Kresge. The reason we're here is because there is a sexual predator at Weston—and has been for five years." I give him a quick once-over. "Interesting that you wouldn't have heard.

Being that you've been on the board a little longer than that and all."

"Headmistress," says Sumi, "how many girls have complained about Brian Tully in the last five years?"

Headmistress Cotesmore looks startled to be singled out, but she quickly recovers. "I don't believe—I don't know that I have that information on hand."

"The disciplinary committee should," I say, looking to Cotesmore's left, where the committee sits. There are five of them, and they look like they have no idea what I'm talking about.

"If it went to the disciplinary committee," says Jade.

"The Weston faculty handbook states," Virginia says, "that any teacher who receives more than three conduct complaints will have a hearing with the faculty disciplinary committee to determine a course of action. That course of action is then reviewed by the headmaster or headmistress to be determined fitting."

"How many complaints have you gotten against Brian Tully, Headmistress?" Sumi asks again.

"I would have to check our records," Cotesmore replies, her expression turning stony. "But I can assure you, the faculty disciplinary committee and I both follow procedure by the book."

"Mr. Tully is a predator," I say to them. "His being on staff puts girls in danger."

"That is a serious accusation, Doe," says Mr. Salak, a member of the faculty disciplinary committee. He was my sophomore history teacher, but I shared the class with Sumi, and we didn't get a ton of work done. Unless the work was driving Mr. Salak crazy.

I never considered how that might backfire.

"It is a serious accusation," I say, nodding. "You're absolutely right, and it's not the first time someone has said that to us. Does anyone here feel worried that we've made a serious accusation?" I motion to the girls on either side of me.

No one speaks.

I look at Mr. Salak. "It seems like we understand the gravity of what we're doing here."

"Do you, though?" asks another member of the disciplinary committee, Mr. Grubka. "This is a man's career on the line. His life and livelihood. If it turns out not to be true, that's slander. You could be charged with defamation."

"It's true," I say. "What we're telling you is true. So, as it turns out, we don't need to be worried about a defamation case, because it's *true*."

"And do you have proof?" Mr. Kresge asks.

"If you're looking for a video or a recording, or pictures, text messages, something like that—no. This isn't TV, Mr. Kresge. Mr. Tully knows what he's doing. He goes after vulnerable girls, and he does it in person. He doesn't leave evidence behind. He invites them to his office under the guise of mentorship and friendship, and then . . ." I swallow, thinking of Noelle.

"And then makes his move," Shawn finishes, reaching over to squeeze my hand. "And we know there are girls who have come to you. We've heard the rumors and talked to those girls, and we've talked to other girls, and even reached out to girls who have long since left—the ones who were here and gone, like that." She snaps her fingers. "The ones who might have been forced out by a bad situation the administration never addressed."

"Our word should be enough," Gemma says, her voice soft but firm.

"And if one girl's word isn't"—Virginia reaches into the canvas bag at her feet and pulls out a stack of papers—some handwritten and others typed, on lined paper and scrap paper and on fancy monogrammed stationary—and slaps them onto the table—"then the word of dozens of girls should be."

"We spoke to current students, alumni, transfers, and dropouts"—I linger on the last one, narrowing my eyes at the adults across the table—"and we collected statements of their experiences with Mr. Tully. It's true that not everyone had one. Not all the girls at this school have a reason to interact with him outside of class. But you'll find we have a lot more from the time he became head of Roseland House two years ago. And, as we all know, the more power a person has, the larger their pool of prey becomes."

"What do you want from us, Doe?" Cotesmore asks me, sounding weary. "You want Mr. Tully fired? Because you demand it?"

"Yes," I say. "That's exactly what we want."

"But it's not all we want," Virginia says, glancing at me.

I give her a small smile and nod. It's her brainchild, after all. I've done enough talking.

Virginia straightens her shoulders. "We want more counselors on campus, and we want them trained by a specialist to recognize sexual misconduct and warning signs for students' mental health. Every student should meet with their assigned counselor once a month to check their well-being, the way we have to meet with our head of house for academic counseling."

"Hiring more counselors would be an exorbitant expense," says Mr. Kresge.

"I don't think that'll be an issue," Virginia says, glancing over her shoulder at the boys behind us. "Considering we're merging next year, and that's to get Weston an influx of funds, right?"

Mr. Kresge's face purples. "That's not the only reason."

Virginia doesn't flinch.

I hold my hand up. "Could someone hand me a copy of the Winfield annual budget, please?"

There's shuffling behind me, and then a hand brushes my back. I bite the inside of my cheek so that I don't smile as Wells sets a copy of the budget in my hand.

"How do you have that?" Headmaster Pritchard demands, glaring past me.

"My father provided it," Three answers. "Is there a problem?"

Headmaster Pritchard's mouth tightens.

"Mr. Kresge, if you'd be so kind as to pull up a copy of the Weston budget for us," I say to him. "I'm sure a few hours is long enough for you to find some wiggle room between these two budgets, don't you?"

"Now hold on a second," Mr. Kresge says. "No one's agreed to your demands yet, young lady."

I pause, staring at him. "What seems to be the problem?"

"A lack of proof, for one!" he replies. Others start to murmur, and it sounds like they agree.

"Our word should be enough. The statements from *dozens* of girls should be enough. Hundreds of girls are locked in the Wellness Center waiting for us to tell them that their discomfort and the discomfort of their friends is enough. We spend more time in this school than anywhere else, and no one who makes us feel unsafe should be allowed to remain on staff. *Period.*"

Mr. Kresge opens his mouth, but Shawn cuts him off.

"Keeping in mind that we have recordings of our protest

and demands, and we're ready to distribute that at any time for anyone who missed our livestream," she says with all the venom of someone asking him to sit down for tea. "To our parents, Winfield parents, and both alumni associations. Do you think your merger will happen if Winfield parents know you're letting a predator remain on campus? Do you think girls won't be pulled out of school when their parents find out?"

"Doe, think about what you're doing," Cotesmore says. "You love this school. You're ready to ruin it over a situation for which you have no proof? Mr. Tully could sue us—the school for wrongful termination, all of you for defamation of character. If the merger is dropped, and we lose students, Weston could close its doors forever."

I level her with a stony look. "I'd rather see this school burn to the ground than let Mr. Tully hurt one more girl."

I push back my chair, and as I stand, the others follow.

"We'll be in the Wellness Center when you come to a decision."

I look at the adults in the room who have stayed quiet—the other three members of the faculty disciplinary committee and the head of the Parents' Association, Iris Tolentino.

"I trust you've all been listening. I hope you consider your options wisely." I motion to the stack of statements Virginia pushed to the middle of the table. "I'd recommend reading those first."

Out in the cool evening air, I sag against Shawn as my friends huddle together in a group hug.

"That took more out of me than I expected," I admit with a breathy laugh.

"You did great," Jade says, squeezing my hand. "Really great."

"You all did," Three says from somewhere behind me.

I extract myself from my friends and turn to him. I'm always reluctant to offer Three any positive acknowledgement, but I owe him today.

"Thank you," I say. "For showing up. For doing all this. I guess we got lucky that your sister's gonna be a Weston girl next year, after all."

Three scoffs, rolling his eyes. "Yeah, as it turns out, I don't need to have a sister coming to Weston to want to help you guys get a pervert off campus. You shouldn't learn to want girls to be safe when you get a sister. You should just want it. Because everyone deserves to be safe."

"Wow," Sumi says, giving a slow clap. "Three has a heart."

The tips of his ears go a little red.

"*Of course* he does," Shawn says, shouldering through the rest of us to wrap her arms around Three's waist. "You think I would've given him a shot otherwise?"

"I'm not sure I'll ever get used to that," Jade mutters.

A hand catches mine as we head down the path together, and I fall behind the group with Wells.

"So," he says, "how do you feel?"

"Nervous," I say. "I don't *actually* want to see Weston burn to the ground."

I lean my head on his shoulder as we walk, our hands entwined between us.

Wells taps his head against mine. "I don't think you need to worry. Don't forget how much sway parents have over our schools."

I glance up at him. "You think the Parents' Association was a good bet?"

"I think *parents* are a good bet."

"Ah. You think we should send out the protest video."

"I'd give it an hour before they cave. As soon as the angry calls start rolling in." He grins, adding, "But you're the master strategist here. I'm just your arm candy."

"Don't sell yourself short. You've got beauty *and* brains," I tease. When I notice the others looking back at us, my cheeks grow hot. I clear my throat, turning my face away from Wells.

"If we involve our parents, it could start a mass panic," Jade says, drawing us back to the subject at hand. "We'd run the risk of girls getting pulled out of school. It could backfire in a major way."

"I also like the idea of us getting what we want because we earned it," I say. "But I don't want to gamble everything on the administration listening to a bunch of kids. I'd hate to let my pride get the best of us."

I don't mention that it gets the best of me often enough already.

"We don't lose anything by waiting, do we?" Gemma asks. "If we release it now, we don't give them the chance to listen to us on their own."

"We can use it to retaliate if they make the wrong decision," says Virginia. "There's nothing that says we have to stop once they decide what they're going to do. We can always fight back—harder, even."

"Good point," I agree. "So, we save it, then. Let's see what they do next."

We part ways at the Wellness Center, the boys heading back to Winfield and the rest of us returning to the lock-in.

Before Virginia returns to her friends, she stops next to me and says, "You did a good job in there. Crazy to think how much we could get done if we teamed up more often, huh?"

I laugh. "We'd have to find something we agree on first."

"Well, just so you know, when I run for office later, I'll be looking for a political strategist." She grins at me. "Somehow I think you'd be good at it."

I frown at her back as she heads off to meet her friends.

"Political strategist," Shawn repeats, sounding thoughtful.

"I should probably focus on getting into college first," I say.

She laughs, looping her arm through mine, and pulls a fun-size candy bar out of her pocket. She holds it out to me. "Better eat it quick before it starts a riot. But you did good today, Doesy. I'm proud of you."

I tear open the candy bar and break it, offering half back to her. "I'm proud of *you*."

She taps her half against mine and grins. "Cheers."

"Cheers."

And we eat.

After six more hours of silence from the administration, I'm positive they're trying to starve us out. Granola bars are scarce. Tensions were running high before we decided to shut off the lights and let everyone try to sleep it off.

It's almost eleven at night. The darkness is pierced by the occasional phone flashlight, but most of us have run out of battery. We have a few power strips in the locker rooms, but there aren't nearly enough for everyone to charge their phones, and we've been taking turns in twenty-minute intervals.

My phone died hours ago. I haven't bothered to charge it again.

"Doe," someone whispers in the dark, followed immediately by a muttered curse.

"Get off my ankle!"

"Hey, watch it!"

"Sorry, sorry," the girl whispers, making her way through the minefield of bodies around me.

When she gets close enough, I see in the dim light that it's Kimberly Meyer, middle daughter of Mrs. Meyer, my physics teacher. She's a sophomore, and her younger sister a freshman. They have an older sister who graduated a few years ahead of me. She was a senior when I was a freshman, and part of the same kind of group my friends turned into—the kind that fought hard in the Winfield rivalry.

"Hey," Kimberly whispers, crouching next to me. "Um, there's someone here to see you."

I frown, climbing to my feet.

"So, I'd just like to preface this by saying I have no control over my family whatsoever," Kimberly says as she leads me to the lobby. "And there was really no way for me to stop her from finding out what we were doing, since, you know, she works here."

I falter as we step into the lobby, my feet freezing on the threshold. On the other side of the glass doors stands Mrs. Meyer, lit by the floodlight that illuminates the walkway.

And behind her are my parents.

"Shit," I mutter, rushing to the door. I push it open and step out into the cold.

"Doe!" Dad shrugs off his coat and drapes it around my shoulders. I realize belatedly I'm only in pajamas and a pair of thick socks.

"What are you guys doing here?" I ask, stealing a glance at Mrs. Meyer.

Kimberly is whispering something to her, looking annoyed.

"Don't give me that look," Mrs. Meyer says to her daughter. "Of course I called them."

"You can't stop us," I tell her. "I'm not the only one who wants to see this done. You can get my parents to pull me out, but you can't stop us all."

Mrs. Meyer looks at me, her eyebrows arching up. "Doe, I may be your physics teacher, but I'm a parent first. Had I known about Brian Tully earlier, I would have done this myself."

I glance at my parents. "Then what . . . ?"

Mom smiles and puts her hands on my cheeks. "You don't really think we'd come all this way to stop you, do you? You've done a lot of crazy stuff, Doe, but this doesn't qualify."

Kimberly sucks in a breath. "Mom, what did you do?"

I look over at her, then follow her gaze down the path.

"What do you think I did?" Mrs. Meyer replies. "I activated the phone tree."

"This is a private boarding school," Kimberly reminds her. "We don't *have* a phone tree!"

Mrs. Meyer grins, pulling her daughter into her side. "We do now."

And we must, because waiting a few hundred feet away and lit by the pathway lamps is a group of parents so large, I can't tell where it ends.

"Why didn't you call us sooner?" Mom asks me. "We're your parents. This is what we're supposed to do."

"We wanted to do it on our own. And we were worried if we involved parents, it might cause a panic," I admit, anxiety creeping back up. "We don't want any of the girls pulled out of school. We just want to make Weston safe."

"Give us parents a little more credit than that," Mom says.

"We want Weston to be safe, too. For you, and anyone who comes after. That's why you should have *called us*."

"We had a meeting with Headmistress Cotesmore this afternoon," I tell my parents.

"We know," Dad says. "Gloria told us." He motions to Mrs. Meyer.

"You did a good job," Mom says. "You may have even done enough to get what you want on your own. But how about you let us lend a little leverage, hmm?"

"What do you mean?" I ask, glancing between my parents.

"We have a meeting, too," Dad says.

"In the morning?"

Mom smiles, brushing my hair back from my face. "No. Right now."

I blink at them. "Wait, what?"

"We're not letting our kids spend twenty-four hours locked in a gym," says Dad.

"Technically it's called the Wellness Center," I say.

Dad scoffs. "If you're sleeping under a basketball hoop, it's a gym."

I let it go.

"Uh, how many parents, exactly, are attending this meeting?" I ask, glancing toward the group.

"Enough that it's being held in the auditorium."

I whistle. "Wow."

"So, how about you tell us your demands," Mom says, "so we can take that in with us."

I give them a quick rundown of what we want. It doesn't take long, considering we only had two demands to begin with.

It's not like we're asking for all that much.

"Okay, get in there and charge your phone," Dad says,

reaching over to squeeze the back of my neck. "We'll text you when we're done."

"How'd you know my phone's dead?"

"We tried calling you as soon as we heard what was going on," he says.

"That's why we had to ask Gloria to get ahold of Kimberly," Mom adds.

"Also, you're not very good about keeping your phone charged in general," says Dad.

I frown. "Could you two take that attitude into your meeting, please? If anyone needs to be dragged right now, it's the people you're about to see."

Mom grins. "Oh, don't worry. I have a whole speech ready. I planned it in the car on my way here."

Dad nudges me with his elbow, smiling. "She ran it by me over the phone earlier. It's pretty good."

"I hope *pretty good* is enough to win."

Mom gives me a look. "Oh, Doe baby, I don't lose. Where do you think you get that from?"

"Hey, I'm right here," Dad says with a laugh.

I hug him, overcome with gratitude that my parents have shown up ready to fight for me. Dad lets out a surprised noise but doesn't miss a beat hugging me back.

Mom closes in on my other side, wrapping me up between them like a Doe sandwich.

No matter what happens, at least I know this: my parents are on my side.

The parents' meeting takes a lot longer than ours did. I imagine Cotesmore and the rest of the panel have a lot more to address in an auditorium full of parents than they did in a conference room with a handful of students. I try to stay awake, and adrenaline carries me for a while, but eventually I flag and fall asleep.

I wake to my phone ringing. I turned the sound on to make sure I wouldn't miss anything. My friends and a few of the girls around me stir at the noise, groaning and protesting.

Jade elbows me. "Doe, turn it off."

I fumble for my phone and put it to my ear. "Hello?"

"You can come out now," Dad says. "It's over."

"Over?" I repeat.

"The police are escorting him off campus as we speak."

I drop my phone. "Holy shit."

"What happened?" Shawn asks, sitting up next to me.

I can hear Dad talking, muffled by my sleeping bag. I scramble to pick the phone up.

"Wait, wait—*what*?"

"They conferenced in the rest of the board of trustees," Dad says, "and they agreed to your terms about the counselors. You can all come out. You won, Doe."

When I don't say anything, he laughs. "Go tell your girls. I'll see you in a few minutes."

I hang up and turn to Shawn. "We won."

"We what?" she asks, blinking.

"We *won*."

"Wait, that's it? We're done?" Gemma asks.

I nod. "We're done."

I stand up and do a slow turn, taking in the sea of girls around me. Some are still sleeping, but the whisper is spreading, and most of them are starting to wake.

I pick my way through the crowd to the wall and flip on the lights.

The room goes stark white and blinding. Several people cry out in protest, including Sumi, who shoves her head back under her blanket. My eyes water.

"Jade, could you . . . ?" I motion to the room.

Jade sticks her fingers in her mouth and lets out a shrill, ear-splitting whistle.

The room goes quiet.

I smile and give her a thumbs-up.

"I know we're all tired," I call, "so I'll skip the big speech about how proud I am of everyone, and how cool this feels. Some of our parents showed up in the middle of the night and met with the administration and the board. We didn't call them, but they came anyway. I wanted us to get this on our own, but it turns out, getting help from our parents isn't all that different from getting help from each other. So, we can go back to our beds, which are only slightly more comfortable than this floor. Because I just got the call that the school is giving us everything we asked for. You guys did that, so *be proud*. Congratulations."

A beat passes where no one moves.

And then the delirious cheering starts, everyone shrieking and hugging.

I go to my friends and collapse into our circle, the five of us crowding in for the most uncoordinated group hug, with one phrase beating in my ears in time with my racing pulse.

We won.

CHAPTER
TWENTY-FIVE

ollowing the excitement of our protest, spring break ended up feeling pretty dull in comparison. I spent it lazing around the house, helping Grandma spring clean, and catching up on homework. But mostly I spent my break waiting to get back to school.

When my train pulls into the Delafosse station, I lug my bags off and head for the parking lot in the sea of other passengers. There are girls I recognize from school, who smile and wave and say hi when they spot me. There are Winfield boys, too, most of whom I don't recognize.

And when the crowd thins, there's a Winfield boy I do recognize, flipping keys in his hand and leaning against a lamppost.

He grins when he sees me.

I want to drop my bags and run to him, but it seems a little over the top after only a week apart. I rein it in and cross the distance between us so I can calmly set my luggage at his feet and wrap my arms around him.

He pulls me close, nuzzling into my neck.

"I was expecting something a lot more dramatic from

you, I have to admit," he says. "I thought you'd at least throw yourself into my arms or something. It's like you didn't miss me at all."

"Hey, you could've thrown yourself into *my* arms," I say, pulling back to look at his face.

"Good point," he says, releasing me. He starts picking up my luggage. "Here, take this and go back. Let's do it over."

I laugh and smack him on the back. "Shut up."

He grins at me, but it quickly falters when he hefts my duffel bag onto his shoulder. "Jesus, what's in this thing?"

My cheeks heat. I busy myself grabbing my backpack from the ground. "Just stuff," I say. "Where's the car? This way? That—"

He steers me the other way, and I spot Christian's car in the quickly clearing lot.

We stuff my bags into the trunk, but before Wells shuts them in, he gives my duffel bag a squeeze around the sides, feeling its contents.

"Hey, stop that!" I smack at his hands.

He gives me a narrow-eyed look as he unzips it.

"My unmentionables are in there!"

"Is that what you're calling these now?" he deadpans, reaching into my bag. He pulls out two well-worn paperback romance novels and holds them up. "Your unmentionables?"

I grab them back and stuff them into my bag. "Incredibly rude. You have no manners at all. What if I had your birthday gift in there?"

His face brightens, and he turns to unzip my duffel again.

"Hey!" I grab onto him, pulling him away from the trunk.

He twists in my arms and traps me against him. "Come on. Give it to me now."

"Your birthday isn't for two more days."

"You can give me something else I want on my actual birthday."

"Like a jumbo box of condoms?"

He groans and drops his forehead on my shoulder. "That joke needs to go."

I laugh, patting his back. "Poor baby. You really want your birthday gift now? Here, in the train station parking lot?"

"Yes," he says, lifting his head. "While we have a little bit of peace and quiet and Christian's car? Absolutely."

He makes a good point. Especially since we aren't allowed in the basement at Rotty's anymore. I'm not sure when we'll get another chance at privacy.

"Fine." I motion to the car. "Get in."

While he turns away, I reach into my backpack and pull out his gift. Grandma helped me wrap it, so it almost looks professionally done.

I climb in on the passenger side, holding the gift to my chest. "Okay, fair warning—"

"I don't want any disclaimers," he says, motioning for me to hand it over. "Give it."

"I'm just saying, I don't know if you'll like the style, or—"

"I'll love it." He flaps his hand again. "Hand it over."

I sigh and slide the small box into his hand.

Wells tears off the bow and sticks it to my forehead.

"Hey!"

He grins and leans across the center console to kiss me. It's so fast, I'm still recovering when he tears the wrapping paper.

Everything goes strangely still as he opens the box.

After Three's birthday and the broken watch disaster, I wondered what happened to Pop's watch. I never saw either of them wearing it, but I wasn't brave enough to ask if it was unfixable, or if Wells had simply returned it to Three.

Until spring break, and one late-night phone call with Wells, when I got just sleepy enough to overcome my nerves.

"At the risk of upsetting you," I said to him, pulling my duvet up to my chin, "what happened to the watch?"

Wells went quiet for a while. I listened to his steady breathing on the other end of the line, the only indication he was still there.

I thought he might not answer. But eventually, he said, "I tried to give it back to Three."

"Tried?"

Wells let out a long breath. "Yeah. It could've been fixed. I offered to pay for it. After everything, it seemed stupid for us to still be fighting over stuff with Pop. We've fought enough. But Three said he didn't want it, either."

I waited.

"So . . . we got rid of it."

"You did what?"

Wells groaned, and I heard him shift in bed. "We just . . . got rid of it. We didn't want it anymore."

It was strange to hear this thing Wells had cared about so much for so long was suddenly gone. Getting the watch from Three was the only thing he wanted.

Until it wasn't.

"It's not fancy or anything," I say to him now as he slides the new watch out of its box and holds it up. "I thought, with the other one being gone, maybe you could . . . I don't know. Use this as a new start. A watch that's just yours, and only means something to you."

Wells turns to me with a small, soft smile and leans across the center console again.

This time, his kiss isn't fast. In fact, we end up kissing for so long that only a sharp rap on my window startles us apart.

A security guard stands outside, an amused smirk on his face. He makes a motion for us to leave.

Wells sighs. "I guess we should've found a better place to park . . ." He waves to the security guard and makes a big show of starting the car.

I click on my seat belt. "We were supposed to be at Phoebe's fifteen minutes ago, anyway."

"Will I ever get a solid hour alone with you again?" Wells complains as he pulls out of the parking lot and heads toward the center of town.

"Sure," I reply. "When we're at college, probably. Maybe over the summer, if my dad lets you visit."

"Your dad loves me."

I don't need reminding. After our protest, my dad hung around for a few days so he could drive me home for spring break. He took Wells and me to dinner one night, and the two of them bonded in a major way. Mom was supremely jealous. She's already planning a big weekend for Wells to visit Chicago over the summer. I haven't told him yet. I don't want him to know my parents are ready to battle it out to be his favorite.

We find our friends at Phoebe's, at two big tables they've pushed together to make room for everyone—my friends, the Wellborn cousins, and Alex and Zamir.

"She's here!" Gemma squeaks when we come through the door. She jumps to her feet to hug me.

"You're late," says Jade.

"My train was a little behind schedule," I lie, taking the empty seat across from Shawn. Wells falls into the one next to me and passes the keys to Christian.

Shawn hums, stirring her milkshake. "Is that why your shirt is buttoned wrong?"

I look down in alarm and swear. I'm not even wearing a shirt with buttons.

I fix her with a look. "Not cool."

She grins. "Just confirming you're late because you and Wells were busy making out in Christian's car."

Christian sighs, rolling his head back. "Really?" he asks the ceiling.

"I was also giving him his birthday gift," I protest.

"Oh, yeah? Is that some new sex code we've never heard of?" Sumi says.

I kick at her under the table, but I end up catching Joc instead. He jumps, banging his knee on the underside of the table, and water slops out of Three's cup.

"Nice one," Three says to me, rolling his eyes as he mops up water with his napkin. He looks unkempt in a way I've never seen him look before, in sweatpants and a backward hat. But as Shawn settles against him, he also grins in a way I've never really seen from him before. Like something in him has loosened.

"Doe, aren't you on probation?" Zamir asks. "I heard a rumor you aren't allowed in town anymore."

"I haven't been back to school yet, so technically I'm still on spring break," I say. "Besides, my going into town is the least of their worries right now."

"The administration is too busy cleaning up their PR nightmare," Gemma says. "I heard my dorm monitor talking about it on the phone earlier. She was saying some incoming first years have already dropped admissions. The school's only saving grace now is the merger."

"Is that still on?" Sumi asks. "I didn't know they'd confirmed anything."

"My dad's pushing for it," Three says. "He'll only send Mer to Weston in the fall if the merger goes through."

"And as long as the Wellborns send a girl to Weston, most of the other families won't drop out yet," says Shawn.

Three's cheeks go pink.

"I guess we won't have to wonder who the new school head will be," says Jade.

Christian snorts. "Pritchard is probably polishing his nameplate as we speak."

The day before spring break started, Headmistress Cotesmore announced her resignation. I wasn't surprised when it happened. After hearing from Mom and Dad how angry the parents were over the mishandling of the Tully situation, I had a feeling Cotesmore's resignation wasn't really an option—more of a courtesy, rather than sacking her outright.

I still have mixed feelings about it. Cotesmore was a Weston girl. We didn't always agree, but until this year, I felt comfortable going to her when I needed to. We had a good relationship for a while. But keeping Tully around, and ignoring the girls who had come to her, was a betrayal. No matter whose decisions those were—hers, the board's, or even someone higher up—she should have fought harder for us.

"Well, I know you hate the idea of merging," Three says to me, "but I doubt the rivalry will die just because we start sharing classrooms."

"It'll probably get worse," says Christian.

The table goes quiet.

I glance around, and I can see the wheels turning in everyone's heads.

"Not our problem," I say. "Not our problem anymore."

Jade shoots me a suspicious look. "Did you just say something about Weston isn't our problem anymore?"

I grin. "As it turns out, we do have to move on eventually."

"It helps that *someone* picked a college over spring break," Shawn says, narrowing her eyes at me. "Not that she'll say where."

I scowl at her. "I was planning to tell you guys later!"

"You picked a college?" Wells asks, turning to me.

I groan, dropping my head in my hands.

"She even sent in her deposit," Gemma says.

I jerk up. "How did you know that?"

She shoots a look in Shawn's direction.

Shawn holds up her hands. "What? I was excited! Our little Doesy is all grown up!"

"Come on, tell us," Sumi says.

"Fine, fine!" I shoot Shawn a smile. "Tell Marcus to get ready for me, because I'll be in Ann Arbor next year. Go Blue!"

But instead of laughter and cheers and congratulations, my announcement is met with groans and protests. From the other end of the table, I hear Biers yell, "Are you kidding me?"

I frown. "What? What's wrong? It's a great school!"

"I'm not gonna be in the middle," Shawn says. "I swear to god, I'm not! I already told Marcus, and I'm telling you. I don't care if you *both* go there! I don't want to be involved."

"Did I miss something?" I ask, glancing from Shawn to Wells to the rest of the table.

Three sighs and lifts his hat to rumple up his hair. Then he turns it forward and settles it back on his head.

I stare at the big red *O* on the front, realization coursing through me.

"You're kidding," I say.

"Go Buckeyes," he deadpans.

I look around at the rest of them. "You're *kidding*."

Next year, Three and I will be attending schools on opposite sides of one of the biggest college rivalries in the country.

"Maybe you two can be the ones to bridge the gap," Shawn suggests with a tad too much hope in her voice. "End a century-long rivalry between two major universities."

Three and I exchange a look.

He points at me. "The dorm halls are carpeted, so don't get any big ideas. Your oil trick won't work this time."

"I've got a great big brain, Three. Don't underestimate what I'll come up with. Unlike you, I don't have to reuse my tricks."

Shawn drops her head in her hands. "I guess I was hoping for too much."

Wells laughs, sliding his arm along the back of my chair. "If it had happened any other way, it wouldn't feel right."

Tonight, after Phoebe's, my friends and I head to the Kingdom. It's as cold as it was in November, but there's something different about spring. The air is damp with the promise of warmth and blooming.

Change is coming to Weston. But it's clear to me now that change was *always* coming to Weston.

The Weston School has been my haven. The place where I've felt the most me. Where I met my closest friends, and where I grew into my real self.

The merging of Weston and Winfield will always be filled with maybes, and we might not know the result for years. Maybe the girls will be overshadowed. Maybe students will be pulled out, and enrollment will drop, and the school will close its doors for good.

Maybe it will be a haven for a new generation of students. And maybe creating a space for everyone is exactly what Mallory Weston wanted when she started The Weston School to begin with. A place for learning, no matter who you are.

I look at my friends as we lounge in the Kingdom. Weston is bound to change from here. Maybe unrecognizably so.

But what I've been holding on to all this time isn't our school. Sure, the teachers, the classes, and the other girls were part of it. But the real Weston spirit is right here with me. It was always my friends.

And no matter what happens to the school from here, we'll always be Weston girls.

ACKNOWLEDGMENTS

I am very lucky to have so many people to thank right now.

To my agent, Ashley Blake, thank you not just for believing in me, and believing in Doe, but for all your guidance in making this book the best it could possibly be. I could not have done it without your eye and your honesty, and there aren't enough words to express how much I appreciate you.

A big, huge, extremely full of exclamation marks (!!!!) thank-you to my editor, Vicki Lame, for loving Doe and the Weston girls as much as I do. Your excited notes got me through so many moments of doubt and reminded me every time why I wrote this book to begin with, and how much I love it, too.

To Kerri Resnick and Lucia Duplessy, thank you for a cover I wish I could tattoo on the insides of my eyelids! A huge, billboard-sized thank-you to Lexi Neuville and Brant Janeway for being marketing royals, and to my publicists, Sarah Bonamino and Meghan Harrington, for being incredible and also for the very early use of the word *obsessed*. That was the booster seat for my heart through this whole process! And a very special, big !!!! thank-you to the wonderful Vanessa Aguirre and the magnificent Angelica Chong, for keeping me and my single, often haywire brain cell on track.

To the rest of the team at Wednesday Books—Devan Norman, NaNá V. Stoelzle, Melanie Sanders, and Janna Dokos—thank you so much for your time and dedication to the book of my heart. Everyone says it takes a village to raise a child, and that sort of feels like what we all did together. This book would not be as bright and beautiful without all of your efforts. I can't thank the entire team enough for carrying me through this wild journey.

And shout-out to Jennie Conway, who bore witness to my very first, extremely excited emails. (Seriously, if you all have nightmares about exclamation points after being on emails with me, I take full responsibility.)

Ah, Whitney. How can I begin to say thank you for everything you've done for me? For every shower phone call, mid-breakdown phone call, and sitting-in-silence phone call. For reading this book chapter by chapter to the tune of my nervous heavy breathing on the other end of the line. For being my number-one fan and champion. Thank you for all that, for everything else, and mostly for being my best friend.

To Ashley and Sonya, thank you for reading every email, even the ones that were white-hot garbage (and for always insisting they were not actually white-hot garbage), and for the last decade of texts that started with "Okay, but what about . . . ?" and all the stories that came next. I can't wait to write with you two for the rest of our lives.

Thank you to the Barrons/Houghs for being my second family, and for loving me like I've always been with you. To Julianne, for the half a lifetime of friendship you've spent being my tiny, mighty champion. To Tori, Dani, and Ellen, for reading my writing however I've given it to you. To Joe and Shy, for every FaceTime that has gotten me through this pandemic, and for all the ones that will come after.

To my friends who have who have supported me through this entire process—I love you all, and I'm so grateful for you.

And to Julian, whom I miss dearly. Words can't explain, but you know my heart.

Of course, I have to thank the fanfiction readers. Being supported by all of you, and learning from you, is what built my foundation as a writer.

A very big thank-you to my family, for never once telling me to find a more sensible path. To have the support of a group as large as ours has always felt like a miracle, and your excitement and enthusiasm about my writing is priceless to me.

A special thank-you to my grandparents, who aren't here to see this book come into the world—to Grandpa, who taught me to believe I could do anything, and to Grandma, who never doubted I could do this.

Most important, I have to thank my mom. I couldn't have written this, or anything else, without you. Thank you for your never-ending love and encouragement, and for always believing this moment would come. I love you most.